The
House of
Two Sisters

The House of Two Sisters

A Novel

Rachel Louise Driscoll

BALLANTINE BOOKS
NEW YORK

Ballantine Books
An imprint of Random House
A division of Penguin Random House LLC
1745 Broadway, New York, NY 10019
randomhousebooks.com
penguinrandomhouse.com

First published in 2025 by Harvill Secker, an imprint of Vintage.
Vintage is part of the Penguin Random House group of companies.

Map by Bill Donohoe

Hardback ISBN 978-0-593-98288-4
Ebook ISBN 978-0-593-98289-1

Printed in the United States of America on acid-free paper

randomhousebooks.com

2 4 6 8 9 7 5 3 1

First Edition

BOOK TEAM: Production editor: Ted Allen • Managing editor: Pam Alders •
Production manager: Jane Haas Sankner • Copy editor: Annette Szlachta-McGinn •
Proofreaders: Deb Bader, Addy Starrs, Barb Stussy
Book design by Caroline Cunningham
Title and part title page frame and chapter opening
ornament: S E P A R I S A/Adobe Stock
Crook and Flail ornament: transiastock/Adobe Stock

The authorized representative in the EU for product safety and
compliance is Penguin Random House Ireland, Morrison Chambers,
32 Nassau Street, Dublin D02 YH68, Ireland. https://eu-contact.penguin.ie

For Mummy and Daddy,

with all my love and thanks

and to Rebekah

"For there is no friend like a sister"

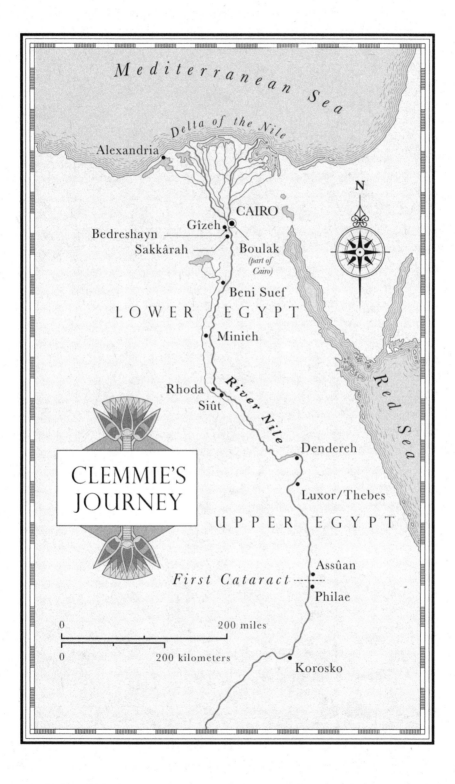

Mediterranean Sea

Delta of the Nile

Alexandria

N

CAIRO

Gîzeh

Bedreshayn

Sakkârah

Boulak
(part of Cairo)

Beni Suef

LOWER EGYPT

Minieh

Rhoda

Siût

River Nile

Red Sea

Dendereh

Luxor/Thebes

CLEMMIE'S
JOURNEY

UPPER EGYPT

Assûan

First Cataract

Philae

0   200 miles

0   200 kilometers

Korosko

PART ONE

Egypt

We drank the Libyan Sun to sleep, and lit

Lamps which out-burn'd Canopus. O my life

In Egypt! O the dalliance and the wit,

The flattery and the strife.

—ALFRED, LORD TENNYSON, "A Dream of Fair Women"

Nephthys is that which is beneath the earth and invisible,

Isis that which is above the earth and visible.

—PLUTARCH, *Moralia*

Unwrapping

1887

THE ROOM IS SO THICK with spice you could take a spoon to the air. *We must evoke atmosphere,* he always says, so she's scattered the cloves and lit the lavender candles: the ones that normally burn at a wake to mask the smell of the dead. It's fitting really, and the headiness mingles with the myrrh oil she's dripped about the place, not bothering to see if it stains the Turkish rug or mars the beeswax shine on the mahogany. The smell will linger for days, but there's something pleasant and exotic about it, as if they've traveled to another land. Her shoulders relax—the oils must be working—and she can almost forget that the audience relies on her as much as the unwrapper.

But who wants to forget? She's a woman doing the same job that philologists once mashed their brains over. When she translates the hieroglyphs, when she retells the myths and explains the meaning behind an artifact, people look at her in astonishment mixed with admiration, the perfect cocktail of reactions. She has no desire to exchange her night of interpretations for one of dancing, or her rapt listeners for a line of men proposing courtship.

It lies there, on the table. Bundled like a caterpillar in its chrysalis, still waiting to emerge. When she was young, she watched a butterfly split the sheath confining it, wings damp and temporarily useless. But it was beautiful. Every occasion they do this, when a new specimen has been procured and they receive the handsome amounts socialites will pay to satisfy their inner desire for the macabre, when her father reveals the embalmed skin, dark with gum and so carefully preserved one might go as far as to call *it* beautiful, she thinks of that butterfly.

Under the first swaddles he reveals small trinkets, each carefully chosen to bring protection to the dead. These he hands to the crowd, letting them enjoy the tactility of the moment before relinquishing them to her. She lays them out carefully, admiring the typical shapes—green scarabs and blue *wedjat* eyes—more of the same beautiful relics to add to her father's collection. There is a space waiting for them in the nearest locked cabinet, glass polished to a diamond's brilliance to best flaunt the treasures within.

He unwinds the folds of cerement, those strips of cloth that bind the neck. There must be many layers left, the neck and head are thick with them. It is here that he finds the last piece and passes it to her, his fingers quaking, reluctant to surrender this new find.

She holds this final amulet in her hands. Larger than the rest. Bigger than any she's ever known. The amulet is perfectly preserved. It is carved from red jasper, that stone once believed to be synonymous with the blood of Isis. The wonder of this piece magnifies the more she looks at it. Perhaps six inches across, even more from base to top. Cut from a large piece of quartz. It's not just the size of the amulet that's impressive. The shape is unusual too. Much like the *ankh*, the stem reaches to a loop. However, instead of the arms stretching out, as they do on an *ankh*, here they fall to the sides. Holding itself. Embracing.

She recognizes the shape. It's called a *tyet*, or knot of Isis. A symbol of life and protection, typical for a funerary token. But what makes this one unique is the duplication. Instead of one *tyet*, there are two carved as one piece. Twinned, sides touching. Her skin prickles with the feet of ancient scarabs, passing unseen. She's never seen a Double *Tyet* before.

That's not all. Her father had no choice but to relinquish this piece, for she is the hieroglyphist, and those enigmatic icons are lying on the surface, winking at her in the lambent light. The amulet is engraved, the characters small and familiar. That mysterious script that she's dedicated her life to understanding. Some people enjoy reading novels, others pass the time conversing with friends, but she prefers to translate an almost lost language. To hear the voices of the dead.

Tracing the hieroglyphs with her fingers, she is oblivious to the buzz from the guests as they watch her father work. It's her role to interpret for their audience. Messages from the past. Sometimes it is the glyphs on a sarcophagus, sometimes cryptic shapes on papyri. She knows what words to expect. They tend to follow a traditional formula referring to the story of Osiris, worded as a plea for the soul of the dead.

She feels each engraving under her finger, like pockmarks on skin. All along the spines of the Double *Tyet* she strokes and translates, finger becoming a third eye. Beginning at the top, she moves downward, from left to right.

A throne. A house with a basket.

Piece by piece, the images make characters, and those make words. Some are words of their own; others are sounds, and she threads them together. Doubting herself at times, looking for the determinative signs, wishing she'd brought along her Birch dictionary, but no. She's studied long and hard. She can do this.

The walls are lined with antiquities from Egypt and books that hold more dust than the local churchyard. In the center of the room, he continues his monologue as he fiddles with the remaining bandages, droning on about the country of sand and Pyramids, explaining the science behind embalming, giving the performance paid for by these women wearing brooches of bees and spiders, and boasting hats made of taxidermied cats and squirrels, and men smelling of tobacco.

The words on the amulet form sentences and she translates them in her head. Slowly, then faster. Building a rhythm. It's as they make sense, passing from ancient Egyptian to English, that she grasps their true meaning. The weight behind them becoming so heavy her wrists can barely hold the amulet up. She has never read an inscription like this before.

Protection. Wrath.

Her eyes widen, nostrils stinging with the shock of realization. She must show him what she has discovered. If only she could talk to him privately. The pits of her arms are damp. Sweat mingles with the spice.

I must stop this, she thinks. *It cannot go on.*

But when she looks up, she sees that he has already unwound what should be the head. And when they see what's there instead, a collective gasp rises from the gathering like a summoned spirit.

She is too late.

Shepheard's

WHEN CLEMENTINE IS STANDING IN the foyer of Shepheard's Hotel, it finally sinks in that she's in Egypt. At first, as she stepped off the train that had carried her from Alexandria to Cairo, she'd felt only nausea—be it from the sand she'd inhaled, the travel sickness, the disorientation of new surroundings, or the warmth causing the boning of her corset to chafe—but now nausea gives way to astonishment. She's actually here.

Hesitating on the tiled floor, she takes in the arch above her, striped in the style of a pharaoh's *nemes*. From the street come the cries of sellers, children demanding *bakhshîsh* despite doing nothing to deserve a tip, and the braying of donkeys lined up for hire. Other travelers might savor the smells of coffee vendors outside, the spices laid out in the bazaars and permeating the hotel, but beneath it all she detects the rotting cadaver of a cat she passed on entering, the day-warmed puddles of urine, and the dusty smells that remind her of nights spent unwrapping relics. This place is alive with people, but it's also heaving with the dead. She should know. If she doesn't succeed, she'll be one of them.

Carefully tucking the wooden box she carries under her arm, she tugs off her gloves, the pearl-gray suede sticking to her skin. Unsure of the etiquette for wearing gloves when abroad in sunnier climates, she peers for examples around the foyer, but even as she does so, she knows she won't put them back on. It may be winter and relatively mild for Egypt, but quite frankly, she doesn't care what people think.

She approaches the clerk, who acknowledges her before she has need to plant her damp palm on the counter bell. It takes her a moment to catch her breath. God willing, the weather will help her condition—but with all this sand and dust and her record of misfortune, how can she be sure of anything?

"I'll need a room for tonight," she says in Arabic.

The hotel book is produced and a room assigned. Signature obtained. Key handed over.

"Madam's first time in Egypt?" the clerk asks, and she wonders if it's that obvious. A man appears next to her, but she pays him no heed until he interrupts in English.

"Pardon me, but there weren't any fresh towels in my room this morning after it was cleaned."

"Apologies, Mr. Luscombe. I'll have it seen to." The clerk bows his head and she wonders how he remembers each individual guest without them bearing some label like a pot of pickles.

With an asquint look, she sees the towel-less man nod, then turn. "Just arrived?"

Only when he doesn't leave the desk does she realize he's addressing her, and she looks at him properly. The man is tall, but something appears to be holding him back from his full height. He's smiling. Clean-shaven white face, white teeth, blue eyes, brown hair. His perfect enunciation a hint of his education, and his tweeds giving him the finish of a country gentleman. She almost expects him to produce a brace of pheasants from behind his back.

"I have just arrived, yes. Now, good day to you."

"Rowland Luscombe," he says, bowing. "A fellow English traveler at your service."

She nods briefly before looking around her for the staircase.

"I'm afraid I didn't catch your name."

She's distracted by the porter when he drops one of her cases and tells him to be careful, then repeats it in Arabic, and then French—just to be safe—before turning back to the man with a brusque sigh.

He has a fascinated smile on his face, a look she's come across before. That expression when someone first witnesses her multilingual abilities. A surprise sandwich, she calls it. A layer of surprise, a filling of either admiration or disgust, finished off with another layer of surprise.

In his case, the filling appears to be admiration. And something else. She tries to put her finger on what, at last settling on inquisitiveness.

"Sorry, what did you want?" She flits her eyes briskly to match her voice, hoping he'll understand that she wishes to be left alone.

"I can see that you are busy, so I won't detain you. I just wanted to ascertain whom I've had the pleasure of addressing?"

"Clementine Attridge."

She doesn't think she imagines the lift of his right eyebrow, or the curl of the left side of his mouth. It gives him a crooked appearance.

"You're traveling alone?"

Something in the way he adds weight to that last word makes her stand taller. She wonders if it's just that he's disappointed. If he already knows the family name, does he wish a different Attridge were here instead? Wincing at the bitterness this question summons, she decides not to answer.

The porter reaches across to take the box from her hands, but she clings onto it. "No," she snaps. "I'll take it."

She glances back at the Englishman, and he's smiling at her outburst. Curiosity scintillates in his eyes.

Angling his head to better see the inscription on the box, he reads aloud: "Table croquet," before returning his attention to her. "Are you a professional of the tabletop sport, Miss Attridge, to guard your balls and mallets so closely?"

The infuriating man is laughing at her! He seems to expect a smile, for her to giggle along with him at her own silliness, but she doesn't oblige.

"It's special . . . for personal reasons."

Which isn't exactly a lie. The box may imply a parlor game, but appearances can be deceiving. She's not here to play games.

His lower lip protrudes, but he appears to accept her explanation.

Now to get away from this unwanted interaction.

"If you'll excuse me, I must change and find something to eat."

"Ah, you're in luck," he says. "I'm on my way to the dining room myself. I've formed a table with a couple of other English travelers. Perhaps, once you're ready, you'd like to join us for luncheon?"

Socializing? She hadn't counted on finding English-speaking people the moment she turned up, much less having to talk to them. Instead, she'd pictured sitting at a table, alone, with a wealth of foreign languages rippling around her. She might have used it as a learning exercise, picking up familiar words and percolating unknown ones until she'd guessed the entire meaning.

A soft wheeze snakes from her chest, and she lifts a eucalyptus-laced handkerchief to her face, inhaling it slowly.

"Perhaps."

Travelers

I N A FRESH BEIGE POINTED bodice and pleated skirt, face washed, and chestnut hair smoothed back into place, Clementine arrives in the dining room. An imitation of a lozenge pattern meanders up pillars bolstering the ceiling's framework. Beyond these is a border of pointed arch windows that, contradicting their Gothic style, let in enough light to make the tablecloths shimmer cheerily. The ceiling bears a beautifully painted medallion and there are gold finishes on the elaborate walls. This is the realm of pharaohs, and everything is aptly ornate.

The brightness of it all, the blithe jollity, is incongruous to the phantoms of her mind. No doubt the people in this room, at first glance, imagine she's a typical English traveler, here to enjoy the sun, pick up a few knickknacks, and purchase a bottleful of sand to take home. They couldn't be more wrong.

Seated at the tables dotting the room are a mixture of European and American travelers, and many more-local visitors wrapped in gold and pure white fabrics. The array of cultures is evidence not just of the lure of this place but also of its war-torn history. From French, to Ottoman, to the current English occupation, with local uprisings scattered in between, it's no surprise to hear different languages battling to be heard, much as they have spent the recent century trying to claim Egypt as part of their empires.

One man, rising against a backdrop of palm leaves, waves. She frowns before she recognizes him. The Englishman from the foyer. With a suppressed groan, she heads to his table, shared with another man and woman, because she still hasn't thought of an excuse to do otherwise.

He pulls out a cane chair for her.

"Miss Clementine Attridge," he says, a reminder that he knows who she is, that he hasn't forgotten, "may I introduce Oswald Lion"—here he indicates a handsome man in tweed knickerbockers—"and Celia Lion. They are both from Bristol."

"Have you been to Bristol?" Celia asks. She is a pretty young woman, and she flashes a bright smile at Clemmie.

"No, I'm afraid I've not traveled much."

Before Egypt, Clemmie had rarely strayed far from her family home in Chelmsford, always preferring to shut herself away from the world and be entertained by the past.

But it has ceased to be entertaining. It has turned into a freak show, something morbid that torments. She tries not to shudder visibly and returns the smiles offered to her.

Celia, seated to Clementine's left, rests a hand on her arm. A gloved hand, Clementine notices uncomfortably.

"I'm so glad you joined us," Celia says. "So far, it's just been myself and Ossie—that is until we met Mr. Luscombe here, who has proved to be such interesting company—but I've been dying for female companionship, for the men talk about ruins and other such things that bore my poor mind and, oh, I'm just so delighted you've joined us."

Clementine blinks in an effort to keep up with Celia's gushing introduction. "I wasn't expecting to make any acquaintances, Mrs. Lion."

Giggling, Celia tosses her head, stray blond curls forming a halo around her face. "Oh, I'm not *Mrs.* Lion. Ossie's my older brother—here to protect me from myself as much as anything else."

Celia laughs as if she's made some joke, although Clementine doesn't quite follow.

"Anyway, you mustn't call me Miss Lion, you must call me Celia. And what do your friends call you?"

Friends? Now that is a joke she could almost laugh at. "My family have always called me Clemmie."

It sounds strange speaking of her family, but maybe this is the right place for it. Egypt is replete with memories, after all. The dead, the buried, and the cursed.

"Well, I shall call you Clemmie, too. Have you noticed how both our names start with C? I'm sure that's hardly coincidental; we must be destined to be friends. I'm nearly one-and-twenty. And you?"

"Three-and-twenty."

"Ossie will be pleased that you're older. He says I need the influences of the mature and sensible to tame me—he really can be callous sometimes—but I think we're going to get on famously. Do tell me you'll join our traveling party?"

Clemmie looks bewilderedly around the table.

"We haven't exactly formed a party, Celia," says her brother.

"No, Ossie, but you know I've been trying to with Mr. Luscombe"—Celia flicks her lashes three times in Rowland's direction—"and who doesn't want to stick with one's own countrymen for an excursion to the Pyramids?"

An excursion? Back in her younger days, as a hieroglyphist and Egyptology enthusiast, Clemmie certainly would have come with a full itinerary to explore. But the years have changed her—or her motives. Possibly both. That, however, is none of their business.

"I'm not here for excursions," she tells them.

Rowland leans forward slightly—enough for her to notice. "If not for sightseeing, then what are you here for, Miss Attridge?"

She chews her mouth as she considers her best response.

"It's no secret why I'm here," Celia interrupts. "My parents sent me for 'an extended trip' as they called it, with Ossie forced to come along to keep me out of mischief."

"Celia, I don't really think—"

"Hush, Ossie. You see, they didn't approve of a certain *romantic attachment*"—she whispers these words with scandalized delight—"and so here I am, though why they felt the need for Ossie to come I'll never know—it's not as if Michael's here, and I doubt I'll run off with a *fellah*."

A waiter interrupts Celia to take their orders, and Oswald visibly exhales while glaring at his sister. Clemmie examines the menu, uncomfortably aware of Rowland's stare. Wine is poured for them, but Rowland puts his hand over his wineglass to prevent it being filled.

Once they have placed their orders and the waiter has left, Rowland shifts a little further forward in his chair.

"You didn't think to bring your table croquet down?" he asks her quietly.

She hates that the privacy of his tone implies a shared secret.

"There's a time and place for games," she says icily, gesturing to the plates and glasses.

He concedes with an amused nod.

"Have you procured a *dragoman* yet?"

"No," she says, and before she can express her reluctance to do so, Celia cuts in.

"Well then, you must share the guide that Ossie has hired. He came very highly recommended."

"Thank you," Clemmie says. "But I've learned enough Arabic to get by, and I intend to learn more by listening."

Rowland sits a little taller, but even so his posture seems to imitate Pisa's tower. "It's true, then?"

"What's true?"

"Your knack for languages, translating hieroglyphs. Does your father still offer mummy unwrappings?"

Her hand freezes over her intricately folded napkin. He knows about her and her father. How much, she's unsure, but he's heard of the old Attridge line of work. She'll have to watch what she says. Clemmie picks up the cloth and smooths it over her lap, her palms turning it damp, before inclining her head to him.

"You know my father's business?"

"Anyone with an interest in ancient Egypt has heard of your father, but I haven't noticed any advertisements for his lectures of late. Is he still the 'Mummy Pettigrew' of our age?"

Mummy Pettigrew. The title given to the most famous mummy unroller of the century. She hasn't heard that appellation used in conjunction with her father for a long time. It summons ghosts. The smell of myrrh and burning wicks. The dust of relics. The stab of a gasp.

"I'm afraid he hasn't been well," she says slowly. "The Russian flu."

The influenza had struck London and surrounding areas hard in recent years. On her way to the docks and the ship that brought her to Egypt, Clemmie had been appalled by the evidence of so much sickness and so little relief. The street sellers wore mustaches of dried slime on their upper lips, coughs shaking their bodies until they risked dropping their wares. It's a plague that she's glad to escape while in Egypt, to be away from her country while it's clasped in the wintry chill of a new year with the flu at its worst.

"I'm sorry to hear that. Is he recovering?"

Thankfully, there are already glasses of water poured for them and she sips hers. It provides an occupation, and she hopes it's enough to cool the rising color in her cheeks.

"My father is dead."

She's always had a knack for killing a conversation. Rowland looks mortified for pressing her, Oswald peruses the menu again as if searching for an appropriate word of condolence nestled among the *Potage St. Germain* and the *Courgettes à la Turque*, and Celia releases an *oh* of pity.

"You're not in mourning," Celia says at last. "Was it some time ago?"

Clemmie nods. Of course, they'll imagine that her father died because of the influenza—better that they think that—but just mentioning his passing reminds her of all they've suffered. Five years of misery and denial.

"I'm sorry for your loss," Rowland says. "It is a terrible illness. I've seen it all over London."

"Is that where you're from?" she asks, desperate to change the subject.

"Originally Devonshire, but I'm in London these days."

She plays with his name in her head. *Luscombe.* Now she thinks of it, he has the sort of face that makes her wonder if they've crossed paths before.

"By any chance, did you ever attend one of my father's Egyptology events at Bickmore House?"

He tosses his head casually. "No, no. I never did manage to get to one."

"Your name. Luscombe. It does seem familiar."

"It's not an uncommon name."

"So will you join us?" Celia interrupts, already seeming to forget the somber tone their conversation had taken. "To see the Pyramids and the Sphinx?"

"Celia, don't force Miss Attridge," says Oswald. His dark eyebrows are set into a constant pleat. It gives him an almost stern look, softened only by the front of his hair tumbling forward.

"Actually," Clemmie says, "I'm here to travel to Denderah."

"Is it your first time in Egypt?" Rowland asks.

"It is."

"Then I don't see how the daughter of Dr. Attridge could come all the way to Egypt and not want to see the Pyramids of Gîzeh!" Rowland says. "I've heard you're quite the Egyptologist yourself."

What else has he heard?

"And you?" she says. "Are you an Egyptologist?"

"A traveler," he replies. "An explorer, you might say. Satisfying a whim. Aren't we all?"

"So?" Celia says. "Won't you come with us?"

Clemmie doesn't take her eyes off Rowland, daring him to be the first to look away. His eyes are intense, so blue a flock of birds could fly through them, and they lock on to her like a magnet to a pin.

"Yes," she says, before she can change her mind. "Why not? As you say, I can't come all this way and not see the Great Pyramid."

She stands at the window of her hotel room. Wanting to enjoy the view, but too busy looking out for the kites. She had first noticed them after disembarking at Alexandria. On the train to Cairo, she'd peered from the carriage window, clutching her wooden box, and two winged shadows had blended with that of the moving locomotive.

Isis and Nephthys.

All her life, she has dreamed of this day. She's lived it in her mind, prepared for it, prayed for it. But not like this. She thinks of what she's left behind. Is she running? Is that why she's here? Exchanging one set of ruins for another?

Looking at the box, she's tempted to open it, to remind herself of what's inside. Of why she's come. She can almost feel the amulet in her hands. Can almost hear that gasp echoing in her ears.

Maybe she should cancel tomorrow's excursion. She shouldn't have yielded to Rowland's needling—stupid, *stupid*!—even if she would like to see Gîzeh. Shouldn't she hire a boat, a *dahabeeyah,* to take her straight up the Nile? Perhaps she could sneak away without her fellow travelers noticing. Yes, that's what she'll do. She'll make the arrangements this evening and leave tomorrow. First thing.

Clemmie looks down and realizes she's rubbing the third finger of her left hand fractiously, easing an invisible itch. One more look at the skies, but there's no sign of the kites. She's just imagining things.

Unwrapping

1887

THE GASP SETTLES LIKE A mist on water. But they still don't speak. The gathered look at the *thing* that's been unwrapped. Her father looks at what he's revealed. And from her chair, Clemmie lowers her hands—the amulet with them—and looks where all the other eyes are fixed.

At last, an older woman in the crowd finds her voice, asking what they're all thinking.

"How is it possible?"

Clemmie knows that she should answer. She wants to answer. Yet she doesn't know what to say, or how to comprehend what's before her eyes. She can only stare, like the rest of them.

"What trickery is this?" demands a gentleman, a spatter of wine on his shirtfront resembling blood.

"No trickery." Dr. Clement Attridge holds up his hands to show their emptiness. "I knew nothing of this. I'm as surprised as you are."

She notes the sparkle of wonder in his eyes, as amazed as his audience. Her astonishment matches theirs.

"What a monster!" gasps a lady.

"Think only of what a grand spectacle you are witnessing," Clement says. "You came tonight to see the macabre. And now you are here for what will be the pinnacle of my lectures."

Our lectures, she thinks. He couldn't tell his paying guests the meaning of the hieroglyphs without her there. He may have excited her interest for all things Egyptian, even taught her the few glyphs that he's familiar with, but she made them the subject of her studies. The focus of her life.

She holds up the amulet.

"Stop," she says, rising and stepping forward. "Bind it up."

It, because what else should she call the mummy?

He looks at her as if she's deranged. The onlookers have paid to see the mummy unwound, and only a madman would stop now. But then, there is a madness to this business. Egyptomania, they call it. This hunger for the relics of that bygone civilization. Perhaps the mania part has become too real?

"It's incredible," says a young redcoat, exhaling his words as he stares. All of them staring. "What I would do to own a specimen like this."

"There," Clement says, gesturing to the redcoat. Triumphant. "Thank you, sir. A gentleman from our Queen's army who knows a rare treasure when he sees one."

It's more than a rare treasure, she thinks. It came with a message. She feels the threat behind the inscriptions, but she knows better than to be disturbed by such things. And yet here she is, horror coiling in her belly. It must be the suffocating warmth of the room, the shadows looming and making the candlelight shiver. A dark night lends to dark thoughts. Why else would she be disturbed by something that she knows is no real cause for concern? Surely it's just that she's shocked to come across such unusual wording.

"Isis and Nephthys," she continues, fulfilling her role of hieroglyphist and pointing at the glyphs that represent those mythical sisters. "The wording here speaks of wrath, pain, and ruin."

What's the use? They don't understand, as if she speaks in that old tongue instead of their own. If anyone acknowledges her—and why would they, when she's an eighteen-year-old woman and they're here to listen to a senior doctor?—they don't show signs of recognizing the names that she uses.

She assesses the small crowd with disdain, her flared nostrils absorbing the spice and melted wax. She feels contempt for herself, too, for being party to this. And then she looks at the amulet and its rare lines, straying from the typical texts. Incantations in relation to the afterlife are relatively common, such as referring to the *ka* or ghostly double coming and going to eat food, but these are different. More akin to something Poe or Alcott might have conjured and deviating from examples of other archeological finds. As she now reads the icons fluently, their interpretation is etched into her mind. She wants to talk to him alone. Maybe she can intimidate the audience with what she has read, enough to make them leave.

"It's a warning," she says. "According to the glyphs, we mustn't touch them."

Finally, she says *them*. For that's what the mummy is. The duplicity of the Double *Tyet* suddenly makes sense.

"Let's see the rest of it," someone says, ignoring her words.

"We came for an unwrapping," the redcoat agrees. "So unroll the creature."

There's nothing else she can do to stop this, and, in truth, she's as curious as the crowd. Biting her lip until she tastes metal, she watches. This is what she sees:

A human body, brown like a carved wooden statue. She finds herself counting as each limb, each body part, is uncovered. One chest. Two arms, and two hands. One groin. Two legs, two feet. Everything outwardly normal apart from one thing. The first thing.

Two heads.

Dahabeeyah

I T'S A RELIEF NOT TO see Mr. Luscombe or the Lions when she slips out of Shepheard's and walks toward Boulak, where, the clerk assures her, she'll be able to procure a *dahabeeyah*. The bazaars are quieting with the sinking of the sun, vendors readying to return home; donkeys with ears as big as their faces splayed tiredly on either side of their heads, no energy left to keep them upright. The smell of coffee lingers on the air, mingling with horse dung cooked crisp in the sun. Around a corner, an amber cat retches up whatever scraps it last ate. She observes with pity, and when its yellow eyes meet hers, the stare is so familiar her breath hitches.

One seller tries to tempt her with the last of his sweetmeats, to make an end-of-day sale, but she shakes her head. A headgear stall catches her eye, and she takes a brief detour to try on palm and pith hats, and traditional *keffiyeh* headdresses, checking the results in a cracked glass that splinters her face into multiple versions of herself.

Seven years' bad luck.

A blessing she wasn't the one to break it, but even if she had, could her circumstances get any worse?

She selects a palm-leaf hat, woven expertly but not remarkably attractive. No bonnets of European fashion will be a match for this exotic sun, and the hat could be prettied up with a ribbon or sash. The seller is helpful and recommends some soft pink fabric so fine she can see her fingers through it, perhaps intended for a veil, which she ties around the crown. It still resembles something a *vaquero* or cowboy might wear rather than a lady on an expedition, but she must be practical and she puts it on. After paying, she gains directions from the vendor and makes for the Nile.

The tops of the *dahabeeyahs* are visible before the glint of water. Suddenly being by the Nile makes her think of the river back home in Essex, and for the second time that evening she remembers a lemon-eyed cat from long ago. Extinguishing the memory, she walks toward the nearest boat, waving a signal to the man atop the deck. He ambles down, grinning.

Forming her question in Arabic, she asks if he's the captain.

"*Reïs*," he says, nodding and reaching into his pocket for a piece of paper that's cloudy with wet spots and yellow fingerprints. It's too marred to make out anything on it, but she presumes it's a certificate of recommendation.

She keeps to his tongue, telling him that she wants to go up the Nile; to set sail tomorrow. The *Reïs* replies that it depends on the wind, shrugging to show it's not up to him, and asks her how far.

"To Denderah." She hesitates only slightly before adding: "No questions asked."

The *Reïs* nods. His tobacco-tinted smile grows as quickly as a squeezed sponge in water as he hurries to reassure her of his discretion, eagerly flashing the paper once more to indicate former satisfied passengers.

"Miss Attridge!"

Turning around in surprise, she spots Rowland Luscombe a few steps away, his leg dragging in the dirt. Not an ugly movement, but still noticeable. After luncheon, when they'd left the dining room, she'd noticed the way he walked. At first, she'd supposed he had a blister or a sprain, but then she realized that the limp was connected to the slight tilt of his body.

She frowns. Has he followed her?

He asks her pleasantly what she's up to. Hands in pockets. Eyes scanning the horizon. Too casual, she decides, and then berates herself for it. Why is she so suspicious?

She nods toward the *dahabeeyah*. "I'm just arranging my transport."

"When do you plan to leave?"

"I hardly see how that's any of your concern."

The *Reïs*, despite obviously not following one whit of their English, is enjoying himself immensely, head turning from Rowland to herself and back again. Rowland frowns at their one-man audience, leading Clemmie away from the bank with a hand on her elbow.

"If you intend to go wandering around, I'd suggest hiring a *dragoman*."

"You might have noticed that I don't need one," she says, pulling her arm free and turning to face him. She's not short, but still only rises to his chin. Without his tilt, he'd be even taller. "I speak enough Arabic to get by."

"I did notice that," he says. "But a lone woman in a foreign country walking unfamiliar streets when the light's fading—I'm sure you're able to envisage the risks?"

She flushes. "You're right. I shouldn't be speaking to strangers. Good evening."

He laughs. "My, you're sharp. I was just thinking of your safety."

Perhaps she should be grateful to him. Maybe that's what he expects: a word of thanks.

"You'd be surprised how capable I am of looking out for myself."

He wrinkles his nose. "No doubt. Still, it might be better if you had an escort. That's why I thought I'd come along."

"You followed me?"

"You're welcome," he replies sarcastically. When she doesn't say anything else, he gestures at the boats. "You're still set on going up the Nile, then?"

Does he mean to be this irritating, or does it just come naturally? Is it merely that she's tired from traveling, that her nerves are taut, that she feels more waspish than normal?

"Of course," she says. "That *is* why I'm in Egypt."

"But what about our excursion? You promised you'd come."

"I can change my mind."

He shakes his head, rubbing his jaw. "Why would you want to? You're an Egyptologist. We'd enjoy it all the more if you came. You could explain the history and myths, interpret any hieroglyphs that we come across."

Just as she used to do at the Attridge events.

"How can you not want to see Gîzeh?" he adds.

"I do, but I don't have much time. I must press on to Denderah."

"One day can't make that much difference."

"I already have my own plans."

His eyes cling like limpets. "Why don't you want the crew to ask you any questions? That makes it seem as though there's reason to."

She pulls herself up taller. Had he been listening all that time? But even if he had overheard, she spoke in Arabic.

He chuckles at her confusion. "I was once a military man," he says. "Serving here in Egypt, I couldn't help but pick up a word or two of the native tongue."

His knowledge challenges her own, and she eyes him warily. What does he want? Why is he spying on her?

"Now, are you going to hire that *dahabeeyah*?" He crooks his elbow at her. "Or shall we head back to Shepheard's and go ahead with our outing tomorrow?"

She wants to stamp her foot, to slap that triumphant smile off his face, to jump onto a *dahabeeyah* and sail away from him that very minute. What would that prove? Maybe it would be better if she found out more about him and why he's so interested in her. A hasty scan of the skies sets her slightly at ease. Empty. Maybe she imagined the birds earlier. And she does want to see Gîzeh. More than a want. A longing. A need to see the high peaks in noontide brilliance bright, as the poem of two Tennyson brothers paints it. To know it for herself rather than accepting the lithographs and descriptions of others. As Rowland said, one day can't make that much difference.

Even so, she can't forget the reason she's here. Her mission. The fascination for ancient Egypt began as a game, grew to an obsession, became a curse. Now it's controlling her every move.

She held her breath, as though it was something that could be bridled. Inhaled it, so that nothing could be heard. Mastered that type of inward breathing that wasn't quite a breath and wasn't not one either.

Is this what it is to be a ghost? she wondered. But she didn't say it. She couldn't risk being found.

This was part of the game, the game of Myths. She was Nephthys. She never had a choice. Never put herself forward as Isis, and she wasn't going to be Set. Playing the villain was only enjoyable to an extent, but the fascination disappeared when the comeuppance came. And she didn't like to be Osiris because he was killed.

That meant that she was Nephthys, and she waited. This part wasn't in the myths. But she took the role seriously, because that's what she was like. Serious. And having studied the character, she filled in the gaps and created the rest of the story, until Nephthys was a part of her, and she of Nephthys.

In the current scene—and they played it often enough that it had become scripted—she was hiding from Isis because she had discovered her love of Osiris. Nurse Pugh would stop playing and say it wasn't proper to play out love affairs, but her father only chuckled and said that he saw no harm. After all, he said, myths are myths, and life is life.

A footstep sounded, breaking a dry twig, and she sucked in her breath again. Fashioning her face the way Nephthys would have worn it. A mixture of fear and pride. They were playing by the River Chelmer—the Nile, they called it—and she'd imagined away the green grass to sand, and the birdsong to the wail of a wronged goddess.

Overhead, beyond the aspens that she pretended were palms, something flew through the sky. She forgot that she was hiding. Forgot that it was only a game, for in that moment life and myth had merged. The bird was unmistakable. Large. Bigger than a kestrel or sparrowhawk. Forked tail. Wingtip feathers splayed like reaching fingers. A red kite.

She opened her mouth, daring to whisper where before she hadn't dared to breathe.

"Isis."

Limestone

THE CARRIAGE RIDE PRODUCES so much dust that Clemmie is obliged to hide beneath her handkerchief. She told the clerk not to have her room cleaned, so she doesn't have to worry about someone going through her things.

Celia, dressed in knickerbockers, which have already won her more stares than she could possibly have dreamed of, chats merrily along the way. Back at the hotel, she'd made a show of turning, hands on hips, asking Clemmie what she thought of her attire, her voice loud enough to demand an opinion from the whole room.

Oswald watches his sister intently like an old spinster chaperone, releasing the occasional *Celia* as a word of caution. He rests a shotgun across his knees that he pats as fondly as a pet dog. Rowland spends the journey seemingly admiring the sights—dust, a passing caravan of camels, the Pyramids and Sphinx looming closer—but sometimes he flicks a pensive gaze in Clemmie's direction.

She hasn't forgotten that he immediately knew who she was, but perhaps it's hardly surprising to come all the way to Egypt and meet someone who's heard of her family. After all, Egypt is likely to attract the types of people who are familiar with her late father's line of work, and her part in it. She studies Rowland's face when he's not looking, knowing that she wouldn't have forgotten if he'd ever been in one of their audiences. Besides, he told her that he hadn't. Why, then, does she get that peculiar sense of vague recognition when she sees him?

Khalil, the Lions' *dragoman,* scatters remarks along the journey, as if to prove that they haven't wasted their money on his services. The bazaars, he tells them, must be explored. The Khedive's palace museum, a site to be savored.

"To see beyond Cairo," he continues, "you are right that the surest way to travel is to take a *dahabeeyah* up the Nile."

"What was that?" Clemmie stirs at the mention of a *dahabeeyah,* lowering her handkerchief.

"Khalil was advising the best way for our group to see Egypt," says Celia.

"Our group?" Clemmie repeats.

"Yes. Didn't you mention going up the Nile? I can't think of anything better—what a lark this will be! Where was it you wanted to go again?"

If she answers, there will be no way to stop Celia from tagging along. But there doesn't seem to be a way of avoiding the question without being rude.

"Oh, just a temple complex I've read about in my studies."

"It must be more than just a temple complex, Miss Attridge," says Rowland. "After all, you almost sacrificed today's excursion so you could set off."

She manages to mask her glare behind a smile. Returning to her haze of cotton and eucalyptus, she gestures to the approaching limestone formations. They're getting close now.

They ride the rest of the way in a silence that's as uncomfortable as the burn of sand sticking to damp skin. Clemmie takes a double breath to fill her lungs, but either the sun is getting too warm or her corset is too tight. She inhales her oiled handkerchief again, but she's grown so used to the camphoraceous odor that she barely smells it anymore.

The carriage stops. Khalil announces that they've arrived and Clemmie clambers out onto the sand. Unaware of anyone or anything else, she stares upward.

From a distance the Pyramids had looked like nothing more than a child's sandcastles on a beach. But now they become everything Clemmie had ever imagined, looking down on the tourists with the conceit of pharaohs. Mystical and impossible, they're delicate enough to crumble to dust, mighty enough to crush them. These mammoth structures that housed the dead, stripped bare now, hold nothing but ghosts. Remembrances. Isn't that what ghosts are?

Here at last, she tells herself. Her eyes sting, like that magical moment when you feel the approach of winter's first snow.

The locals here are prouder of their wares than the ones from the bazaar, and justly so. Here they offer a chance for the traveler to climb the limestone structures, to enter the Great Pyramid, to provide *bakhshîsh* for a worthy cause. By the lofty tombs resides the Sphinx, its sagacious face watching the trespassers. Alert. Eyes holding an unspoken story that has been guessed at for centuries but will never be proved.

"How long do we stand here staring at them?" Celia asks, shielding her eyes with her hand.

"Aren't you impressed?" says Clemmie, annoyed at the interruption.

"They're very big and old, I grant you. But they are just a pile of stones."

"You'll have to forgive my sister's ignorance," Oswald says. "Unless this tomb holds some tragic account that she can romanticize, you won't get much enthusiasm out of her."

"I did read a story about a Pyramid before we came," Celia says, "and I can't help but wonder if it was inspired by true events."

Her expression is hungry. Hungry to feed on a sensationalized history, relishing the horrid and macabre. Clemmie's seen that look before in her father's study. She tries to swallow, but her throat is thick with dust.

"It was about getting lost in a Pyramid," Celia continues. "It also had the most dreadful curse and was quite frankly terrifying."

Oswald chuckles. "See? What did I tell you? If you can turn this trip into a gothic romance, she'll adore every ruin you can offer her. But please tie it all up neatly at the end with a dead hero, a broken heart, and the sense of all hope being lost."

Perhaps he expects Clemmie to laugh along with him—Celia certainly does at her own expense—but Clemmie has no inclination to join in. How can they talk so lightly of curses? What fools they are.

"Well," Rowland says, "what are we waiting for?"

They all turn to look at him, and when she meets his eye, she knows that he's been watching her. Has her face given her secrets away? She'll have to be as unreadable as the Sphinx if she wants to keep him from finding out her real reason for coming to Egypt. She can't risk anyone knowing, for there is no one she can rely on. After all, she trusted her father and look what happened.

They start to climb. There's a team of Egyptians to guide them. They speak in English, with the odd French word thrown in, which is rather disappointing for Clemmie and proves her point about there being no need for a *dragoman.*

Still, jubilant to be here, she can't resist sharing her knowledge.

"Did you know," she says as they ascend, "that if the Great Pyramid were in London, it would cover the whole of Lincoln's Inn Fields? The Greek historian Herodotus was told it took as many as one hundred thousand men twenty years to build."

At the entrance, they can feel the air coming from inside. A stale and undiluted heat that suffocates. Peering through at the dark passage, Celia declares that she's not going in. That it's a thing of nightmares.

It's also a thing of dreams. Clemmie imagines the people who built this phenomenon, the mummified pharaoh once laid inside for his eternal rest, the embalming that came before as devised by Anubis on the body of Osiris in the stories. Everything she's read, every childhood reenactment of these myths, each night of unwrappings and translations, has led to this moment. She sets a foot on the threshold, startled at the wall of heat hitting her, as sure as if it were a physical force. Her corset feels tighter than ever. She fights for breath.

They keep going. Upward. Aiming for the top, to look out over the plateau and then enter the Pyramid on the way back down. The Egyptian guides are patient, showing them where to put each foot or hand, how to scramble up. Clemmie reassesses Celia's knickerbockers with grudging approval.

"Look at that." Celia points to two circling specks in the sky. "Some kind of hawk."

Breathless, Clemmie stops her ascent and follows the trail the birds make, as if spectating on a pair of dancers in a ballroom.

"Black kites," she says.

"Black kites? Can you really tell from that distance? You're sure?"

Clemmie doesn't take her eyes off the birds, nodding briskly. "Oh yes. Quite sure."

They're swirling. So high up it would normally be hard to say for certain what they are without some magnifying aid. But she knows. She was a fool to linger, she should have gone straight to Denderah. It isn't her corset and the heat anymore. Her lungs are tightening by themselves. She tries to lift her handkerchief, but it's too late. She's already coughing.

"Goodness, Clemmie—what's wrong?"

It's nothing, she wants to say, but she can't fit the words between her wheezing coughs. Clemmie searches her pocket frantically, pulling something out—a flash of a locket that she senses Rowland doesn't miss—before pushing it back in. She must have left the bottle in her hotel room, and she tries to express her alarm to the others with her wide eyes.

Rowland clambers quickly next to Clemmie, not hesitating before gripping her forearms and pulling them above her head.

"It'll get the air in."

She thinks he's explaining to the others, but maybe he's apologizing to her for their close proximity. For being bold enough to touch her. Their guides produce flasks of water and offer her sips. One has a lady's fan tucked into his white garments, which he flaps furiously in Clemmie's face, perhaps accustomed to corseted Europeans fainting mid-climb.

It takes some fifteen or twenty minutes, but at last the coughing subsides.

"I'm so . . . so sorry," she gasps. "What a . . . oh . . . fuss I've caused."

Rowland's frown seems to be one of concern rather than displeasure at having their excursion interrupted. "Let's just return to Shepheard's, shall we?"

She knows better than to argue. Even though they didn't enter the Pyramid or stand before the Sphinx, Rowland is right. The Egyptians seem disappointed that they didn't get to show off the view from the top, but cheer up enough when Rowland and Oswald both hand them a generous *bakhshîsh*, insisting that they visit again when *mademoiselle* is better. Rowland leads her back to the carriage, and she's aware of his hampered gait, but also relieved by it, giving her time to breathe.

How to explain to the others what happened? She doesn't try to, but in her fogged head she realizes that this attack was more acute than the last one. They're getting increasingly worse, lasting longer, and leaving her weaker, fatigued, her lungs scarred and scratching. She imagines a day when her lungs will collapse in on themselves, when her windpipe will freeze and she'll choke on oxygen she can no longer inhale.

This is her fate if she doesn't succeed at Denderah. And that's why she's here. To bring healing. To undo the wretched past.

If she plays her part right, if things work out the way she's calculated, she may change the course her life has taken. The future altered for the better. Then she can look back on recent years, not as the horror that they are but as something distant and obsolete. A myth.

She thinks of Celia's story about a curse, but it's not just a thing of fiction. Not for her. When the carriage starts up, she turns to look back, fighting the fatigue that's pushing her down with an invisible fist. The sun is bathing the stone-hewn mounds in shades of grayish buff.

Above them, two winged specks begin their descent, and she knows even from this distance that their talons are open, eager for the kill.

Unwrapping

1887

SHE HAS NEVER KNOWN A mummy like this one. Never seen anything that looks like it. Yet here it is. Here *they* are. In the heart of an old manor house in Essex lies a preserved, double-headed body.

How old? she wonders. Just children.

These mummified remains are those of siblings. Siblings, like Isis and Nephthys, those names etched in hieroglyphs on the amulet. The myth of Osiris is often represented in funerary texts, Isis and Nephthys beckoning to him. But on this amulet the mention of the goddesses feels almost personal. Beckoning to *her*.

"What happens next?" the redcoat asks.

Clement, her father, looks pensive. She wonders if he's thinking of money to be made. He could take the mummy to London. The broadsheets would be pinned up, pointed at by curious fingers, and torn down to be examined by eager readers. She can see it now:

The Two-headed Mummy Exhibiting at Such-and-such-a-place
Admission One Shilling per Person

She can read the thoughts going through his mind so easily, the idea growing. One shilling? No, not a small any-man exhibition. So many fakes in those displays, and this is no fake. Something more fitting, then. Viewings at the house, perhaps? Maybe in this very room. Yes, she sees it all going through his head, and only when those in the gathering press closer does he awake to their inquiries.

"Could it be separated into two beings?"

"That's right. Cut in two. Could it be done?"

"If alive, would it have survived such a thing?"

"Didn't Barnum have some twins like these? Never heard of a mummy like this, though."

"Weren't you a surgeon, sir?"

He nods and shakes his head. Dazed. The words that she wants him to say are nowhere near his thick tongue. Why can't he tell them that the evening is over? That they've had their money's worth. That they'll have to pay again to have another peep. Why can't she have him to herself so she can impress on him the importance of what she's translated? It could further knowledge in the field of Egyptology, comparing this text to other finds. Does the unusual wording pertain to the era or the location?

"Ladies and gentlemen," Clement says, squeezing his hands together. She sees them tremble despite his effort to hold them still. "Dear guests. You've paid tonight to see something spectacular, and you've been amply rewarded."

"We know what we've seen," says a man. "Now cut them apart the way Mummy Pettigrew used to do."

She watches her father's face. He's always treated his collection with the utmost respect as a scholar and enthusiast, so surely he won't cave in to their demands. Something about this night feels different, however. Why must they compare him to Mummy Pettigrew? They need only stroke his ego and he'll do things they'll come to regret.

"I'm not Pettigrew," he says, and it's true. He's not. Never before has he cut into a specimen the way that the former antiquarian and surgeon would, revealing the cavernous space where they once whisked the brains like beaten eggs, and dating the period the body was from based on what was found inside. If just the heart remained it could be declared an earlier specimen, the other organs removed to be kept in canopic jars. If the various organs were intact, then it could be pronounced a later example of mummification.

"Call yourself a surgeon? If Mummy Pettigrew were alive, he'd not waste this opportunity."

"Will you sell it, sir? I'll buy the mummy to start my own collection." This here from the redcoat.

"And what good will that do us?" The old woman speaks again, her voice becoming high-pitched in an effort to be heard. "Cut the creature apart. Dissect it."

They sound frenzied. Egyptomania is catching.

Clemmie tugs on his arm, begging his attention. "Please, Papa. Trust me. This piece is too special. You need to listen to me and replace the bindings."

"*I* need to listen to *you*? Perhaps your mother is right and I have indulged you too much. You're eighteen years of age. I am the doctor and your father. Remember whom you're talking to."

Tears sting her eyes at this rebuke, but she blinks them away. Yes, they are father and daughter, but are they not colleagues as well? Anger replaces hurt, and she fails to hide this from her tone.

"Do not forget the years I've spent studying. I've translated countless amulets at our former events, and none has been worded like this one. We need to take the time to study it and understand what we've uncovered."

The tip of his nose turns red, the way it always does when he is furious. He turns back to the crowd and she braces herself for his address.

"Friends, I repeat, I am not Pettigrew."

She holds her breath. Has he heard her words of warning after all?

"Did Pettigrew ever produce such a specimen as this?" he continues. "You're looking at the new Mummy King. The name 'Pettigrew' will be dust when we are through tonight."

There's a cheer as he produces his old doctor's bag, swiftly brushing away a layer of dust to reveal a history of use in cracked leather. He opens the bag, metal permeating the spice. From inside, he lifts an array of tools. First, a surgical knife, long and straight, the tip forming a point. Next, a saw that looks more fitting for building fences than dismantling bodies. A trephine is third, the tool that's always made her think of a corkscrew. A scalpel follows.

He rolls up his sleeves as if for surgery, shaking slightly. It's been a long time.

She rests a hand on his, and he looks at her with irritation. She might as well try to reason with a drunk man.

"You can't do this," she says.

"It's just a mummy."

"If you do, there's no going back."

He shrugs her off and makes the first cut.

Companions

CLEMMIE TRIES TO REST WHEN she gets back to Shepheard's, but no matter how tired she is, she can't sleep. In her mind's eye, she can see the raptors circling, their haunting cries echoing in her ears.

Giving up on sleep, she paces. Slowly. Her efforts hampered by her bruised chest. Corset removed to help her breathe. She remembers Rowland holding her arms as though she was a child's puppet. The memory of his touch stains. In her chemise, she checks her bared arms in the mirror, but there's no mark. She rubs her face with her hands and groans.

Clemmie sits at the dressing table, opening her portable leather writing case. Working methodically, she smooths out paper, removes the cap from the ink bottle, and dips her mother-of-pearl pen into the black liquid. Her fingers twitch. She drums them on the blank page, then lowers the pen, walking to the window so she can peer out. Cairo is alive with its people and visitors, and the calls to the mosques with their pearlescent minarets. Manure besmirches the ground outside the carpeted steps of the hotel. It is beautiful and filthy all at once. It's a world of opposites and she's here, at last. But she can't enjoy it.

She'd linger in Cairo if she could. She'd take her time seeing the sights and wonders, admiring art, history, and sculpture. Her whole life she's dreamed of this opportunity. It's cruel that she's come so far but has no time to explore.

The surest way to travel is to take a dahabeeyah *up the Nile.*

If it hadn't been for Rowland, she'd already be on one. Her mind is made up. No more delays. Today has been proof enough that she shouldn't have tarried in Gîzeh. Tomorrow, she'll return to Boulak. To the Nile. And this time no one will stop her from hiring a boat to Denderah.

☍

Shepheard's might be full of people, but among so many eyes it's impossible to blend in. No sooner does Clemmie step foot in the foyer than a familiar arm threads around her own.

"Clemmie, how are you this morning?" cries Celia, as Oswald and Rowland amble over to join them. "I was so worried when you didn't come to the dining room last night. Have you quite recovered from your turn? Do you have any idea what happened? Are you still well enough for our trip?"

Our trip? Clemmie's stomach sinks as she recalls that Miss Lion has already invited herself along to Denderah. Oswald asks if she's feeling better, but Rowland doesn't speak. She's almost certain he noticed the locket back at the Pyramid. Instinctively, she slides her hand into her pocket now and grips it. The cool metal calms her, providing a familiar relief.

This is her moment to detach herself from the group.

"I've been enough of a bother," she says, "and you must forgive me for cutting yesterday's excursion short. I have clearly proved to be quite the encumbrance, so I promise that I shall trouble you no longer. I intend to hire a *dahabeeyah* this very day and be on my way, so I shall bid you all a farewell and Godspeed on your travels."

"But my dear Clemmie," Celia whimpers, "I thought we were going together. We did say it would be such a lark. I was rather upset about being sent all the way to Egypt on account of Michael . . . but it won't be nearly so dull now we have such a splendid traveling party."

"I agree with Miss Lion," Rowland says. "Traveling in a group is surely preferable over solitude? Why, first there is safety in numbers—surely something worth our consideration when the journey ahead is so unfamiliar to us all! And we can all share and gain from each other in knowledge. I, for one, would love to understand more about your study of Egyptology, Miss Attridge. And then, of course, we do make a fine party, the four of us, don't we?"

He's right, of course. Years ago, she never would have imagined herself coming to Egypt unaccompanied, yet here she is with no compeer, no chaperone, not even a maid. She tries to think ahead. It would be easier if she were on her own. Nothing must hamper her mission.

Something else answers for her. It's not that she doesn't like being alone, she's used to it. It's how she's spent the best part of her life, tucked away with her books, learning about Egyptian artifacts, hieroglyphs, myths; studying different languages, because they were her way to travel before coming here. She's never had a hankering for friends. Growing up, she had all the companionship she ever needed at Bickmore with her family, Nurse Pugh, and her cat, Bast. And before everything went wrong, the family was set to grow rather than shrink. All her life she's told herself that she has no need for friendships beyond kin. Yet she's aware of a peculiar confliction stirring within her breast.

Having others around might prove wise. Her asthma is only getting worse, each attack more frightening than the last. Mr. Luscombe, the Lions, and the Pyramid guides certainly were helpful when she had her last episode at Gîzeh. And if she agrees to travel with them, they could share the costs. She has limited funds these days after all, a thought that sours her tongue with fizzing rancor. Besides which, she can keep an eye on Rowland Luscombe if she has him in her sights. She ignores the voice in her head warning that it will be easier for both sides to observe each other at such close quarters.

"I suppose it would make sense to join forces if you were going up the Nile anyway," she says slowly. "Let's hire a vessel."

"On the way can we visit the bazaars?" Celia pouts to win the others over.

"I'd prefer to make haste," says Clemmie. Already she's behind schedule. She remembers the kites at Gîzeh yesterday. Her deteriorated health. The reason she's here. The fear that persistently coats her insides, turning her organs hard and resinous.

"There isn't a wind today," says Oswald. "We can't set forth without one, so we might as well visit the bazaars on the way to select a boat. Trust me, Celia will be a nightmare to be around if we don't humor her."

They have no idea what real nightmares are.

Cairo

THEY'VE SEEN GLIMPSES OF THE bazaars, and there's been no escape from the noise of the stalls, but a morning spent browsing the Arabian market on the way to Boulak seems so luxurious it's almost sinful. There's a bitter tang of coffee brewed freshly by a *Kahwagee*. Here stands a line of donkeys for hire, a little boy shoveling up their dung into a steaming heap that attracts the loud buzz of flies, the sellers swatting them away from tobacco, foods, sweetmeats. The streets are shaded by tall, narrow buildings, upper stories projecting like the jettied floors of Tudor structures, giving them a strangely familiar, almost English feel. Everything else about them is foreign. Yellow stone. Yellow earth. Yellow sun.

The bazaars are busy, too vast and overwhelming to do them justice in a short, sweeping visit, and as there's no wind, they take their time. Ambling. Picking up trinkets, admiring examples of *khayamiya*, that form of textile sewn in elaborate designs and vivid colors, and trying on *keffiyehs*. Amid the smells of coffee, sugar, and manure, the Egyptians selling everything from carpets and slippers to dates and smithed goods, Clemmie wants to feel happy. To enjoy herself. It seems wrong that the pleasure should be squeezed out of her trip when she's wanted it all her life. But maybe she deserves this. Maybe it's her penance to be here and not be able to appreciate it fully.

"You're feeling better?"

Unconsciously, she's walking in step with Rowland. Celia has delayed Oswald at the slipper bazaar, and is trying to persuade him to buy her a gold pair, curled up at the toes and fit for a court jester.

"I'm much recovered, thank you," she says, apologizing again, still embarrassed about what happened at Gîzeh. She searches his face for validation. A slight frown forms a dune on his forehead, and she wonders if it's from the effort of walking. His hobble is an irregular melody, but it sets a rhythm that suits her lungs. With anyone else she'd be gasping to keep up, but next to him she can breathe calmly and take in the sights without requiring a constant supply of eucalyptus.

"I should thank you," she adds, rubbing her arm at the memory of him holding it up. "You stepped in quickly. I'm grateful for your help."

He seems not to notice her thanks, limping to a stall laden with sweets. A pyramid of white-dusted jelly squares takes pride of place in the center. He buys a bag of them, yellow and pink, and then returns to her, proffering his purchase so she can help herself.

She reaches into the paper bag. "What are they?"

"Lumps of Delight. Have you never tried them before?"

Shaking her head, she opts for a yellow one, a cloud of white dust dancing to the ground. She watches the powder, imperceptible the moment it meets the dirt from the street.

"Well?"

She pops it in her mouth. Plump as a cushion, it's gummy on her teeth and tastes of lemons. Not sour but vaguely citrusy, like oversweetened lemonade. Too delicious to chew for long, it melts away in seconds.

"Delightful, aren't they?" he says, white crusting his lips. "Have a pink one."

She expects strawberry, instead uncovering elegant notes of rose water, the taste of an English garden in her mouth.

They begin walking through the streets again, stopping on occasion to stroke a carpet, or to admire an elaborate saddle fit for the purest-bred Arabian stallion, or to dip their fingers into the bag of sweets.

"How long have you suffered with asthma?" Rowland asks.

She looks at him, surprised.

"I've seen it before," he adds, "and you can't mistake the smell of eucalyptus."

That's how he knew what to do, stepping in to lift her arms above her head.

"You mentioned before that you were in the military. Are you a doctor? Were you in a medical corps?"

How else did he know eucalyptus is used to ease the airways?

"No, no. Nothing like that. Was it the dust that brought it on, do you think?"

She ignores the question. He'd never believe her if she told him. Sometimes, she wonders if she believes it herself, and then she remembers all that's occurred over the last five years, and she can't doubt it.

"I stupidly left my bottle of eucalyptus behind in my hotel room."

"You should be more careful. You never know when you could have another attack."

"Well, you needn't worry. Celia has seen to it that I shan't be alone on my journey up the Nile, so you can keep an eye on me if you want."

She doesn't mean to sound petulant.

"I thought you didn't mind having our company?"

Clemmie considers her earlier turmoil. She doesn't know what she wants anymore. Just to get to Denderah. That's all she can think of.

"It's not the company I mind, but I don't like being interrogated."

"Interrogated?"

"You've seemed intent on questioning my motives ever since we met. Why?"

A vendor interrupts, thrusting some beads into Clemmie's face. They're the shade of that traditional Egyptian blue, the pigment often used on amulets and vases of long ago, and they glimmer in the brilliance of the day. She shakes her head and sidesteps him.

"What about you?" she asks. "You've told me nothing about yourself. Do you have secrets, Mr. Luscombe? And if you do, would you tell me?"

She's proud of her riposte. Proud of the small smile that creases his mouth, proof that her words have sunk in.

"I suppose we all have skeletons in our closets," Rowland admits. "Yet I ask that you humor me for a moment. You're a hieroglyphist who used to host mummy exhibits. You've only just come to Egypt despite it being, presumably, a lifelong fascination; and you've come alone, with no chaperone. Your asthma may be improved by the warm climate—then again, the dust might not help. You would claim to have a passion for the subject you've obviously dedicated your life to, but you were going to bypass the Great Pyramid and the Sphinx. I concede that we all have secrets, Miss Attridge, but I'm sure you can understand why I find yours so intriguing."

The sugar residue on her tongue is cloying. Does he see her as a riddle to be solved? She's worked hard to wrap up her life and secrets over the last few years so that they won't be unraveled by outsiders. Far better that no one knows what's been happening at Bickmore. Heart beating against its double cage, she searches his face to gauge how much he knows, but his features leave no clues.

It is unsettling that he's learning about her, but she doesn't know him at all. He's an Englishman from London. His name is Rowland Luscombe and he used to be in the military, serving at some point in Egypt. For some reason, he walks with a limp. She knows nothing else about this man. He has a knack for interfering, she'll give him that, but shouldn't they be talking about him? Her mother always advised that men like to talk about themselves.

She recites her excuses. The ones she's practiced in her mind.

"I've always wanted to visit Egypt, but there have been delays. Recovering from the influenza, serving at my father's sickbed, mourning. These things have prevented me from coming until now. Finally, I am free to travel, and perhaps, as you say, the warm air will improve my breathing."

None of what she tells him is a lie. It's what she doesn't say that stands out.

"And, specifically, you want to try the air at Denderah?"

What is it he really wants to know?

"I'm sure you and I both know that the air at Denderah will be no different from the air at Gîzeh. But I'd like to see the depictions of Isis and Nephthys in the ceiling artwork whilst I'm here."

May the knots of Isis and Nephthys know rest.

"Isis and Nephthys? Why them in particular?"

Clemmie looks away, scanning the sliver of sky visible between the jetties. Clear. Just blue and nothing more.

"They're favorites of mine."

✗

The *Reïs* Clemmie had formerly spoken to isn't at Boulak when they arrive, no doubt already hired and well on his way with a party of tourists. There are plenty of other *dahabeeyah*s of varying sizes to choose from, however, each captain eager to show off the cabins, scrubbed decks, and modestly furnished saloons. After they've shaken hands with a promising *Reïs* by the name of Captain Youssef, and eaten their luncheon at Shepheard's, the group retire to their rooms to write letters and refresh themselves while the sun is at its zenith. Over dinner they'll make the final arrangements for setting forth up the Nile the next day.

Clemmie approaches her closet, removing the box within. As she toys with the catch, her mind wanders from what it contains, instead pondering Rowland's limp, Celia's regular references to Michael, and Oswald's frowns of disapproval. She's spent another morning with her new companions, yet she still knows next to nothing about them.

"We all have secrets," she mutters to herself, running her hand over the sleek wooden design. *Table croquet.* The label on this ordinary box lies about its extraordinary contents.

People come in hordes to steal from the land of Pyramids, but she's come to give something back.

Unwrapping

1887

IT'S OVER. AT LAST, IT'S over. The people file out, one by one, some muttering about the things they've just witnessed, others as mute as Zacharias after his interview with the angel.

But this was no angel. They've seen something they couldn't even have conjured up in their nightmares. They've witnessed two heads being uncovered from a mummified child's bandages, and they've observed a scientific dissection. It was a dreadful thing, really. Flakes of the preserved skin—or was that the resin itself?—peeled with each cut, dropping onto the table and the floor. Mummy dust. Some might consider calling in artists to scrape up the remnants to turn into that highly craved paint, which Rossetti lauded so much in his life.

Clemmie watched her father work, his actions feverish, exclaiming with wide eyes over the division of the twins. Of the sisters. She knows they're sisters because the body is naked, and because of the hieroglyphs on the amulet. It's too late now to think about the warnings, and she's not even sure why she reacted to them the way she did. Curses are just an invention of sensationalized stories, after all.

"What a night," her father says. She glances at him but he isn't looking at her. He speaks to himself. Perhaps still cross with the way she addressed him.

She looks back at the remains and shudders. Her father did this, but

she failed to stop him. Disrespect is infectious; if anything, her imper-
tinence incited him to this irreverent act. She rubs her hands on her
skirt over and over, wanting to rid herself of the contagion, the association. When she's through she turns her palms slowly, inspecting them.
Pale. Spotless. But they don't feel clean.

"I wish you hadn't," she says.

His exhale is loud and nasal. "I'll have no more of your lip, miss."

"But Papa—"

He strikes the air with his hand, cutting her off. "Are you so blind
that you can't see what this has done for the business?"

"Your rarest specimen is in pieces. What good will that do our business?"

"You don't know what you're talking about."

"Am I so ignorant? You used to believe in me and encourage my
learning. Have I not assisted you for years?"

She remembers the consequences of her earlier rage and reins in
her temper. Trying to placate him, she hurries over to nestle her hand
in his elbow.

"Please, Papa, don't be cross. Only remember the way we built up
this profession, and how you introduced me to Egyptology."

She reminds him how he would take her to visit the British Museum,
or borrow books for her to study, or even purchase copies for her very
own library. Everything from *Précis* by Champollion to the fifth volume
of *Egypt's Place in Universal History*, complete with *The Book of the
Dead* and hieroglyphic dictionary, grammar, and selected texts. That
was the book he brought back from a London trip, failing to remember
the ribbons her mother had requested. He had presented her with the
brown paper package, crinkling beneath her fingers as she untied the
string, his own lips twitching in the delight he knew she felt. That moment she knew, knew that he believed in her, that she could master the
forgotten language that only a few were beginning to revive for the
current age. She plies him now with memories of when he would teach
her the myths or reveal a new addition to his collection, a papyrus or a
ring bearing hieroglyphs, ones she would use to practice and master
her knowledge of the script. This passion is one they've shared and it
has made them close.

"How could you cut up the mummy when you've always valued them so highly before? And this one, such a unique specimen. It seems such a . . . waste."

His move away from her is subtle, but enough for her hand to drop. He doesn't want to forgive her. Not tonight, when she has got in his way and failed to share his elation, or to praise him the way his paying guests did.

"I don't know why I ever indulged you." He steps to the mouth of the door where the hall beyond is a dark throat. "Your mother was right, you know. This isn't a matter for young women. I refuse, *refuse*, to discuss this any further."

"Papa!"

"We'll clear up tomorrow," he says as he lights a candle to take to bed. He pats the remains of the dicephalous mummy—or mummies, she's not sure whether to use singular or plural in this case—fondly as he leaves the room, expecting her to be the one to turn out the lamps. She's the assistant, after all. The darkness swallows him and his meager flame, as his murmurs about what a grand night it was grow faint.

She takes in the mess they've left behind. Embalmed limbs splay across the table. Two heads bear frozen gasps. They found two hearts—no other organs, so it is an early specimen—and she considers those two hearts nestled inside one body. What does it mean for two hearts to be part of something that is one?

Her eye falls on a mosaic quilt hung over the back of her father's chair, one he drapes across his knees in cold months. She walks to his desk, picks the quilt up—each patch a story of childhood garments— and lays it over the twins, tucking them in to their chins and placing the amulet on top. Her movements cause more flakes to fall from the table, and her efforts seem futile, this token of protection come too late. Her vision clouds with tears, and when she blinks, a dark spot marks the table, round and wet amid the dust.

It is late, and she turns out each lamp, one by one, until a single pale light is left. The shadows have substance, and the shape of the quilt twitches in the corner of her eye. She spins to face the resting mound, watching closely. Nothing. She steps back, shakes herself. Foolishness only breeds foolishness. She's spooked by what they've seen tonight. All she needs is to sleep.

One hand hovering by the last lamp, she clutches the silver locket at her throat with the other, unable to take her eyes off the mutilated sisters. Thinking, also, of two mythical sisters. The ones that the hieroglyphs named.

A throne. A house with a basket.

Isis and Nephthys.

Letters

My dearest E,

It is unnecessary for me to say that I wish you were here with me, but I am writing it down just the same. There have been moments— when I stood at the foot of the Great Pyramid, when I tasted Lumps of Delight in one of Cairo's bazaars, when I inspected dahabeeyahs on the bank of the Nile at Boulak—that I felt you with me. And so, as I promised myself that I would, I am writing down what I see here in Egypt, so that you will read about it, and know it as I have.

Shepheard's Hotel is a fine establishment, right at the center of the comings and goings of this busy city. No, I should start before that. In my last letters I described the monotony of the steamship, and the dreadful motion of it upon the waves, and how I feared I would never arrive in port or manage to stomach a meal again. I also wrote to you when the shore was in sight, just as I was starting to become accustomed to the swell of the sea. And now I can confirm that I arrived in Alexandria and from there boarded a train that brought me to Cairo. I have not hired a dragoman, as many travelers do, and I think you would be proud of how much I understand and the number of phrases I can speak in Arabic. Today, I learned a new word: lazeeza. It means delicious, but I will explain more about that in a moment. I wish I had all the time in the world to examine every ruin along the Nile, to study the hieroglyphs and gain an even greater understanding of this early civilization. But we both know that I am here for other reasons.

Which is where I announce that I have formed a group with three other English travelers. Ha! You will laugh at me when you read this. Could it really be me that I am talking about? you will say. Has your little Clemmie had a whiff of some strange sea air, or tasted some food laced with a magical potion that has changed me? No, I am not entirely converted. For despite joining up with these people, I am still suspicious of one of them. He is called Rowland Luscombe and he knew who I was when I told him my name. He seems to guess things about me before I even tell him. If you were here, you would say that I am a fool, that many people with interests in Egyptology would know who Clementine Attridge is, and perhaps you would be right. I never have been one to want to spend time with people, apart from you. For years I have studied a forgotten language, and I declare that easier to understand than my fellow creatures.

We have hired ourselves a dahabeeyah after some deliberation. Each vessel was so impressive, it was hard to decide which to engage. The Reïs we settled on is called Youssef and he has the finest vessel, with enough cabins to suit us all (myself, Rowland Luscombe, Celia Lion, her brother, Oswald Lion, and their dragoman). Like me, Celia has come without a maid, and the men haven't brought valets. We were informed that the crew will sleep on the lower deck. There is a saloon, a bathroom, and of course, the hold for our luggage. I have inspected my cabin, which has a closet for me to conceal my precious cargo in, as I swear it will not be left to be rifled through in the hold.

There is also a small kitchen on board, so we have no fear of starving on our journey. This is how I came to learn the new word, for Captain Youssef's daughter sails with him as the cook. This practice surprised me, for I am aware of the female segregation common in this part of the world, but Mariam—that is her name—explained that they are Copts, and so she enjoys a few more liberties than other women. She tells me that she even went to a school for girls in

Cairo as a child, for there is a girls' Coptic school, which opened some thirty or forty years ago. Mariam let us sample a curried dish that she was preparing, which was quite excellent, and when I tried to express this, she introduced me to the new word: lazeeza. It is my aim to expand my vocabulary by learning at least ten new Arabic words every day. Perhaps improving my Arabic will distract me from what I am really here to do.

Now I must close this letter, for if I am to be fresh in the morning, then I should like to have an early night. At last, I can really say that tomorrow we set forth. You are with me in my heart, and I know that a part of you will journey up the Nile with me, accompanying me to Denderah.

Yours always,
Clemmie

Instead of sealing the letter, she fixes it inside a scrapbook. Then she flips through the earlier pages. It already holds former examples, each one addressed to *E*. Letters pasted into each page. All unsent. Letters that, if her quest to Denderah works, she hopes will one day be read.

Dear Stone,

I congratulate myself on leaving you behind to tend to things in London whilst I am away. As it happens, I require you to make some enquiries for me. Whilst at Shepheard's, I have had the good fortune to meet some fellow English travelers and we are agreed to make our journey throughout Egypt together. One of them, an Egyptologist and hieroglyphist by the name of Clementine Attridge, has with her a rather interesting wooden box, which I suspect holds more than she would have me believe.

Using the funds I left behind, take yourself to Chelmsford in Essex and, using discretion, ask about there—especially in the public houses and among the servants at Bickmore House—as to any rumors of artifacts or suchlike going missing. It would be better if you kept my name out of these enquiries, so I suggest you adopt a different name, history, and purpose throughout your investigation, the particulars of which I shall leave to you.

My thanks for your trusty services. I await your response with impatience, and whilst I appreciate your subtlety, would also be grateful for much haste to be applied in this matter. These instructions have proved too long to fit in a telegram, but I dread to think of the duration of mail traveling both ways, and suggest you wire your response in brief terms. Meanwhile, I will arrange for all communications to be forwarded as I make my travels. Tomorrow, I begin a journey up the Nile. Our destination: Denderah.

Sincerely,
Rowland Luscombe

Hapi

THE BREEZE IS BLOWING THAT morning, carrying a whisper of hope and a tremor of excitement. Khalil is sent on ahead of them with their luggage, the hired carriage piled high. Clemmie is unwilling to part with her table croquet box, even when Rowland clearly picks up on her unease, eyes sparking with interest. Maybe she should have tucked it out of sight in one of her cases, but she can't bring herself to have it far from her.

They leave Shepheard's with promises that they'll be back after their voyage, passing through the bazaars one last time as the vendors are setting up and the smell of mutton kebabs cooking on their skewers adds the savor of meat juice, garlic, and cumin to the breeze. That same wind carries them forward, propelling them to Boulak, hardly permitting Rowland to hobble let alone pause at the sweetmeat stall to buy another bag of the white-dusted squares, and with rose gumminess on their teeth and powdered sugar on their lips, they arrive at the port. The rows of *dahabeeyahs* bob like ducks on an English stream, their masts emulating rushes. Here, their very own vessel is waiting for them.

"It's such a funny-looking boat," says Celia.

"Magnificent," says Rowland.

"Not bad," says Oswald.

And Clemmie toys between the thrill of the moment and the unease of why she's here. "Shall we set off?"

It's not quite as simple as that. Their *dahabeeyah* is moored on the opposite side of the river, so they board a *sandal,* a miniature version of what's to take them up the Nile, and make their crossing with the wind nearly dislodging Clemmie's palm-leaf hat. If it keeps blowing like this, they'll get to Denderah sooner than she dares to hope.

"What did you say our boat is called?" asks Celia.

"*Hapi,*" Oswald replies.

"What a jolly name," Celia says, brushing strands of hair from her eyes. "Proof that we're destined for happy travels."

Clemmie tries not to smile and catches Rowland's eye, his face bearing the same look of restrained mirth. She turns her attention back to Celia.

"I think the spelling of it—H-A-P-I—suggests the Nile god."

The *sandal* pulls up alongside *Hapi* and they climb aboard. There's no sign of Mariam, no doubt busy preparing their luncheon, but Youssef is ready to greet them.

"*Sabah al-khair,*" he says, welcoming them with smiles and nods, his voice spilling over his beard and matching his large frame. Clamped in his mouth is a *chibouk* pipe, so long that the bowl almost touches the floor. His bare toes drum the deck eagerly, and while he seems ready to release a cry of *yalla* so they may be on their way, he takes time to gesture around the *dahabeeyah,* to the sky—a fine day—to the river ahead, uttering a handful of Arabic words that Clemmie and Khalil vie over translating for the rest of the group.

"Well then," says Rowland, when they're all standing on the upper deck, the crew busy preparing to set sail. "Let's get settled."

Yalla. On their journey, that word will become the rising sun of each day, the wind in their sails, the skim of vessel through river. It's a word that sets Clemmie's chest clenching with anticipation and apprehension. The beauty of another language transforms the ordinary "let's go" into the extraordinary. *Yalla,* her heart responds. *Yalla yalla yalla.*

It doesn't take long for Celia to turn *Hapi* into a floating hotel, rearranging the vessel's furniture along with their own added comforts. Her instructions are delivered with teasing command: *Move the pianoforte over here. Turn it slightly. A little more. Ossie, I told you to get the crew to move this into the hold. Mr. Luscombe, I don't suppose you'd carry this to my cabin for me, would you? It's much too heavy for me.*

Clemmie observes with something between admiration and resentment. She feels incapable of flirting and making jokes the way Celia does. Despite journeying up the Nile being her idea—the others inviting themselves along—her presence still seems like the epilogue to an already complete story.

Having made the most of the bazaars, Celia has purchased all the necessary furnishings to make the vessel feel comfortable. An amateur depiction of Waterhouse's *Cleopatra* graces the wall, so cheap it would have been a crime to refuse it. The paint is chipping already, the frame splitting along the grain, but from a distance, with narrowed eyes and a healthy imagination, it could be fancied as the real article. Celia has even bought a rug, an affordable imitation of the more luxurious examples sold in Cairo's marketplace, and the splendid array of maroon, indigo, and gold adds a richness to the main communal room. A Bible and the three volumes of *Jane Eyre* have been carelessly left behind by a former traveler, and Rowland adds Scott's *Waverley* novels to the *dahabeeyah*'s narrow bookcase to form their own little library.

Having hidden her croquet box under some folded undergarments as a deterrent in her cabin's closet, Clemmie settles in the saloon with her personal copy of Edwards's *A Thousand Miles up the Nile,* the perfect handbook for the occasion. Over the top of the pages, she observes Celia coyly tuck her arm into Rowland's to be led *for some air on the deck*. Some moments later, Oswald enters the saloon, hesitating longer than necessary before passing awkwardly through to the cabins beyond.

Obviously, she makes them feel uncomfortable. *They* make *her* feel uncomfortable. Why did she ever agree to this?

"Miss Attridge, won't you join us?"

She looks up from her book in surprise as Rowland sticks his head around the doorway.

"Don't tell me you came all the way to Egypt just to read that book?"

She snaps it shut, nearly dropping it in her haste as she stands.

"It's . . . um . . . a little hot," she jabbers, hoping that her explanation also accounts for the color in her cheeks. But it's January, not exactly the hottest season in Egypt. They both know that she's lying.

He offers his arm. "The awning is up."

The cabins' roof forms the upper deck, and this is furnished with rattan chairs that look a little too fine for the old *dahabeeyah*. Instead of sitting, Clemmie stands at the rail, watching a *fellah* on the bank as he operates a *shâdûf* to irrigate the land. A lever system, the *shâdûf* is made from a long pole with a bucket on one end and a weight on the other resting on a wooden prop, used to raise the water into troughs. It looks like heavy, tiring work. Nearby, foreign birds with long necks wade in the shallows, imitating the mythical *Bennu* bird that Nephthys supposedly guarded. The scenery forms the sort of image Clemmie imagines captured in a tinted lithograph by David Roberts.

"Where's Ossie?" says Celia. "He's missing it all."

"Why don't you find him?" says Rowland. "And I'll ask the cook to get us some fresh lemonade."

Celia's eyes sparkle. "I'll just be a moment. Don't have too much fun without me—and sing out if I miss anything."

Once Celia has disappeared down the steps to the lower deck and into their living quarters, Rowland joins Clemmie at the rail.

"So?"

She barely turns to look at him. "So what?"

"Are you pleased to finally be on your way?"

Pleased is hardly the word, but she can't tell him that. "Of course. I've always wanted to explore Egypt."

"You've always wanted to, or it's what your father wanted for you?"

She whips around to stare at him. "That's very bold."

He holds her gaze a moment and then deflates. "You're right. I apologize. I just thought that maybe you're really here to honor a dead father's wish."

Clemmie returns her attention to the *fellah*.

"It's true, my father did want a son to share his name and interests, and then I was born instead. Clementine instead of Clement Junior. For a time, Father treated me like the son he'd never had. Not so far as to name our business Attridge and Daughter. No, that was a step too far, even for him. I'd thought it had a ring to it, but he wouldn't concede."

She tries not to scowl, but the pain is still raw. She loved her father, but she also resents his memory for numerous reasons. This is one of them. Partner in everything but name. Apparently, men don't usually go around advertising that they work closely with a woman.

"Even if my father was determined that I'd inherit his passion for Egyptian antiquities, that doesn't mean that I only followed in his steps for his sake. I willingly fell for Egypt and its history."

He smiles to make amends. "So, how did you come to study a lost language?"

"I'm no pioneer," she says. "That accolade deservedly goes to the French and English hieroglyphists, Champollion and Young. You've heard of them, of course? They fought for the title of 'hieroglyph decipherer,' much in the way that their countries fought to occupy this country. The Rosetta Stone was the key."

"Yes, I did know that."

"The ancient language of the Egyptians," she says excitedly, "in all its written variations—the famous hieroglyphic script, from the Greek *hieros glyphos,* meaning sacred words, and the less iconic hieratic, demotic, and Coptic script—is a lock that people are still trying to pick. The more keys you have, the more access there is. I thought about that when I was growing up, and realized that when you need another key, you just have one made. I decided to be one of those keys, to help unlock the past."

"Your gift is admirable," Rowland says. "Especially if one considers your knowledge of Arabic and French as well. Do you speak any other languages?"

"I'm fairly proficient in Latin and Greek, but my German is only passable. It really needs more work."

His eyes widen. "More work? That's most impressive, to be so young and yet have accomplished so much."

"Ah, but I have a guilty secret, Mr. Luscombe. Never have I actually finished stitching a sampler, and I cannot entertain you all on the pianoforte, or paint watercolors of the sights that we shall see on our journey. I confess that the only novels I read are in foreign languages to further my understanding. You see, the many hours that other young ladies spend in recreation have, in my case, been employed in various linguistic studies. I am quite inept when it comes to the arts, I'm afraid.

But languages come easily to me, the way some people have an ear for music, or others an eye for perspective and sketching. Hieroglyphs captured my heart. I had no choice. I had to pursue the study of them."

"I presume you're one of these fanatics with hieroglyphs carved into the walls of your house, and a pet dog called Anubis."

"Not quite," she says, mouth twitching. "But I did have a cat called Bast."

He chuckles. "Of course." Then: "Did have?"

"She died. Doesn't everything eventually?"

She doesn't tell him the whole story.

Thankfully, he moves on, perhaps deterred by the bitterness in her voice, asking her how her father came to be an antiquarian and mummy unroller. It's strange, reliving a history of her dead father in the land that he was fascinated with. Dust meeting dust. The words tumble out of her, like the myths she used to narrate at Bickmore's events. Familiar. How he was a respected surgeon, then he met her mother, they fell in love, married, and with her dowry Clement was free to focus on the estate and give up medicine.

"And become the master of Egyptology," Rowland interjects. "Rendering his scalpel to the dead rather than the living."

Sickened at the turn the conversation has taken, Clemmie longs to discuss something else. But the past leans on the bit, and her hold on the reins slips as Rowland nods for her to continue.

"He'd always had an obsession for the myths, an obsession he passed on to me."

She doesn't say *love* because she's come to realize that love and obsession are two different things.

"And the new Mummy Pettigrew was born."

She stifles a shudder, forces a smile. Her chest is starting to feel tight, and she reaches into her pocket for her handkerchief. The other item, the one she always keeps with her, falls out. Before she has a chance to move, Rowland stoops and picks it up. Turning it over. Reading aloud the tiny engraving.

"*No one else hath loved thee more than I.*"

She snatches it from his hand.

"A locket?" he asks.

Briefly, she runs her fingers over the snapped silver chain before stuffing it back into her pocket where it belongs. The broken chain represents her family. Represents her.

"It's none of your concern," she says.

A sting travels through the tingle of skin to her eyes and she strides across the deck, the silence embossed by the cut of water and an occasional shout from the crew.

"I found him!" Celia's voice interrupts the stillness, footsteps following. "What's going on?" She laughs. "Look at you two on opposite ends of the deck. Anyone would think you've quarreled."

Rowland and Clemmie meet the Lions with stiff smiles.

"I was just cleaning my shotgun," Oswald says brightly.

"*Again!*" Celia tuts. "You care more for that firearm than you do for me . . . Mr. Luscombe, where's the lemonade you promised?"

Clemmie volunteers to order it, glad of the excuse to step away. She heads for the little kitchen as a healthy chatter rises from the others.

"I didn't even think to bring a gun," says Rowland. "What do you plan to shoot?"

"I'm here to hunt a crocodile," Oswald replies.

"Ossie's quite the shot back at home."

"Celia, there's a big difference between pheasants and crocodiles."

The three of them laugh. Clemmie listens to them wistfully. Resenting them for their skill. Wondering how they do it. They make it sound so easy—but then, for all her knowledge of languages, she's never had much practice at trying her words on people.

Lemonade

SHE FOLLOWS THE SMELL OF hot oil. Captain Youssef meets her on the lower deck, approaching with strides so weighty she's surprised they don't compromise *Hapi*'s stability. When he speaks, he removes the *chibouk* from his mouth and tugs at his beard. On his wrist is a small blue tattoo of a cross.

"How do you find the *dahabeeyah* and the river?" he asks her in Arabic, clearly glad to have a traveler whom he can speak to without the need for a *dragoman* to interpret.

"I'm glad to be on my way at last," she replies. "I'm actually in search of your daughter."

He gestures to the little structure from where the savory smells are coming. Only when she sees the flicker of pride in his eye does she linger to ask him how his daughter came to work with him.

Youssef's laugh is the equivalent of firing a cannon, and if Clemmie is his target, then his aim is true. She beams despite herself.

"Do you think it's strange for a daughter to work with her *baba*?"

Clemmie hesitantly shakes her head, unsure what to tell him. It's not so very strange to her.

"My Mariam used to stay at home with her *mama* whilst I escorted travelers up the Nile. But then we were hit with the cholera and her *mama* died."

"I'm sorry," Clemmie says.

Youssef continues to smile. How can he be happy after losing his wife? Maybe the river is healing. Perhaps Mariam is a comfort to him, too.

"When her *mama* died, I told Mariam that we'd better find her a husband, but she didn't want to get married."

"Not want to get married? Whyever not?"

Youssef laughs at her astonishment.

"Mariam said, 'No, *ya baba*, let me come and cook on the *dahabeeyah* for you and your guests.' It was an interesting idea, and the more I thought about it, the more I liked it. The last cook I'd had made my travelers sick from the *kunáfah* because the cream had soured, but Mariam is a good cook and never uses cream that's gone bad."

Clemmie makes mental notes of the words she's not quite sure of, but mostly she understands what Youssef has to say, only interrupting to ask what *kunáfah* is.

"Ah, *kunáfah* is a pudding made with rice and almonds, cream and cinnamon. Mariam is bound to make it for you on this trip. When she proposed working on the *dahabeeyah*, I pictured how the kitchen could be hers to cook in, live in, sleep in, how I could sleep across the doorway to protect her, and she could look after me too. I realized how good it would be for us to be together, so I agreed."

His readiness to accept his daughter in his business is an aching reminder of Clemmie's father. A man who encouraged her learning, but as she grew older, couldn't quite bring himself to include her in everything.

The others are waiting for the lemonade, so she excuses herself. Following the aroma of fried onions, she considers Youssef's words. The kitchen is so small, Clemmie wonders how Mariam manages to live in there. She pictures Youssef sleeping along the entrance, like a faithful guard dog, and smiles at the thought. Her father would stand up for her when her mother argued against Clemmie's involvement in the business. He was her own guard dog, to a point.

Mariam is a tall woman, like her father, but unlike him she's slender and graceful. She wears a white headdress across her brow and over brown hair that is visible just above her ears, the draping fabric matching the rest of her garb.

When Mariam hears Clemmie approach, she looks up from stirring what will no doubt be their dinner tonight. Her heart-shaped face shows the smoothness of her years along with an almost childish glimpse of her front teeth beneath her lips. Despite this youthfulness, her bearing is balanced with maturity in the way she holds her head. She may be dressed plainly, but along with her quiet confidence, she is quietly beautiful.

"You want something, *ya aanesa* Clementine?"

"Please," Clemmie replies, following Mariam's lead and keeping to Arabic, "call me Clemmie."

"You want something, *ya aanesa* Clemmie?"

Clemmie gestures outside. "My companions were hoping for some lemonade."

Mariam reaches for a jug and fills it with water from a nearby barrel. She then adds sugar and begins slicing lemons in half, the sour tang mixing with the caramelization of onions. Mariam's movements are musical and fluid. Woman and river are one, and Clemmie wonders if that's what happens when you live alongside something.

"Your father told me how you came to work with him," she says, glad of an opportunity to practice her Arabic. They're close in age, she guesses. Mariam the elder by a couple of years or so.

Mariam nods, but continues working in silence. Squeezing cloudy tears from the lemons, tasting, and adding more sugar.

"He said that you chose to work with him instead of marriage."

"That's true. Marriage is a holy commitment, and I already have commitments of my own. My religion, my father, one to my country, and even one to myself. Maybe one day, I will make room for another responsibility, but I cannot leave my father yet. We need each other. For now, I have found my place, and it makes me happy."

Returning to mix her lemonade, with her back to Clemmie and shoulders squared, Mariam's stance is a clear sign that their conversation has ended.

Clemmie fumbles for something else to say, not wanting to watch the lemonade making in silence.

"I understand your commitment to Egypt. Similarly, it has a deep meaning for me. I've dedicated my entire life to its history."

Mariam looks up fleetingly, her eyes narrowing. "How have you done that?"

"I'm a hieroglyphist." She goes on to describe her father's collection, but even though she leaves out the details of unwrapping the mummies, Mariam stiffens and a shadow crosses her face.

"Many Europeans find my country a rich source of entertainment."

Clemmie falters before rushing to explain. "Not at all. At least, I don't. It's more than that to me. My interest in the history is genuine, I'm not a naïve collector. In fact, I have a purpose in being here. It's why I have to get to Denderah."

Has she said too much? Perhaps, but she doesn't want Mariam thinking she's an inexperienced ingénue when archeology has shaped who she is.

"Forgive me, *ya aanesa* Clemmie, but you are a visitor. I do not doubt that your party will be respectful travelers, but I do not think you are aware how much my country is hurting because of tourists and their demands. Even the race to interpret the hieroglyphs was based on politics and power. Empires have fought for their right to claim us and our buried history. It isn't enough that they have us now, they want to take our past from us too."

Clemmie pauses, several of the woman's words beyond her present repertoire of Arabic. After a moment, she gathers the essence of the statement and summons a response. "Surely the international study of archeological finds here will increase our chance of understanding your history and only lead to an increased admiration for it? Isn't that a good thing?"

"Some time ago, the export of our antiquities was banned if the excavators didn't have a permit, but there are still many who dig and smuggle without a license. It's not just the stealing that pains me. The *khat* or corpse was supposed to be safe once it was buried, and back then they believed that the *ka* and *ba,* those ghostly aspects of the dead, wouldn't recognize the *khat* if it didn't stay intact. I do not believe the same things my ancestors did, but their wishes should be honored. Artifacts are being damaged, provenance is being lost, and history is undone because everyone wants to claim their own Egyptian treasure."

Clemmie straightens her shoulders, keen to defend herself. "I have never sought to undo history. Far from it. I've studied hieroglyphs to preserve Egypt's history—and of course it elevated my father's enterprises."

"Your knowledge is commendable, *ya aanesa* Clemmie, but more so when put to good use. Your expertise could be of value if used for more than personal satisfaction and entertainment."

Clemmie frowns. "What do you mean?"

Mariam turns away. "The lemonade is ready."

She puts the jug on a tray with four glasses, and when she proffers the tray, her lower arms peep from her sleeves, revealing a small blue tattoo on her right wrist.

"What is that?" Clemmie asks, mostly to ease the tension but also out of curiosity. She saw the same mark on Youssef.

Mariam looks down, considering the tattoo as if it's a freckle that she'd forgotten she had. "This? As a Copt, we wear the cross on our right wrist as a sign of who we are."

Clemmie has seen the Coptic cross before and has even seen a heavily tattooed man once when a circus passed through Chelmsford—apparently, he had tattoos everywhere and she'd wondered how far he would go to prove it—but she's never seen a woman with a tattoo, or realized it could have a sacred meaning.

She takes the tray from Mariam.

"*Shukran,*" she says. Thank you.

Mariam smiles briefly, front teeth peeping like seed pearls. Yet it's clear she views Clemmie as just another insensitive tourist. Clemmie hesitates, feeling a pang, a need to share. It's been so long since she's had someone near in age to unburden her heart to. Mariam returns to the pan, adding minced garlic and seasoning, and Clemmie shakes the thought away. How could Mariam help her? She heads back toward the others.

A cheer rises from her traveling companions as they spy the lemonade, and she molds her face into a smile. There's no time to be distracted by Mariam's criticism. She must focus on why she's here.

As she pours the lemonade, Mariam's words echo in her mind.

Your expertise could be of value.

Unwrapping

1887

CARRYING THE LAMP TO LIGHT her way from the study, Clemmie moves up the gallery and to her room, where she picks out someone waiting in her bed, and the mound of a cat at the bottom.

"Mmm, you're finished at last," Rosetta says sleepily from the quilts.

"It was a late night."

"I had quite the night myself. Mamma could hardly contain herself from interrupting your evening when I told her, even though we all knew it would happen eventually, and Papa had already given his blessing."

Clemmie takes off her dress, petticoat, and corset, finally released and in her nightgown. Her silver locket lies cold against her exposed chest. She blanks the memory of the conjoined sisters as her father cut them apart, and feels the approach of a different scalpel coming for her. Knowing it even before her older sister reveals the news.

Rosetta stretches her left hand out. A hand that sparkles in the lamplight. Not a scalpel. A ring. What's the difference?

"He asked you?"

"He did."

"Tonight?"

"Tonight."

"Oh, my darling . . ."

When Clemmie was growing up, on the few occasions when she wasn't learning languages or playing the game of Myths, she liked to visit the stable block to pet the horses. One time, as she passed by the feed shed, she heard a scampering in the oat barrel, and when she lifted the lid there was a mouse inside. She wanted to free the creature without squeezing the soft flesh of its body or being bitten, so she measured its movements and finally let her hand dive in, grabbing the mouse's tail.

Before she could set it down on the ground, however, the little mouse must have panicked, dangling as it was upside down from her hand. It rocked its body forward and back, and suddenly it was gone. She saw it scamper away, not quite sure what had happened, until she realized that she was still holding something.

The mouse had bitten off half its own tail in its bid to be free.

She now feels like that mouse, losing and gaining in the same instant. Her joy is for her sister, but she also senses the loss before it has happened, no doubt as the mouse must have done before its teeth severed its tail from its body.

Severed. She tries not to think of the twins downstairs.

Burrowing beneath the sheets, she's glad that they nearly always ignore their separate rooms, choosing instead to share a bed. Rosetta leans across to kiss her cheek, and Clemmie inhales her sister's scent: musk perfume, and beyond that, a hint of rosemary water on her hair.

Slipping her ankles further down the bed, she's surprised that Bast doesn't react as she usually would, shaking the quilt playfully between her teeth. She reaches to stroke the soft slate-blue fur before extinguishing the lamp, prepared for a sleepless night after everything that transpired downstairs . . . but the fur is so cold she must be mistaken. This is a lifeless thing, not a cat.

As realization dawns, as the discovery is usurped by tears, as Rosetta sits up beside her and releases cries so loud that the whole house is roused, she remembers a line from the amulet.

Let what is sacred be brought to ruin.

Bloodstone

WHEN IT'S DARK, AND THE horizon has turned the many colors that the sinking sun deems to paint it, they moor near a place called Bedreshayn. Mariam's tiny kitchen is alive with clanging pots, and the four travelers retire to their individual cabins to ready themselves, the promise of lamb and starchy rice on the air.

Clemmie changes into her dinner dress, remembering how much easier it was when she used to have a maid. That was before her father died, before the inheritance was mutilated like the mummy that came before it. Back then, life was normal and Bickmore was a house that collected more than antiques. It stored memories, love, and happiness. The walls, every panel and surface, each chair and rug, bore motes of the past that were more than dust. The attic nursery, where Nurse Pugh would sip her hot chocolate while Clemmie drifted off to sleep. The gardens, which were a stage to enact the game of Myths. The study where, until that night, she spent so many joyous hours holding pieces from her father's accumulated antiquities, imagining the hands that fashioned the clay or chipped away at the stone until it was a polished piece. Connecting her to historic times. Bickmore saw all of that, it was part of it, an extension of her kin. It was a place she felt safe in. She hasn't felt safe now for a long time.

Her dress is sage and carnation pink, and Clemmie tries to be pleased with the reflection that looks back at her in the long mirror. It's been a long time since she's had a new dress, and she wishes she had something in that fashionable eau de Nil shade—how appropriate that would be in this setting—but the sage is the closest she has. There was no time or money to have a new dress made before she came, and she never anticipated socializing. It's fortunate as it is that she thought to pack one of her best gowns. If only she'd brought more.

There's a faint bobbing beneath her feet that reminds her of being rocked in Nurse Pugh's arms as a child, the echo of a Welsh lullaby stretching the bare skin across her clavicles. She picks at her nails, an old habit that has recently returned.

A rapping on her door interrupts her thoughts.

"It's only me, Clemmie dear," Celia's voice sounds outside her cabin. "Do let me in. I can't for the life of me decide which earrings to wear and I wanted your opinion."

Clemmie opens the door and in sweeps Celia, no longer in her knickerbockers, the prettiest peach dress making her hair look even lighter and her cheeks more rosy. Back at Shepheard's, Celia wore a stunning array of dresses, but this one exceeds them all. Clemmie's mouth waters as she drinks in the latest style, the ribbons at Celia's shoulders showing so much pale flesh, the trained skirt deliciously extravagant.

Celia sits down on Clemmie's bed, uninvited, and holds up two pairs of earrings. "Which do you think will look best?"

"I was wondering the same thing myself," Clemmie says. She pulls a wooden jewelry box off the table by her bed and sits next to Celia, who puts a gold earring in one ear, and an opal drop in the other, tossing her head dramatically.

"I like the opals," says Clemmie, lifting the lid. Inside, her jewelry box is lined with bloodred velvet, serpentine chains curling in the individual trays. She hasn't bothered pawning them because they're base metals set with paste and she doubts she'd get much.

"What's this?"

Celia's hand dives for something before Clemmie has a chance to see what she's found. But she knows. In a sudden rush of her heart, she knows.

"You dark horse," Celia says. "An engagement ring?"

Clemmie swipes for the gleaming object but Celia keeps it out of her reach, prattling about the warm weather swelling her own fingers, asking if that's why Clemmie isn't wearing the ring, then leaving no time for her to answer before declaring that Clemmie might have told them that she's engaged for she'd already started to pair her up with Ossie in her mind, and there she was thinking that she was the one with a secret amour.

Celia holds it up so that the ruby, the one genuine piece in Clemmie's box, catches the light. And it does, a tricking play of light on stone so that it's almost liquid. A pool of blood surrounded by diamond-cut teeth and set in lips of gold.

It's when the ring is in this position, vulnerable to the citron glow cast by the lamp, that Clemmie successfully seizes it, hiding it in a fist that turns white at the knuckles.

"I'm not engaged."

Celia's eyes widen at the possibilities. "But you were? Oh, do tell me, Clemmie! Did he die? Did he betray you? How tragic. Or did your family not agree? I sympathize fully. My parents are determined that I'll forget Michael on this trip—"

"I'm not engaged!" Clemmie says forcefully. She pushes the ring into the box's drawer, hidden away where Celia can't help herself to it again. Then she gathers up some pear-cut paste stones, holding them to her lobes in an effort to distract Celia from her discovery.

"Ah, these were the ones I was looking for. What do you think?"

Donkeys

THE FIRST ALARMING THING THAT Clemmie notices when she leaves her cabin the next morning is that the crew are not making ready to sail from Bedreshayn. This observation is quickly followed by another. When she steps onto the upper deck, she discovers a line of Egyptians along the bank. Some sport grins, others frowns, some are shouting, and others let their elbows speak for them. They all have one thing in common. Donkeys.

She asks what the parade is all about, and Rowland says that the donkeys are for hire. Following his line of gaze, she sees Khalil bartering with them. After pointing at a few potbellied beasts, he sends the rest away. Youssef is happily puffing on his pipe on the lower deck, evidently in no rush to set sail.

"For hire?" she repeats. "We're not landing here, are we?"

"Don't you know where we are?" Rowland looks genuinely surprised.

"Of course I do."

He wears a look then, as if he understands, and starts to chuckle.

"What's so amusing?"

"Your time limit," he says. "I almost forgot. But don't tell me the great Miss Attridge doesn't want to see Sakkârah?"

She ignores the title he gives her.

"We can see all of this on the way back," she says. "It makes more sense to visit them downriver."

He nods at the book in her hands. *A Thousand Miles up the Nile.* She brought it with her to read on the deck, before she knew her traveling party had other plans.

"I'm not sure Miss Edwards would agree with you," he says. "As I believe she puts it, the history of Egypt goes against the stream, and the Pyramid in platforms is the oldest building in the world. Thus, I agree heartily with her. We should view it before anything else along the Nile."

She flushes. It's just her luck that he would be familiar with the Egyptologist's memoir. Yes, Amelia Edwards did consider it better to stop off on the way up the Nile and view the sights chronologically, but why should they do the same?

"I would prefer it if we reached Denderah sooner."

That's putting it mildly. She needs to get to Denderah. She's running out of time. So far from Essex, other than by sending a costly telegram, she has no way of knowing if things are as they were when she left. And there is so little money, she must reserve every penny for this trip, and trust that the same frugality is being used at home. She took what little they had to get here. A telegram can wait.

He laughs. "Then maybe you should have taken a steamer rather than a *dahabeeyah.*"

"Steamers may be considered swifter, but I've heard that they get stuck on more sandbanks than *dahabeeyahs.* I'd rather bet my chances on the traditional vessel."

Still, it was a hard decision. The debate over which is best has been argued ever since Thomas Cook introduced the steamers. She came with the intention of hiring a *dahabeeyah,* but the day they engaged *Hapi,* she was tempted to try one of Cook's tours instead. The price was more favorable, but the risks of getting stranded on sandbanks less appealing. As things stand, she's glad they chose Youssef's boat, but it's just as well that she did agree to travel with her new acquaintances. The luxury of a *dahabeeyah* comes at a cost that is more manageable spread between them.

On the bank, the donkeys release a chorus that sounds somewhere between sawing through wood and one of her own asthma fits. They swish their ropey tails valiantly, but it does little to keep the flies away from their hindquarters. One kicks its belly but the horseflies are experienced, finding juicy places that hooves and tails can't reach. Already she's found bite marks on her neck and wrist where she's dared to let her flesh be exposed. It's just another reminder of how vulnerable she really is.

"I still say we should press on and see Sakkârah downriver."

"Clementine . . ." It's the first time he's used her given name and she's more than a little startled by it. "I don't know why you're in such a rush to get to Denderah, but you're an Egyptologist in Egypt. Enjoy this trip."

She doesn't know what to say. Something in his words calls to that inner part of her that wants to listen. But which is the deceiving voice? The one that stays true to her dreams, or true to her mission? She can't forget what she's left behind, what she hides in her cabin and in her heart.

"No one calls me Clementine," she says, knowing that she sounds truculent. Why does he bring out the worst in her? Trying to soften a little, she adds: "At least, they haven't since I was a little girl."

"All habits need to be started by someone."

She meets his eye, and there's something peculiar in his face that she feels mirrored in her own. If this moment were a papyrus, then she would need to take her time translating it. Studying it closely, mulling over the intended meaning and consulting her Birch dictionary. If only there were dictionaries to assist with interpreting people.

He tilts his head, like a dog begging for scraps. "Come on. Have a bit of fun."

Clemmie glances at the waiting donkeys. A breeze blows off the bank, carrying a whiff of dusty animal hair and fresh dung. She looks beyond the mealy-colored animals to the sand and pictures what's waiting beyond. The hieroglyphs she could read, the structures she could touch, the remains she could pray no one will find and take away.

"Very well."

When he smiles, his teeth glint in the sun. It is a warmth that radiates from him, leaving her flushed and smiling, and, in that instant, undeniably happy.

Roots

THE DONKEY THAT WILL CARRY her is fawn colored, a dorsal stripe emerging from beneath the saddle to its hindquarters. It's been an age since she's sat in a saddle, and riding a donkey will be a first. She asks the Arab holding the lead rope if the jenny has a name. The man smiles at her use of his tongue and pats the donkey's neck firmly, as if attempting to squash a horsefly.

"It is called Queen Victoria."

She tries not to laugh, wondering what the Queen would think to know that a *fellah* has named his ass after her.

"I expect you wish you had knickerbockers like me," says Celia, mounting with ease and looking extremely comfortable seated astride her gray donkey.

Clemmie eyes the saddle and gathers up her dress as she climbs into it, trying not to shriek as her guide gives her what's no doubt intended as a helpful push. She arranges her skirt and petticoats into two equal parts. There's something freeing about sitting astride, and if she were on a hot-blooded Arabian horse instead of this sleepy donkey, she'd have been tempted to kick both legs and see how fast they could go.

Once they're all mounted, Oswald steers his donkey to ride alongside Clemmie.

"Tell me, then," he says. "How did this all start for you?"

If this question had come from Rowland, she'd be suspicious at once. But Oswald is smiling blithely. He's just trying to make conversation. As such, she allows her mind to slip back to where it all began.

"I was just a child," she says. Her father had always collected artifacts, so she was used to seeing them. Beads, pottery, papyri. All exquisite examples of craftsmanship that would grip her with awe. Carnelian, jasper, faience, colors that have painted her world. Will the things made by her contemporaries still be beautiful in one thousand, two thousand, five thousand years? Are they fashioned well enough to last that long? The Egyptians had skill. They built Pyramids that have perplexed generations, and everything, right down to a tiny carnelian bead in her father's collection, was perfectly made. Made to last. Made to tell stories. Did the artisan ever wonder, as they polished, polished, polished the stone: Who will hold this in years to come and will they think of me, the one who first held it?

"My father stored the artifacts in his study, and when I asked for stories, he'd tell me Egyptian myths instead of fairy tales. I might have been young, and whilst the edges of the memory have blurred slightly, I can't forget where the love for Egyptology took root. He beckoned me into his study one day. Said he had something to show me and I ran in, thinking it was a present. It was better than that."

Queen Victoria trips on a rock, and Clemmie pulls on the reins to lift the donkey's head. Once the jenny has regained her footing, she continues with her account.

"My father showed me a mummified cat that had just arrived for his collection, and he let me hold it."

Even though she was young, she won't ever forget how that felt. It was small. Long. Thin. Wrapped so tightly you couldn't guess what was inside but for the shape of the head on top. And all she could do was think: *This was a cat. A cat from another time, and it is here in my hands.* She was young, and perhaps some children might have been frightened by the mummy, but not her. A fascination leaked from the cat into her bones. That is how it all started.

"Remarkable," Oswald says. "I'm not sure I comprehend the attraction, but I do respect that the hieroglyphs have an air of mystery to them, which makes it all rather intriguing."

"What about you?" She glances at him. He's too big for his donkey, and if his stirrups weren't so short, he could let his feet trail along the ground, carving sand. "Your love of shooting. Where did that begin?"

A sentimental smile sweeps across his face, and she wonders if the same one passed her own when she reminisced about the cat.

"Ah," he says. "That goes back to my childhood as well. I was a boy and my father was hosting a shoot. He let me go along, to watch the beaters flush out the game. Suddenly, he passed me his shotgun and said: 'Take it, son. This one's yours.'" Oswald shakes his head fondly at the memory. "The weight of my father's gun in my hands, the feeling of taking aim, waiting, listening for the jagged cry of a pheasant. I might have set out on the shoot as a boy, but my father was giving me a chance to become a man."

Because, in this world of death, wars, and empire building, killing is a rite of passage.

"He knelt behind me, held the gun with me, showed me what I needed to do. When the next bird took flight, I was ready. I got my first bird. And I'll never forget the look of pride on my father's face."

Are they so different, with their twisted pull toward dead things? Oswald might not understand her passion for Egyptology, and she certainly doesn't understand what's so irresistible about killing animals, but there is something in their interests that unites them. Even as she struggles to fathom where the hunger for power over the past meets power over life, she does appreciate the need for a father's approval. And she misses the bond that she once shared with hers.

Nothing has been the same since that mummy unwrapping five years ago. The amulet has seen to that.

Unwrapping

1887

THEY BURY BAST BY THE river after clearing away clumps of silver-spiked nettles. Just the two sisters are present, although they know that had their old childhood nurse still been in employment, she'd have been proud to mourn with them. Clemmie speaks through her tears, a final word of thanks to Bast for being more than a pet and companion and rather like a third sister, but Rosetta doesn't speak. She cries through it all.

Clemmie would have liked to have had Bast embalmed, but the current age hasn't quite caught up with the respect shown to cats in former times. It was with great delight that she came across Louis Wain's *Kitten's Christmas Party* in the *Illustrated London News* last year, and perhaps that, along with the rise in Egyptology, have inclined people to wonder: Is there more to them than catching vermin? What did those pharaohs see in them?

The mound of earth is patted down. She turns to look at her elder sister, whose face is smeared with tears and mucus.

"Any words?" she asks.

"No."

They stare at the heap awhile longer, wondering how long it will take the soil to settle flat again. How long till the grass and nettles reclaim the naked earth and hide this tiny grave?

"Only," Rosetta says, "I feel as though this is the end of an era. The end of our childhood."

"Our childhood ended some time ago."

"But our lives are changing. I became engaged yesterday. Bast is dead. Today's the start of a life where I won't be a part of this family, and Bast is no longer with us."

She loops her arm through the circle of her sister's. "You'll always be part of this family."

"You know what I mean."

A kite flies overhead—no, two of them—and she shields her eyes with the flat of her hand. Watching them swirl, forming a vortex. She recalls the candlelit horror of last night, and considers the mummy. A mummy that, as her arm slips out of her sister's, makes her think of the two of them. Sisters, joined and then not.

"Come for a walk," she says.

"No," Rosetta replies. "I'd rather not. I want to lie down before Horatio comes."

It's odd to hear Horatio's name and to think of him and her sister becoming a new entity that she won't be a part of. Clemmie brushes this thought aside and asks if Rosetta is quite well.

Her elder sister massages her temples. "Ever since last night I've had this dreadful headache."

She doesn't think anything of it as she watches Rosetta go into the house. Why should she? After all, they're both upset. They've experienced nerves and excitement, sadness and tears. A recipe for a headache, that's all.

But then, as it will turn out, the headache is still there the next day, and the next.

And the following week.

And the month after that.

Even a full half year later.

In fact, the headache never goes.

Decay

THE RUINS ARE HALF BURIED in sand that hides its treasures under a blanket of gold. These crumbled remains aren't what touches Clemmie the most. She thought they would be. She imagined staring up at the oldest Pyramid, touching statues, tracing hieroglyphs, and breathing air trapped inside tombs that was once exhaled by a long-gone people—but it isn't any of these things that sets her heart throbbing and summons tears to the dam of her eyes, waiting to spill. Instead, she's overcome by what isn't there. By how ravaged it is.

Vandalized graves tell a history of shame. She remembers what Mariam said about excavators and permits. Until she'd spoken to Youssef's daughter, she hadn't understood that smugglers were such a problem, but standing here she comprehends the truth of Mariam's words. Tourists and dealers have destroyed what well-managed digs would have been able to save. She wonders how much has been lost.

The ground of Sakkârah is littered with what's left behind, like dropped remnants of loot from a conquered city. Rags, stones, bones, worthless chips of amulets, and even chunks of discarded embalmed flesh. This is the path that they walk once dismounted. Rowland stoops to pick up scraps of pottery, filling his pockets.

She's ashamed at his insensitivity, even as she knows that years ago, she'd have done the same. Now her perspective has changed. She's changed.

Clemmie steps on the desecrated ground, all too aware that she might be treading on a preserved finger, a human tooth, or a lock of ancient hair. It takes her back to a room that smells of lavender and myrrh. The same disrespect that was shown that night has happened before, over and over. It's happened here. She's walking in the footsteps of curses, trailing her own in her shadow.

"It looks as though a lot of people got here before us," Oswald mutters. "Damnably shameful really, what they've done. It's a sorry mess."

Oswald's right about it being damnable. This kind of irreverence and the calamities it can cause, that's why she's here. Clemmie spies something brown, knowing that it was once ripe flesh like her own. She longs to bury it, but where would she begin? For there is another piece. And another. Her companions are somber enough, aware of the pillaging that's happened here over the years, but they can't grasp the gravity of it the way she does.

As the wind whips up the sand to sting her skin, some of it sticking to a damp patch on her cheeks that she hadn't realized was there, it makes a sound. A stifled moan. And she hears it. This gaping land groaning for what it once was, begging for its stolen ancestors to be returned.

Scraps of cerement that once wrapped bodies scud across the littered plateau. Every step they take presses a broken amulet or lump of embalmed flesh deeper into the sand. This ancient people mummified their dead to protect them, to preserve. They chose amulets to guard and guide them on their way to the afterlife, they laid them in coffins to shelter them. Her father once told her of his father's friend who sat on his wife's grave for a month for fear of body snatchers in the days of the London Burkers, but what about here? Who is there to honor the wishes of the dead, to sit on their graves, to protect them? Despite embalming, destruction has still come. Not through death's rot but through the blight of the living.

Mummification is like taxidermy, conserving what would otherwise putrefy. The sands that have blown for centuries and the river that has inundated and receded; the hieroglyphs that tell a hidden story of what came before and the embalmed bodies of humans and animals; the lofty structures now tumbled, buried, and incomplete and the legends and myths that are told to the next generation: all of it is a preservation of decay.

But that's the point, she thinks as she stands on the violated ground. We pretend to have control, but ultimately the decay has already happened, and still happens. Can anyone stay the inevitable?

Something blue stands out on the ground and she steps over to it. Picks it up. A broken piece of an amulet. Two figures snapped at the necks so only the heads remain, she knows at once who is depicted by the glyphs they wear as crowns. A throne. A house with a basket. Were they worshipped here? Are there images of these two on what remains, on tombs not yet uncovered?

One of the guides sees what she has found. "Ah," he says in French. "That is a good find."

"Isis and Nephthys," she whispers.

He nods. "That is correct. Very popular funerary goddesses. You'll find them all over Egypt. Their icons are wherever you go."

A current runs through her belly, icy and churning. What the guide says is true, and his words make her doubt herself and her plan. It's crucial that she gets her quest right, but her confidence dwindles. If the images of Isis and Nephthys truly are everywhere, then is the right place to return the amulet to really Denderah?

They're a solemn party when they arrive back at *Hapi*. For the most part they're tired, tired from staring at lumps of limestone and from treading a broken history. Clemmie would like to think that they all feel a little ashamed, if not for their own violation—stepping mindlessly on remnants of the dead and Rowland pocketing anything that looked marginally of value—then for those who have been before. Amelia Edwards was right when she said that the work of destruction goes on with no one to prevent it.

There's a suggestion of dinner, something smells *lazeeza* from Mariam's quarters, but Clemmie stays on the deck while the others disappear to their cabins to refresh themselves. A horsefly lands on her hand and she pauses. Watches it settle. Waits for the moment when it will taste her blood. And then she acts suddenly, squashing it beneath her fingers. Killing the creature before it has a chance to fly away.

Some minutes later, another comes, oblivious to its brother's demise. Having learned from the last one, she times her movements perfectly, capturing the fly between her finger and thumb. Feeling the juice of it as she squeezes.

Is she so very different from this horsefly? Her family have sucked the blood of Egypt, tasted its delights, and that is their sin, their folly. They have been squashed for their audacity. Every day she watches and waits for the moment when it will come. Being ground to oblivion. The hieroglyphs fulfilled. Her punishment delivered.

It won't be long. She feels that in the tightening of her lungs, in the knowledge of what she's left behind, and in the memory of funerals, stopped clocks, and black crape. She doesn't have much time before the curse strikes again. She's here now, to give herself—to give *them*—a chance to fly away to safety. Will it be enough, or are they nothing more than gadflies, their destiny to be crushed?

The day is old, the shadows gathering. Her self-doubt increases. Is Denderah the wrong site? As she ponders what's to be done, she spies a stain on the decking. She walks over to it, the awning removed so that what's left of the sun for the day can be enjoyed. The stain is dark, and she bends down to touch it, but it's not wet. It feels of nothing. And her own shadow distorts it. Makes it move.

She realizes, then, that her shadow isn't alone. That the stain is itself a shadow. Not wanting to, she looks above, the dying orange sphere forcing her to cup her hand over her brow. And then she sees it, alone this time.

The kite hovers on a current of air that doesn't reach Clemmie's lungs. She wonders where the other might be, fear gripping her heart.

She was a fool to delay any further. Either the curse will be broken, or she will.

Irrigation

AFTER DINNER, CLEMMIE HEADS OUTSIDE to the kitchen. She moves quickly, afraid that she will change her mind. Fearful that the wine is acting instead of her. Too scared to turn around.

She can't get Sakkârah out of her head, and it builds on the shame of her own part in this. She keeps thinking about that piece of a funerary charm she found on the ground, how it made her question where the amulet belongs. She longs for reassurance that her plan might work. Who else can she turn to? Certainly not Rowland.

Mariam is cleaning up by the light of a candle, the flame so small and dim that Clemmie can hardly see her face. Every now and then she sees a glimmer of front teeth, a flicker of an eye, or the ghostly sheen of Mariam's headdress.

When Clemmie reaches the threshold of the kitchen, Mariam stops working and turns. Her eyes are guarded.

Clemmie doesn't fully understand why she's approached Mariam until she's standing here before her. Only that Mariam has knowledge. Clemmie may be considered clever and an impressive scholar, but she's still the traveler in a foreign country. Mariam is a local. Mariam could help. Besides which, she wants to show Mariam that she's not like other tourists.

"It's wrong," Clemmie says in Arabic. "Sakkârah was dreadful."

Mariam nods, almost warily.

"I'm trying to make things right. I told you that there's a reason why I'm here, and I want you to know it."

The crew are playing instruments nearby, seated around the lower deck singing songs. Lit by nothing but the night sky and the vague glow of burning tobacco. Youssef's large outline looms over his men, smoke curling from his smoldering *chibouk* like a spirit leaving a body. Occasionally, the men exchange words or stories and Youssef's laugh ricochets off the shadows.

"Come with me," Clemmie whispers, beckoning for Mariam to accompany her. Mariam is silent, and Clemmie interprets that as her opening. She walks ahead to her cabin, trusting that Mariam will follow. That she'll give her a chance.

Clemmie opens the closet and pulls out the wooden box. The lighting is better here in Clemmie's cabin, the lamp affording them the yellow glow necessary to see each other's faces. To see what Clemmie has been hiding.

She doesn't tell Mariam about the evening she translated the amulet and all that ensued. The contents of the box can speak for themselves, and when she lifts the lid, she waits to see the reaction flicker on Mariam's face. Only the eyes betray her, sparkling with wonder. In Clemmie's heart is a rushing sense of release mixed with fear. She's guarded this for so long. Has she made a mistake?

"A Double *Tyet*," Mariam says at last.

"You know it?" Clemmie is surprised for a moment, so unfamiliar is she with discussing Egyptology with people who know the subject as well as her. Perhaps even better.

A ghost of scorn shadows Mariam's face. "This is my history, my passion as well. Do you remember, *ya aanesa* Clemmie, that I said I have a commitment to my country?"

Clemmie nods, thinking back to the first time she spoke with Mariam, when she was making the lemonade.

"What I said is true," Mariam says. "This commitment is to protect my country's history, to see it restored. The stories and physical evidence of those stories are my heritage. The river runs through Egypt.

It has done so for centuries. It flows. Our culture is the river. I want it to never stop flowing, to feed the land. But the more people take, the more the river recedes and the land dries out. It becomes barren. There is a cultural drought, and we need enough vessels to reverse that. If we irrigate, not with water but with stolen antiquities, educating people, halting the theft and destruction of history, then we can feed what's been bled dry."

She says something then that stirs Clemmie, even as she hurries to piece together the words that she's still uncertain of. To make sense of them in the context of the sentences. Mariam explains how each *shâdûf*, or irrigation vessel, helps to reinstate what once was. One bucketful of the river will be followed by another, and another. Soon, there will be enough to connect the land with the river again.

"Rare pieces like this amulet shouldn't be in the homes of foreigners, hundreds of miles away."

"I'm returning it," Clemmie says. "That's what I've been trying to tell you. It's why I've come."

ॐ

Together, they sit on the floor of the cabin with the amulet between them. Mariam is fascinated as Clemmie points out the hieroglyphs and their meaning, how to translate them. It's also a lesson for Clemmie, learning to translate from glyph to English to Arabic. The hieroglyphs run down the center of each *tyet* in two columns, carved into the red jasper, and she shows the order they are read in. Tracing the *sa*, similar to early petroglyphs with stick limbs, only in this instance there are no arms, only a head, and two spreading horizontal strokes for the legs. Its meaning is protection. Then there's the sign for brother, *sn*, an arrowhead turned feminine with the use of the letter t, drawn as a half circle. The addition of the coil, or w, indicates the plural. *Sisters*.

Still, Clemmie doesn't admit what her father did to the mummy, or describe all that's happened since that night. She just shares the amulet, the inscription, and her intentions. Don't the hieroglyphs reveal enough once their mystery is laid bare?

The protection of Isis and Nephthys be upon the sisters. If any disturb these sisters, let the wrath of Osiris's sisters be upon his household's sisters and the pain of Osiris upon his own body. May the knots of Isis and Neph-

thys know rest where Osiris rises to meet Isis, or let what is sacred be brought to ruin.

Clemmie waits for Mariam to take it all in, and then explains her intention to find the right place at Denderah to bury the amulet.

Only now does Mariam frown. "Why Denderah?"

"In the Hypostyle Hall the ceiling depicts Osiris whole again and Isis and Nephthys restored to each other. It's symbolic of healing and forgiveness, and is the only site I can think of that comes close to Osiris rising to meet Isis."

Mariam's brow remains rumpled. "But Denderah is the Temple of Hathor."

Clemmie knows that. But there's a connection between Hathor and Isis, and she's read in such great detail about the artwork on the ceiling.

Pointing to one of the columns of hieroglyphs, Mariam asks Clemmie to translate them again. She does so, indicating the throne for Isis, the house with a basket for Nephthys, the throne with the eye for Osiris. She shows how to determine the direction of reading according to the way the glyphs are facing. In this case, left to right.

"You say that this speaks of restoring the Double *Tyet*?"

"It speaks of the knots of Isis and Nephthys, so yes, I believe so."

"Where Osiris rises to meet Isis?"

"Precisely. The ceiling at Denderah depicts Osiris, revived and in the barque. Back with Isis. Meeting with her."

Mariam shakes her head. "It doesn't mean Denderah."

Clemmie's heart sinks, and she stands, snatching the amulet back and laying it once more in the croquet box. Ignoring her earlier doubt, she focuses on the logic of her choice. Of course the text means Denderah. She's spent her whole life studying Egyptology, she knows her subject. How could it mean anywhere else? She wishes she'd never asked Mariam. Why did she, anyway? Because she felt sentimental and ashamed after Sakkârah, so she stupidly thought that to unburden herself to an Egyptian might make her feel less guilty. Maybe absolve her.

"If not Denderah, then what could the inscription mean?"

She's afraid of the answer. Afraid that Mariam doesn't know, or that if she does, it will be a harder mountain to climb. Something impossible and unachievable.

But Mariam doesn't slump in despair. Her smile is a *shâdûf* lowered into the river, coming up overflowing.

"The place where Osiris rises to meet Isis? That can mean only one thing. Osiris points to the river, and Isis speaks of her temple. You must go to the Temple of Isis. You must go to the island of Philae."

Unwrapping

1887

AFTER WATCHING ROSETTA WALK AWAY, Clemmie makes her last farewells to Bast. Alone. How can her life have altered so dramatically in one day?

Eventually, she returns to the house. In her head, she hears the chanting echo of the hieroglyphs she translated last night. A warning. But what if the flickering lights from the lavender candles tricked her eyes, or she isn't the great hieroglyphist that she thought she was? Isn't it possible that she's made a mistake? Possibly even been influenced by the nonsense printed in *Punch* cartoons and by gothic tales; just part of the current fashion for all things Egyptian.

There is no one in her father's study. No one, apart from the mummies in his display cabinets, those that he has kept for his collection and not sold to other Egyptologists. The ones unwrapped before last night. She puts the amulet to one side and peels the quilt away from the table, hoping she remembered it all wrong, but the twins are still in a mess from the dissection. She's not sure if the sight is worse in the daylight, or in the memory of last night's haunting shadows.

She hears the front door shut and steps into the hall. There he is. Horatio Devereux. His stride is long, his carriage confident as he tosses his riding gloves onto a hall chair and heads toward her, hands extended and face eager. She's glad to see him and the comforting familiarity he brings, and after all the recent upsets, would rather like to rest her tired head on his broad shoulder.

"Well, aren't you going to congratulate me?" he says, clasping her hands in his large ones and squeezing them repeatedly.

Of course. The engagement. She falters, trying to think what she should say. *Thank you for making my sister happy by taking her away from me?*

She has no words.

Of course she's grateful to him, truly she is. Horatio is the answer to her sister's prayers and dreams. Their fathers are best friends; their mothers drink Assam tea and eat Victoria sandwich cakes together weekly while sharing notes on the unattached in Chelmsford, scribbling records of who is courting whom, and striking names from the eligibility lists in their notebooks as they pore over engagement announcements in the newspaper and draw connecting lines between those who are left—an employment that they believe to be highly beneficial to the single members of their neighborhood. In effect, Horatio feels like family, he has spent so many hours at Bickmore. A proud member of the Queen's army, only his training and deployment have kept him away from the Attridge home. In more recent years, Horatio has shown a personal interest in the business side of her and her father's studies, making suggestions on hiring out some of the artifacts to help balance the books. She has come to look forward to their moments together, when he will inquire about the latest mummy unveiled or ask her to pen a description for an amulet he is valuing—a rarer thing since he started courting Rosetta.

They grew up with Horatio almost always around, tagging along when their fathers met to smoke their meerschaum pipes or their mothers convened to decry the hopelessness of a local bachelor who would take no hints about the pretty Miss Harriet Plumb, who was very much ripe and ready and on the verge of festering if not soon plucked. As such, perhaps she should have known this engagement would happen. It makes sense. Rosetta is the elder, after all, and should be married first. Still, Horatio is the scalpel to their sisterly ties. Of course it hurts.

"Aren't you going to kiss me, sister? For you shall be my sister soon."

She smiles weakly and obediently pecks his cheek. "Rosetta's taking a nap. She has a headache."

He slaps his head. "The cat. I'm sorry. The groom did mention it when he took my horse."

Putting a gentle arm over her shoulders, he guides her toward the study.

"I want to hear all about the unwrapping," he says. "It will be a healthy distraction for you from the upset of your cat."

She's glad he has come, even if he represents the approaching change in her life. After last night, she needs him and his sympathetic ear. He asks where her father is, but she neither knows nor cares, waiting for the horror to register on Horatio's face when he sees the limbs on the study table. When it does, something akin to relief flutters in her breast. He feels the same.

"What happened?"

In brief words, she describes the events of last night. Waving the amulet at him—which he seizes excitedly from her hands—she confesses that she could do nothing to stop her father from cutting the twins apart. If anything, she provoked him. Almost in tears, she reads to him what the hieroglyphs say. No different in the daytime, they etch the same message that she deciphered the night before.

"My word," he says. "I've never seen an amulet like it."

The winter sun shines brightly, albeit coldly, into the room and onto the crimson stone. Horatio lets his hand rest on her arm, sharing this moment with her. His breath is the pattern of a bird's quivering wings.

"This is worth more than a hundred ordinary amulets," Horatio murmurs, but she barely hears him. The hieroglyphs are an art and mystery of their own, and their peculiar text drowns out anything her future brother-in-law says.

Perhaps she could compile a paper on amulets and funerary texts not yet explored, and possibly even have it published. Yet her interest is trimmed with a malaise that lingers from last night. Excitement fails to come.

Sphinx

THE WIND THAT HAS CARRIED them thus far to Bedreshayn ceases. From her rattan chair Clemmie observes the crew assemble on the banks, working in a similar manner to the way horses draw barges on ropes back at home. Hauling them along by the sheer manpower that has made generations marvel. The Pyramids were constructed this way, and in the strain of their backs Clemmie sees an echo of history.

Celia parades around the deck in her knickerbockers, checking over her shoulder that Rowland is watching, and pouting when his attention isn't fixed on her. Oswald polishes his shotgun so often it's surprising the metal doesn't wear thin. Rowland seems the happiest of them all, taking to whistling a tune that Clemmie recognizes but can't place. She seems to be the only one put out with the delay the lack of wind causes. Even the crew don't seem to mind, mixing effort with bursts of howling song, which the traveling party listen to with fascination.

What should take one day's sailing may translate into two or three of tracking. Clemmie wishes she could sprout wings the way Isis and Nephthys would in the myths, so she could fly to Philae.

Philae. Now that Mariam has suggested the island, it makes perfect sense. Plutarch himself highlighted the connection between Osiris and the Nile. Grateful for Mariam's guidance, she pictures her new destination. The Temple of Isis. She thinks of the images depicted on the temple walls. The piecing back together. The work of healing and restoration. *Yalla,* she thinks. *Yalla!*

As she fidgets in her chair, Rowland casts her a quizzical frown.

"You're in the land of your dreams—try to enjoy yourself like the rest of us. What has got you so flustered?"

Hardly a surprise that Rowland would notice her impatience—how like him! Distractedly, she tries to brush him off.

"I'm just anxious to get to Philae."

"Philae?" he says, raising an eyebrow. "But I thought you wanted to go to Denderah."

Of course. Her change of plans. She hasn't mentioned it to anyone other than Mariam and, just this morning, Youssef. She tries to remain casual as she replies: "I do. I still do. But I want to see Philae now as well."

He gives her such a look, as if he's making a mental scrapbook of the things she says in order to peruse at his pleasure.

The tracking continues past Beni Suêf, a town claiming the usual coffeehouses, palm trees, and thirsty buffalo and donkeys lining up at the water's edge to drink. It's here, as the crew pull at their ropes and push the *dahabeeyah* away from sandbanks with long poles, that Youssef voices his concerns to the Lions' *dragoman.* A villa blinks a white face at them from a mass of green palms, and Khalil nods in its direction, cautioning that they should hire guards from the Khedive, or pass through these parts as quickly as the crew can tow them. Celia asks why they would need protection when they haven't required any thus far, and Khalil mentions a group of bandits known for operating in the area.

"They make their living by robbing tourists," he explains. "It is very bad to stay around here too long."

Rowland, Oswald, and Khalil gather confidentially to decide if they should hire men, while Youssef puffs his giant pipe, bare toes hammering the deck, waiting for Khalil to report back to him in Arabic. She can just about overhear the men's discussion, Rowland admitting his reluctance to sail through as he wants to check the post office ashore. Khalil opens his mouth to impart advice, but he's stopped by Oswald brandishing his shotgun.

"Who needs guards when you have a beauty like this one?"

Youssef seems to understand that movement. He gives a shrug, and whether satisfied or not with the decision, he returns to overseeing his crew.

Even with Oswald's trusty firearm, they still only stop briefly at Beni Suêf, mooring just the one night. Next, they track past Minieh—a town of mud huts that smell of stewed lentils—pausing for short spells at each stop so that Rowland can arrange for the forwarding of correspondence further up the Nile. He comes back empty-handed each time, and whistles a little less.

The villages north of Siût are not paved with gold, but they come close enough. Equine dung. Human waste. Dog muck. If the price English tanneries pay for feces to treat their leather was taken into consideration, there's enough excrement in these villages to be a pure finder's paradise. Enough, no doubt, to line a poor Londoner's pockets with money that would pay for a room, for meals, and perhaps even fund membership with a burial club to ensure his body wouldn't be claimed for an anatomist's education. But here it sits in steaming piles, fed on by flies and cracking in the sun, its value unnoticed.

In one such village, they disembark to remind themselves what solid ground feels like. Even the sand shifts beneath them, a grainy river that they sink in. Clemmie knows what it feels like to sink. To be sucked into something that can't be escaped.

Passing through these Egyptian villages summons a strange reminder of England. She remembers the London she traversed to get to the ship that brought her here, and shudders at the memory of her homeland: a place reeking of the influenza, of whatever the Thames chose to vomit up, and of death. Not the kind of death that is remembered in monumental tombs but the kind that smells of decay before it's even happened. One country has its poor folk clinging like mold to its damp and darkest corners, and the other lets them bake in the sun like the mud houses of their villages.

She's startled from her thoughts by a small cry, similar to that of an infant. It reaches inside her, pulls at her heart, loosens it from its customary setting. Only it isn't a child, she knows that full well, it is why the sound has touched her so. This is the mew of a creature that has always been special to her. Something almost sacred. The Egyptians saw them that way, after all. And Clemmie bends down to stroke the cat circling her legs. A scrawny thing, it's the color of Egypt's ruins. A living Sphinx.

After spending some minutes fussing with the cat, its ears two pyramids rising from a dusty coat, she notices that her companions haven't stopped for her and are almost lost among the Egyptians eagerly promoting their wares. Each vendor tries to shout louder than their neighbor, shoving dates, beads, and scarabs in the tourists' faces.

She straightens to go after them, and has only taken a few steps when she hears the cry again. The cat is once more pressing itself against her. Clemmie bites her lip. Looks around her for an obvious owner. But the modern-day Egyptians don't seem to view cats in the same light as their ancestors. Maybe this poor creature has never been shown kindness. It's certainly a skinny thing, a remnant of blood on its whiskers suggesting that the only way it gets its food is by hunting for it.

She can't take it with her, though. She just can't. As she catches up with the others, the cat trots after her, tail aloft.

By the time they get back to the *dahabeeyah*, Clemmie has the cat in her arms, and a ferocious rattle escapes its chest that's both comforting and painful.

"You can't keep it."

This protest comes from Rowland, and Clemmie feels all the more determined now that he's set against it.

"She's a she," Clemmie says. "And I can."

"Well, *she* probably has fleas."

"I think she's darling," Celia declares.

"They're useless," Oswald comments. "Dogs have a purpose, but what do cats do?"

Infuriated at Oswald's ignorance, Clemmie bites her tongue and focuses on scratching beneath the cat's chin. The desert-colored feline rubs her face against Clemmie's, her nose a damp kiss.

Rowland settles in a chair opposite, something about him softening as he observes the display of affection. He places his hands on his thighs, and raises an eyebrow.

"I suppose she could be the ship's cat and make sure we're free of vermin."

Just as Clemmie's about to snap that she doesn't need his permission, he reaches out and rubs the cat's ear, asking if she's thought of a name.

"I'm going to call her Sphinx."

He nods thoughtfully.

When Celia and Oswald leave the deck to ready themselves for dinner, Rowland leans back in his chair, staring at the cat. And at her. She asks him what's on his mind.

"I was just thinking," he says. "Given they say the Sphinx guards Egypt's old secrets, it's rather fitting that you have a Sphinx of your own."

Clemmie holds the cat close to her, and Sphinx purrs more loudly. "If I have secrets to be kept, then I'm not going to admit it. Am I?"

"Did you have a favorite artifact in your collection at home?"

She's surprised at how precise and sudden his question is, and fumbles for a response.

"There was a mummified cat—"

"Not a human mummy, then? An amulet?"

"We had those too."

"Many?"

She narrows her eyes and stands, holding Sphinx out toward him. "Why don't you ask her?"

"The Sphinx never gives up her secrets."

"Precisely." Clemmie pins him with a stare. "Neither do I."

Dog Star

MOORING AT RHODA, THEY SEE yet another bank lined with Egyptians who water their camels, but take their time watching the *dahabeeyah*. Are these the bandits Khalil warned them about, or is Clemmie just feeling jumpy? Oswald carries his shotgun with him constantly and suggests the women stay in the saloon. Clemmie refuses. Her mission may prevent her from making the most of this trip, but she'll be hanged if she's to spend the journey shut in a stuffy cabin.

Oswald takes aim at a pied bird swooping overhead. When he pulls the trigger, it falls on the deck with a dull thump, but instead of stooping to inspect his kill, he returns the stares of the locals while patting his weapon.

His shot made Sphinx scurry into the saloon, but now she emerges to inspect the kingfisher. In moments, there's blood on her maw, the entrails forming a puddle, and feathers skip across the deck like a parade of black and white ghosts.

"Why did you kill it?" Clemmie asks.

Oswald smiles at what he clearly considers to be a show of feminine delicacy. "To make a point. It's just a bird."

Just a bird. Just a thing. It makes her think of Bickmore.

It's just a mummy.

Shelley wrote about Egypt's ruins, calling them "these lifeless things." That's how people see them. Specimens. Antiquities. *Things.* Just something to be lorded over, controlled, misused.

She glances at the men on the bank, to see if killing the bird was worth it. They are murmuring among themselves, and there are more of them now, attracted by the shot. Most are dressed in the garb of *fellaheen,* but one man in particular stands out from the others. He's athletic in build, his robes befitting a merchant with a rich turban wound on his head. His arms are woven across his chest, one hand holding the reins of a beautiful bay Arabian mare. The brown of her body is a burnished copper, her mane, lower legs, and lifted tail pure ebony. He isn't watering his horse, merely standing there. While the others are watching the *dahabeeyah,* his gaze settles on something more specific. Trained on her.

When she notices this, when their eyes meet, a gape slices his face, teeth gleaming.

𓋴

The evening is haunted by the special star of Isis. Sirius, the Dog Star, sits below the moon and looks down upon the *dahabeeyah* and those inside. Clemmie sits with her companions in the saloon, her skin pricking. She can't forget the stare of the man on the bank, nor the way Oswald's shot seemed only to breed trouble, enticing more men to the shore. Something about the evening is menacing. Darkness is the breeding ground of ghosts, terror, and memories, and she's tormented by all three.

Celia is bored, and trips her fingers restlessly over the pianoforte, a tune in a minor key that adds to the melancholy of the night. Perhaps she agrees it's too somber, for she changes her mind and closes the lid with a huff. Oswald looks more on edge than ever, no doubt concerned that a bored Celia might be even less discreet than usual.

"I know," Rowland says. "We should play a game."

With a mischievous sparkle in her eyes that outdoes her earrings, Celia proposes a game of Forfeits. Rowland hardly registers her suggestion, fixing his eyes on Clemmie as he makes his own.

"I was thinking more of a tabletop game. You're partial to croquet, aren't you, Clementine?"

She stiffens, registering the calculated look in his eyes. He's testing her. Maybe he knows there are no croquet accessories in her box. Does he suspect what she keeps in there instead? She decides to ignore him, and opens her mouth to encourage Celia's choice when a cry stabs the evening. It's a desperate sound, that bloodcurdling howl. Searching her companions' faces, Clemmie sees the fear in her own breast reflected there. All except Oswald. He slaps his knee excitedly, and tells them that it's just a jackal.

"Anubis," Clemmie whispers dreamily. "It's the sound of Anubis, calling for his mother."

Celia looks at her blankly, as does Oswald. Only Rowland seems to have any idea of what she's just said, a glimmer of recollection on his face. Almost nostalgic.

"Who's Anubis?" Celia asks.

She decides it's forgivable. Not everyone knows the myths as well as she does, so she licks her lips and tries the name out loud. The name that's haunted her for years.

"He's the son of Nephthys."

Still no clarity sweeps across the brows of her fellow travelers. It was verging on offensive to be unaware of Anubis, but not to know the story of Nephthys, well, that is a crime.

Forgetting about Forfeits, she decides to recite the myth, just as she always used to. It's a story she's told many times, and the thoughts it conjures are not welcome. They're the images of a childhood spent playing Myths, and the events at Bickmore when she regaled an audience with these tales to add to the entertainment. *Entertainment.* Even now, she winces at what they once thought those nights were.

She can see the room so clearly it's as if she's there, back in her father's study again. One wall stacked with shelves of jars, both the Egyptian canopic variety and the modern glass types. The latter holding fluid-preserved specimens from Clement's surgical days. As a child, she would stand before them, counting the limbs and organs and pretending that they belonged to dismembered Osiris. She'd peer at the mummified remains lying in cabinets along the other walls. Dogs. Cats.

People. The cerement yellowed, wrapped in intricate patterns that rivaled anything her mother sewed in her quilts.

Where to start but at the beginning? Not Anubis, then. Not even Nephthys or Isis. She takes them back to Nut, the Egyptian goddess of the sky, and Seb, god of the earth, closing her eyes and her heart to the pain this story summons.

Invisible

I N THE MYTHS, EARTH AND sky were born of the same parents, she tells them. They copulated and inside the womb of the sky there grew offspring that could put the sun to shame, so the sun forbade the sky to give birth on any day belonging to the year. The god of wisdom, whose only weakness was his love for the sky, gambled his wit against the moon—and won. With his winnings, he fashioned five extra days. And over the course of those five days, the sky was free to give birth.

Four children. Four siblings. Two pairs.

Osiris and Isis.

Set and Nephthys.

Osiris was the firstborn. Set followed, although not on the second day, nor between his mother's legs. He forbade his sisters from emerging before him, and on the third day he found a tender spot in his mother's side. The sky was pierced the day Set was born. Next came Isis, and finally, when the earth and sky were already busy adoring Osiris, calming the screaming Set, and kissing the beautiful Isis, Nephthys was delivered.

But no one had time to notice Nephthys. No one ever did.

Seb and Nut were finally parents. With a child in each arm, they spoke their names for the first time. Seb, god of the earth, held his two sons and knew that they would etch their stories throughout his many regions. Nut, goddess of the sky, cradled her two daughters and felt their inner calling for her domain, like fledglings desperate to try out their wings.

Osiris, Seb said, admiring his green-skinned son. His name is Osiris.

With the firstborn named, the other son's animal head wrinkled in an ugly fashion as he screamed his indignation, the elder daughter gurgled with joy, and the other one? They didn't stop to observe how she reacted, for they were too busy considering Osiris's future. What were the possibilities?

At last, once the other two were named—Set for the second boy and Isis for the elder girl—they gave the fourth-born the name of Nephthys. Mistress of the house. It was a poor choice of name, for a mistress is in control and has a say in things, and as the youngest she had no say in matters. She was an outsider. Later, when worshipped as a triad, Nephthys was included with Osiris, Isis, and Horus. But *tri* means three. She was an afterthought.

Not many people know Nephthys's story. Her brother Osiris is famous. Her sister, Isis, lauded. Even Set, while despised, is well known for his villainy. Nephthys is the forgotten one. The oxygen to the body of the myth, invisible but necessary. Always present, but shadowed by her siblings. For when up against the loudness of Osiris's grandeur, Isis's beauty, Set's wrath, how could she compare? She didn't try. She just went along, forming her own untold story. Adding to theirs. Helping.

Maybe they did give her the right name after all. The mistress of a house keeps things running smoothly. She performs tasks that no one ever gives her credit for. If you remove her, the place goes to ruin, but when she's there everything moves as a smooth-flowing river, no one truly understanding all she does. Holding the house together like the cement that joins the bricks. Many will praise beautiful stonework, but no one ever compliments the mortar.

In the legends of Osiris and Isis and their archenemy, Set, Nephthys was there too. Without her character, there would be no story.

Clemmie stops. The jackal releases its dreadful ululation once more, and her own heart longs to howl with it. For she is the Nephthys of her story, invisible and forgotten, and had she been just a little more like Isis, then maybe her father would have listened to her.

Unwrapping

1887

THE MYTH HAS DIFFERENT WAYS of explaining how Isis and Nephthys became rivals. Some say Osiris mistook Nephthys for Isis—who was both his sister and wife—and slept with her instead. Others consider it likely that an affair took place. And some view Nephthys as a deceiver. If she could change into a kite, then she could no doubt disguise herself as her sister to sleep with the man she loved. Clemmie, however, tells it differently.

In her interpretation, the one that formed her childhood games, and has entertained guests at one unwrapping after another, she imagines the River Nile, and a bruised Nephthys bathing wounds inflicted by a god of violence: her brother and husband, Set. It is then that Osiris passes by and sees her as if for the first time. It does not excuse the wrong of them coming together, but it is the version that makes the most sense in her mind.

Clemmie puts lavender water on a handkerchief and smooths her sister's head.

"Nothing will ever come between us, will it?" Rosetta asks.

"How could it?" she replies, but she doesn't speak of the fear inside her. That sense of unease that she's had since that night. Is she afraid because of some cautionary hieroglyphs, or because she's on the cusp of losing a sister?

Rosetta has laid fashion plates across the bed, the latest styles extracted from *The Ladies' Treasury,* a whole quilt of them. She is admiring bridal gowns while rambling about how they will still see each other all the time when she is married, how her engagement and wedding won't alter their relationship, that nothing will really change. Clemmie wonders whom Rosetta is trying to convince. Because Isis and Nephthys had once been close, and then things did change. Once, the twins were whole, and now they have been riven apart.

She is about to comment when they hear something smash downstairs. Clemmie doesn't bother to light a candle or throw a dressing gown over her nightdress. She hurries out of the chamber, fashion plates twirling in her wake, passing through the gallery, down the stairs and, following the yellow glow, to the site she has come to dread. Her father's study.

Clement is inside, in that room that stinks of dust and faintly still of spice, and now of preserving fluids, nursing a hand that looks more like talons. Scattered at his feet are a million shards of glass, glinting like crystal teeth. A jar ruined beyond repair. The severed hand that was inside imitating his own, stiff fingers splayed upward, as if someone reaches through the floor to grab him.

"My hand," he is saying. "It hurt so much I just dropped it. This damned rheumatism."

She doesn't comment, but she notices how his shoulders are starting to curve, his back folding. He looks old, something she hadn't realized until now. It frightens her. She wishes she could embalm them all, capture them in some preserving fluid. Her parents young and well, Rosetta unmarried by her side, Horatio assisting her with the collection. If there was only a way to contain them as they are before they run through her fingers like cupped water. It is useless. Life breeds change, change produces maturity, maturity leads to a certain end. Everything has consequences.

He is muttering and muttering to himself and her eyes fall on the amulet and twins, lying together in one of her father's cabinets.

Nothing will ever come between us, will it?

Her sense of disquiet intensifies. What if it already has?

Jackals

NOT ALL JACKALS CRAWL ON four legs but, be they man or beast, they all excel at hunting. A new cry emerges from the night, and it isn't the wild dogs this time. When a shot is followed by more shouts, they know that something is amiss. They are all on their feet in moments, the same word on their tongues.

Bandits!

Rowland is closer to Oswald's shotgun and he grabs it and a handful of cartridges from a box on the table, barely hampered by his limp as he rushes out onto the deck. Toward the hold. Oswald is close behind him. Clemmie stands in the doorway, Celia a step behind her. She can see nothing in the darkness outside, but hears heavy feet, splashing, the report of a gun going off.

"Ossie," Celia whispers, her voice tremulous. "Ossie. Is everything all right?"

A gun replies, but this one splinters the wooden frame of the door. Celia shrieks, and in the echoes that follow, Clemmie realizes that she has screamed too. They are lit targets in here. She hurries across to the lamp and extinguishes it. The darkness is immediate and absolute.

"Oh dear," Celia murmurs. "I feel rather queer."

There is a tumbling sound, hitting the floor. Celia must have fainted. Crouching, Clemmie pats the mound at her feet and tries to shake the limp body, but she can't rouse her. On the deck she can hear Youssef's angry voice, cursing any bandits who dare to invade his vessel. Khalil is insisting that they should guard the hold, and Rowland and Oswald are arguing over how many bandits they saw. From the sound of it, Oswald seems convinced he saw two figures scrambling away on the bank, but Rowland swears there was a third.

A floorboard creaks in the saloon. Clemmie freezes. Heavy breathing follows and a shadow moves. Someone else is in here with them. Is it one of the crew? She doesn't dare speak.

It dawns on Clemmie that Oswald's display earlier proved to the bandits that they'd need to come armed. What is it they want? Is this anything to do with the man who stared at her brazenly from the bank?

The shadow springs to life, issuing a dull thud as the intruder knocks into the table. A chair tumbles, cracking against the boards.

Leaving Celia senseless on the floor, Clemmie picks up the chair as both weapon and shield, and thrusts it at the darting figure. She can feel the weight of him pressing it back at her, shoving her body until she hits the wall behind her, pinned in place by the chair. Using the wall to her benefit, she pushes back, hearing her opponent grunting in return. He is so close that she can smell him. The exotic perfume of castor oil, unusual to her olfactory senses but a luxury in these parts, is thick on his skin. She imagines that if she were to grapple with him, were they to touch, her hands would slide right off like trying to grasp a snake.

And for a moment, she isn't on the *dahabeeyah*. She remembers a different struggle, not unlike this one, during the Osirian darkness of a thunderstorm back at home in Chelmsford. The stabbing pain of the chair at her sternum is the weight of a hand that pinned her down. The heavy breathing of her opponent is the ragged panting of her attacker from before.

Bitch!

She can still hear the voice ringing in her ears. The hum builds in her head, and she expects her ears to burst, blood oozing from the canals and dripping from her lobes. He's pressing too hard, squeezing the memory from deep within her. One she's tried to keep buried.

Shoving aside the memories, she summons all her strength and pushes back. The man opens his mouth, his breath hot on her face as he sibilates three words.

"Where is it?"

Has she heard him right? She isn't a match for his strength. Even though she braces her back against the wall to push against him, she's getting weaker, so she frees one of her hands, searching in the folds of fabric for her pocket. Her fingers close around her eucalyptus bottle. She has more in her cabin, surely it is worth the loss. Smashing it against the side of the chair, she ignores the pain of glass on her palm and brandishes a shard.

The glare of the Dog Star is bright, helping her eyes adjust to the darkness. As the star pours its luster through the window of the saloon, Clemmie sees the outline of the man's face and thrusts her weapon at his face. He releases a horrible sound, a shriek of agony that puts the jackals to shame, and the pressure from the chair is released. Her fingers come away damp from more than her own sweat and blood.

The shadow melts into the darkness before pounding feet invade the room. She feels that he has got away, knows it before she sees it. Youssef is shouting into the night, and she pictures Mariam huddled in the sanctuary of her kitchen. Where did the thief come from, and where did he go?

Someone fumbles for a light and the darkness gradually gives way to an orangey glow, illuminating the travelers and their *dragoman,* and Celia's limp form on the floor. Oswald drops beside his sister and slaps her cheeks repeatedly until she blinks and whimpers. Rowland fires a final report outside into the darkness—a warning shot—before resting the shotgun on the floor beside its owner. Looking up from reviving his sister, Oswald claps Rowland on the back, drinks from a flask, pours some into Celia's mouth, which makes her gasp, and offers it to his friend. Rowland shakes his head. Clemmie thirsts for the reviving bite of liquor, but Oswald doesn't offer it to her.

"There, there. You quite all right, Celia? Bit shaken, were you?"

The chair slips from Clemmie's grip, and she can't stop shaking. Clutching her skirt, she tries to stem the bleeding from her hand, but no one notices the blood. All too busy fussing over Celia.

Oswald seems proud of himself, Rowland quietly confident, and rightly so for guarding the hold and chasing off the bandits, but she was the one who confronted one of the men, who drew blood. She's on the cusp of telling them, but stops short.

Where is it?

Maybe the man wanted her money. Surely that's the only explanation for his question, if she even heard him correctly. After all, she went after him with the chair, foolishly, thinking she might scare him off with her crude weapon. Still, she decides not to tell her companions about her encounter. If it was more than chance, she doesn't want them to know. Was she targeted for a reason, or is she being irrational?

She can hardly breathe, but what little oxygen enters her lungs she feeds on. The prowler left with a reminder of his visit, one he'll bear for life.

"It was the gang Khalil warned us about," says Rowland, trying to calm Celia. "They're gone now."

The men discuss how slippery the bandits were, still debating how many of them managed to board. Khalil says they should check any money or valuables they brought with them, just to be safe. Oswald comments how glad he is that the women were inside the saloon while they searched the deck, and teases his sister for fainting. Celia, now mostly recovered, babbles praise about Rowland's valor, equally oblivious to the fight that took place in the shadows while she was lying insensible on the floor. They're all so busy talking that they don't seem to notice that Clemmie remains on the periphery.

She remembers the feel of the man on the other side of the chair. How he fought against her. And she can't shake off the memory it triggered, a memory that makes her want to hold herself and weep.

"The gang have been working these parts of the Nile for some time now," Khalil is explaining. "They target Europeans or Americans who might have a good deal of money, or even possessions they can go on to sell."

Clemmie doesn't know what cargo the others have brought with them, but she's painfully aware of the rare item that she hides. Slipping away, she hurries to her cabin. While her traveling companions are congratulating themselves on their near miss with thieves, she's not ready to accept that they have escaped so easily.

She strides over to the closet, corset pinching. Sphinx jumps down from the bed, getting under her feet, nearly making her fall. Her heart masters a staccato rhythm while her lungs transmute into fists. Ignoring her cat, she reaches out her bloody fingers and throws the doors open.

Everything is as she left it. The box is still there.

Fortunes

AT SIÛT THE CREW MAKE their demands. The ovens are waiting, the sun is warm, and they must stop to make bread. Mariam cooks only for the travelers, their *dragoman,* herself, and her father, so the crew rely on these stops to make and replenish their stocks. Khalil tries to placate the tourists, promising that the bazaars here are excellent, that they'll find plenty to keep them occupied.

Each bazaar that they've visited along the Nile has looked much like the last, so Clemmie isn't convinced that this one will be any different. Still, they're nearly out of coffee, and Celia never turns down an opportunity to do some shopping. Taking Sphinx with her, Clemmie visits Mariam's kitchen to see if any supplies are required.

"No need, *ya aanesa* Clemmie. My *baba* will buy whatever we need to get to Philae."

Mariam winks, and Clemmie can't help but feel reassured by the woman's certainty. They need only to get to Philae. Then everything will be well. This is what she tells herself, yet she can't stop thinking about the attack at Rhoda. Maybe it was just bandits, like Khalil said. Yet why does she feel that the attack was personal, that it was related to the man who watched her from the bank? Who would know about the amulet she carries, and how?

"Will you watch Sphinx whilst I go ashore?"

Mariam looks delighted and scoops the cat out of Clemmie's arms, giving her a piece of leftover meat. Sphinx growls with pleasure, licking her whiskers and eyeing the counter for more.

With Sphinx in good hands, Clemmie pairs off with Celia. Just before she disembarks, she sees the smooth surface of the river unsettle to her left, something long and gray splitting the calm. She squints. Surely it's too big to be a fish? Oswald's objective comes to mind.

I'm here to hunt a crocodile.

Whatever it is vanishes, the river restored to its idyllic glassiness. She blinks. Maybe it was a crocodile—or perhaps it was the way the sun glints on the water, distorting things. Glancing at the others, she wonders if they saw it, but they're talking among themselves, too busy having a good time to imagine monsters lurking.

Khalil guides the women ashore, and Rowland and Oswald beg to be spared from hanging around the jewelry, fabric, and slipper stalls, and go in search of a post office instead. As they part ways, Clemmie catches Rowland staring at her in a way that leaves her flushed. Not probing, as is his usual manner. Rather, in a fashion that is deep, lingering, and hard to interpret, even for a hieroglyphist. She turns quickly and takes Celia's hand, glad when the younger woman starts babbling away, distracting her from the curious sensation of Rowland's look.

In the distance they can see *fellaheen* preparing the ground for planting, the demand for Egyptian cotton booming over the past thirty years since the Civil War in America affected supplies. Dogs run to greet the tourists, leaping around them, barking and begging for scraps of food. Clemmie is glad she left Sphinx in Mariam's care.

As they walk toward the bazaars, Celia turns to her favorite topic: men. She mentions Michael first, a wicked smile begging Clemmie to ask about him, but Clemmie doesn't have time for scandals. From there, Celia moves on to their mutual acquaintance, reciting what little she's learned about Rowland thus far; that his family home is in Devonshire but he presently lives in London above a jewelry business on Bond Street, how he was a military man and she supposes he got his limp from his fighting days.

Clemmie nods, only half interested. There's a beggar on the ground up ahead, and she has the distinct feeling that the figure has noticed them and is waiting for a *bakhshîsh*.

"Rowland wouldn't talk about his time in the military, though," Celia continues. "He merely said those days were dead and buried."

They're by the beggar now, an old woman who holds her hand up to them and mutters a few words from a toothless mouth. She couldn't have seen them coming, for where her eyes should be there are empty slits, flies feeding at the tear ducts.

"Fortunes," the woman calls out in English. "Fortunes."

"How droll," Celia says, clearly excited at the prospect of having her fortune told. Careful not to make contact, she places a coin in the center of the proffered palm. The woman's other hand appears, grabbing her before she has a chance to move away, perhaps afraid her customer might change her mind. Celia shrieks slightly.

"Pretty English lady," says the woman as she pulls off Celia's glove and strokes the soft skin beneath. "You love a man who is far away. But you will see him again."

Celia mouths *Michael* at Clemmie, ceasing to try to pull her hand free.

"Yes, soon you will see him. Not long now. This man loves you too."

Celia is delighted and shakes the woman's hand heartily before collecting her glove from the sand.

The woman turns her empty sockets at Clemmie. Her skin doesn't even twitch as a fly runs over the hollowness and comes up the other side, tracing the ravine of wrinkles branching out to her ears.

"I don't think I really need my fortune told."

"Oh, go on," Celia says. "Mine was rather promising. Who knows what favorable things she might say to you."

"I don't think it's a good use of my money. Besides, shouldn't we keep up with Khalil? He can't have noticed that we've stopped."

"Nonsense. Khalil is still in sight, and this is my treat!" Celia drops another coin into the woman's hand.

Clemmie swallows, sacrificing her wrist to the woman's grip. "Very well. But . . . in Arabic, if you please. I'm trying to improve my knowledge of the language."

Celia forms her lips into a moue, disappointed that she won't understand the fortune teller's words, but that's exactly why Clemmie begged the change in vernacular. What if the woman really can read into the future? What might she say that Clemmie wouldn't want Celia to hear?

There are gaps in Clemmie's repertoire, words she doesn't under-stand, but being in Egypt, talking to Mariam and listening to Khalil, Youssef, and his crew, she's already picked up more than her studies ever taught her. She readies herself for whatever the crone might say.

"A man. A man in a uniform."

Clemmie rolls her eyes. Just as she thought, the coin is wasted. This prediction is no different from Celia's.

"What of him?"

"You don't love him. But you will."

No doubt the woman says the same sort of thing to every person who pays for her time today, tomorrow, and as many days as she has left. A vague prediction like that could be made to fit any person's hopes for the future.

"What does she say?" Celia interrupts.

"Oh, just the usual silly romantic lines that she thinks we all want to hear."

She can feel the woman's long nails pressing against her skin till her flesh pulses beneath them, and she tries to pull away, but as she turns to go the scrawny hand tugs her down to her level. Clemmie notices the grind of bones where flesh lacks. What little remains hangs from the teller in loose flaps, like a turkey's wattle.

"You've been paid," Clemmie says in Arabic. "What more do you want?"

The woman smiles a toothless smile, a smile that has felt the rise of many suns over the Nile, that has tasted the dust of pharaohs long gone, that has known too much to be considered a fool.

"A curse."

Clemmie feels the chill of her blood despite the heat.

"You dare to curse me?"

The woman laughs hoarsely, a croaking sound like the wind through an abandoned building. "Not I. You cursed yourself."

"Let go of me," and she pulls herself free. How easily the woman lets her go without any struggle.

"Mind what I say," the fortune teller says, her empty sockets seem-ing to focus on something beyond Clemmie. Through her. "You cannot run from curses. They're not easily undone. You think you're in control, but you never are."

Unwrapping

1887

A T NIGHT SHE DREAMS OF that dreadful unwrapping. On windy days she hears the trees by the river rustling, making the sound of feathers. Sometimes there's a rush of air passing around the house, and it resembles a collective gasp. Her eyes are stained with hieroglyphs.

If any disturb these sisters, let the wrath of Osiris's sisters be upon his household's sisters.

Not that she believes in curses. Bast is dead, but otherwise all is as it was. There have been no more unwrapping parties. She refuses to perform in any more, and surprisingly, her father does not insist, too distracted by his rare specimens. Without a hieroglyphist to assist, the event pales. Clement is planning an exhibition around the twins. Each time he finds a venue to host, they pooh-pooh his propositions, either disbelieving his claims or not agreeing to his terms. His nose colors with rage as he wads these letters into balls. Perhaps they would make more of his specimen if the twins hadn't been cut apart.

If only you'd listened to me, she wants to say, but her father refuses to talk about it, thinking only of some other way of getting the acclaim he wants for his spectacle. His pains distract him, slowing him down, the plans never materializing.

Before Horatio was called away on military service, she tried to discuss with him the ramifications of her father's handling of the twins.

Wanting him to confirm that she was nervous for no reason, that the glyphs were just words and nothing more. He only half listened. Yes, he'd said, her father was a fool to cut up the mummy. But the amulet? That's still in perfect condition. With a hieroglyphic inscription like that, in such an unusual design of the Double *Tyet,* they should think carefully about what to do with it. It could be highly desirable to other collectors. They'd pay a handsome price for such a piece.

She is frustrated with them both. Neither of them has listened to her. Once, her father enjoyed her involvement, and Horatio doted on her the way any big brother might a little sister who shared an interest. Now things are shifting.

In her father's study, she tries to find some record of where the twins came from. The more she thinks about the mummified sisters, the more she wants to understand them and the life they once lived. Searching her father's desk is more impossible a task than uncovering a lost language. He has no obvious system, receipts for tobacco filed clumsily along with his accounts for the estate. How is Bickmore running smoothly when the paperwork is so chaotic? She comes away no wiser about her father's dig, ignorant of where the twins were discovered.

The glass panes of Bickmore's sash windows rattle in their frames, shivering like an animal that knows a predator lurks. Rosetta has gone for a walk, her headache so strong that she asked Clemmie not to come with her. This pushing away unsettles. Usually, they will talk through their problems, but perhaps the shutting out began with her. She's kept the words of the amulet from her sister. Rosetta has an aptitude for superstition, and Clemmie wouldn't want to alarm her.

It's a surprise when her mother calls her to the drawing room, and she obeys, stiffening in preparation for whatever lecture will come.

Her mother pats the rococo chaise and she joins her there, uncertain. Beginning to pick at a nail, an old habit returning. The smile on her mother's face is as unsettling as the summons. Not that Flora never smiles, only her smiles are usually reserved for her elder daughter. The one who has followed a path she approves of: society, balls, courtship, and now an engagement.

"It's occurred to me that your misguided business endeavors have been brought to a natural halt," Flora says as she pours Assam tea, as formal as entertaining a guest.

Clemmie says nothing, afraid that the most simple, obvious reply might be misconstrued and used against her.

"Thus, you're free to move on from a whim that your father has entertained and I've permitted for long enough."

Aha, Clemmie thinks, accepting her teacup. She knows what's coming.

"Mrs. Devereux knows a family whose eldest son is not acquainted with your . . . interests and pursuits. We can forget the whole sorry error of involving yourself with your father's line of work and begin anew. Will you have a piece of Victoria sandwich? Cook made it with blackberry jam today. Now, where was I? Ah, yes! The gentleman in question need never know about your little pastime and—"

"If I marry," Clemmie says, "and believe me, Mamma, I hope to one day, then I won't deceive a man to think me anything other than what I am."

Flora puts down her teacup. "You are a foolish girl, Clemmie. An ungrateful creature. If you are not careful, you will doom yourself to spinsterhood."

"She isn't the only one."

They both look up. In the doorway stands Rosetta, a wry grin on her face. A letter is in her fist and she waves it dramatically, caressing a brow, which Clemmie instinctively knows pains her.

"Horatio has written," Rosetta says. "He isn't coming home when he thought. His leave has been denied. Apparently, Britain won't evacuate their troops from Egypt until next year, and now that he's been sent over there, he thinks we'll have to postpone. The wedding . . . it can't happen when we hoped."

She's trying to keep up a brave front, but now the words are out, Rosetta's face wobbles.

"It'll only be a short delay, darling," Flora says. "Next year will be here before you know it."

Clemmie watches mutely as her sister enters the room and buries her face on their mother's shoulder, crying out her disappointment. Flora smooths her elder daughter's hair, hushing and murmuring words

114 RACHEL LOUISE DRISCOLL

of encouragement. Inside Clemmie's heart sparks a flicker of hope—
hope that she may keep her sister for herself—but she snuffs it at once.

Let the wrath of Osiris's sisters be upon his household's sisters. The hieroglyphs never spoke of a broken engagement. They are just words.
Yet she cannot help herself.

What if there is more to the hieroglyphs than her father or Horatio
is willing to acknowledge? Something that she thought was impossible,
but that now makes her skin crawl as she considers Bast's sudden death
and Horatio's letter. It is nonsense, and yet she cannot stop her mind
from navigating these absurd paths now she has begun. If her family
are cursed, then maybe no happiness can reach them. No wedding. No
love. No courtship for her. Only the opposite.

The opposite of courtship? Spinsterhood. The opposite of love? Bitter hatred. The opposite of weddings?

She shudders.

Denderah

I
F GÎZEH IS FAMOUS FOR its Great Pyramid and reticent Sphinx,
then surely Denderah is known for its temple complex. Despite recollections of the human jackal and the fortune teller, Clemmie can't
help but feel delighted when they dismount from their newly hired
donkeys to stand in front of the great temple. After all, this was her
original destination.

It sits in a plain—part sand, part grass—the columns still buried and
peeping from the ground like shy mushrooms. Palm trees stand as living guards for the dead, but they've failed pitifully if they intended to
keep the grave robbers and defacers at bay. People have been here
before, invaders who have undone the work of masons.

Where to turn the eye? Here are carvings of characters wearing tu-
nics and crowns and carrying scepters. Some of the intricate details
have managed to withstand the wear of time, sandstorms, and intrud-
ers. There stands a wall of hieroglyphs just begging to be translated,
shapes that mean nothing to Celia, Oswald, or Rowland, but that promise whole stories to Clemmie's darting eyes. They move in separate directions, each drawn to different things.

Standing in the center of the vestibule, Clemmie looks upward. Can
anyone dare to call these buildings ruins when the ceiling is as well
preserved as this? It's so high above her she has to strain her eyes, but

she knows what she's looking for and finds the chiseled barque as easily as if she'd been here before. Each carefully sculpted shape—a crown, a scepter, each glyph—is depicted in blues and that sandy orange of these parts. The turquoise and rust of a kingfisher.

She's so rapt on tracing the ceiling's artwork that she doesn't hear Rowland approach. He offers a pair of opera glasses and she takes them greedily. Between the Hathor-headed pillars, the faces flattened by former mutilators, are two arresting scenes in that same teal and buff stonework. First, on the right, there's a line of deities. They're all facing a large eye, with ibis-headed Thoth on the other side of it. Clemmie counts the characters, knowing them by the icons they wear on their heads. Nephthys, Isis, Osiris. In total, there are fourteen figures on the ramp leading to the eye, and to Thoth.

The artwork on the ceiling reminds her of a story she heard many years before, and as she blinks through the opera glasses, she can hear her father's voice once more.

Seated on her father's knee, she was aware of how she fitted there perfectly as he held a precious papyrus in his hands, his arms on either side of her. Within this comforting enclosure, she nestled against him.

"Will it break if I touch it?"

"You just need to be gentle."

She hesitated. Her chubby hands so small against his.

"What about gloves?"

She heard the smile in his voice without turning to look at his face.

"We can feel the fragility more easily without them. And I like to think that the oils in our hands are good," he said. "They keep them conditioned and preserved. Like saddle soap on leather."

"Like resin and skin."

He'd taught her well.

"Do you know what this is?" He pointed at the image of an eye. The dramatic curl beneath it forming an ambitious tear. The brow striped blue and white, just like a nemes.

"Horus!" she said, so excited she nearly jumped off his lap. "The falcon-headed son of Isis!"

She was always delighted when the myths linked with her favorite characters. Isis and Nephthys. They were the best figures in these tales because they didn't let anything—not even death—get in their way, and she wanted to be like that. Not to let anything stop her from achieving in life, and always to put family first, just as they did with their brother Osiris.

That was a whole different story, and her father was on the cusp of telling her a new one.

He chuckled. "That's right. But the name of the eye. Do you know?"

She thought back over the many lessons. The hundreds of times she'd sat on his lap when her mother had rolled her eyes and left the room in a huff, trailing a new dress or a doll that Clemmie had hardly registered. She'd seen this eye before and knew it was important to the ancient Egyptians. What was it called?

"Wedge . . . wedgy . . ."

His belly shook against her back, warm breath blowing a wisp of hair into her eye. "Wedjat."

She loved learning about hieroglyphs. Her father knew some of them, but not many. One day, she would learn this bygone language for herself.

"Once," he said, "it was believed that Horus fought with Set."

A story. All her father's stories began with once. Perhaps the very best things always happened in the past, or maybe some were still to happen, and the next generations would recall them as once.

She lay against him, feeling the rise and fall of his chest against her shoulder blades. He asked her if she remembered who Set was, and she turned herself around to see his face properly. Then she put her fists on her hips and gathered her brow into a stern frown.

"The evil god who killed Osiris."

He tapped the point of her nose. "That's right. Well, Horus hadn't forgiven Set for killing Osiris, so they had a duel. And do you know what Set did?"

She bit her lips, waiting for him to go on.

"He ripped his eye out."

Her father reached for her eye and pretended to grapple for it. She shrieked, writhing on his knee and giggling.

"But Thoth restored the eye."

"Thoth!" she said excitedly. "The one with the ibis head. The writer."

"Yes," he said. "The scribe. He returned the eye to Horus who gave it to Osiris in the afterlife and it restored him. Thus, it is a symbol of healing."

"But he could have kept it for himself," said Clemmie seriously. "That was a very generous gift."

"What did you say?"

Clemmie turns, surprised to see Rowland standing next to her, and remembers where she is. In Denderah. With the traveling party. Not with her father, on his lap. These simple remembrances have taken on the feel of her father's tales. Recent years reducing her happiness to nothing more than a story that begins with *once.*

"You said something about a gift." Rowland looks amused.

She must have spoken out loud and she lifts the glasses to her eyes again. Ignoring him.

"Well, here you are," he continues. "The place you couldn't wait to get to. That is, until you decided Philae was the main attraction."

Clemmie keeps her eyes on the ceiling. She won't give in that easily.

His silence asks the questions he isn't voicing. Was her hurry really just to look up at this ceiling, or did she have another reason? What's made her suddenly decide to press on to Philae?

She still keeps her eyes averted, determined to keep him wondering. Through the glasses, she looks to the second scene. Pointing, even if it's too high up for Rowland to view clearly, she asks if he sees the barque.

"The boat? Yes, I see it."

"In that boat is Osiris, and on either side of him are Nephthys and Isis, his sisters who could both change into kites."

Celia and Oswald join them.

"How do you know who's who?" Celia asks.

She swallows. How can she forget?

A throne. A house with a basket.

Isis and Nephthys.

Explaining that the crowns they wear are their glyphs, she gives up the little binoculars to be shared around, watching their faces as they pick out what's there.

"The house with the basket—that's the rectangle standing on its short side with a half circle on top—the figure wearing that glyph is Nephthys."

No one speaks as she talks them through it.

"On the other side is Isis. Her glyph is the throne. See the shape of a seat on her head?"

They have that look in their eyes again. The one that shows their ignorance. She thinks of where she left off last time, when the jackals and intruder interrupted her. This is the perfect backdrop to continue, really, with the carvings of mythological figures around her.

She launches into the story, picking up from Nephthys's betrayal. Something she's no foreigner to. The myth has never felt so real in her head, on her tongue, as it does at Denderah.

Nephthys waited for Set to find out about her union with Osiris. When he acted no differently toward her, she realized that he didn't know. When she encountered Isis, her sister kissed her as always and there was no sign of resentment, so she wasn't aware either. On the occasions when she saw Osiris, she searched in his face for what they'd shared, and while he was discreet, while he rarely met her eye, there were moments when they did look at each other and she knew that he did remember. That he thought of it too.

For all of her marriage to Set, Nephthys had been barren, but finally she began to notice the changes in her body and she knew the truth.

Her *kalasiris* was of the most fashionable style. Woven so finely that it was translucent. Nephthys was afraid of that. Fearful that Set would notice the swell of her baby. Terrified that when it was born, it would be obvious that it was Osiris's. So she hid her pregnancy. She covered herself with feathers, and somehow her time passed without anyone asking questions or suspecting. After all, no one really noticed Nephthys. She was just Set's wife, the sister of Osiris and Isis, devoted to birds, last-born. She was invisible.

When she knew her time had come, she crept away and found a cave dripping with mineral fingers. There she gave birth to her son. He didn't have green skin like Osiris. Nor did he have Set's animal features. But he did have the head of a pup that would grow into a jackal, and the power in his dark face reminded her so intensely of Osiris that she was afraid that Set would take one look and know this was not his son. That she had consorted with her sister's husband behind her own husband's back.

Nephthys called her son Anubis, meaning decay, perhaps because she felt certain that his future would be connected to the dead—or maybe because she wasn't sure if he would live that long, and if he did and was ever discovered, it would be better for them both if they had already passed through to the underworld.

<p

Rowland raises an eyebrow. "They're as bad as the Olympians. Set did find out in the end, didn't he? Isn't that why he murdered Osiris?"

Clemmie nods. Thinking of the carving knife, a part of the myth. The scalpel, a part of her own life.

The scene above them takes place after Nephthys's affair, Osiris's murder, his dismemberment and revival. Isis and Osiris face each other, restored after all they've been through, but Isis and Nephthys are also facing each other. The sisters restored to each other as well. Apparently, Isis has forgiven Nephthys for her adultery with Osiris.

It's so remarkable that, while the discovery of this simple detail excites her, it also uncovers a host of questions that she can't make sense of. Questions that sit deeply, like the buried complex they stand in.

Nephthys betrayed Isis, and yet they worked together to save Osiris. How did Isis forgive Nephthys for stealing her love? How did they piece their relationship back together? Was it done gradually, just as Osiris was put back together piece by piece? Or did she never blame Nephthys in the first place? And if so, why was she so good? She didn't deserve the pain her sister brought upon her. How can a sister forgive a wrong so great?

Rowland is watching her intently as she silently frets over these troubling questions, his eyes fixing on her like a camera lens ready to capture a portrait. Can he see every thought reflected in her eyes? If he can, then that's a dreadful thing, to be so transparent. She returns her attention to instructing her companions.

"In the barque alongside them you'll see Maat."

"A mat?" Celia asks.

"No, no. Maat, the goddess. She wears a feather, and her feather is used in the weighing of the heart when Anubis judges the dead."

"Why is she there?" Oswald asks. "What does Maat symbolize?"

"Truth."

Clemmie almost chokes on the word. Is it just her, or does Rowland look at her strangely? If Anubis were to place her on his scales, what would her weight be against Maat's feather?

She hurries to translate the other symbols. The winged scarab holding a *shen* ring: signs of rebirth, power, and eternity. This is a scene of hope. She holds out her hand for the binoculars and lifts them to her eyes. Looking for something specific. There it is. In Isis's hand. In Nephthys's too. That plus shape with a loop at its head. When she was little, she described it as a small *t* with a halo, like the *tyet* but with arms extended. Both sisters hold one as they stare at each other. Not in defiance. In unity.

"The *ankh* is an important symbol in this scene."

"And?" Rowland prods. "What does the *ankh* mean?"

Clemmie doesn't take her eyes off the sisters or their *ankh*s.

"Life," she says. "The *ankh* was believed to be the key of life."

Unwrapping

1888

I T IS A YEAR SINCE that dreadful night. Nothing has changed as such, so she knows she was foolish ever to wonder if the hieroglyphs could harm her family. There has been nothing else like the moment she found Bast curled up dead. Neither has there been a wedding. Horatio continues to serve overseas, and Rosetta's health has not been the best. Flora says it's the anxiety of the delay, or the melancholia of a long winter. Both explanations are perfectly reasonable, but Clemmie misses the cheerful, carefree sister who used to spend happy hours with her instead of easing headaches in a darkened room.

In his letters, Horatio remains as much a part of Bickmore as when he's home on leave. He thinks of them all. When the mail comes, it does so as a packet, the envelopes within to be passed around. Usually, one for Rosetta containing a pressed leaf or flower from his travels, which she twirls and twirls as she reads, failing to share the contents with anyone. Sometimes Clement's chit promises the smell and bulge of tobacco. Often the message to Flora is an interesting account about a hat he saw a general's wife wear, or detailing, down to a sketch, the attire of a local woman. Horatio is still serving in Egypt, for, despite the foreign secretary's promises to evacuate British troops by this year, Britain continues to occupy the country on the grounds of establishing order after the uprising. The revolt undermined the Khedive and threatened Britain's shares in the Suez Canal, and Kassassin and Tell El Kebir are still in the minds of people on all sides. There are no claims of annexation, the British government not having any desire to aggravate the Ottoman Empire, but they still retain Egypt as a colony.

There will even be a letter for Clemmie. Hearing from Horatio is always a pleasure. It makes her more than a little jealous that he is in Egypt, and she devours his words hungrily. He writes of tombs and temples, asks her how business is going, and in her response, she asks for sketches and details of the sights he sees, omitting that the business has in fact dwindled.

Her father's aches are dreadful. One in his hand, a swelling in his knuckle, a stoop of his back, a thud in his head, a shooting pain up his leg, and more besides. She hates to see him age, this man who has always been a constant in her life. Requests arrive by post for Egyptology events, but there are no more. This is partly because she won't help her father with another unwrapping, but also because he is in so much discomfort that he sits in his chair all day and moans.

"I have another pain," he tells her one morning as he pours a dose of laudanum. He has become almost obsessive about his afflictions, counting them, naming each one. Tallying them feverishly.

"This one is sharp, cutting through my spine." He rubs at his back. "Right here."

"Oh, Papa," she says. "Perhaps you should be in bed rather than your study. If you rest, you shall be well again."

"Do you know how many pains that is now?" he says. "Fourteen of them. Fourteen! How is a man to live with so many pains?"

She falters.

Fourteen. Like the fourteen body parts of Osiris. Butchered, like the mummy.

The pain of Osiris upon his own body.

It's just a coincidence, she promises herself.

She remembers the words on the amulet, and she chooses to forget them. She walks through the scarlet-painted walls of the house she has always called home, and instead of paint she sees blood. She looks at the winged scarabs depicted in the plaster coving, and the border comes to life, crawling until she blinks. She avoids the study where the twins lie, because she knows that their silent faces will ask her why she didn't stop her father from his destruction. She still pictures them, though, lying there in one of the mahogany cabinets.

She wants to tell her sister her concerns, the way they've always shared everything, but when they sit with fingers entwined, she loses the power of opening up. A bud that forgets to bloom, unable to share the possibilities of what's hidden inside.

"Nephthys," Rosetta says, and Clemmie realizes that she's trying to distract her. Is her unease so obvious that her sister is attempting to take her back to the days when they would play games? "Nephthys, let's go to the Nile."

She pats her sister's hand and smiles. "We did always have fun, didn't we?"

Rosetta moves to the window and looks out.

"Where's Osiris?"

She's strangely irked that Rosetta is still pretending.

"Let's go to the Chelmer," Clemmie says, purposely using the river's real name instead of the one it wore in their childhood.

"Osiris is missing," her sister repeats.

Clemmie goes over to her, touches Rosetta's arm, and for a moment there's a shadowing in her face. A glazed, distant look. Then it passes, and she is her sister again.

Cataract

THE CATARACT IS NOT WHAT the name would suggest it to be. Celia expressed fear at the thought of confronting a waterfall the height of Victoria, but it turns out that whoever gave this section of the Nile its name was feeling lyrical that day. There are no waterfalls, merely shallows with waters trying to make up for time with a facade of rapids. The liquid path to Philae is dotted with islets and rocks that protrude from the riverbed, threatening to ground *Hapi* and render the *dahabeeyah* just another of the sites that people will pass and talk about for centuries to come. Youssef is unwilling to sacrifice his vessel to the Nile, even in exchange for fame, so the crew maneuver, *Hapi* twists and turns like a fish on a line, and sometimes they flounder, often they glide, and they press onward.

Before the cataract, at Assûan, Rowland was the only one to dash onshore, and when he came back, he was sporting the kind of smile that's almost boastful and whistling that tune again. Clemmie wanted to ask him what had made him so pleased with himself, and when she saw the flash of paper in his pocket—a telegram—she could only presume he'd received the news from home that he'd been waiting for. Is it from a sweetheart? News on an investment? She feels a little out of sorts at his good humor, but isn't sure why.

They're so close to Philae now that Clemmie can't keep still. She paces the deck and then gets frustrated watching the crew working. Doing their best, no doubt, but sometimes it seems as though they intend to get stuck on every sandbank they find. At last, she sits in the saloon to escape the heat of the day.

Mariam brings her some lemonade, smiling surreptitiously so that Clemmie knows she's thinking the same thing.

We are almost there.

"You know what you said about being a *shâdûf*?" Clemmie asks.

Mariam nods.

"I've been wondering how you go about it?"

"I wondered if you would ask. Most tourists aren't interested in talking to me. They see me as a cook, nothing more. To them, I am invisible, but that helps me to observe. I know people by their frowns, the things they say, and the things they don't. I listen. It is something we can all do, but many don't choose to. My kitchen is a place to view, to hear, to understand what happens on the river and beyond."

"And how does that help with the preservation of antiquities?"

Mariam's head rocks as she weighs her response. "I look out for anything suspicious, and there is a contact my father and I can report to who helps end the work of unlicensed sites."

"You're a spy, then?"

Mariam's laugh tinkles like a stream. "Not exactly. I don't search for illegal traders or even try to track them down. But when a dealer comes on my *baba*'s *dahabeeyah* and wants to sell to our tourists, which happens from time to time, we write a description of the person and the location and send it to our contact."

Clemmie can see how well the role suits Mariam. Working on a tourist vessel means she can keep her eyes and ears open and serve what she so longs to protect without anyone suspecting. Celebrated archeologists like the Scotsman Rhind clearly worked with permission—but there must be many who are smuggling antiquities out of the country to meet the demands of the world.

"If you're willing, when we get to Philae, I would be grateful for your help."

"Of course, *ya aanesa* Clemmie."

Mariam carries her tray out onto the deck, where Oswald can be heard detailing the pheasant shoots he hosts back at home. Clemmie can't hear Rowland respond, and wonders if he's an avid listener, or just pretending. Celia has gone to lie down, complaining that the cataract makes her feel queasy, although Clemmie hardly notices the change. Only that they're not moving as much as she'd like. She sips her lemonade, but the sweetness of the drink is almost sickening in the heat.

She goes through her plan. The one she concocted back at home in England before she even purchased her ticket to come to Egypt; the one she's had to adapt now that she has company and since Mariam advised on the location. Everything must happen at night, in the shadows, where she can be like Nephthys. Invisible.

Why did she ever agree to share the *dahabeeyah*? It would have been far simpler if she'd said: *No, thank you, Miss Lion, I wish to travel alone,* or: *Mr. Luscombe, I don't care what you think, but I'm hiring this* dahabeeyah *right now and I'm going by myself.*

But she didn't say that. Why? Because in her heart, even though she's resented every conversation where she doesn't fit in, she wants them here. Handsome Rowland—did she really just admit that?—for all his irksome questions, shares her appreciation for Egyptology. She enjoys observing the way Oswald watches out for his sister, that older brother figure she might have liked for herself. Celia's coquetry is almost unseemly—it's a wonder Rowland manages to ignore her constant flirtations—but her undeniable warmth is inviting. Dare Clemmie say it, she's almost fond of them all. She wanted not to feel invisible, and in those moments when they've listened to her recounting the myths, she hasn't been. She desired to come up the Nile with a traveling party like any other tourist who'd made some connections, and she has. Was that so very wrong?

It's too late to berate herself now. Still, her wheezing starts up again, inducing a bout of dizziness that she's glad no one is around to witness. Clemmie reaches into her pocket for a handkerchief. It's not another attack, she pacifies herself. It's just the nerves.

The handkerchief she pocketed this morning when she dressed isn't there. She must have dropped it.

Heading for her cabin, she pushes open her door, barely noticing that it was already slightly ajar as she mutters to herself.

"Where is my—"

She stops. Someone is in her room. Someone other than Sphinx, although the cat trots over to welcome her. Clemmie physically jumps when she sees Celia facing the closet. The aftertaste of lemonade turns bitter in her throat as she realizes what Celia has been doing.

The closet is open. On the floor is the box. The table croquet box that she'd placed beneath her undergarments. The box that she wouldn't store in the hold for fear that someone would find it. There it lies, empty. Celia slowly turns around, the amulet in her hands.

Clemmie shuts the door behind her and hurries forward, snatching the Double *Tyet*. It's too late. She realizes that. Celia has seen what she's been hiding.

Neither of them says anything while Clemmie struggles to think. And then they both speak at once.

"What are you doing in my things?"

"Where did you get it?"

"Celia, answer me. What are you doing going through my belongings?"

"I was looking for you."

"In the closet?"

"Well, I came to find you." Celia speaks quickly, but doesn't look at Clemmie. She's still staring at the amulet. Mesmerized by it. "I was feeling a little queasy, as you know, and of course I don't have my maid to look after me. She betrayed me, you know. Did I tell you that? She's the one who told my parents about me and Michael. I'll never forgive her."

"Celia!"

"Your episode when you couldn't breathe came to mind, and I thought: 'Clemmie will know what to do. Maybe her bottle of oil will help me.' Your father was a doctor or something, didn't you say? And you're so clever, you're bound to know things about sickness and suchlike, so I knocked, I really did, but no one answered so I came in."

"Why? If no one answered, that meant no one was in here, so no one could help you."

"I didn't want to trouble you. I thought if there was a bottle of oil in here, I could just sniff it and go."

"Eucalyptus oil is for the airways, not for nausea."

"How was I to know?"

"And then?"

"I couldn't see what I was looking for, but—oh, I don't know. I just saw the closet and I opened it. I wasn't doing any harm. It was just there and I was bored so I opened it and there was the croquet box and I thought: 'What a lark that would be to play!'"

"So you opened it."

Instead of apologizing, she glances at Clemmie with a look of awe. "The hieroglyphs. I recognize them. Aren't they the ones you showed us at Denderah? The names of the sisters."

She's surprised that Celia remembers. Brushing her fingers over the throne and the house with the basket, Clemmie kneels down to place the Double *Tyet* back into the box, carefully returning it to the closet. She closes her eyes. Remembering that night five years ago—is that all it's been, these five years of torture?—and how since then her life has crumbled like one of Egypt's ruins.

Forcing herself to her feet, Clemmie leads Celia over to her bed. They sit side by side, both silent at first. Clemmie takes the younger woman's hands in hers. They're clammy, but her own are no better. She has to think clearly. Sphinx jumps onto the bed between them, kneading the sheets and nuzzling their arms for attention.

"Celia, I need you to do me a favor. This was my secret. The amulet is very rare, and I don't want people to know what I'm about to do with it. I can't risk someone stealing it."

"Did *you* steal it?"

"It was my father's."

"You didn't find it here?"

Clemmie shakes her head, explaining just enough without giving her whole story away. She admits that she's here on a secret mission, one that Mariam knows about, but no one else. It can be Celia's secret too, she says, and she can join her if she promises not to tell a soul. Not even Oswald or Rowland.

"Is it dangerous?"

How can she lie?

"I honestly don't know. I just have to see it through, no matter what."

"You mean, like an adventure?"

"Yes," says Clemmie slowly, trying to tempt her. "An adventure. I could do with your help."

"Very well," Celia says. "I promise. What would you need me to do?"

PART TWO

Egyptomania

The work of destruction, meanwhile, goes on apace. There
is no one to prevent it; there is no one to discourage it.
Every day, more inscriptions are mutilated—more tombs
are rifled—more paintings and sculptures are defaced.

—AMELIA B. EDWARDS, *A Thousand Miles up the Nile*

At the dawn of light, I am thy protection each day.

—*The Lamentations of Isis and Nephthys*

Unwrapping

1889

TWO YEARS AFTER THE UNWRAPPING—when Rosetta's head-
aches still haven't ceased, when she has fits of rage that never presented before, and she's been known to refer to her absent fiancé as
Osiris; when the wedding has been delayed countless times due to
Horatio's service and Rosetta's poor health; when Clemmie has caught
chill after chill that leaves her breathless; when Clement has been almost crippled with aches that tingle and throb in various patterns
throughout his body, each pain distinct and different, fourteen of them;
when the influenza is sweeping through London and the districts
around—Clement is taken to his bed, and Clemmie quickly follows
him to hers. They spend two weeks of fevers, coughs, and pains, before
she comes around and wonders where those days have gone.

When she is stronger, Clemmie sits by her weakening father. Her
mind returns to her hieroglyphs and languages and myths, but the
cough doesn't quite go away. It leaves a wheeze behind, the scratch of
sand. She tells them to keep Rosetta from her until she is quite sure
that she will not catch it, because if she could not protect the twins, if
she could not protect Bast, then she must do all she can to protect her
sister.

That's what Nephthys would have done.

"It's just influenza," Clement mutters from his bed, not managing to look her in the eye, but she wonders if he thinks what she's thinking. If he feels the way Bickmore has become a shadow of what it once was. How they are becoming shadows with it. Shadows are more easily distinguished in the light, but when the darkness comes, they form a larger whole.

Clemmie holds her father's cold, cold hand, senses his weakening grip, and watches as he fades.

Philae

THE ISLAND OF PHILAE IS nothing remarkable. There's no great Dog Star shining over it, as Isis's beacon, to say that her temple rests here. No sacrificial smoke billows from its core, no clowder of cats graces the banks with their sacred bodies. It's just another rocky sand-pit of an island, occasional palms or grasses breaking up the gold and softening the harshness of it. And Clemmie has never seen anything more beautiful.

They unloaded themselves from *Hapi* rather wearily. There's a hunger inside Clemmie that isn't a need for food, but it strips her of strength just the same. Is everyone watching her? Celia now knows a part of it at least, but are Rowland and Oswald waiting to see what all the fuss was to get here?

The temple isn't alone, kept company by a scattering of buildings that show a history of defacing, just like Denderah. Clemmie winces, hating the missing faces on the columns and the efforts to inscribe signatures where once only hieroglyphs and Egyptian artwork stood. What did these reliefs look like when the chisels had first completed their work? Was each glyph etched so clearly you could run a fingernail through the indentations to trace its outline? What expressions were on the faces that are now crumbled? So much has survived, but there is also a good deal missing. What she'd give to see Philae's temple in its original state, before generations of hands marred what was.

Is the destruction that has happened here any different from what transpired in her father's study five years ago? What was it Mariam had said about each *shâdûf* making a difference? If that's the case, then how can Clemmie be a part of that? Is her quest to Philae enough?

The inner court boasts the sky as its roof, the surround made from the same yellow stone forming the Pyramids by the Nile. Along one wall is a stele, one of those tablets the like of which Moses carried down from Sinai with God's Commandments inscribed.

"Is it an exact copy of the Rosetta Stone?" Rowland asks.

"Oh, I've seen the Rosetta Stone," says Celia. "It's in the British Museum, isn't it? Ossie, you took me. Remember?"

"It's not an exact replica," Clemmie says.

She points to the blank space at the bottom, hesitating before tracing the winged scarab at the top. She shows them that the hieroglyphic and demotic writings are present, but there's no Greek.

"Without the Greek, the Rosetta Stone wouldn't have been deciphered," she says. "This stele is incomplete."

"But you can read it?" Rowland asks. He looks eager, genuinely interested. Is this some kind of test?

"If I had a long time . . ."

"Well, there's no rush," he says, limping away. "We're here now. That's what you wanted, wasn't it?"

In one chamber, the story of Osiris is told on the walls. His revival, and the part his sisters played in it. Rowland reaches into his pocket and draws out a bag of sweetmeats, offering them around. Clemmie takes one absentmindedly, hardly tasting it. The gumminess melts between her teeth.

Celia points at the fragmented body parts scattered over the tableau, asking what's happening in the scenes, and Clemmie tells them about Osiris, one of the most famous myths. As she talks, she walks alongside the wall. Following each carving with her eyes. Describing how Osiris was murdered and cut into pieces. How his sisters searched for his scattered body parts, even when it seemed all hope was lost.

"This one is Isis." She reaches toward the one wearing the throne glyph as her crown. "And the other is Nephthys." Her hand hovers longer here.

If her mission here works tonight, then she's just hours away, after all these years, from making things right.

Beneath Osiris's body are canopic jars, the carved pots bearing the heads of mythical deities, and under the funerary bed lie *was* scepters and *ankhs*. Symbols of power and life. These illustrations are filled with hope as Nephthys and Isis piece their brother's body back together. Hope that she dares to inhale, filling her lungs the way they haven't been filled in a long time.

Opposite her, Rowland seems to be puzzling her out, but maybe he'll just accept that all she's ever wanted is to see these depictions of Isis and Nephthys, just like at Denderah. The enthusiastic Egyptologist.

Better for him to think that.

Maybe Rowland expected her to be rejoicing, or laughing, or crying, now that she's here, but Clemmie continues to keep her feelings corseted as tightly as her waist. She might be at Philae, but it isn't over yet.

She's played out this day in her head so many times, and as the hours crawl by, she feels the tension growing inside her. If her plan works, she'll return home to a semblance of the life she once knew. If she fails . . . but no, that isn't worth thinking about. She can't fail.

Mariam excels herself that evening, preparing a meal fit for a celebration. Maybe it is, and Clemmie almost smiles at this subtle message of recognition. Over roasted lamb, skewered kidneys, tomatoes, and rice, and a dessert of preserved apricots that Mariam calls *mish-mish*, the others converse cheerfully, their chatter bright with laughter. Clemmie doesn't join in. She feels in two places tonight, busy with thoughts of Bickmore and also of the island. Her chest throbs with the fervor of two hearts. So much rests on tonight going to plan.

Oswald complains that he hasn't seen a single crocodile yet, thumping the table with his disappointment and drawing her attention back to her companions. Rowland promises that if Oswald doesn't get his trophy, he'll visit the Lions in Bristol and the two men can go shooting together. At this suggestion, Celia becomes more animated than ever and says Rowland must come to Kearly House often, crocodile or no crocodile. This muddle of conversation blurs into a medley of voices that Clemmie hears but doesn't retain. She thinks only of the closet and what's inside. Of what she has to do tonight, under the cover of darkness.

"What happens next?" asks Rowland. "Clementine? Are you with us tonight or did we leave you behind on the island?"

They all laugh and Clemmie forces herself into the moment.

"Mr. Lion, would you pass the water?"

"I think we've known each other long enough to drop such formalities," he replies. "Call me Oswald."

She smiles briefly, accepting the jug and pouring herself a drink. Meanwhile, Rowland voices his question again. Should they stay at Philae, press on for Abou Simbel, or go back the way they've come?

"Do let's carry on," says Celia. "I thought it would be frightfully dull staring at all these broken-down temples, but with our marvelous company it's been such fun." She gifts a smile to Rowland that glitters in the lamplight.

Clemmie refrains from sharing her plans. After tonight, she must remain near the island and send a message to Chelmsford to see if she's been successful, waiting for the response that can put her mind at ease with three words: *All is well*.

Unwrapping

1890

SHE DOESN'T RECOGNIZE HERSELF IN black. It turns the rosiness of her cheeks to alabaster, and her eyes darken to match the fabric of her mourning. Her father, Dr. Clement Attridge, is dead, and she misses him with a hollowness that no language—known or forgotten—will ever describe.

Dolor. Douleur. Dolorous. *Tristis. Triste.* Triste. Over and over she plays with the words but they have no meaning. The languages she knows let her down.

Horatio is on leave at the time of her father's death, a blessing because he is home to mourn with them, to support his bride-to-be and her family in this time of grief. He spends many hours at Bickmore, wrapping one arm around Rosetta, who leans into him, absorbing his touch, and one around Clemmie. She appreciates his thoughtfulness and sensitivity. When Rosetta whispers to him—*"Let's be married, please. Do help me escape this misery"*—he strokes her cheek with his thumb, promises her better times are coming, and insists they honor Clement's memory.

"He was a second father to me," Horatio says, his voice chipped with emotion.

Rosetta's double grief—mourning her father and her delayed wedding—sends her to her bed, to a darkened room smelling of lavender. Clemmie wonders if they should call a doctor, and Horatio smiles sadly at her tenderness, but says all Rosetta needs is to be cared for and loved. What medicines might a doctor prescribe for grief? Isn't having her loved ones nearby all the balm she might need?

They've always had an easy relationship. As young girls, the sisters would beckon Horatio over to the river, ask him to play. Despite being older, he'd occasionally indulge them, other times he'd just watch. When Clemmie grew out of the game of Myths and turned her hours to studying them through iconography on papyri, pottery, amulets, and jewelry, Horatio would sometimes join her. His isn't a deep passion the way hers is, although his interest in Egyptology has grown steadily over the years, even more so after his experience in the army. Yet he's been there, a part of it all.

By the river that she once played at, near the spot where Bast was buried, watching her happiness trickle by like the current at her feet, Clemmie lowers her face into her hands and sobs.

Flora doesn't want to remember Clement with her daughters, to fight the depression. She goes for walks around the estate, wishing only to be alone. She is disoriented, often stumbling and bumping into things. At night she sleepwalks, and come morning there might be a new bruise on her forehead where she has walked into a doorframe, or a swelling to her ankle where she misjudged the stairs. She becomes clumsy, frail, mumbling to herself. A ruin of what she once was.

Bickmore's very wood and walls seem to groan along with them. When she lies awake at night, Clemmie hears the manor sighing. She is aware of these sounds as she passes through the redbrick, hoary-tiled house, and treads the rheumatic staircase, avoiding the study. She hungers for the symbols of Egypt, but she cannot face the twins.

She needs her mother to be strong, but she isn't. She needs Rosetta to be strong, but she doesn't act the part of elder sister. That leaves her. Her and Horatio.

"I'm so glad you're here," Clemmie says. He rubs her back, then folds her in to his chest. For just a fleeting moment she wonders if it is wrong, but why shouldn't he? He is like a brother to her, and right now she needs a sibling. She needs not to be alone.

"I'm not going anywhere," Horatio promises, and it's true. He's managed to get transferred. He'll be working at a military college nearby, just a few hours away on horseback.

His words are meant to comfort her, and in a small way they do—but something oxidizes them, tainting their shine. She peers over his shoulder and sees two birds with forked tails in the sky, scanning the earth for prey.

Something is looming. Something deadly. It's not going away, even after claiming her father. Perhaps, at the taste of blood, it wants more.

It steps closer. She feels the certainty of it as sure as Horatio's breath on her hair, and she doesn't know how any of them can stop what's coming.

Burial

"THEY'RE ALL IN THEIR CABINS."

Celia is standing over the bed where Clemmie has been resting. She hasn't slept. She hasn't even tried to. But it helped to lie down with her eyes closed and go through the plan in her mind, Sphinx pressed up against the curl of her body. A part of her wants to stay like this. To remain in the realm of shadows where dreams are at their height, imagining that she's a child again with her cat tucked in next to her.

"You're sure?"

Celia nods, her face lit by the paraffin lamp she holds. Clemmie feels the warmth it casts, aware of her own stickiness. The Egyptian nights are cool, but dressed in a thick layer of anticipation, she feels as sweaty as a farm laborer.

"I'll fetch the box," Clemmie whispers.

It's easier to call it the box. Stated simply, it could be anything. A box of ribbons, a crate of books, a case of Lumps of Delight. As she picks it up, all the imaginary contents melt away.

She never has feared mummies and their funerary amulets. Whenever her mother voiced her concerns, her father would say: *At least she isn't afraid of being around death, Flora.* Maybe she hadn't had a choice, with a surgeon and mummy collector for a father. In recent years, she's changed. Nowadays, she *is* afraid of death. Her morbid fascination has come back to haunt her, stealing her loved ones along the way, stalking her minutes and hours with a sneer that seems to say: *You're next.*

She tells Celia to go ahead with the lamp, to look out for anyone, and to be quiet.

Celia nods, taking the role of "silent lookout" literally. They shut Sphinx in the cabin, and hear her scratching at the door, wanting to follow.

Guided by Celia and her lamp, Clemmie steps onto the deck. Wheezing over her burden. The amulet isn't heavy, of course, but it weighs her down in a different way. Every few steps she stops, catches her breath, and then carries on. Already fretting about selecting an appropriate spot to return her offering, wanting to get everything just right. She never expected this to be easy. Making amends isn't supposed to be, is it? Especially when the penance should be death.

Something on the deck moves, and for a moment, Clemmie thinks they've been discovered. She anticipates Rowland's quizzical eyes, or the glowing end of Youssef's *chibouk*, but the figure that steps into the light is only Mariam. She has come, just as she promised.

They leave *Hapi*, crossing the plank that connects vessel to shore. The night is mostly silent, garnished with the Nile's breathing, the creaking bones of the *dahabeeyah* as it strains to see what they're up to, the harsh call of a lamenting owl. The darkness preys upon her imagination, and the silhouetted bulk of the temple looms dangerously, sand growing fingers that scratch her bare feet. The distant cry of a jackal— probably far away on the mainland—is a reminder of Anubis carried on the wind.

Death isn't far away.

Once ashore, they hesitate. Celia waits for guidance, and Clemmie suddenly feels incompetent, eager for the counsel of Mariam, who scans the island, the lamp carving the evening's glyphs across her face.

"Where do you think is best to bury it?" Clemmie whispers.

"The text was not specific," Mariam replies softly.

"I agree. It only stated that the amulet should be restored to Isis where Osiris rises to meet her."

"We should avoid too close to the temple," Mariam suggests. "In case of looters."

"Over here," Clemmie says, and Celia carries the lamp in the direction of Clemmie's jerking head. It's far enough up the shore not to be overheard by the sleepers on the boat, but the ground is still soft enough to dig. As well as the box, Clemmie is carrying a hand trowel brought with her from England, and she gets to work.

By the light of the moon, the stars, and Celia's paraffin lamp that quivers in the night's gloom, Clemmie—on bended knees—digs a grave of sorts. She tears strips from her petticoat to imitate cerement and wraps the amulet in the manner of a *khat* or corpse before replacing it in its sarcophagus-type box. Like a strange reversal of grave robbers, they slink in the shadows and cast furtive glances at each other as the funerary token is interred. In the presence of Isis's temple, encircled by the liquid representation of Osiris, she lowers the amulet ceremoniously into the hole.

"Mariam?"

The captain's daughter reaches out, twining a loose lock of Clemmie's hair around her finger. There's a dull flash of something in her other hand. Mariam has brought it with her, just as they'd agreed. A knife. Mariam's eyes are asking her permission, and she nods.

She had worried, all along, that returning the amulet wouldn't be enough. Over and over she'd tried to reason with herself. Should she have brought the mummy with her too? But how could she, when the twins had been cut apart and were so terribly fragile? She would have needed expert shipping to achieve this safely, which, of course, would have cost dearly, and her funds are stretched tightly as it is. She had argued with herself that restoring the Double *Tyet* was what was required, that if the twins were harmed further, it might only deepen the blight. So this is her final touch. A mark of respect and of mourning.

Mariam comes to stand behind Clemmie and takes out pin after pin. For the last time, Clemmie feels her long tresses tumble down her back, and then the painful yank at her scalp and the sound of tearing as Mariam's sharp knife hacks at her hair. Celia gasps slightly, but doesn't intervene. If every muscle wasn't already strained, Clemmie might notice the release as the physical weight disappears. She fingers the new ends, surprised to find them just below her shoulders.

It's an old funerary rite, one associated with Isis and Nephthys. A sacrifice to honor the dead twins, but even so Clemmie feels the burn of shame and tears at this loss. She prays that her burden may fall along with it.

Swiping at her eyes with the back of her hand, she feels foolish. Here she is, crying over hair—something truly lifeless—when throughout her life she has aided the desecration of the dead. Mummies are people once mourned. A long time ago, the twins were alive in this country. Did the sisters once wade among the sedges by the Nile, the way she would as a child among the reeds by the Chelmer? Did they play games together, those of make-believe, or the board games Senet or Mehen? Did they share the same tastes, or bicker over their choices? What were their favorite animals? Their favorite foods? Colors? How did they die?

She imagines their family arranging their burial. The mummification was carried out, the amulet designed and carved according to the specifications. Did their mother demand a Double *Tyet,* so that each daughter could be represented and yet still be joined as one? Did their father write the text to be inscribed in glyphs, so that he could still perform his duty to protect his offspring? How can she weep over lost hair, when the mummies she's handled and gaped at weren't things at all? They were people. They knew pain, and loss, and what it was to feel the Egyptian sun on their skin, the Nile on their toes. If she didn't understand that then, back when she was her father's assistant, she does now.

When she's finished, Mariam passes Clemmie the hank of hair trailing from her fist. About to lay it on top of the box, she hesitates, thinking of something else.

Reaching into her pocket, she draws out the silver locket on the flat of her palm, naked in the lamplight. For a final time, she reads the inscription.

No one else hath loved thee more than I.

Feeling braver, she says the words aloud. Meaning them.

"No one else hath loved thee more than I."

She flicks the locket open, a curl of blond hair nestled inside like a sleeping cat. Her thumb sweeps over it. She kisses it. A tear wets it. Then she closes the locket, trying not to think of the moment when the chain was broken, pulled from her throat. Her entire life she has taken from this land. This is just a small gift in return.

She uses the snapped chain to bind her cut mane to the locket, tying a knot. Joining them, brunette and blond. Making what is broken, mended.

It's a symbol of her life. Of the twins once bound along with the Double *Tyet*. Of her own family. Even of the mythological names inscribed in stone. Betrayal. Brokenness. Healing. That's the story that formed the framework of her childhood games, the myth that has echoed in her life since the unwrapping.

She lays her bundle on the box and the amulet within. Releasing a shuddery breath, mucus thick in her throat, she scrapes the sand and grit to cover them up. The amulet is returned. Back, Clemmie hopes, where it belongs.

It is done.

"Do you say something now?" Celia asks, her first words since they left the boat. "A speech or a prayer?"

"I've prayed to God in my heart."

She waits for the question that she knows Celia wants to ask. Why? Why have they done this? What has it all been for? That's something that she can't tell them. This is something she's borne silently for years. It's better to keep it that way. If Mariam thinks this is just about restoration, that there's nothing more to this, then so be it.

"May I have a moment alone?" she asks, both in Arabic and English, gesturing to the mound.

Mariam steps back slightly, indicating for Celia to do the same. She's vaguely aware of the light receding as they move a few paces off. Not deserting her, just lending some privacy.

"You're back now," she whispers.

She considers how she has tried to do what the hieroglyphs said. Is it enough? She doesn't know, but she hopes it is. She doesn't know what else to do.

"Clemmie . . ."

"Shh." She frowns in Celia's direction.

She closes her eyes, and her mind flips page after page of her life before her, like a kineograph. Dozens of images flicker before her eyes, dancing through the shadows. Two girls, hand in hand. Faster and faster the images move, blurring, the girls blossoming into women. They no longer hold hands.

"Clemmie, really, I think there's something out there."

Her eyes snap open. She drops the trowel and rises, looking around. It's Rowland, isn't it? He's followed them. But in the spectral glow cast by Celia's lamp, there's no sign of a man. No leaning silhouette.

"You're imagining things. There's nothing . . ."

She stops. Celia's right. There is a soft dragging sound. Maybe it is Rowland after all, towing his bad leg. His footfall is easily discerned, that slow tread followed by a pause and then a shuffling step.

Yet there's no movement on the *dahabeeyah*'s outline. Maybe it's the river that makes that sound, caressing the shore. She tries to see Mariam's face, but she stands too far from the lamp for her features to be visible.

The shuffling is getting closer. Like a boat being dragged up the bank. Pebbles grinding. They're not alone.

"Can you hear it?" Celia asks.

Clemmie nods. Her thoughts turn to the thief at Rhoda, how he came upon them silently. Was he one of the bandits Khalil warned them about, or was there more to it? Did someone know about the precious cargo she carried?

"Mariam," she says. "What *is* it?"

Now that the noise is more distinct, their eyes follow the direction of it. And it can't be a person, unless they're crawling, because it comes from down on the ground. Gone are the thoughts that this could be Rowland—it would almost be a welcome relief to see him. It's something else.

"Do you see that?" Celia points to a shadow creeping toward them in slow motion. Like a snake, only bigger. Much, much bigger. Mariam mutters something unintelligible. A prayer, perhaps.

Clemmie has come to stand by Celia and she relieves her of the lamp. Holds it higher, her arm stretched out in front of her. The brightness makes the crawling motion stop. Rocks. So many rocks. Large, bulbous ones, and a long one that could also be a log. Or something else. Clemmie steps marginally closer, and the light picks out the detail on that terribly long shape. First, horny scales. The flicker of a third eyelid. Then something white. A necklace of teeth.

Celia screams before Clemmie or Mariam have a chance to say anything. Her screams awaken the shadows, and the night becomes alive.

Things seem to move in the darkness, things that either aren't there or shouldn't be there, and Clemmie's skin tightens against the touch of imagined fingers and insects and teeth. The creature is still some distance from them, but if it attacks, they'll have little chance against its speed. Should they run, or remain perfectly still? Their only weapons are the lamp in Clemmie's hands, and the knife in Mariam's—but while the latter was sharp enough to cut her hair, could it pierce a monster? Mariam calls out something, but in the fug of panic, Clemmie struggles to piece together the Arabic. Is she saying they should freeze, or make a dash for it?

There's the sound of men's voices. Clemmie hears Rowland shouting and Oswald calling for Celia with a panicked voice. The night is illuminated by lamps and candles as the *dahabeeyah* comes to life. She sees the forms of the men hurrying toward them, Youssef eclipsing the others with his large frame. The crocodile sees them too. It turns, not charging at the three women—but heading straight for the men.

"Look out," she hears herself calling. "Look out!"

In the lamplight, there's the gleam of a metal barrel, the spark of ignition, and a splitting crack.

Crocodile

"**W**HAT THE DICKENS WERE YOU DOING?**"

Oswald is at their side sooner than Rowland, despite hesitating to watch his prize crocodile scurry off. He drops his shotgun, then grabs Celia's shoulders and shakes her several times before pulling her close and holding her. Youssef chides Mariam, speaking so quickly it's hard to keep up with his Arabic, but the tone—anger, washed with relief—is easy to interpret.

"I'm sorry," Clemmie murmurs, first in English, then offering it in Arabic to Youssef. No one pays her any heed.

The oil sloshes around in the lamp, and Clemmie wishes she could pass it to hands that are steadier than her own. As Oswald embraces his sister, and Youssef cups Mariam's face in his hands, Clemmie feels something inside her contort, her heart throbbing rather than beating. She wouldn't mind the scolding if someone would care to hold her right now.

Rowland catches up with them, standing awkwardly as if some giant were lifting the island, and he were tilting with it.

"Exploring at this time of night?"

He's looking at Clemmie. Of course he is. This wouldn't be Celia's idea.

Blast the crocodile, Clemmie thinks. And blast Rowland Luscombe!

"I had to see the stele again," she lies.

"At night?"

"I brought a lamp."

"And Celia and the captain's daughter with you?"

"Mariam knows the island. And Celia was curious, weren't you?"

Celia nods, her face glistening in perfect streaks. She looks like such a child in her brother's arms, Clemmie feels instantly guilty. What if Celia hadn't screamed? What if Oswald hadn't fired his shot in time? This is her fault.

"I suppose you didn't know any better," Oswald says.

"I hardly think that's the case," Rowland declares. He rubs his hand over his face. She can hear the scratch of his evening stubble. Clemmie doesn't meet his eye, she's too ashamed to. She has put them all in peril. It seems that, no matter how hard she tries, danger follows her everywhere.

"Right," Oswald says, "back to the *dahabeeyah* now. Celia, no, don't give me that look."

"But," his sister wimpers, her lip wobbling, "aren't you men coming with us?"

Oswald releases a shaky breath, as if aware of what he could have lost, and brushes away a tear from his sister's cheek. His voice is gentle when he speaks. "I'll be along soon. I promise. But first, I want to see if I hit it." He glances at Rowland. "Coming, Luscombe?"

"Yes, in a minute. You carry on."

Clemmie watches Youssef lead Mariam toward the boat, Celia behind them, but before she can follow, Rowland stops her.

"Clementine, wait." He hobbles forward, peeling something from her shoulder. She turns to see what it is.

He's holding a lock of her hair. It must have fallen from her head during the cutting, and he twirls it now between his fingers and thumbs. Considering it.

"Not the best light for a haircut," he says skeptically. She clutches her shortened mane instinctively and snatches the hair from him. Hating how he makes her feel so exposed.

Wrapping an arm around Celia, Clemmie guides her back to *Hapi*. As Youssef steers Mariam toward the prow to ensure she's safely inside her kitchen this time, she turns and winks. A simple gesture, but it unites them. The three women. Clemmie bobs her head in appreciation.

Once it's just the two of them on the main deck, she squeezes Celia's hand, a show of affection she'd forgotten she was capable of giving. There was a time when she knew how to love. When she was loved in return.

"Thank you," she whispers.

"What for?"

"For not telling."

Celia turns her damp eyes at Clemmie in surprise. "Why, Clemmie, of course I didn't tell. You really are like a sister to me. Clemmie and Celia—C and C."

There's a sound onshore. Possibly just a rock tumbling down the bank, but it makes the two women stiffen. At least, Clemmie can blame it on that. But her mind is elsewhere, and while she'd hoped that tonight would lessen the weight from her mind, the drama on the island, the pressure to hear from home, and even Celia's little speech, have all unsettled her further. She'd rather not think of sisters right now.

"I would never tell," Celia insists. "You'd do the same for me."

Would she? Clemmie hopes Celia's right, but her friend—yes, *friend*, she realizes now that she does have friends, both Celia and Mariam— seems to trust her more than she trusts herself.

"What do you say? Sisters?"

Clemmie can't quite bring herself to respond. Putting the lamp down, she holds Celia close. Let that be her answer. Closing her eyes for a moment, she inhales herbal soap and the saltiness of sweat. Savoring the embrace. When was the last time someone held her? She stifles a sob and squeezes tighter. Even if she wishes for other arms tonight, she's still grateful.

In the distance, she hears Oswald and Rowland onshore.

"All this time and not a sight of a crocodile," says Oswald. "Then the women find one. What are the chances of that?"

Unwrapping

1890

WHEN CLEMENT'S FUNERAL HAS COME and gone, Clemmie, now familiar with bowls of steam and bottles of eucalyptus, looks out of her bedroom window. She spies two red kites painting a pair of spectacles in the sky.

"What has become of our family?" Rosetta asks.

They wrap their black-sleeved arms around each other, becoming a single form, and this is what it is to be siblings. To hold each other in silence and have no need for words because the embrace is a language of its own, and they are one the way they always have been. Clemmie would not change this moment for anything, not even to have her father back, because she has her sister and the funeral has delayed the wedding again, and while she knows it's wrong, she is glad.

Then they shift. Rosetta moving first.

"I might as well not be engaged," she spits bitterly. "My marriage is cursed."

"No!" Clemmie says. "Don't say that word."

Because if she continues to pretend the curse doesn't exist, perhaps she can outrun it.

Her sister's eyes spark at the reprimand, and her hand swipes across Clemmie's face, nails catching and drawing blood from her lip. They stare at each other in shock. In all their years, even if they had small quarrels, they have never struck each other before. It is evident in Rosetta's face that she isn't sure what happened, or where her rage came from.

"I . . ." She struggles to speak. "I'm sorry . . . I don't know . . ."

In Clemmie's mind comes a thought, chill and terrible. Something is happening to her sister. Something that isn't grief, or frustration over a delayed wedding, or the pain from her headaches.

The curse has claimed Bast, and it has taken her father. It isn't a thing of fiction, or lying dormant. It's here, all around them.

What if her sister is next?

Telegram

**THE EASTERN TELEGRAPH COMPANY, LIMITED.
CAIRO.**

It is done—How is E

Excavation

HOPE IS SAND, COLLECTING OVER time, millions of particles
building a dune. Fashioned into castles. Also, so easily blown into
a lessening drift, a cloud, then dispersed over a barren desert. Fickle
and vacillating, its truest merit is that, even when reduced to a meager
few grains, it's hard to get rid of entirely.

The crocodile troubles Clemmie. It shouldn't. She knows it was one
of those things that could so easily happen to any tourist along the Nile,
but she's come to regard any form of danger as a sign. Was the crocodile
part of the curse? Does that mean she's failed to remedy the Attridge
wrongs? Or is she reading too much into the reptile's appearance? Her
hope is wind-tossed and, just as sand erodes, it's wearing her down.

There's something remarkably peaceful about the way Korosko
looks, all palm trees and tumbling black rocks, braying donkeys and
excitable dogs. The skies are bluer than an English summer, the sands
so gold they're in danger of starting a rush that would rival the discovery at Sutter's Mill. A hint of silver touches the surface of the river before disappearing again. A Nile perch? A catfish? Perhaps, even, that
legendary fish that was said to have swallowed the fourteenth body part
of dismembered Osiris.

The journey to Korosko was a compromise. Clemmie needed to find a post office and the others wanted to press on into Nubia, so they finally came to an agreement not to backtrack to Assûan. They have made their way to the first Nubian village where she could send her telegram. A short but vital message, to which she impatiently awaits a reply. Rowland asked her who she was contacting, and when she kept her lips sealed, he looked vexed and his eyes darkened to lapis lazuli. Perhaps he suspects she's contacting a lover. What does it matter to him?

Now that they're moored, gently bobbing like a baby's cradle, Clemmie dares to hope that the burial, her peace offering, has given her the *ankh* that she came to seek. The key of life. She'll only know for certain once she gets a reply.

She feels strange, and it's more than just the shifting sands of hope within her. Now her closet is empty, with no sense of purpose and no rushing to Philae, she's almost bereft. It's a release, of course it is, but she's clung tightly to the amulet for so long, kept her precious cargo close, that being parted from it is like saying farewell to a loved one. Burying the amulet was a funeral, then. And she mourns it, even as she hopes for peace.

It was like that with her father, mourning his death but hoping that the curse had had its satisfaction and would leave them be. Remembering this, the ache inside her increases. Memories are darned holes, reappearing to haunt the one who wears them.

The others seem disconcerted by Clemmie's change in character. So far, she's only wanted to hurry, to press on, to ignore the precious sights and keep sailing, keep tracking, keep poling off sandbanks. Now she wants to wait. And she anticipates their questions. Maybe not from Celia, happy with her involvement in Clemmie's secret, but certainly from Rowland. Prying, piercing-eyed Rowland. He's bound to quiz her shift in priorities, to try to excavate the truth from her.

Yet he doesn't.

Oswald, restless after coming so close to obtaining his hunting trophy, suggests they do something other than sit in their rattan chairs and watch caravans of camels passing.

"We should ride them," he suggests, and as a transatlantic cable takes several hours to deliver a message and then send a response back, Clemmie agrees.

The camels are bad-tempered, matching Clemmie's impatience. In truth, riding a camel and admiring the sights is exactly the sort of thing she once would have yearned for. But how can she focus on anything as she wonders about her message?

Where is it now? She's not exactly sure how telegrams work, but she pictures the message as a collection of little sparks, flint on flint, and those sparks charging through a copper cable. A miniature, fiery train in a burnished tunnel. She imagines them building speed as they left Korosko and hurried back through Egypt, and then plunging down into the water at the port of Alexandria. Somehow, the blazing locomotive of her words isn't put out, but keeps its form as it charges through cables planted in waters, waters uncharted by anything other than giant fishes, monstrous sea creatures, and whatever else lives deep within the folds of the Mediterranean. Finally, through passages her mind cannot comprehend, the sparks will arrive in England to be delivered to a thatched cottage neighboring a grand redbrick house that she's always called home.

So where is it now?

As they pass through the hot sand, the barefooted locals lead them by thick, frayed ropes that seem hardly substantial should the camels bolt. The high vantage point allows Clemmie to see all around her. A pale apricot fox scampers by, hiding behind a rock as they pass. Overgrown ears peep above the boulder, distancing the creature from its English cousin.

"A fennec," Oswald shouts from his camel, his face flushed with pleasure. "Such a spot for game."

Something interrupts the natural lie of the ground up ahead. Celia is shrieking, convinced that her camel will dismember her with its ferocious teeth as it reaches back to investigate her bazaar-bought slippers, but Clemmie ignores her friend, keeping her focus, instead, on the strange mess in the distance. As they get closer, she can make out some moving figures through the shivering curtain of heat. It's once they're almost upon the scene that her suspicions are confirmed, and she tries to swallow the sand-thickened bile.

Here, lying on the ground, are two sarcophagi. Shovels, picks, and other tools are discarded about them. Near the large hole, worked by Egyptians, some overseers discuss their recent find—a fragment of broken pottery. The coffined bodies are almost forgotten in the excitement of this new piece; evidently the men are trying to determine its age, and they don't seem likely to reach an agreement. Their French accents and vernacular are thick with excitement and greed.

What has the sun witnessed these many centuries but a constant cycle of pillaging? Conquerors, all of them, whether in the name of war, or of peace. Thieves and plunderers, licensed or not, where disrespect has been shown to these antiquities, they are all guilty. The sun has seen it, it has hoped to rise on change, but with each new dynasty, era, and empire, there have always been looters. Arriving hungry. Leaving gluttonous and gouty on treasures.

The dig is a gaping wound, just one of many pocking the land, bleeding it dry. Still, she can't help herself, and her heart surges at the wonder of it. What else is beneath them? What might be found? How old are the relics? Her excitement is no different from the rug, a tourist piece, that Celia purchased at the bazaar to furnish their *dahabeeyah*. It comes cheap, the colors lush at first, but wearing thin after a short while, raveling, till at last there are holes and emptiness.

And what will happen to the artifacts? Where will they go now? The museum? Europe? To some collector who has managed to procure a license to fund this dig? Is it one of the Frenchmen before her? Is this even a legal site? Will the remains be kept intact or will they be unrolled for all to see? Perhaps, even, dissected? What is their fate?

A part of her wants to stop, dismount, and watch the work of excavation. To help. There's a staggering exhilaration in this spectacle, to uncover the hidden history, buried by the sands of time. But another part of her longs for gales to come, to stir the sands and bury all of this, so that no one will ever find them again. Excavate comes from the Latin *excavatus*. To hollow out. Hollow, from the German *hohl*, meaning empty. Emptiness, as in hunger, desolation, barrenness, words infused with pain. *Desertum, desertus.* Is it any wonder that the word for this sandy wilderness is the same as the one for forsaken? They are taking what they want from the desert, and when they are through, it will be left ravaged and devastated.

At least the Double Tyet is safe now, she thinks. As they continue to ride through the desert, leaving the arguing excavators behind, something cold settles beneath her breastbone. A strange feeling in this land of sun and dust. Has she done the right thing, leaving her amulet to the mercy of this place? Will the Nile swell and cover the island? Will the excavators set their sights on Philae next? Has she done enough?

Unwrapping

1890

T<small>HEY ARE WALKING BY THE</small> Chelmer. All three of them: Clemmie, Rosetta, and Horatio. It is like old times. Horatio visits whenever he can get away from the military college, helping with the estate,
but he says nothing about his nuptials. Their year of mourning is ending, their crape already turned to half mourning, which in turn will give
place to colors that feel unfamiliar and sinful. If their mother were
herself, then she would be urging Horatio to set a date—but she is not
herself, and so the wedding becomes something of a myth.

They pass the gardener, and Horatio stops him. "Tell the groom to
saddle my horse."

"Are you going so soon?" Rosetta asks.

He kisses her cheek. "Forgive me. I must."

Spurred on at the thought of his departure, Rosetta raises the topic
again. "If we were married, I think I could manage you having to leave
for your work just a little better."

"He was your father," he says. "How can you think of a wedding
when you are still in half mourning?"

"He would want me to be happy," Rosetta says.

Horatio's fingers lace with Rosetta's. A gesture that makes Clemmie
feel like an imposter. She falls back slightly, out of step with them.
Watching.

"You are still young and beautiful, Rose. The delay will not change that. I, for one, feel Clement's death keenly. It hasn't even been a year yet. We must show his memory some courtesy and wait."

He heads for the stables, leaving them to contemplate his words. Rosetta doesn't look guilty. As it always does, his demurral leaves her in a state.

"Has he changed his mind, do you think?"

"Of course not," Clemmie assures Rosetta as they walk. "Horatio is considerate, that is all. He is grieving like us, and he doesn't wish to do anything offensive when we're not quite out of mourning, and our mother is still so—"

She breaks off to watch a tenant's cat padding through the grass, a welcome distraction from having to find a word to describe their mother's grief. Flora is wrapped up in her misery, bound like a mummy, and no matter how the sisters try they cannot reach her.

It's hardly surprising that Clemmie finds it impossible to ease Flora's suffering, for she has never found her mother reachable. Not since she chose her path in life and opted for hieroglyphs over courtship. Always time for romance later, she has told herself. She isn't sure if she still believes that, not when her own sister's happiness, which seemed so certain, is now shredded to a gaunt shadow of what it was.

Her sister, though, she has always been close to their mother. The favorite. The one who enjoyed the stories of ancient Egypt, but put beaux and balls and dancing first. It's strange, really, for the two sisters are opposites, and yet in their incongruity, they fit.

Despite her bond with their mother, however, Rosetta has not managed to ease her suffering. Flora pushes them away, disappearing to wander, lost in her thoughts. Returning with the scratch of brambles on her skin, or mud on her skirts where she has slipped. She is thinner. Fragile.

Clemmie forces a brightness to her voice. "Look, do you see?"

She points out the cat and Rosetta actually smiles, saying that it reminds her of Bast.

"It's the wrong color," Clemmie says.

"True, but the eyes are the same."

"Do you remember when we'd play out here with Bast?"

A silly question. Of course Rosetta remembers.

Her sister draws herself up into a regal pose. "I am Isis."

Clemmie laughs. Then throws herself into the old role. Just as they used to play it. She falls to her knees and clutches her sister's feet, just peeping from the gray hem.

"Will you not forgive me, sister?"

She looks up, and for a moment, Rosetta seems confused. Then it passes. Perhaps she has forgotten the next line. Clemmie gets back on her feet, brushing mud and grass from her skirt. Is there any better medicine for an aching heart than the balm of nostalgia? And these are the happiest of memories.

"You always know how to make me feel better," Rosetta says, squeezing Clemmie's hand.

They weave their arms together, joined at the elbow, and turn for a leisurely stroll back toward the big house. It watches them with a familiar face, age spots of lichen freckling the red, but only now does Clemmie realize how much the windows resemble wide eyes, the front door a black gape.

Even before she has crossed the threshold, Clemmie knows something is wrong. Their maid is crouched on the hall floor. She is wailing. Imploring an indistinct shape at the foot of the stairs to move, to stir.

The sisters approach. Clutching each other tighter.

When Clemmie was nine or ten, her mother once tried to tempt her with a porcelain doll, to entice her away from the study and its antiquities. Bast ran under Flora's feet, and she lost her balance. The doll slipped from her hands and its beautifully painted face smashed. Such a delicate thing, so easily broken.

Clemmie remembers that porcelain doll now—that is what the shape on the floor reminds her of. A remarkable representation of the human form, but shattered.

Rosetta snatches her arm free, wringing her hands fretfully. Clemmie steps closer. It isn't a doll. The broken figure with its porcelain pallor is Flora. Lying frightfully still, twisted into a grotesque shape.

Clemmie bids the maid to call for a doctor, quickly, but the maid is shaking her head and whimpering and saying she is so sorry, so very, very sorry, and Clemmie finally comprehends her meaning.

It is too late for a doctor.

Rosetta charges forward, throwing herself across her mother and howling. It is an animal sound, deep and guttural and something that makes Clemmie want to recoil. She longs to run, from all of it. Instead, she tries unsuccessfully to prize her sister from their mother's corpse. Each of Rosetta's shrieks reverberates through her very being.

"She fell," Clemmie murmurs, looking up the long staircase to the gallery above, where her father's portrait hangs, watching her. Was that the last thing her mother saw? Could she bear his face no longer? Was it a case of tripping, or had her grief become too much to bear? Clemmie hates herself for even suspecting such a thing, but now the thought is in her mind, she cannot free herself of it. Her hands are cold and she is shivering. She feels empty and dazed and needs to cry, but can't.

Flora is dead. She's overwhelmed by a throbbing sensation throughout her being. Her heart? The pounding of something far, far worse?

Let what is sacred be brought to ruin.

She thought it referred to Bast. Perhaps, even, to the breaking of her parents' marriage through Clement's death, or the delay of her sister's wedding. But life is sacred, isn't it? And now Flora's has been ruined, stopped abruptly, shattered.

First Bast. Then their father. Now their mother.

With just the Attridge sisters left, Clemmie makes herself a promise as she stares at the wide, frozen eyes of her mother, at the image of her sister strewn across. She will stop this before there is another victim. Clemmie will fight for her sister and for herself.

The curse has met its match.

Egyptology

*H*API WELCOMES THEM BACK from their camel ride by nodding on the river's surface, so that Clemmie feels inclined to bob her head in return. Rowland holds her back on the bank of the Nile, and she casts him a questioning look that he doesn't hurry to answer. Again, her thoughts turn to copper cables, and she impatiently hazards a guess at the location of her telegram. Halfway to England? Perhaps further by now?

He still doesn't speak, and the hairs on the back of her neck arise, expectant for a coming fight. *Why is it you want to wait here? What made you leave Philae so quickly? I still don't believe you wanted to read the stele in the dark.*

"Clementine."

He's awkward, and she's never seen him quite like this before. Unsure of himself, embarrassed. He's usually cool, collected, seemingly in control and making her flustered and tetchy. She asks why he's detained her, but he just rubs his leg in a way that makes her wonder if it's painful and avoids her eye.

If he's not going to speak, then she'll let their surroundings talk to her, and she turns slowly to absorb them. A moment she'll remember forever. It seems unlikely that she'll ever get tired of the horizon. That orangey-buff lie of the land, dotted with palm trees here and there, leading down to verdant banks feeding off the black soil and river. A nearby field of young barley shimmers in the stiff breeze, and above the green dance titmice and sparrows—birds that remind her of home. Strange, that two diverse continents should claim the same species of creatures. Home reminds her of the telegram; the birds stir recollections of the larger variety she fears so greatly. Even with no predacious birds above her, Clemmie's stomach is a snake coiling in its nest.

He breaks the silence at last, asking her what she's thinking. She nods at the sky, indicating the sun.

"The ancient Egyptians would say that Ra is sailing in his Day Barque. They called it *Mandjet*."

"That's what I love about you," he says.

She stiffens slightly, not sure why. Preparing for one of his rounds of questions. Waiting for him to validate such a statement.

"You know. Your knowledge of everything. How accomplished you are in this sphere."

Clemmie answers with her shoulders, tossing his comment to the wind. She's never known anything different. Can't even comprehend life without hieroglyphs and myths. As a child, she would visit her father's study, even in the night when she should have been asleep, and stare at what was kept there.

Preserved. The past in the present. It would leave her speechless and gaping. Sometimes, her eyes would sting with tears that she couldn't explain, and she'd rub them away, confused at the intense emotions stirring deep inside. How could anything have that much sway over her? The artifacts connected her to people she could never meet, a vast distance of time narrowed by what they'd left behind. She loved to imagine their stories, their names, the families they'd provided for by crafting these vases of faience, that striking glazed material, often blue in color, that the Egyptians called *tjehenet*. Scintillating, bright, dazzling, brilliant. That's what their word for faience meant, just as they'd describe the moon or the stars.

Something touches her hand, bringing her back to the present, and she jumps. Looking down, Rowland is holding her wrist. Not tightly. A bangle of fingers. Her heart quickens as he tugs gently, and they sit in the sand together. She feels the grains sifting into her shoes, sticking to sweat on her skin where it finds an entryway.

He doesn't let go at first, looking at her hand as if he's only just noticed her gloveless *faux pas*. She studies it along with him, the freckle on the knuckle below the index finger, the blue veins a map of tunnels, and that tiny scar, white and almost unnoticeable, where Clemmie once cut herself on a piece of broken Egyptian pottery.

Her hand grows moisture like a second skin and she slides it free.

"I need to talk to you."

She waits for him to say more, starting to fret as she notes the seriousness on his face, in his voice.

"Egypt, all of this, it means more to me than I've told you," he says.

Rowland gestures out to the Nile and she follows where he points. Where the sun is reflected and journeys begin. She thinks of when they first met, when he said he was an explorer of sorts.

"Egypt has so much to offer the world," Rowland says. "I want to help share it."

"A museum?"

"In a way, I suppose, but more of a traveling exhibition. I could journey around America and Europe showing off the wonders of this place. Artifacts, hieroglyph translations . . ."

Her heart increases with the speed of his words. He's speaking a language she understands, singing a song that woos her.

"Why are you telling me this?" she asks.

"Just picture how it could be. The antiquities safe from thieves, illegal diggers, and dealers."

They've seen evidence of shady dealers onshore hinting at specimens that can be purchased for private collections. Mariam points them out with an accusatory finger as she and Youssef add to their report. Clemmie considers the excavation they witnessed today, the mummies tossed to one side. Surely they never imagined being dug up and exhibited far from their chosen graves. If it had been foretold to them, would they have laughed and thought the teller mad? If the body snatchers of decades ago are now frowned upon in Britain, why not the body snatchers of today in Egypt and Nubia? Time does not lessen the fact that what remains was once alive. In the fever of Egyptomania, everyone seems to forget that important truth.

She keeps her hands busy, watching the sand trickle through her fingers.

"Imagine a traveling museum," Rowland says. "Just picture the possibilities. It could be used to educate the world on the brilliance of Egypt's culture. Many people see Egyptian relics as an opportunity for sensation and entertainment, but I want to do something new, to enlighten the world on a real history, backed by legitimate study."

Anything to keep some artifacts safe is surely preferable to having them stolen and sold on by dealers.

"If you want to protect antiquities, then I admire that," she says.

"I'm glad you've said that, because I want you to be my partner."

She stops sifting sand. Partner? Rowland wants her, Clemmie Attridge, to be his partner? Blinking several times, she waits for the scene to pass. To wake up and find that she's been dreaming. It doesn't go away. This is really happening. She's sitting with Rowland Luscombe on the banks of the Nile with the offer of a partnership between them.

He's telling her that she could help him, come on his tour. That he has an eye for business and opportunity, but she's the one with a skill for the subject. How they'd be the perfect match.

She can picture it. Everything she's prepared for in life, with her and Rowland at the helm. Translating glyphs, explaining the history, even acting as an interpreter in countries where Rowland doesn't know the tongue. It could work. She never was her father's partner, not really. A Clement Junior in skirts—he could never truly see beyond that, torn between their shared passion and the norms of society. Shutting her out of his ledgers and business plans. But Rowland is looking at her, and he isn't put off by the shoulder-length hair fraying from the stubby knot at her neck, by her petticoats. His invitation is a dream realized and now within her reach. If her heart were Nephthys, then this is the moment when it would transform from flesh to bird, testing the air's possibilities.

She lands, as all winged things do. Maybe that's all this is. A dream.

"I can't be your partner."

He wasn't expecting that answer, she can tell from the way his face falls and his shoulders with it.

"Why not? I thought you'd jump at the offer. Don't you want it?"

Doesn't she? Clemmie's been burned. No matter how much she loves Egyptology, that passion is tinged with fear these days.

"You wouldn't do mummy unwrappings?"

"Not if you didn't want to."

"It would be to protect the antiquities?"

"Of course."

"Why America and Europe?"

"You have a better idea?"

She thinks of what she came here to do. Returning the Double *Tyet* to where it belongs.

"Why not here in Egypt? Beyond Gîzeh's museum, there will always be tourists who need educating, and that way the artifacts are kept in their country of origin."

He approves of the idea. She can tell from the way his smile expands, mirroring the inundation of the Nile. Her and Rowland, in business together. She could laugh, so delighted is she that he'd want that, and also amazed that she might want it too.

Bickmore looms into her mind, and Clemmie throws a fistful of sand at the water.

"I just can't."

"Why?" He still doesn't believe her. "I'd do it however and wherever you wanted."

It's flattering that he so badly wants to work with her.

"It isn't the location."

"What is it, then? What can I do to persuade you?"

His face is hopeful, perspiration standing in relief on his brow. She never thought something like this would mean so much to him. Is this why he's had so many questions for her on their journey? Was he, in effect, interviewing her?

"I have to go home," she says gently. "I would dearly love to stay in Egypt—I'd remain for the rest of my life if I could—but I'm not free to do whatever I choose."

He lends his ear, crestfallen. She feels guilty for disappointing him, but, in truth, she is just as disappointed. At herself, for saying no. Also, because she feels as though there's something left unsaid, but she doesn't know what it is. She can't help but suspect that Rowland's holding something back from her.

Frustration seeps from his pores, his disappointment souring his voice.

"What has got its hold over you? What has it got to do with Philae?"

He's implying that she's being controlled, and she's ready to spit out a retort when she realizes that he's right. Her life isn't entirely her own. Some might call it loyalty. She has other names for it. Responsibility. Sacrifice. *Fides* might be translated to faith and trust, but it also relates to fidelity that shows devotion, reliance that proves unity, allegiance that speaks of ties. Her allegiance is already sworn.

"What do you know about Nephthys?"

He frowns at what he thinks is a change of subject. Her and Nephthys's stories, they're bound together, and she longs to show him that. When she insists, he humors her, and his recital is impressive. She could change into a kite. Seen as the helper. Sister to Isis. Often forgotten, but the one who offers protection to those she loves.

"That's right," she says. "See, you don't need me for your tour after all."

"Everyone needs a helper."

Clemmie tries to look away, but Rowland's holding her captive with his gaze. Why is he looking at her like that? Does he realize what she's on the cusp of telling him? Can she really bring herself to spill her story? She's aching to tell someone. Something within her longing to break free of the cerement she's bound herself with.

"Well, I'm my family's helper."

He stands up, rubbing his knee.

"I thought your father had died. You never speak of your mother."

Clemmie picks at the hem of her skirt, the stitches coming undone the way she is. Secrecy is tiresome. She felt too ashamed to admit everything to Mariam with her commitment to the land, knowing the part she's played in its undoing. As for Celia, she means well, but other than the unavoidable discovery of the amulet, she'd rather not let her history feed Celia's appetite for scandal and gossip. Can it hurt to tell Rowland? Would he understand?

He's saying something about her love of Egyptology, how he can't grasp her refusing the chance he's offering her. Maybe the only way she can explain is by laying everything bare. Sitting in silence, she wonders if Rowland would make a fair partner. She hasn't trusted him for most of their travels. Could they work well together? Would he take all the credit in the way that her father used to?

Attridge and Son is one thing, her father would say. *But men don't go around proclaiming that their partner is a woman. It just isn't done.*

I'm like a son to you, though, she'd argue. *And Attridge and Daughter sounds just as good, doesn't it?*

It didn't matter how hard she'd tried to be that son. She was still only Clementine.

"When I was injured, the doctors said I'd never walk again," Rowland says. "At first, I didn't even want to. I thought it would be better if I was dead. But after a while, I found that I did want to live after all. That I wanted to walk again. That maybe I was still alive for a reason. To walk, and live my life, succeed, and do something with myself."

She's surprised to hear him divulge this, and tries to picture Rowland lying in a hospital bed, the wounded soldier home from the wars. The fight gone out of him, used up on the bodies of rebel Egyptians. The man who stands before her, for all his lopsidedness, doesn't seem to connect to such a picture.

"I did learn to walk again, step-by-step. Sweating, swearing, defying the doctors. People don't always have to be what others expect. You can make of your life what you want if you work hard."

That's why he's told her this. To encourage her to change her mind and choose the partnership over being the woman society would have her be. He's mistaken if he thinks that's what holds her back. She's never cared what people think.

Standing up, she brushes away his offer along with the dust.

"I can't. I just can't."

Her rejection places them on opposing banks, and she senses an expanse, like the Nile, broadening between them, where mere seconds ago it had seemed that they could almost touch.

He speaks with confidence, as if he can see into her heart and count what's buried there, packaged tightly and tied with string.

"I see I was a fool to think we'd work well together. Partners have to be honest with each other. You. Me. We're no different, keeping our secrets. Just like the mighty Sphinx."

She thinks of the human-headed cat that's watched the centuries pass and guards what it's seen behind limestone lips and eyes. Fired by his words, by a need to see the river bridged, she bares her limestone heart before she can regret it.

"The truth is, I can't accept because someone at home is waiting for me. Someone whom I love."

His jaw tightens. He squares his shoulders, the way a crumbling column bears the weight of an architrave.

"I'm saying no because of Rosetta."

Rosetta. Like the stone in the British Museum, like the city at the Nile's mouth, like the tender bloom of summer. The name is out, and the wind picks up on it, reeling at the sound of her name. His face is a question mark. She's begun, so she might as well continue.

"Rosetta is my sister."

Mania

THERE'S A MADNESS IN HER family. People call it Egyptomania. Clemmie calls it a curse. Her father passed his obsession on to her, but he didn't love the artifacts. He can't have loved them, because loving is caring, and he didn't look after them and he didn't teach her to love them either. If he had, things might be different. She wouldn't be here now, with death lurking in the shadows, trying to make amends for his mistakes.

When they were children, Rosetta and Clemmie would play outside whenever the weather was pleasant, and sometimes when it was not. They liked to play by the River Chelmer, a platinum snake cutting through their estate, which to them was a delta-less Nile.

They never could say when the game of Myths started, but there must have been a first time, as there is to all things.

I am Isis, Rosetta would say.

You're always Isis, Etta, said Clemmie. She had always called her older sister Etta. That, or Big E. She was Clemmie or Little C. It was nothing to do with height, only the hierarchy of their ages.

Well, Isis is the elder, and I'm four and a half years older than you.

Etta never forgot that half a year. It made all the difference.

Clemmie wouldn't argue. After all, Etta was older and prettier. A sociable girl who knew what to say to people. Clemmie wasn't like that.

There was one thing that united the two of them—even if there were four and a half years spanning the gap, and Etta loved parties and Clemmie preferred books, and Etta was her mother's pet and Clemmie her father's—and it was that they were sisters. Clemmie didn't want friends because she had Etta, and Clemmie was Etta's best friend. Invisibly, they were conjoined. Their bond was so great that they even moved at the same time, or thought the same thoughts, or spoke simultaneously. If they hadn't looked so different—her with her brown locks, and Etta with her golden ones—they could have been mistaken as twins. They often said they shared a brain.

Another person Clemmie loved dearly was Nurse Pugh. Childhood friend, playmate, nanny, and surrogate mother, she was always included in the game. As there were only three of them, and Etta was Isis and Clemmie was Nephthys, that left Nurse Pugh to be all the characters in between. At times she was Osiris and would lie flat out on a picnic blanket so the girls could pretend to sew her back together. Sometimes she was Anubis, and they borrowed the kitchen scales so she could weigh the heart against the feather of Maat (said heart was a piece of offal also borrowed from the kitchen, which Clemmie said made their game more realistic and led to Etta vomiting when she smelled the rawness). Other times Nurse Pugh was forced to juggle multiple roles at once, and would carry a token to differentiate her characters: a quill for Thoth, a clod of earth for Seb, a piece of wire fashioned into a star for Nut.

The only other accessory to the game was Bast, their cat, who had beautiful slate-blue fur. Because the cat-headed goddess had little to do with the story of Isis, Nephthys, and Osiris, the feline was usually forced to be an accessory, a headdress, or a mummy, and once ate the stand-in heart right off the scales, which they all agreed meant that Bast had decided for herself that she would play Ammit, the crocodile-headed goddess who devoured the hearts of the impure.

Life was perfect growing up, and the sisters made themselves a promise. One day they'd exchange their pretend Nile for the real Nile, and they'd travel to Egypt together.

The night of the unwrapping, everything changed. As she tells Rowland about the mummy, about what was hidden beneath the layers, and how she tried to stop her father, she's surprised not to see more emotion cross his face. Mortification. Shock. Horror. She expects all of these, but his expression is passive. Just listening.

She relives the event as she tells it. The room wearing the cloak of evening. The candles making the wall of jars blaze, their contents dancing in liquid fire. Cloves and myrrh, lavender and book dust, expensive cologne and musty cerement. Silence, but for a gasp. The cold weight of the amulet. The feel of their own future in a bloodred stone.

The smirk of a blade, the menace of the hieroglyphs. A throne. A house with a basket. Limbs everywhere. Mummy dust on the table, on the floor, on a lady's gloved finger and a gentleman's shoe. The redcoat offering a price, a value rising, but nothing, nothing could be enough for this . . . this what? This once preserved, now butchered, both plural and singular, previously living *thing*. A lifeless thing.

And then there was the amulet, just as unique and desirable as the mummy. She had etched its message in her mind by this point. Soon it would be a chain around her heart, a knife in her belly, a scourge on her back.

The protection of Isis and Nephthys be upon the sisters. If any disturb these sisters, let the wrath of Osiris's sisters be upon his household's sisters and the pain of Osiris upon his own body. May the knots of Isis and Nephthys know rest where Osiris rises to meet Isis, or let what is sacred be brought to ruin.

The first part came true that very night, even as she refused to believe that curses exist. Bast, their precious pet cat, and an animal so sacred to the Egyptians, died. Progressively throughout the year, her father began to complain of his rheumatism increasing. He kept to his study for longer, went riding less.

1888. A whole year after the unwrapping. Her father was now stooping, his hands becoming claws, his back resembling a dromedary's. But rheumatism can do that to a person. She caught a cold, a chill that settled on her chest, as they sometimes do. She never could shake the wheeze. Her sister had headaches, sudden fits of temper, memory lapses, a way of trailing off into their childhood game, muttering about

Osiris and Nephthys. All no doubt due to the stress of waiting for a fiancé serving overseas and her postponed wedding.

1889. The year of the influenza. It stole across borders, a stowaway on ships, a tourist come to see London Town, to take in the sights, to enter the beds of whores, courting ladies and gents alike, wrapping its arms around the friendless, the parentless, the homeless and hungry. It was a trespasser, a tramp, a sojourner with nowhere to stay, and people opened their doors in innocence, they shared their homes and their lives. They paid for it.

It wasn't satisfied with London. Catching a train to Chelmsford, a carriage to Bickmore, squeezing through the wrought iron gates and creeping up the drive. No one saw it or the bags it carried, intent on staying awhile.

Sickrooms, sweating, just turning in bed an effort requiring the stamina of Shu holding up the sky. The body a shipwreck, flesh sinking, bones the flotsam surfacing. The tide ebbing, ebbing away. She and her father, on the brink of death, and she knew then. She knew, even as she tried to persuade herself that it was influenza and nothing more. The threat had bided its time, it had haunted her mind to torment her, but now it had come with full fury. Rosetta's wedding was postponed again. *Until the sickness passes,* they said.

1890. Blackest black. Crape and bombazine. Jay's, the place that *makes mourning a specialty,* supplied everything. The handkerchiefs: black. The petticoats: black. The jewelry: jet, woven with hair, the image of an Egyptian sarcophagus, an inscription. *Embalmed in our hearts.* And how can you walk down the aisle in black? Rosetta wept for her father, but also for the marriage she feared would never take place. Her mother withdrew from the world. They would find her wandering about, muttering, crying, barely eating, tumbling over herself in her stupor. *Talk to us,* they'd say. *Come and have some broth. Here, try some lavender water on your temples. Lie down and rest.*

She has often pictured how it happened. One day, near the end of the year of mourning, the sisters returned from a walk to find their mother on the floor. Fallen down the stairs. She imagines it like this: her mother walking in a daze, cheeks sticky from tears left to dry, thinking that she will go for a walk. Yes, that is what she thought. She passed through the gallery and at the stair she saw the portrait of her deceased husband all draped with black, and it brought everything rushing back. She took a step backward, not a thought for the stairs until she knew that she was falling and she rolled, smacked, bumped, finally hitting the bottom with a crack. Her neck was broken. Did it happen partway down, or did she feel each step slam into her bony frame until she reached the tiled floor? Was it quick, or did the life peter out of her as she waited to be found?

When they did find her, her face was so pale it made the widow's mourning attire look blacker than normal. So black that Jay's might have wanted to capture the image, to prove that the *Illustrated London News* hadn't lied, and they really did stock materials *excelled by no other house in London or Paris.*

1891. Was it over? Hardly. Rosetta's headaches worsened as they entered another year of mourning, this time for their dead mother. Yet another year of waiting for the wedding. Clemmie's breathing tightened. She wrote to their old childhood nurse, asking if she could visit to discuss her sister. She was worried, and clearly Nurse Pugh was too once she arrived, for she unpacked her bags and insisted on staying to watch her former charge. The reason for their concern was this: Etta kept calling Clemmie Nephthys, and while she'd thought that her sister was reminiscing and referring to their childhood game, it had become a habit. Etta started using the names of mythical figures for other people too. Osiris, Set, Nut, Seb. And Isis. Always Isis.

I am Isis, said Rosetta.

Clemmie's mouth is dryer from her bitter history than from the sun and sand. She aches for water, or the sweetness of Mariam's lemonade, the tang of coffee. There's that strange stinging in the top of her nose that comes from needing to cry but holding back the tears. Perspiration breeds in her cleavage. Her lips crack and the taste of her own blood is oddly saccharine. Her veins have flowed with vinegar for years, but the release of her story is freeing.

"You see," she says, "we can't set sail until I know that Etta is well again. And I can't work with you because my sister comes first. Before Egyptology. Even before myself."

He looks confused, and she realizes that she hasn't told him one final thing. The missing puzzle piece. The reason she's here.

"I brought the amulet back to Egypt. I buried it by the Temple of Isis to make things right."

Something in his face clicks, the story fitting together. Rushing first to Denderah, then to Philae. A midnight adventure by the light of a lamp. The cutting of hair. The crocodile.

"I hope I've done enough."

There's a madness in her family. People call it Egyptomania. Clemmie calls it a curse. That's why Clemmie had to come here. Because Etta's forgetting herself more and more, going months on end when she believes she's Isis, remembering Clemmie and Nurse Pugh rarely, more often than not mistaking them for Nephthys and Nut. Becoming violent in her rages as she screams for an Osiris who will never come to her.

If any disturb these sisters, let the wrath of Osiris's sisters be upon his household's sisters.

Rosetta bears the mark of Isis on her mind, and Clemmie the stain of Nephthys on her lungs. Perhaps it was inevitable, after their childhood games, playing those roles. Rosetta, ever the sociable one, and Clemmie always keeping to herself and her studies, unseen. One noticed and loved, the other invisible.

Egyptomania.

Madness.

What's the difference?

Curses

N OW THAT SHE'S UNWRAPPED HER history, unwinding the truth
so that it's in a heap before them, her story naked in all its macabre honesty, she waits for him to tell her that all will be well. This is the
moment when he'll praise her fortitude, her grit in coming here after
suffering so much. He'll squeeze her hand in a friendly manner—for
haven't they reached that stage now, if he felt able to call her a business
partner and she's bridged the river between them by confessing her
secrets?—and say that they'll wait for the telegram together, that he
understands why they can't work together now, that Rosetta is probably
already restored to her. No longer believing herself to be Isis, but Etta,
once again.

Rowland doesn't move, doesn't smile, or even offer a gesture of sym-
pathy. She waits for him to speak, and he does so at last. His voice
precise and measured, like a surgeon making a cut.

"Curses don't exist."

Has he really heard her painful truth, just to dispute it? Just to say
that her sister's mad and she must accept it. That her asthma is unfortunate, but it was just the result of many chills and a bad case of influenza. That the same goes for her father's afflictions and death, her
mother's fall. That Bast was old and going to die anyway. All of them
devastating but natural calamities.

"All of mankind is cursed," he says. "But not by some amulet meant to protect embalmed twins."

"You weren't there."

"No." He speaks slowly. Thinking. "No, I wasn't. Yet you must see how mad it is to think that stripping a mummy has made a myth a reality in your life."

He sees it, the madness in her family, but that's all he thinks her theory is. Madness and mania. He's calling her insane.

She's been tracking her way through her narrative, but now her words become water at the cataract.

"All I know is what I read. The hieroglyphs spelled out a warning, and then my sister changed. That can't be a coincidence."

He still doesn't understand, she can see it in his eyes, so she breaks it down for him one more time.

"Mine is the plague of Nephthys, who was the guardian of the canopic jar that held the lungs. The accumulation of chills and influenza left me with asthma. My parents suffered the blight of Osiris; my father's body was racked with pain, my mother's body literally broken. Regarding my sister, they say that Isis was at her wits' end, mad with grief, when she lamented Osiris's death. And Isis's own sister betrayed her. Rosetta's malison is twofold, and I am party to it."

His eyes ask her: *How?*

That is one truth too many. The past has been bled from her, and she feels robbed like the ground she stands on. There may be more to tell, but if he doesn't have the courtesy to believe her, then he doesn't deserve to know.

For one brilliant moment, she thought she could trust Rowland Luscombe, and now she feels violated. She picks up her skirts and runs on board, away from him. Her family's secrets are out for him to taunt her, for the land to feed on, and the wind to share. What a fool she was to think he'd understand.

The truth is, no one's ever truly understood her. No one, except for Etta.

It was somewhere between a lifetime ago and yesterday when Clemmie knelt beside Bast's sleeping figure and beckoned Etta over. The fire was

crackling in the hearth, lending the only light, turning the nursery into one of shadows. Believing the girls to be asleep, Nurse Pugh had slipped downstairs in order to fetch herself a cup of chocolate, and Clemmie saw it as the perfect opportunity to stretch the playtime hours.

"What is it?" Etta asked.

"It's Osiris," Clemmie replied. "We've put his body back together, but now what?"

Etta grinned, catching on to the game at once. "We're his sisters. We can bring him back to life."

"How?"

It was tempting to run fingers through the cat's fur, but then Bast would stir and the game would be over. If they listened closely, they would have been able to hear the soft growl that cats make, which isn't a purr but isn't fully a snore either. They shut their ears to it, though, and in their minds Bast became Osiris, exchanging slate-blue fur for green skin, and whiskers for a plaited beard.

"Let's hold hands," Etta suggested.

They did so. Clemmie's left one entwined with Etta's right.

"We should sing songs to our brother," Clemmie said, remembering something her father had told her once. Lamentations, he'd called them.

Inventing their own tunes, they started to sing, coming up with the same lines as if rehearsed—but then their minds always worked that way. They sang notes that were far from harmonies, notes that might have kept the dead where they were rather than convinced them to return.

"What are you two doing out of your beds?"

They sprang around, rubbing their hands nervously on their nightdresses, hopping from one foot to the other. Nurse Pugh held her cup of chocolate in one hand, her other forming a fist on her hip, and it was hard to tell if she was really angry or just feigning it.

"Into your beds this minute, and go to sleep before I get cross."

They didn't need to be told twice. They even went to their separate beds rather than diving into the same one, just to be extra good. But when Clemmie had counted to sixty—a full minute, she told herself, would be enough to satisfy Nurse Pugh that she was indeed going to sleep—she allowed herself to peep toward the fireplace.

Bast had lifted her head and was looking around.

"It worked," Clemmie whispered to herself. And she fell asleep smiling.

Ɣ

It comes at last. A miracle, really, how progress has made it possible for a message to pass such a distance so quickly. In a flurry of trepidation, hope mixing with dread, Clemmie tears the telegram open. Nearly ripping the whole thing in half in her haste.

She reads the words so quickly that she cannot comprehend them. Standing in her cabin, with Sphinx jealous over the attention given to a piece of paper and releasing mews that Clemmie's deaf to, she tries to read the words again. A sob comes from deep inside her, so deep she didn't know such a place existed. It builds, spurting from her so violently that she's thrown to her knees. The paper tumbles, and Sphinx scampers after it across the floor.

It doesn't matter. Clemmie has read the words. She knows what's there, and as she cups her hands over her mouth to muffle her cries, she repeats the telegram in her head.

E has been better—Herself again

Sand

I F ETTA IS RESTORED TO herself, then Clemmie can go home. She can hardly believe it, and her heart sings a song of triumph. She has thwarted the curse. She has mended what was broken. She has made things right.

Youssef and his crew prepare to sail back downriver, but while Clemmie's spirits have lifted, her friends are unhappy to leave. She's blissfully unaware of this, or at least, she ignores Celia's pouts, Oswald's mutters about not getting his hunting trophy, Rowland's sudden moodiness. Mariam won't meet her eye when she passes the kitchen, and she senses an air of reproach that she doesn't understand.

If her compatriots want to go upriver to Abou Simbel, they can find another boat—but she made it clear she wasn't going that far; it was her idea to commandeer this vessel, they invited themselves along, and there's nothing that can stop her from going home now.

They're on the deck when it happens. Celia reaches to select a treat from Rowland's paper bag of sweets. He's formed an addiction for the Lumps of Delight and purchases them at every bazaar, coming back with his pockets full, white dust crusting his mouth. Rather than picking up a pink or yellow square, however, Celia slowly retracts her hand, extending a finger.

They look where she's pointing. On the horizon there's a strange cloud, not unlike the smog of London streets. It looks misplaced here, with the openness of the desert before them. Smoky. For a moment, Clemmie wonders if there's a fire nearby and pictures a whole village erased, remnants of buildings forming a new generation of ruins.

The palm trees start to bob, their heads wagging savagely. Clemmie's stomach fills with unease, and something in her head tells her that she should be hurrying for the saloon. For shelter. Yet she can't move. Small waves form in the river, making the *dahabeeyah* rock.

Out of the corner of her eye, Clemmie sees Oswald pick up his shot-gun, but how can he fight a cloud with lead? The crew start to yell. Odd, panicked shouts that Clemmie doesn't understand. *Khamaseen.* She doesn't know that word. What is a *khamaseen*?

The dust hits with realization. Sand filling their nostrils, ears, mouths. Scratching and stinging their eyes and faces.

"It's a sandstorm," Oswald shouts the obvious.

Someone pushes Clemmie forward; she thinks it might be Rowland. They battle with the strong winds that have sprung up from nowhere, the air full of swirling grit. Blinded by it, they stagger to and fro, but somehow make it into the saloon, where the men bolt the door.

It makes a difference, but still the pressure of the wind finds gaps, puffing the yellow mist into the room, adding to the book dust and making them all splutter. In the haze, the replica painting of *Cleopatra* really does resemble the original masterpiece. Their hair is full of sand, like the powdered wigs of the last century.

They're all choking so badly that it's easy for them to initially miss that Clemmie's cough is different. That she's stuck somewhere between the need to inhale and the force of coughing; a strange space between the two that leaves her gasping.

"She can't breathe," Rowland says, thrusting his hands in her pocket, not caring for propriety. He pulls the bottle out, smothering it on his own handkerchief and holding it over her nose.

"It's no good," says Celia. "She can't inhale it."

"Oswald, help me carry her."

Clemmie feels hands on her back and her legs as the men lift her between them and convey her to her cabin. Celia hastens after them.

"Get her corset off her," Rowland says.

Celia appears momentarily appalled, but does as she's told, fumbling for the buttons at Clemmie's back. Through the mist of dust, Rowland looks torn between helping and stepping aside, a twitch of impatience on his face as he watches Celia struggling with the mother-of-pearl buttons. Clemmie is numb, modesty far from her mind as she focuses her efforts on one thing.

Inhale.

Don't cough.

Inhale.

The blouse is off and Rowland gives orders, moving forward to remove the Swiss belt from her waist and untie the strings at her back, telling Oswald to get a bowl of boiling water and Celia to light a lamp.

The release of the corset coming off is immense. Clemmie feels her body roll forward, and Rowland supports her, lifting her arms the way he did at the Pyramid. Instructing Celia to hold the handkerchief in front of Clemmie's face.

It's easing slightly, small breaths sliding their way in. She's not sure how long she sits there, Rowland holding her arms above her head, Celia adding more oil to the cotton square while juggling a lamp. Oswald reappears with a wide-eyed Mariam carrying a bowl of just-boiled water, dust sitting on its surface and covering their skin and clothes entirely. He must have ventured from the cabins to get it—the kitchen being situated on the other end of the deck—and Clemmie wishes she could thank them both. Words are impossible.

She's in her chemise and skirt, her modesty scandalously jeopardized. Now that the water is delivered and set before her on the bed, Oswald steps back into the doorway, looking unsure whether he should remain. He keeps his eyes averted while his cheeks bloom. Rowland stays by her. Never letting go.

"Pour some drops into the water," she hears him instructing Mariam. "That's it. A few more."

He guides her body over the steaming bowl, telling her to breathe. The heat from the water flushes her face, and Mariam places her own headdress over her head, creating a little steam tent. Clemmie's cheeks become damp with perspiration and condensation. Eucalyptus fills her nostrils, coating her tongue, the vapors reaching the back of her throat. Her windpipe. Her lungs.

Perhaps Rowland feels the change in her for he lowers her arms.

The lamplight returns as the headdress is removed from her head. She lies back, breathing properly now. Her chest bruised inside. Her lids heavy.

Rowland says something about her getting some sleep, that she must be exhausted. Clemmie feels the need to apologize for all the fuss, but she just lies there. Later, she'll look back on this scene and recoil, but she doesn't have the energy to face that now. Sphinx jumps onto the bed, shoving her face in Clemmie's, then curling up on her chest. It's not exactly comfortable, and as he leaves the room, Rowland carries Sphinx away, whispering something in the feline's ear.

Exhaustion swallows her. As she drifts, she thinks of the sandstorm, of her asthma episode. Has she failed to end her family's misfortunes?

Because of the storm, everything is coated in dust. Fine particles that scratch. Sand is hard to get rid of, filling crevices, sticking to skin, grazing everything it touches. She'll carry the itch of the Nile with her all the way home.

Plagued

H OME IS A LONG WAY off, made longer still by the series of storms
that attack the Nile and the little *dahabeeyah* on its surface. In
their own version of the ten plagues of Egypt, where each plague is
dust, sand clouds rage around them sporadically for ten days. Each
time they make progress downriver, the winds blow them back off
course, diminishing them to nothing more than a leaf skimming the
water. Always, they're borne back to Nubia.

The mark of Nephthys haunts Clemmie's lungs. Between storms,
the old star of Isis glints in the night sky, and kites puncture the day.
Clemmie twists her handkerchief until it becomes threadbare and
chews the whites of her nails. Her room reeks of eucalyptus.

She has that sickening sensation, the one that has formed stratum in
her belly over recent years, turning it cold and leaden. Something bad
is in the air, as sure as the smell of death. Etta is well, though, Nurse
Pugh's telegram assured her of that, so why is she so afraid?

At night she dreams that she is locked inside the chest that Set built,
the same one he made to trap Osiris in. When her eyes adjust to the
darkness, she realizes that she is lying next to Osiris's corpse. Entombed
and left to suffocate.

During the day, when they're stranded on a sandbank, she thinks she
sees a figure on the bank watching them atop a bay mount, and it re-

minds her of the man at Rhoda. When she peers from a window to look closer, he's gone. She practices pinning her lopped hair, but the ends come loose quicker now it's so short. With a desperate ache she misses the locket that she always kept so close. She misses the familiarity of the amulet hidden in her closet. She misses her sister and how life used to be.

The days blow themselves in and out, all bluster and no words. The traveling party keep inside, unsure when the next dust cloud will hit. *Hapi* bucks on the water like a spooked horse. Ten days of this and Clemmie doesn't know what to do with herself. She holds Sphinx close, thinking of Bast. Of how quickly those she loves can be taken from her.

Mariam comes to her, bringing hot coffee, black and strong. She offers a little jug of cream but Clemmie shakes her head. Taking a sip she swallows the bitterness, and it mingles with the gall in her belly.

With the small jug in her hands, Mariam turns to go, and Clemmie lowers her cup.

"Wait. Mariam. Stay a moment."

The captain's daughter turns slowly. Unwillingly. Her eyes peer into the creamer, as if waiting for its contents to curdle before her eyes.

"Have I done something to offend you?" Clemmie asks.

There is a pause, finite but noticeable, before Mariam inhales and stands taller.

"It was one amulet, *ya aanesa* Clemmie," she says. "I thought you cared about the antiquities. I thought you were different from the other tourists. But just like the others, you leave once you've had your satisfaction."

"I have responsibilities."

Mariam beats her chest twice. "I know about responsibilities. If I marry, my *baba* is alone. When I joined him on the *dahabeeyah*, he smiled at me. He learned to laugh again. The work I do on this vessel is more than just cooking and cleaning. It holds worth for my *baba* and for my country. You said you care for Egypt's history. If that's true, there is so much more you could do than bury one amulet. This land needs irrigating with more than water."

Maybe Mariam is right, but Clemmie can't think about that when there are other things pressing on her mind. She really needs to get home.

After ten days, a little boy stands on the bank at Korosko, staring at the boat. Clemmie notices him with a sinking feeling. Khalil disembarks to see what the boy wants, and after rewarding him with a *bakhshîsh*, he enters the saloon with a square of paper in his hands.

Clemmie knows what it is before he's even offered it to her. That's what it is to be sisters, conjoined in mind and spirit, despite the distance between them. The paper slices her finger when she opens it, but it's the words that do the most damage. They cut her heart, and this time she's not sure how to repair it.

How often can you mend a broken thing?

Unwrapping

1891

THE WIND HAS PICKED UP, and it shivers around the poky cottage that is now their home, drawing whispers from its walls. Whispers of those who once lived here, whose names and faces Clemmie doesn't know. Whispers of the past and present, and the whispers in her head.

Isis. Nephthys. Osiris. Set.

The storm is nearby, she can feel its lurking presence. She misses her four-poster bed in the big house, the bed curtains that felt like a shield, and she hides under the canopy of her quilt. Her lungs tighten and she rubs her chest, wondering how she can save her sister and herself. They haven't shared a bed in a while. Rosetta has become distant, confused by her grief, altered.

The pressure of responsibility makes it harder to breathe. She tries again. Breathing in and out. In and out. In . . .

She's aware of a peculiar smell. It puts her in mind of the farrier, when he presses an amber shoe against a horse's hoof, instigating that odd stench of burning keratin. Stinking, yet oddly pleasant. As a child, she loved to sit in the stable yard and see a horse, leg trapped between those of the smith, fidgeting on its rope as the smoke billowed away from the curl of metal. She'd pick up the trimmings, those giant equine fingernails, and see the creamy white where the cutters had parted them from the overgrown hoof.

The smell is more than a memory. It is present, in the now. Some- how, it is in her room. She freezes beneath the quilt, afraid to look.

"Who's there?"

The smell of burning—is that hair?—becomes stronger. Far off, somewhere, is the first rumble of the coming storm. The pull to know what waits beyond is too strong. She yanks the quilt down.

There is a flash, mere seconds before the thunder follows.

Standing in her room is a glowing figure, like a Christmas ghost. Only this ghost is made of flesh and blood, the flash of teeth a chilling smile. It's her sister, holding a candle, twirling a feather into the flame. A wisp of smoke curling upward.

"Rosetta?"

"My name is Isis!" The candle gutters with the power of each sylla- ble. Her sister's eyes spark with meaning, then calm just as quickly. Maybe the storm comes from inside her. She turns her head to one side, lifting the smoking feather and watching it smolder.

"What are you doing?"

The lightning emphasizes the shadows, the thunder speaking next. "I know you've consorted with Osiris," Rosetta cries, spittle leaking from her mouth.

Consorted? She locks eyes with Rosetta. Remembers these words from the game in their childhood.

"Traitor!"

This last word is a strangled scream, and she ducks just as her sister flings the lit candle at her. It lands on the quilt, and she smothers it, hearing the fizz of it being extinguished. Now in shadows, she turns back to the figure—but Rosetta is gone.

The storm lights the room once more, but so briefly she sees noth- ing, quickly surrounded by darkness again. She focuses her eyes as the heavy downpour begins outside, watery fists hammering on the win- dow.

A movement. A book fallen to the floor. She jumps. In her agitation she kneels on the candle, feels it snap in two beneath her. The thunder is loud, so close now it must be at Bickmore's gates. Lightning and rumbles follow each other in quick succession, and she makes use of the flickers to scan the room. The thunder plays tricks on her ears and the lightning blinds so that she can barely tell what she sees.

Then a shadow springs at her, and they're rolling. A tangle of quilt and hair and arms, fabric and flesh. They hit the floor hard. In between bouts of darkness and bright light, Rosetta presses against her sternum, repeating a dreadful word:

Bitch!

How long they struggle together, she doesn't know. They never fought as children, so her heart breaks all the more, hardly believing that this is happening. Her sister has changed. She thinks that she is Isis. A cruel twisting of a game that once brought joy.

The curse has already claimed her sister, after all.

Telegram

**THE EASTERN TELEGRAPH COMPANY, LIMITED.
CAIRO.**

*E relapsed—New doctor diagnoses tumor—Operation
must happen soon—Await your consent*

Decisions

G RIEF IS THE NILE RIVER that floods and recedes but never
dries up. Clemmie knows that whatever decision she makes, it will
haunt her for the rest of her life. The outcome may be kind, thanking
her for choosing well, blessing her for bearing the responsibility—but
it could also be vindictive, dooming her to a lifetime of inescapable
misery.

And what about the curse? She knows that Etta's mania, her Isis
episodes, have come and gone in waves. That lately she's spent more
time believing herself to be Isis than Etta, but there are always those
moments when she returns for a short while, confused and dazed and
unsure why Nurse Pugh and Clemmie look at her in that wary way, why
they ask her repeatedly what her name is. Is this new doctor right?
Does Etta have a tumor, not a curse-induced mania? The headaches,
the melancholia, the confusion of living two characters, has it really
been an illness all this time?

Her mission didn't work, but something else might. An operation
could save Etta. It could also kill her. She wonders whether to talk it
over with someone—Celia or Mariam, perhaps, to fill the sisterly role
that she so misses. Confidante. Adviser. Friend. Or Rowland? He
knows her family's history now, after all.

Yet she's handled things by herself for so long. It's true that Nurse

Pugh has been a support, but her entire life she's felt solitary in a way. Pretending not to mind when her mother shook her head at her, when Etta apologized for forgetting that they were going to spend the evening together when she'd also arranged to go out with Horatio, and when her father excluded her from the important things—after all, he said, she didn't need to worry her head over the numbers, the bookkeeping, the logistics of procuring mummies for their events.

Invisible. Alone. Surrounded by her hieroglyphs, her books on languages, the antiquities, and her cat.

Once more she's alone, surrounded by sand, the Nile, ruins, and a different cat.

"What should I do, Sphinx?"

The cat looks at her with bright green eyes that say it all, just like the limestone formation she's named for.

In your heart, you know.

Clemmie nods her head.

Ghosts

HER HANDS ACHE FROM THE weight of writing the telegram, and she rubs them till her joints click. She feels old. Older than her three-and-twenty years. The five winters since that awful night have felt more like fifty, spring never coming. In telling Nurse Pugh to arrange the operation, is she sentencing her sister to death?

She is anxious to return home. The urgency of Nurse Pugh's message has spurred her to sanction the operation, but Youssef says the storms have damaged the *dahabeeyah* and they'll have to stay moored at Korosko for another day while the crew see to repairs. She wonders whether to hire another boat, but in this narrow part of the Nile, none are going downriver to Cairo. The few vessels that sail by seem bent on passing this mostly uninhabited part of Nubia and exploring upriver.

The delay provides a chance to think over Mariam's words, of what Egypt itself is saying to her. There's a cry emitted from the desert when the wind blows, a howling that makes her ache, a hole that she understands because it matches the one inside her. She can't stop thinking of the excavations, of Sakkârah's looted ground. She and this realm, they're bound together, be that by the amulet or something else. Perhaps there is a desire inside her to help mend this country after all, just as she wants to mend what's left of her family.

A *shâdûf*. Irrigation. The river flowing, feeding, restoring.

Mariam challenged her love for Egypt. And maybe she was right to. Even if she has dedicated her life to studying its history, what was her motivation? Does she owe Egypt more than returning one precious antique?

There is so much more you could do than bury one amulet.

For so many years Egypt has been her entertainment, the subject of her studies, her life's work. She might be a hieroglyphist and Egyptologist, but is she really any different from the other tourists who come up the Nile hoping to purchase a stolen mummy to take home?

After sending her decision at the Korosko post office, she meets up with the others amid the heaving bazaars. They've procured more coffee, Lumps of Delight, dates, and other delicacies. Walking back to the *dahabeeyah* together, they ask each other what to do now that the storms seem to be over. Once their vessel is repaired, are they going back to Cairo as originally planned, or shall they press on, further up the Nile? There's a hopefulness in the others' voices when they suggest the latter, but she insists that she must go home.

Hapi is nestled beside a neighbor at the bank, a steamer that must have moored for its tourists to stop off at the Nubian post office and check for letters or newspapers. Youssef is on the deck, looking out for them. As they approach, Clemmie notices the eagerness of his eyes, the twisting of his hands, the way he rocks onto the balls of his feet and back again. He seems different without his *chibouk* clamped between his teeth. When they're almost at the boat, he beckons to them, his hands telling them to hurry. Something is wrong.

Youssef rambles in his tongue as they board the *dahabeeyah,* and maybe it's the way he mutters, or the noise inside her head, but Clemmie can't understand him. Can't make him out. Khalil steps in, and even his translations pass through her like a ghost through walls. Mariam emerges from her kitchen and joins in with the chatter, only adding to the confusion. Something about Clemmie's cabin. How Youssef couldn't stop him. How he said he knew her.

She walks with hardened limbs, a mummy come to life. She's hollow inside, as if Anubis has pulled her organs from her body, one by one.

There's no need to open her cabin door. It's already flung wide, the room in disarray. The closet where she once kept the amulet in its box is bared, her clothes on the floor. The little dresser by her bed, even that has been emptied, the drawers turned upside down. Undergarments, stockings, the scrapbook of letters, her copy of *A Thousand Miles up the Nile*, all scattered. The mattress has been torn off the bed frame, revealing the emptiness beneath. Sphinx sits on a pile of petticoats and looks questioningly at Clemmie. She doesn't look back.

Instead, she stares at *him*. At the man who has done this, appearing as a ghost from her past. His red coat burns in the sunlight, buttons bright as blades, wearing his uniform loudly to speak of his position when his civvies would be more appropriate—especially in this heat. He's an image of Bickmore, that bloodred manor that pulsates like an open wound in her memory, and he stands in the chaos he's caused, breathing heavily.

He notices her as he turns, and she's startled by the familiarity of him here on the Nile. Her two worlds colliding. Is it really him, with his tall, muscular physique, eyes mirroring the shade of his dark wavy hair, and clean-shaven jaw with that mild cleft in his chin? The man before her is handsome, could be even more so if he attempted a smile of greeting.

He doesn't. The room darkens. For a moment, Clemmie thinks it could be another sandstorm approaching. But it isn't that, it's him.

"Clemmie," Horatio says, nostrils flaring. "I've found you at last."

Legacy

B EFORE SHE CAN UTTER HIS name, before she can say anything, question him, accuse him, he strides forward. His boots cut through the white sea of her strewn undergarments, leaving his brand in blacking and dust. He takes her upper arm and pulls her into the room, gesturing at the mess he's made. She waits for him to apologize.

"Where is it?" he demands. "I've turned this place inside out. Where is it?"

She knows what he's looking for. The greed in his eye is a replica of the one she saw in her father's when he unwound the two heads, saw the Double *Tyet* to match, and knew what treasures he owned.

He gives her a little shake, as if she's a money box with a stuck coin. "Well?"

"How dare you rifle through my things."

"Where is it?"

"Get out of my cabin."

"Clemmie! Where is it?"

"I won't talk to you until you get out."

He huffs but obliges, taking her with him and letting her cabin door slam behind them.

"Is everything all right?"

In the tiny corridor feeding to the cabins stands Rowland. For a moment, in her astonishment at her life catching up with her, she'd forgotten about the others. But now Rowland is there, barely leaning as he straightens his spine to almost its full potential height, filling the passage. Oswald and Celia gather behind him, curious and frowning.

Horatio steps forward, still pulling Clemmie with him, and his movements own the space. He speaks with confidence, reversing things so that he's the host and they the guests. Making the *dahabeeyah* his property.

"And you are?"

Rowland introduces himself, Oswald, and Celia, but he doesn't look at this intruder. He's eyeing Clemmie. Silently asking: *Are you quite all right?*

"This is Horatio," Clemmie says, filling the silence. Because she knows Horatio expects her to introduce him, and because she senses Rowland needs to hear her speak, that she needs to add her voice before Horatio takes over completely. "Horatio Devereux. He's . . ."

What? An old family friend? The son of her father's best friend? The son her father never had?

Out of the corner of her eye, she sees Horatio shake his head. She's disappointed him yet again.

"It's *Major* Horatio Devereux," he corrects. "I'm Clemmie's fiancé."

She's winded by Horatio's statement.

"Horatio and I . . . I mean, he isn't . . ."

He waits for her to finish, but she's too shocked to disprove him. The fact is that he's said those words. Her traveling companions believe he has cause to say them. Celia's eyes twinkle with the memory of a ruby and diamond cluster ring, Oswald looks puzzled but accepting. And Rowland? Clemmie wordlessly pleads with him, not sure why she so desperately wants him to believe her, but something in his face, in his stance, is guarded. He doesn't want to listen. He won't. Her three friends disappear into their respective cabins to let the *lovers* be alone.

"Why did you say that?"

She's angrier with him for this than for going through her things. He ignores her question.

"I know why you're here, Clemmie. I went through the collection. I know you have it with you."

She doesn't want to talk outside the cabins where the others might hear, so she enters the saloon, and he follows, still grasping her arm.

"My father's collection is nothing to do with you," she says after shutting the internal saloon door. "You had no right."

"You're reading too much into the amulet. Returning it is madness, I told you that. It won't change things."

How can he speak so easily of madness? She tries to remind herself that Rosetta loves this man. That she has loved him herself in her own way.

He scowls as he brushes her cheek with a finger, the way one might check for dust on a mantelpiece.

"Look at you," he mutters. "You're so freckled. Don't you ever wear a hat?"

She glances at her forearms, where her sleeves are rolled to the elbow. Reddened and peeling in places, her skin's darker than when she left England. Egypt has left its mark in more ways than one.

"I'm not your fiancée, Horatio," she insists, twisting out of his grip. It hurts, coming free, and her skin pulses from the liberation.

"You accepted my ring."

"I turned you down."

He produces something from his pocket, and she sees the glimmering stones. Ruby. A circle of diamonds. He's been through everything, then, even her jewelry box. It's true that she's been keeping the ring safe, but not for herself, and she takes it from him. Putting it in her pocket. The ring isn't hers to accept. If she did, then she really would be the Nephthys that her sister thinks she is. Betraying her.

They stare at each other awhile, both thinking of the person whom they haven't named. Clemmie knows she'll never get him to understand, and she heads for the doorway that leads to the deck, but there's a crackle of paper behind her. Glancing back, she sees that he has produced a letter. She takes it, thinking it could be from Etta. It isn't, of course. The writing is his father's.

It's a lawyer's letter written with intimacy, because she's more than just a client, she's the daughter of the lawyer's deceased friend. She scans the words, all of them a reminder of her situation. That she'll be *more comfortable,* that she'll be *providing for her sister,* if she stops fighting her *inevitable nuptials.* The letter angers her because she doesn't need reminding how difficult things have become, and doesn't want to think about her father's betrayal.

Her father had never been a stickler for society's rules, otherwise he would not have let her study hieroglyphs in the first place. His wife cared, however, and he considered this to an extent, not wanting her to grieve over his decisions as well as his memory should he die before her. Thus, he thought about his will carefully. He constructed it with the consideration a man gives these things when he's trying to please everyone: his darling wife, his beloved daughters, society, and the surrogate son who would soon enough be a son by marriage.

The natural course of things, he concluded after discussing with his best friend—who happened to be his lawyer, and who also happened to be the actual father of Clement's *adopted* son—was to leave his estate to his wife, as it was possible to do these days. On the unlikely event of her death—a precaution, these clauses, his friend would say—then the estate would be left in control not of Clement's daughters—again, possible by law, but frowned upon by society to trouble the brains of delicate young females with such complexities as property—but to his soon-to-be son, Horatio. His daughters would be provided for, of course. Dowries for both of them, a small income to live off in the meantime, and a carefully constructed list of each and every antiquity in his collection to go to Clemmie. Property, however, is not a thing to leave to young women, and so he signed it off to Horatio gladly, knowing full well that the major would be married to his daughter soon enough, and that his wife was unlikely to die anyway, and even more unlikely, that his will would be required anytime soon. Unnecessary precautions, all of them.

He never accounted for a creeping curse that would snuff out first his life, and then his wife's. Neither did he expect a mania to change the character of his elder daughter, preventing a marriage. The estate passed into the hands of a man who had not married into the family, a man who, out of the kindness of his heart, allowed the Attridge sisters and their childhood nurse to move into a leaky tenant's cottage on the estate. Clement never could have accounted for any of these things.

While he'd done his best to make everyone happy, he'd very much muddled things, getting tripped up in the web of society, and practicalities, and, perhaps, in the daze of thinking Horatio *was* his son, when he'd always so desperately wanted one of his own.

And what of the legatees?

Rosetta was none the wiser. As far as she knew, the damp cottage was her temple, and the continuous drip of a leak into a copper bucket was the insistent knock of Osiris in his chest, begging to be released. She searched for him and called for him, but, locked in her room in the cottage, she never found him.

Horatio was content, to a point. He had the estate, but he didn't have the artifacts, and one in particular was worth more than the most generous dowry a doting father could bestow.

Clemmie was discontented. She yearned to get Bickmore back, the estate that was hers and her sister's by rights. Still, she had the artifacts, and that meant that they were safe for now.

There is an answer to both Horatio and Clemmie's problems. Marriage. But while Horatio is willing to squeeze a ring onto her finger that once belonged to another, can Clemmie betray her sister, and the fate of the antiquities, just to regain the family home and a secure future?

Betrayal

S HE FOLDS THE LETTER, ADDING it to her pocket where the ring already sits.

"You don't make things easy," Horatio complains.

What if Etta never gets better? At some point, Clemmie will have to marry him if they want to reclaim Bickmore.

"It's wrong," she says.

His breathing turns into a ragged sigh. "I'll tell you what's wrong. Not getting the collection. I worked closely with your father. That amulet is mine by right, and we will get married."

She tells him about the telegrams, the tumor, and the operation, that there's a chance his former love might recover. His face is unresponsive, failing to share her excitement at the prospect of healing, or her fear at the risks.

"I know about the doctor, I paid for the quack. How else do you think that Welsh nurse got the money? She came begging and I did it for you. That doesn't change things. Rose is mad, Clemmie, and I'm not marrying a madwoman."

If she was touched by his financial assistance, that quickly fades. "What if I'm mad too?" she asks, squaring her shoulders. "Aren't you taking a risk marrying into my family at all?"

He frowns, and she can feel him scrutinizing every part of her that's on show—and those that aren't. Her sun-washed complexion, gloveless hands, the naked finger that he wants to bear his ring. She's not alien to the glances men have given her and her figure. Sometimes the glimmer of desire is followed with one of regret when the man discovers her unwomanly scholarliness, as if confused that God would bestow both ample bosoms and a capable brain on a woman in equal measure.

He recites his reasoning. Her parents weren't mad. Her mother's grief was a melancholia that would have faded over time. Mania doesn't run in the family and his private physician said Etta's was an unfortunate, isolated case.

Always so practical, so thorough. He's taken great pains to make sure he doesn't propose to another woman that he'll have to jilt. Yet his words rankle. She barely recognizes the man who was going to be her brother. When did Horatio become a stranger?

"It's time to grow up," Horatio says. "You're nearly four-and-twenty, Rose is insane and may not survive this new treatment, I want the collection and a wife, and you want to get the house back. Marry me. It's not as if anyone else wants you."

Should she feel honored by his comment? Horatio wants her, the first man to propose or offer courtship. His reminder of her age cuts sharp. Young in many ways—running out of time when it comes to finding love. Love? The only love she comprehends is what it is to love her sister.

Clemmie plays with her finger, the one that should be wearing the ring. She's tempted to reach for it. To brush her fingers against the metal claws holding the diamonds and ruby in place. To feel the scratch of them, rough and containing. Rather than diving her hand into her pocket, she voices her reservations.

"Do not forget your former promise to my sister. The ring you have since given to me was pulled from Rosetta's finger. Is it really surprising that I hesitate? How can I betray my own sister that way?"

In her head she sees Nephthys and Osiris. How they went behind Isis and were joined—just the once—but they were joined. Isn't this the same?

"Wear the blasted ring," he says. "You know you're going to eventually. I thought you were fond of me. Don't you want to come home to Bickmore?"

Of course she wants Bickmore back, but can she really marry for the sake of the estate? God willing, Rosetta will survive the operation, but what if Etta recovers only to discover that Horatio is married to Clemmie instead? She'd make an enemy of her sister forever.

When Horatio proposed to Etta, Clemmie felt a loneliness that all her books and knowledge couldn't fill. In a way, she was jealous. Not in a thieving manner, an envy that wished it for herself *instead*. But she wanted it for herself *as well*. She wanted to be engaged. To be loved.

Horatio offers her his vow. His companionship. The old family estate. It's what her deceased parents would have wanted. To see her married, Bickmore their home, to have the two families united. Rosetta will be more comfortable, they won't have to worry about money, they could even pay for nurses to look after her. For just a moment, she allows herself to remember the years she's spent with Horatio, their shared smiles over an artifact, the moment when she explained how the type of script could help date a piece—hieroglyphic being the oldest, developing into the hieratic, then demotic, and finally the Coptic—and his face brightened with understanding. They could share the collection, work on it together, maintain what her father started.

What is she thinking? He's not the man she thought. Was his gesture of letting them stay in the cottage really a kindness? Couldn't he have refused the inheritance, admitting that things hadn't turned out the way her father had expected? Besides which, there's still a chance that Etta will recover, and because of that she can't accept.

She needs to get away from him, his presence is confusing. Picking up her skirts, she leaves the saloon, hurrying onto the deck. Stepping across the detachable plank used to board and disembark, observed by the Korosko peaks, she reaches the banks of the Nile.

He's right behind her, not even the sand able to soften the heaviness of his steps. He grabs her, stops her from running. Turns her around, making her body bend to his will. He presses his lips onto hers. Rough, more forceful than words. She jerks her head away, wide-eyed. Sullied.

Almost four-and-twenty and, until now, she'd never known the taste of a kiss. What cruelty for this to be her first. His eyes widen as he reads her expression.

"Have you really never been kissed before?" he snorts. "In which case, I should kiss you more often. Make you appreciate what I'm offering."

This time, he holds her face in his hands so that there's no backing out. His grip is too strong for her to pull away, and his lips part hers intrusively. Flesh against flesh bruising. Thumbs indenting her cheeks and fingers crushing her jaw. By the silence of the Nile, to the thrum of two unsynchronized hearts, and beneath the brand of the Egyptian sky, his kiss impresses what he expects her to do.

Strangely, the words the crone spoke to her at Siût burst into her mind.

A man in a uniform. You don't love him. But you will.

Was she right? If Clemmie can believe in hieroglyphic warnings, can she also accept the words of a fortune teller? To not marry Horatio is to betray their rightful claim to the estate. To marry him is to betray her sister.

She pushes his chest, tearing away from him. Breathing heavily, but not from her asthma.

"I won't marry you, Horatio. And if you don't understand the loyalty I feel toward Etta, then you're more of a stranger than I thought."

He makes a low noise in his throat, the sort of animal noise she imagines Set might be capable of releasing.

"You can't turn me away that easily," he says. "I will have what's mine by right."

Something stirs on the lower deck, and they both see Mariam at the rail. Watching. She doesn't say anything, but her presence is enough. Horatio rubs his chin, distracted now their exchange is being witnessed. With a final bruise of his mouth on Clemmie's, marking his territory, he steps away. His point made. Striding back to the boat.

Above, the sky is moving. Two kites symbolizing what Clemmie is trying to defend. The bond of sisterhood.

Waiting

HORATIO CAME BY STEAMER, BUT with *Hapi*'s minor repairs set
to be complete before the day is out, Clemmie refuses to transfer
to his vessel. She'll make her own way downriver without him, setting
sail in the morning. He isn't easily deterred, however. Paying his crew
off, he gathers his cases and boards their *dahabeeyah*. She tries to stop
him, but he's thought of everything and bribes her with the mention of
Etta's operation.

"Who do you think is funding it? If you want me to pay the bill, then
you'd better keep quiet and let me join you."

Is he really that heartless? She doesn't fight him, not wanting to find
out. There's a cabin that Khalil has been using, and Horatio soon de-
motes the *dragoman* to the lower deck, moving in with an assured gait
that says more than words.

Clemmie's companions are not impressed, and she feels the stain of
association. They're judging her for lying to them, but how can she
deny his claims? Horatio's very presence seems to verify his words.
Why else would he come after her unless they had an understanding?
And there is the ring, a key detail that Celia knows about. She's probably already told Oswald and Rowland about it to make it look as though
she was in on Clemmie's secret.

"Horatio, please," Clemmie says, standing in the center of the cabin as he opens his cases and starts to unpack. "Just stop and listen to me."

He throws down a shirt. "I've told you, it's entirely up to you. I'm coming if you want my money to pay for your sister's treatment. It's not as if you can afford it, not after frivoling away your money on this trip."

"That's hardly fair! I came for Etta's sake."

"Rose has nothing to do with this. You came for yourself. You've always wanted to see Egypt and saving your sister was just an excuse."

"You really can be cruel sometimes."

"Frankness only hurts when it's the truth."

Is that right? Do his words sting because there's a measure of truth to them? Have her motives been selfish?

"Clementine?"

They both turn to see Rowland limp through the entrance. His gaze sweeps over the cabin, from Clemmie to Horatio, taking in the mess of unpacked belongings.

"I couldn't help but overhear your happy reunion," he says wryly. His eyes come to rest on Clemmie again. "You don't seem entirely comfortable about your fiancé joining the voyage. Is something wrong?"

Horatio laughs. "A mere lovers' tiff. But, of course, you want to know I'm who I say I am." He produces a letter from his pocket that Clemmie soon realizes was penned by her own hand.

"Bickmore isn't the same without your presence, Horatio," he reads aloud. "I am sure you can imagine how your own loved one pines for you."

She wrote that so long ago, when he was serving in Egypt, and she can't remember what else she wrote. *Your own loved one.* She meant Rosetta, not herself, an act of sacrifice encouraging her future brother to return and wed her sister, but how is Rowland to know that? Hot with embarrassment, she snatches the letter to stop him reading more.

"Typical Clemmie," Horatio says, winking. "She does prefer to keep everything a secret."

And when she catches Rowland's eye, she knows that Horatio has done what he set out to do. He's convinced him. As far as Rowland is concerned, Clemmie has always kept secrets, so Horatio must be one of them.

✗

While Horatio is sorting his things, she gathers Sphinx into her arms and heads outside into the sun. There's no sign of the Lions. Celia likes to nap in the afternoons if she gets too hot, and Clemmie can only presume Oswald is tending to his shotgun. Honestly, he gives that contraption more attention than some men offer their sweethearts.

Other than the crew, Rowland is the only member of their traveling party on deck, and she's relieved because she feels the need to explain, most of all to him, who Horatio really is. She joins him at the rail but he doesn't even look at her. Scratching Sphinx's head, she pretends not to be offended. He shields his eyes with his hand, watching the activity on the bank at Korosko. There's a Nubian giraffe, an actual giraffe— something she's only seen in paintings and engravings—passing by. It's a rare and beautiful sight, but wasted on her at this moment.

She wants to touch Rowland's arm, to make him look at her, but he's doing his best to focus on anything but her.

"Horatio's not my fiancé, you know."

He looks at her then, and his face is drawn. His jaw so tight she expects it to creak when he talks.

"You don't have to explain," he says, pushing away from the rail. So desperate to get away. "It's nothing to me."

✗̂

Stuck at Korosko until they set sail tomorrow, she thinks of how close they are to Philae. She recalls how the night prodded her during the burial, how she felt as though she was committing a crime in the shadows, even as she knew that she was doing what she believed to be right. If the sandstorms, her asthma attack, and Etta's relapse are redolent of the curse, then her actions that night were futile. A valuable amulet is in the ground, and it was all for naught.

What about the excavation she saw here in Nubia? Just the sight of all those picks and shovels, the crates of antiquities, made her shudder, worrying what their fate will be. History's discovery isn't so very wrong, but the way it's carried out, the thoughtless misuse of bodies and their funerary goods—well, she has the benefit of hindsight. She hopes that her amulet is safe from the whims of those who would dig it up, that Philae will never be excavated. Even if returning the amulet hasn't ended her sufferings, it had to be the right thing to do.

The deck creaks behind her. She turns to face Horatio.

"I'm a patient man, but I've looked everywhere. The hold, your cabin. Have you given it to one of your friends to look after?"

"Of course not. I wouldn't trust anyone with the amulet."

"Who are they anyway?"

"We were strangers passing through Cairo. They're just tourists, Horatio."

"The collection is wasted on you."

"Wasted? I've spent my whole life studying Egyptology."

"You can't grasp the financial side of things. Why else do you think your father left Bickmore to me?"

Even though it hurts, what he says is true. Her father never did explain the accounts to her. The little she knows about money is self-taught since moving into the cottage and managing her petty allowance.

"That amulet is priceless."

It reminds her of something he said years ago, something she barely paid attention to at the time.

This is worth more than a hundred ordinary amulets.

"I won't ask again," he says. "Where is it?"

It's just money to him. A Double *Tyet* associated with a two-headed mummy and inscribed with maledictions makes a unique combination. What would people pay for such a piece? Could the amulet make Horatio outrageously rich if he found the right buyers and had them bidding against each other? She takes in the frustration chiseling his features, making his chest rigid through his uniform, greed darkening his eye. The relief is so immense, knowing that they're at Korosko rather than Philae, that the amulet is safe in the ground and Horatio can't have it, and that the twins are well hidden back in Essex, that she feels her face break into a rare smile. A laugh filtering through the gaps.

"You'll never find it. The amulet and the twins are safe."

She hears it before she feels it. A crack, a blur of movement, a burn spreading through her face as the back of his hand meets her cheek. She gasps. Her hand nurses her face, as if touching it will help her comprehend that he's struck her. He's panting. They both are. Their eyes meeting then not meeting. He steps forward and she flinches, but he doesn't strike again. An apology, then? No, she knows better than that.

His face is in hers, spit sizzling on her skin.

"I have ways of getting what I want, Clemmie. Don't make me use them."

With that threat, he's gone, and she turns back to the river. One hand cradling her offended cheek, the other arm dangling over the bar. Reaching down to a reflection that looks up from the water, as if she sank in the Nile's depths long ago and is trying to claw her way back.

Unwrapping

1891

THEY CANNOT FIND HER.

It was Nurse Pugh who raised the alarm. Nurse Pugh who sleeps in the same room as her troubled charge. Since Rosetta accused Clemmie of stealing Osiris, after coming to her during the thunderstorm, her marbled eyes gleaming between flashes so that the storm was a part of her, Clemmie has known to keep her distance.

Nothing will ever come between us, will it?

Her heart breaks differently from how it did when they lowered her parents' coffins into the ground. This separation is a different type of loss, and now Rosetta is missing.

They list all the places she might have gone. Back to the big house? The village? God help them if she has, for they have tried to keep her condition a secret. When people ask after her, they say she is suffering from a case of fatigue, and the villagers nod sympathetically, clasping hands to their breasts and murmuring: *So many heartaches, poor dear girl.*

"The river. She'll have gone to the river, I know it," Clemmie says, and she doesn't know why she is so afraid. The Chelmer was always a harmless part of her childhood, but nothing seems harmless anymore. Nurse Pugh hides the kitchen knives, she puts her sewing needles and scissors in a locked box. They have to think of everything, like when an infant first starts to toddle and may touch anything. Danger is every-where.

Clemmie doesn't delay even to pull on her dressing gown. Alongside Nurse Pugh, she hurries from the cottage and runs in her nightgown through dewy grass to the water.

What is a sister's intuition? Is it shared blood, something silent and unseen inherited from parents, or a sagacity from being raised the same? Does it begin with conception, or at birth, or does it come over time through shared experience? Who can explain the phenomenon? Yet Clemmie knows it exists, for, as she arrives through the trees at the riverbank, she spies a ghostly figure wading through the river.

Rosetta.

"Osiris! Osiris! Where are you?"

Choking on sobs she cannot afford to indulge, Clemmie opens her mouth to call to her sister. Nurse Pugh stops her.

"Hush, *cariad*, we mustn't startle her. She could be sleepwalking."

Sleepwalking. That is what they blame it on. Melancholia. Head-aches. As Nurse Pugh lowers herself into the river and guides Rosetta out, Clemmie watches tearfully from a distance, afraid of making things worse. She tries to put a name to what her sister suffers, and there is only one word. *Mania.*

They don't send Rosetta to an asylum. Clemmie won't hear of it, and their childhood nurse continues to take care of her. They produce a key—oh, wretched thing—and their hearts turn along with the lock when they secure Rosetta in her room.

Somehow, they make it work, through the hard times and the better seasons. The few doctors they consult, spending their limited resources, are useless. They're all the same, passing them a pamphlet for the Essex County Lunatic Asylum, or prescribing laudanum to help her sleep. When Rosetta screams for hours that Osiris is gone, Clemmie stands outside the door and hears Nurse Pugh insisting that Osiris is well, that he will return, followed by the silence of an embrace that Clemmie cannot be a part of.

The time of mourning their mother's death passes, and Clemmie exchanges her grays and lavenders of half mourning for something more colorful. Pinks. Blues. She puts aside her jet and mourning jew-elry. She stands in her room, where she now keeps some of the antiquities, the rest stored in the attic for want of space. The eyes of olden days watch her when she sleeps, when she dresses, when she reads a book.

If Flora were alive, she'd say it is a man's room. A piece of broken pottery here, a papyrus there, amulets complete and incomplete, a string of beads, the mummified cat that started it all for Clemmie. It began as a hobby, became a profession, and she contemplates the collapse of it all. A study of ruins reduced to such.

She sits on her bed, counting the money that she has so carefully saved from the modest income her father's will stipulated, scraped together after paying the doctors. As she considers the mummy and their amulet, the hieroglyphs that she has gone over and over to deduce the true meaning behind the text, she knows that she is ready. She needs to be ready. Rosetta's health is at stake.

It takes no time at all to pack her luggage, to empty the table croquet accessories out of their box and carefully rest the amulet within. She finds a spare case and, with all the tenderness she'd want someone to use when handling her own sister, she lowers the twins inside. She bound them back up when she inherited the collection, but moving them now requires time, and she rewraps each strip of cerement as best she might, trying not to disturb them. Thinking of the care once taken when they were first embalmed. Trying to be just as respectful. The case is the best she can do for a coffin, the best she can offer to hide them in. And they need hiding.

Horatio has been coming to the cottage more and more. He has a good deal to say, things she doesn't want to think about that involve Bickmore, Rosetta, herself, and a ruby and diamond ring. He talks about doctors and nurses, care for Rosetta, a better life. His words are like eating too much rich food, tempting and delicious, but they soon turn the stomach. He moves on to the collection, the twins and the amulet, reminding her of Clement's dreams, of the plans the men used to make together in the study. Of exhibiting the twins and their Double *Tyet*.

When she was little, she once played in this cottage between tenants. In the game of Myths, the part where Isis was looking to confront her, she turned it into hide-and-go-seek. Finding the key beneath the cast-iron boot scraper and slipping inside, she ran through the furnished rooms looking for a place to hide. There was nowhere good enough on the first level, so she hurried for the stairs, tripping over in her haste. Her leg struck the bottom step as she fell, and it made an odd creaking sound. When she looked closely, tears for her scraped knee deterred by curiosity, she saw a space beyond where the panel of the first step had shifted. Kicking the panel away entirely left a gap big enough for her to slide through.

Clemmie carries the twins downstairs, careful not to knock or disturb them. Then she kneels at the foot of the stairs and kicks the panel out of the way. It's snug, but the case just slides through. She covers the hiding place back up with the panel. This is the best she can offer for now. What else can she do?

"There," she whispers. "No one can hurt you anymore. I'm going to make peace in Egypt."

Perhaps she should know better than to bid Rosetta farewell, but how can she not? What if her sister is stolen entirely from her while she's away? What if Clemmie's lungs are crushed for good?

Their last time together, Rosetta looks at Clemmie with a stranger's eyes, and that is why she has to go.

Eventide

A S *HAPI* FLOATS ON THE NILE, a different vessel floats in the sky; the Day Barque exchanged for the Night Barque, *Mesektet*. The saloon lamps make the shadows tremble, but they don't disappear. Lingering. Waiting for the moment when they can take control.

There's protection in numbers, so Clemmie hovers with the Lions, with Rowland, keeping to their sides, trying to follow the strain of their languid conversation. It feels like a weakness, to admit that she doesn't feel safe with Horatio anymore, that she could do with the help of others. Still, maybe the bravest thing Nephthys ever did was reuniting with Isis after all Set had put her through, after Osiris was murdered. Maybe there's more to company than she ever realized.

Horatio claims the head of the table for dinner, and because she doubts that he'll bully her in front of the others, she joins them. Bully. It's a strange word with a peculiar etymology. Once meaning sweetheart or fine fellow, now it has come to mean a harasser. One of those terms that can be good and bad, that change so utterly over time. Isn't that what's happened with Horatio? In her childhood, she never once would have imagined him capable of striking her. The redness has receded, the stinging with it, but she keeps replaying the moment in her mind, expecting to wake up and realize it was all a dream.

She's hungry, and whatever Mariam has prepared smells good.

Clemmie has come to love the spices, the garlic lentils, and the buttered rice. Everything so fragrant, the fish flaky, the lamb tender, rice fluffy and soft—one could mistake them for having been cooked in a palace kitchen rather than on their humble vessel. Mariam's skill is no different tonight. The *kunáfah* that Youssef once recommended is creamy and delicious. Heady cinnamon and sweet nuttiness from the almonds remind their palates that they're far from their own country with its bland version of rice pudding served with jam.

Celia, easily won over by the scarlet of a uniform—and undeterred by any possible attachment between Clemmie and Horatio—focuses her attention on the major. No doubt she'd flirt with Ossie if it would make another man jealous. First, she twitters to Horatio about his achievements on the battlefield and, not wanting to leave Rowland out, mentions his former time in the army. Horatio sits up taller at this information and assesses Rowland with fresh scrutiny, asking what regiment he was in.

Rowland takes time to swallow. "The Seventh Dragoon Guards."

"You fought in Egypt?"

"At Kassassin. Yes."

Now Horatio is interested, having served here himself. "The Moonlight Charge. I wish I had been a part of it. Were you injured there? Tell me about it."

Of course Horatio's sharp eye didn't miss Rowland's limp. He never misses anything. That's why Clemmie must be careful not to let anything slip about Philae. She can't risk him unearthing the amulet and undoing the one bit of good she's achieved.

Rowland moves his *kunáfah* around his bowl. "I don't talk about it much."

Clemmie glances at Horatio, despite having avoided his eye all evening. He has no sensitivity. Unaffected by his own brush with combat, he doesn't see how some men would prefer to forget about their time in the army. Should she stop his careless questions? She's torn, because the more the men talk of Kassassin, the less likely it is that the amulet will be mentioned.

Ignoring Rowland's reticence, Horatio lifts his glass emphatically, spilling wine on his hand. He sucks it clean. "The cavalry saved the day. It was a glorious moment in our history."

"We did," Rowland says, "but behind the golden curtain of every military triumph lie the wounded and the dead."

Horatio pauses respectfully to mark Rowland's statement.

"Very true. What was it Kennedy wrote in his poem last year? *'Ha! 'twas a glorious ride, Though I miss an old friend from my side, And sadness is mingled with pride.'* Come, I'm sure you could regale us with a tale or two."

Rowland doesn't look up from the glass of water in his hand. If it were big enough, he looks as though he'd drown himself in it.

"He said he didn't want to talk about it, Horatio."

Everyone looks at her. Especially Horatio. And he tilts his head, nodding slowly, as if he's beginning to comprehend something about her. Something that she doesn't even know herself.

Celia asks for another myth that evening, and Clemmie considers the right part of Nephthys's story to tell. There's a hint of danger on the air tonight, and she doesn't know whether it comes from Horatio after what happened on the deck, or whether it's something else, but it puts her in mind of Osiris. Of death. Of what people are capable of. She folds her hands in her lap as she retells Osiris's murder.

Once, she says, thinking of how her father would begin his stories that way.

Once, Nephthys was alone, thinking of all that had happened. She thought of her unhappy marriage to Set, of how her affair with Osiris had been discovered, and how Set had lately made a curious chest to be given as a prize to whoever could fit inside. Set had always been the one to defy the rules. He'd pierced his way out of his mother's womb rather than be delivered naturally, and now he'd murdered his brother. Osiris was dead. Nailed inside the chest that Set had made, like a corpse in a coffin. There, trapped inside, he'd suffocated.

Isis had searched for the chest so that Osiris's body might be restored to her, and on her travels she had discovered Anubis, stealing him for herself. In her rage over the affair, she even spread tales that

Nephthys had exposed her son to die. Because of this, Nephthys didn't help her sister hunt for the chest. Isis needed time away from her.

Nephthys was found out.

Anubis was no longer hers.

Osiris was dead.

And for all these things, Nephthys would be blamed. She could see it now, the future foretold. Through the rolling centuries people would look back on the infamous story of Osiris's murder. They would blame the strumpet who had instigated Set's wrath. They would look at Nephthys's neglect and see her as a dreadful mother. They would view her with scorn.

Yet she was still a daughter of Seb and Nut. Surely there would be devotees, even in small numbers. Some would recall her shape-shifting magic. Her care of the *Bennu* bird. And what else? For what else could Nephthys be known?

Whatever animosity lay between the sisters, that didn't erase one thing. That there was the same blood—the blood of siblings—coursing through their veins. They both loved Osiris as a brother. He was dead, but his corpse had finally been brought home. It was after retrieving his *khat* that Isis came to Nephthys again. Something else had happened.

He's gone, Isis told her.

Gone?

I hid the chest. I left it for a short time. I barely turned my back, and it was gone. Set has butchered him and scattered his body far and wide. We are sisters, and our brother's body has been dismembered and distributed throughout Upper and Lower Egypt. I need your help.

This is what Isis offered to Nephthys. An opportunity to heal what was broken. To focus not on being wife, lover, or even mother, but to be joined in sisterhood. They needed to unite, for the sake of Osiris.

That's how, as they stood side by side, flesh melting to feathers, the sisters were rejoined. Their mission was clear. A fire burned within their breasts that they both felt the heat of, and their birds' eyes gleamed with recollections of a childhood spent running around naked and carefree. Memories that they shared, something that was both of theirs, that neither could disown. They opened their hooked beaks to release a scream that sounded as one.

As they took flight, it wasn't obvious that they were parading as birds, or even which was which. They were just two kites soaring over the Nile.

When her story is over, they sit in silence for a few moments. The lamps cast a glow on Oswald's shotgun as he polishes it, massaging oil into the wooden stock. Rowland offers a Havana to Oswald, passing over Horatio, then cuts one for himself. The night smells of linseed, cigar smoke, and coffee. Horatio, drawn always to weapons, comments on the shotgun, and Oswald hands it over to be admired like a proud parent.

"Had much chance to use it?"

Oswald shakes his head. "No, no. I almost got a crocodile back at Philae, but I missed."

Horatio tuts his condolences. Alarmed at the mention of Philae, Clemmie is about to move the subject on to something more comfortable when Oswald continues.

"Of course, I wouldn't have even got that close if it hadn't been for the women."

Horatio cocks a questioning eyebrow, and before Clemmie can signal to remain silent, before she can cut in, Oswald explains what happened. How Clemmie, Celia, and Mariam irrationally decided to go ashore one night at Philae, the darkness lit by a solitary lamp, and that's how they encountered the crocodile.

She's seen the way Oswald holds his body when he takes aim with his shotgun. The careful positioning, the way the body replicates ice. Solid, but capable of being liquid. Horatio is like that now as he angles his body toward her, and she doesn't look at him because she knows that he's on to her. That he'll flush her out.

Castor Oil

H ORATIO DOESN'T HAVE TIME TO ask Clemmie questions about
Philae. She prays for a distraction, some kind of intervention, and
the answer comes with the sound of splashing, the creak of wood. Is it
another *dahabeeyah*, perhaps? Have they got a neighbor mooring
alongside them? Or is someone boarding?

Oswald tells the women to stay inside, loading his shotgun. All three
men head onto the deck, stretching themselves to their full heights,
filling out their chests and shoulders. Fear infiltrates Clemmie's lungs,
leaving little room for oxygen. Perched on the piano stool, Celia drums
her fingers on its wooden leg. They share a look of mild concern, both
thinking of Rhoda. Perhaps, also, of Philae. Burying the amulet on the
island wasn't illegal, was it? Would that count as tampering? Surely not.

There are voices, but the blood in her ears has a way of masking
words, so that all she can hear is noise. Clemmie almost jumps up from
her chair to join the men, but she's afraid of stirring, of missing anything important in the rustle of her skirts. She keeps still and waits.
Listens.

At last, the three men, joined by Khalil and Youssef, reenter the saloon.

That's when she smells it. Not Youssef's pipe—she's grown accustomed to that. The unmistakable odor snakes around the room, perme-

ating everything at once. Reminding her of Rhoda, the pressure of a chair trapping her, the warmth of blood on her hands. She can't forget the smell of castor oil.

It curls beneath her nose now, laced with a whiff of nightfall. The men settle back into their chairs, Youssef and Khalil still standing, and she tries to read their expressions. Oswald unconcerned, Rowland attentive, Horatio alert, Youssef sucking his *chibouk* with a vehemence that's unsettling. Khalil snorts, unimpressed. That's when she sees him. A man emerging from behind the *dragoman*.

He wears what appear to be expensive clothes, the robes of a businessman, a turban on his head. He plants himself in the room, and his single eye is energetic as it sums up the travelers, landing on Clemmie. The other eye is covered by a strip of leather, and she wonders at the level of damage beneath, inflicted by her own hand. He grins at her, knowing that she knows.

She wants to say: *It's you!*

But she doesn't. Maybe it's the evening that makes her wary, or the way Horatio is acting, one moment watching her, the next glaring at the newcomer, annoyed at the intrusion. Instead, she speaks calmly. Surprised at how composed her voice is, how the words slip out easily on the oiled air.

"What's all this about?"

"Apparently he has something to sell," Rowland says, resting the end of his cigar in an ashtray.

"Sell. Yes, yes," the man cries in English, tapping his fingers together eagerly. He walks the curve of travelers and stands first before Rowland, then Celia, Oswald, Horatio, and finally, before her. Khalil observes with arms folded across his chest, a knowing frown on his face. Youssef puffs harder.

"A mummy," the man says. "I sell beautiful mummy. It is wrapped and ready to go into collection, to unroll, to go back to your England."

Clemmie blanches. He has some nerve, trying to make customers out of them when she's certain he's the man who tried to steal from them with his gang of bandits. Unless he isn't a bandit at all. In which case, why did he creep onto *Hapi* at Rhoda?

"Very cheap. I give you special price. Two hundred pound."

Oswald splutters with outrage. "Two hundred? I could let a town house in South Kensington for a whole year with that sort of money."

"Very rare. Very popular. You say no, I find fifty other buyer."

He's a shrewd seller, and no doubt he's right. When something is faked, the value of what's genuine goes up. Mariam's told her about some dealers who make the corpses of criminals and the poor look like ancient mummies. Apparently, the market is so popular that sellers can't meet Europe's demand. Thus the price goes ever higher. Clemmie's seen the greed on people's faces when they witness these unearthed bodies, viewing them as something otherworldly. No doubt many would be willing to take the mummy off his hands. This is wrong, though. To be bartering over human remains under the cover of night.

How did he get it? If he comes at this hour, in this way, it's unlikely he has a license to dig. She tells him that they're not interested.

"Now wait just a minute." Rowland puts out a hand to stop her. The seller's face, which had momentarily fallen, broadens into a smile again.

Once, she might have been excited. She wouldn't even have thought about the humanity of this, merely picturing another specimen to grow the collection. Yet this isn't a piece of broken pottery or a papyrus that they're being offered. It's the remains of a person, a person who was once laid to rest, like her father and mother in the Essex churchyard. She'd just as soon see them dug up and sold.

"You want two hundred for it?" Rowland asks.

"Yes, yes. Two hundred."

"Don't buy it." Clemmie's voice cuts faster than a butcher's cleaver, fingers turning to ice. Her palms are beaded with sweat. Bile gathers in her throat.

She has to do something. The night of the unwrapping, maybe she could have translated the amulet faster, before the two heads were revealed. If she hadn't lost her temper and been disrespectful to her father, then the twins might never have been cut apart. Perhaps she should have taken the scalpel from her father's hands, wrested it from his grip and thrown it through the window. What if? What if! *What if.*

Tonight, she won't add to her list of regrets. Clemmie stands abruptly, knowing the man before her as the villain he is. She isn't sure why he attacked her at Rhoda, nor why he's been haunting the Nile on his bay mare, stalking her movements. Neither can she guess why he's here now. A reminder? A warning? A threat? Whichever it is, she won't be cowed by him.

She herds the dealer away. "We don't care for your type of business," she declares in English before repeating it all in Arabic. "Get off our boat and don't come back."

Khalil is impressed, she can tell from his expression. Youssef too, nodding and grinning broadly. The man is unwilling to go, though, and before he disappears completely, he addresses the other travelers. An invitation.

"I don't go far. You want me, I find you."

She ushers him onto the deck with more speed, feeling the eyes of her companions on her back as she watches the man go. Needing to be sure that he does disembark.

At the low end of the deck, he turns just before stepping across the plank. She can see a silhouette of a waiting horse ashore. Hears the impatient stamp of a hoof muffled by sand. The moon depicts the man's movements, his mouth a crescent of his own, and he tugs at the leather on his face. Clemmie can only imagine the scarring, the cloudiness beneath, and knows that his subtle movement is a message. He knows exactly who she is, that she did that to him. His final words echo in her head.

I find you.

The dealer's smile is no longer a smile but a set of teeth that remains in her vision, even after he's gone.

Tuat

IF DREAMS ARE PREMONITIONS, THEN hers is one tonight. Clemmie's mind reaches the end of Nephthys's tale, traveling alongside Osiris on *Mesektet,* the Night Barque that passes through the underworld. She sinks into the darkness of slumber. Into the darkness of a realm within a realm.

Across the mountains, through a murky valley with a river running by, here the monsters lurk. They hide in caves that are unseen until too late, darting from sepulchral mouths. They slide through crevices, breath appearing mere moments before they do. A ghost of their existence, warning of what's to come.

To harness the darkness, to defeat the monsters, you have to get close enough to touch them. Even then, knowing that the dark can't be eliminated entirely. Darkness is a battle that light strives with each day.

That's what she, as Nephthys, thinks as she travels by these mountain ranges. As she sees the creatures stirring in the shadows. As she watches Apep, that dreaded serpent of darkness who tries night after night to prevent the sun from rising, gliding toward his archenemy Ra.

Apep is huge, scales shining. Wounds that will never heal seep gore, leaving a trail that feeds the ground. Knives protrude from his body, one for each time Ra has battled with him. They've fought every night for more years than they can number, and they'll continue to do so. That's what it is to battle the darkness.

Here, there's a whole underworld waiting for a mistress, this place called *Tuat*. It calls to her blood, telling her that she can have a purpose here. That she can make a difference.

The dream ends abruptly, and Clemmie wants to know more. Wants to discover that unknown realm. To grasp what such a place might mean, and how Nephthys might have been mistress of the underworld: controlling the darkness, avoiding the monsters, caring for the sibling she loved, protecting the dead, and bringing about good.

Has she slept for five hours or five minutes? It's hard to tell. Her cabin is dark, and Sphinx growls softly at her feet, in a dream of her own. The night whispers, or the things that live in the darkest hours do. She listens more closely to the rustle of shadows, that wispy, smoky sound that can almost be touched and yet remains shapeless. It hardens to something with substance, something beyond the night, and she strains to pick up the threads of a voice, to weave them together to make words.

It comes from outside. Whether outside her cabin, or out on the deck, or even on the bank, she's not sure. She pulls her nightgown off and, not bothering with her corset, squeezes into some clothes. The buttons don't fully fasten without her torso cinched in, her chemise no doubt showing at the back through the open flaps of her blouse, but she doesn't have time. She opens her cabin door, grimacing when it squeaks, and shuts it carefully behind her. With quiet haste she heads along the corridor for the saloon, stuffing the loose ends of her blouse into her waistband as she goes. Once there, she stops by the door that leads to the deck. Holds her breath. Listening to a voice that is all too familiar.

"Look, I need to build a full collection. Can you help me or not?"

She waits for an answer, and can only presume one is made by the nod or shake of a head. More whispering. Indistinct. The edge of an accent. Castor oil still lingers in the room from earlier, like one of *Tuat's* waiting monsters. There's movement outside, a sense of the interaction ending, and she creeps to the window. Sees a figure heading toward the edge of the boat, a single lantern in his hand. Footsteps sound outside the door, and she crouches down by the pianoforte, hoping her shape won't be spotted among the shadows of the room.

Afraid that her eyes will gleam and give her away, she squeezes them shut, letting her ears be her vision. Hearing the person's tread—a step, then a drag—as they cross the room and disappear into their cabin. When she's certain that she's alone again, she runs on her toes onto the lower deck. She didn't bother to put shoes on, and maybe it's just as well, for it lends a silence to her movements.

Up ahead, there's a little light. High up, taller than a man. It could be mistaken for a firefly, but judging from what she's just heard, and by the events of the evening, she believes it's a lantern, lighting the path of the mummy dealer she wounded back at Rhoda as he rides his horse away from the *dahabeeyah*.

Why would Rowland be foolish enough to do business with someone like that? For that's who she heard, whispering on the deck, shuffling back through the saloon. Rowland Luscombe, the man who asked her to be his partner in Egyptology.

"*Ya aanesa* Clemmie."

She jumps at the suddenness of the whisper, but she knows the voice and feels for Mariam's hand. They squeeze each other.

"He was here again," Mariam says. "The man from earlier."

"I know. I'm going to follow him."

Mariam shakes her head. "It's too dangerous. Let me wake my father. He will act as a guardian."

"No, don't do that. Your father will only stop me from going."

"Then let me go with you. I know this man. I have suspected him of illegal dealing for a long time, but I have never been as sure as I am now."

Clemmie has endangered Mariam once already at Philae. How can she risk her safety a second time?

"No, I should go alone."

"It is dangerous. I don't think it is safe for you to go."

"Don't you want to know where he operates? If I follow him, I can find out. Besides which, he was one of the men who boarded the *dahabeeyah* at Rhoda. I need to know why."

"Then I am going with you," Mariam insists.

Something catches the moonlight, gleaming from Mariam's hand. A

228 RACHEL LOUISE DRISCOLL

kitchen knife. Clemmie hears her own breathing increase, Mariam's matching hers. By following the dealer, they'll be entering the den of smugglers and thieves.

"Very well," Clemmie says.

She hoists up her skirts, putting aside fears of crocodiles, serpents, and other lurking monsters of the Osirian hour. Stepping across the plank, the two women leave the *dahabeeyah* behind them.

Nephthys entered *Tuat* to take control of that dark realm. As Clemmie scrambles up the bank, keeping her eyes on the dancing speck of light and glad of Mariam's presence and knife, she enters an underworld of her own.

Apep

T HIS IS THE TORTUGA OF mummy dealers, a world of nocturnal
  activity. She doesn't know where they are, can only just make this
place out as they pass by shapes of tents, darting past lit shelters and
campfires, ducking behind crates, jumping at voices. It doesn't seem to
be a village, at least nothing like the ones she's come across along the
Nile thus far. The feel is more temporary. Nomads, perhaps? Or, quite
possibly, an excavation site?

They marched after the glare of the man's lantern, rocking rhythmi-
cally from atop his horse, but now Clemmie is unsure where the light
has vanished to and what to do next. They just keep going, the viscid
darkness lending them invisibility.

For years she's lived in fear, so where has this courage come from?
Promising herself that she'll find answers for the dealer's attack at
Rhoda, she follows her sixth sense.

Shadows hang between tents like sable laundry left to dry. They
gather here, they saunter there, always just a whisper away. Are there
ghosts of pharaohs and their slaves in these parts, and if so, would they
deal kindly with her? Which is worse to meet in the dark: the living, or
the dead?

A dog starts barking, a deep, throaty sound, as they pass by one tent.
They scurry away, afraid of discovery. An entrance flap is thrust aside, a

pocket of light pervading the night, and they duck low among some woven baskets, hoping to avoid detection. Mariam lifts a finger to her lips. The flap closes again, the light inhaled with it. Clemmie releases a shuddering breath.

Where has he gone? She turns her head, using all her senses trying to detect what's hidden by the darkness. Orange fires send sparks fizzing into the sky, and flickering patterns across their arms. Something brushes Clemmie's shoulder, but maybe it was just her own hair, loose and tickling. A scratch on her feet, but it's probably only the sand.

The air is thick with beer, campfire smoke, and the earthiness of cooked lentils. Her head battles with itself. They should go back, she knows they should—but without a light, which way would they go? Could Mariam direct them through the desert in the dark? What else, then, but to investigate this place, to find answers, and then to return to the *dahabeeyah* when dawn comes. For she must find answers. Why did this snake, this Apep-man, come for her in the first place, and what has made him track her all the way to Nubia?

Mariam points toward the last tent in the compound, and together they move, catlike, toward it. This is the largest of the dwellings, and it's here that an equine silhouette is tied, shaking a long neck. A nearby campfire lights the horse enough for Clemmie to see her flicking sand with a pointed foreleg. Everything about the mare speaks of her Arabian hot-bloodedness. Her pastern forms the perfect pointe, digging beneath her. Ears that curl subtly inward are pricked for sound; she'd even hear a scorpion bend its tail to sting its prey. The campfire turns her coat penny-colored, worthy of bearing the Queen's head.

The mare senses them. She pauses her digging. A soft whicker vibrates through her muzzle. Clemmie reaches out a hand, approaching at the shoulder so that the horse can see her. The coat is warm, dusty, alive, nostrils hot and moistening her palm. She hadn't realized she missed Bickmore's stables until this moment.

Someone inside the tent is humming. Having won the mare's affection, Clemmie crouches by the canvas and feels the presence on the other side, knowing that nothing but fabric parts them. She hears footsteps within. An indulgent yawn.

"We should go," Mariam whispers in her ear. "It isn't safe."

Clemmie shakes her head and edges, slowly, so slowly, until she is by the entrance. There is a strip of light where the tent flaps don't quite meet, and she presses her eye against the slit. She can't see much—the flaps are almost kissing—but the room beyond is lit. A dirt floor wears a rug that has seen better days. A pacing body periodically blocks the light and narrow ribbon of view. Whoever is inside is restless. Mulling over something. Or possibly waiting. For what? For whom? Mariam joins her, and Clemmie feels each of her friend's rapid breaths fanning her hair.

The mare kicks over her bucket, water reaching Clemmie's toes. It makes a clattering noise that in turn causes the person within to pause. She stiffens. Has he spotted her? Are they found out? What would happen if they were discovered? What might a man like that do to them? Despite the knowledge of Mariam's knife bolstering her courage, she doesn't intend to find out. They both scramble onto their feet and to the side, just in time.

The flap is flung wide, light throwing a yellow pool onto the dust. A shadow cuts it. They press their bodies flush to the canvas wall. His shadow solidifies into a silhouette and he moves to the left. She can just about see the gleam of his garments, the way the light from the hut glances off his robe and turban. As he moves, she catches a glimpse of a darker shade at his face, a line of shadow that she knows to be the leather eye patch circling his skull. Castor oil oozes from him, like the gore from Apep's wounds. She glances at Mariam and sees her friend grimly nod.

It's him. They've found the right place.

He murmurs gently and pats the mare on the rump before picking up the bucket and heading to a barrel. As he works, wooing his mare with soft words, she sees only his back or the side of his face. Once he is through, when he turns around to enter his abode, he'll be facing them. They could run now, around the side of the tent. Mariam nudges her and jerks her head at a stack of packing cases across from them, which Clemmie can only presume hold or will end up holding excavated relics. They could dart across the site to hide by the coffin-sized boxes while his back is turned. There's one further option, but it's ludicrous.

Maybe there really is a madness in her family, for while sanity screams to choose one of the first options, curiosity wins over survival.

She starts to move toward the opening, seeing Mariam's eyes widen with the realization of what she is about to do, furiously shaking her head. Clemmie gestures for Mariam to stay where she is, and dives inside the open entryway. Relieved to see another pile of crates, she ducks behind it.

Once here, she doesn't know what to do next. Any minute, he'll come in. The crates are made of slats hammered across more slats, small gaps between providing a convenient way for her to spy without emerging. She looks around her, hemmed in by boxes of all descriptions, and lifting the lid off one of the smaller ones at her back, observes that they seem to be full of papers. It's like an office of sorts, one that can be packed up easily and moved around from site to site. This, then, is the man's study. Where the dealer circles his maps, totals his figures, and sets his prices.

The Apep-man has finished talking to the mare, but he doesn't re-enter. She can hear him humming, a faint, haunting tune that makes her shudder. Mariam doesn't follow her inside either, keeping watch from without. When Clemmie has waited and waited, counted to thirty, then sixty, she allows herself to move. Remaining behind the empty crates, she keeps her head low, expecting his one-eyed face to appear at the open tent flap. It doesn't. She scans his quarters. On a nearby table lies a bowl of dates, untouched. A cup of beer, smelling sickly sweet.

She pulls out some of the papers from the box. They're more organized than her father's study back at home, easier to make sense of. Numbers, tallies, expenses—this must be a collection of his accounts.

Still no sign of the man returning. She can hear the scuffing of his feet, impatient and bored. Tobacco fills the air, smoke snaking into the tent. Clemmie wonders if she should run out while she can. Maybe his delay is a gift, an opportunity to escape. Surely she'd be seen, though, and then what?

She reaches out cold fingers, lifting the lid off the next box. This one reveals a stash of candles and English-made lucifers. She pockets one of the candles along with a packet of matches. They might help her and Mariam get back to *Hapi* without waiting for daylight.

On to the next box, she uncovers stack upon stack of papers tied with string. More accounts. She's about to replace the lid when her eye catches on something, the handwriting leaving her spellbound. Her heart pounds so violently that her chest hurts and a wheeze scratches her throat. Salt blurs her vision and she blinks, pulling the paper from its place and unfolding it.

It's a letter. The year etched in the corner bears numbers that make her feel old, even if it wasn't that long ago.

1886

An agreement of sorts. As she reads on, she can see that the purpose of the communication is to arrange for the procurement of a specimen. An insistence that the mummy should be kept intact. The wrappings undisturbed. A date by which it'll be required. An assurance that the payment will be made as per their usual terms.

She traces the arc of the hand, what first caught her attention, the leaning slope where the t's are crossed, the fervent blot of each punctuation mark where the pen was pressed in deeply. A pattern in the penmanship that she can almost hear, that scratch of nib so familiar. It brings the past back to her, screaming in her ears at her own naïvety.

At the bottom, the writer has signed his name eloquently.

Dr. Clement Attridge

Discoveries

WHEN THEY UNROLLED THE MUMMY, they thought they knew what to expect, but they never could have predicted what was waiting beneath the layers. A rare amulet. Two heads. A hieroglyphic warning. Now she knows that her father had two heads as well. And that is the root of her family's troubles.

She almost gasps, but catches herself in time. This letter from him, here in this place, it's staggering. She sways at the revelation and the meaning it holds. Her father smuggled illegally procured antiquities to build his collection. The same collection that Clemmie inherited was acquired by illicit means. To his clients, his audience, his own family, he was a learned historian and ardent follower of Egyptology, but beneath his reputation and renown, he was willingly involved in a trade of destruction and disrespect, one that has harmed those same artifacts he claimed to hold dear.

Furthermore, her father did business with the very man who tried to attack her.

Before she can truly comprehend what this means, as a whole host of fresh questions surges through her mind, a dreadful silence interrupts her thoughts. She realizes that the smell of smoked tobacco has disappeared and the shuffling has paused. Her head snaps toward the entry, but there's no one looking in. Maybe the man has stopped to refill his pipe. To take a stroll through the shadows. Or has he spotted Mariam?

"You came."

She recognizes the voice of the mummy dealer. He's been waiting for someone, then, and she glances around her, knowing that he's likely to come inside. To welcome his guest. She should have run when she had the chance. Now she'll have to hide and pray that she isn't seen, or that Mariam is able to get help.

Crouching as low as she can, she hugs her knees to her. The shock of the letter has made her wheeze. A cough grates in her throat and she tries to inhale slowly and silently to regulate her breathing. Nestling the letter in the safety of her cleavage, she isn't sure if she wants to preserve this evidence or burn it.

Her father worked with thieves. No wonder they're cursed.

Footsteps enter the tent. A shuffling from Apep, as she thinks of him now, and then the heaviness of boots. An Englishman? She thinks of *Hapi,* of the voices that disturbed her dreams. Rowland.

But the voice that cuts through the tent, filling every crevice and chilling her to the bone, is not that of her traveling companion. Instead, she hears a voice that's just as familiar as the penmanship of the letter.

Horatio is loud and assured when he speaks. "What the devil were you playing at? Coming to the boat like that was a damned risk. I never gave you permission."

"I work for myself. I do not need your permission."

"You work for me."

"With you. Not for you. For years I watch you foreigners make money off my country. Why should I not have my share in this trade? You would not even have an interest in this amulet if I had not provided the mummy it came with."

"I know where the amulet is. She's buried it on an island called Philae."

"Philae? Where on Philae?"

"Well, I don't know. Just on the island, *somewhere.* You'll have to dig."

"You need to pay."

"Don't you trust me after all these years?"

"I follow her. I tell you where she is. This is different work than my usual trade, and you never ask me to do work like this for you before. Get you mummies, yes. Hunting a woman? My price has gone up and you need to pay."

"But you didn't get the damned amulet, did you? I'll pay you when you finish your job."

Clemmie squeezes her mouth shut with her hand.

"Where? You tell me where, and then I dig."

She can barely see between the crates, she's too busy holding herself still. Trying to stay unseen and unheard. Even if she can't see clearly, she hears the slap of skin against skin, the scuffle of feet as someone is shoved backward.

"Dig up the whole damned island for all I care. You failed to get the amulet before she buried it, so I won't pay you one penny until you've found it."

"What so special about this amulet? I get you another."

"You're not paid to ask questions."

"I have special site here. New tomb we found. Many mummies and amulets. You have half price. As many mummies you want. Yes?"

This time, pottery breaking. Bone hitting bone. Can Mariam hear this forceful exchange? Even if Clemmie doesn't dare to look, she can picture it. Horatio pushing Apep against the tent pole, a ready fist and hot breath in his face.

"I want that amulet!"

"And the woman?"

"What about her?"

"She did this to me."

"Bested by a woman? That's starting not to surprise me."

Her toes curl against the cold, hard floor. She once liked Horatio. Liked him because he was the charming addition to their family. Then he took her place. First coming between her and Rosetta, and then her father and Horatio spent more and more time together in the study. Whispering. Frowning if she dared to enter. Her father's arm slung across Horatio's shoulders. The look of pride in his eyes.

"Well? The woman?"

"I need her. Her father was a fool. I thought I'd persuaded him to leave me everything, but he stupidly left the treasure to her."

There's a strange sound, and she realizes Apep is laughing. It's a cackle. Mocking. Horatio won't like that at all.

"You kill him for nothing. That very funny. That very, very funny."

Her heart stops. It must do, for something around her shifts. There's a dull, thumping sound, and she dares to peer between the slats.

Horatio has Apep by the throat. He throws his head against the table. Once, twice, more times than she cares to count. Apep's single eye lolls back, and she thinks Horatio's going to kill him, thinks she might be sick, but then he stops. Takes his hand away. Apep rolls to the floor like an eel, and Horatio watches him for a few seconds before marching out into the darkness.

Apep doesn't move. Neither does Clemmie. She's paralyzed from the recent violence echoing in her head, and beyond that, the man's words.

You kill him for nothing.

Unwrapping

1891

Bᴇғᴏʀᴇ Cʟᴇᴍᴍɪᴇ ᴍᴀᴋᴇs ɪᴛ ᴛᴏ her sister's room for a farewell, she staggers to her knees. An invisible blow dealt her, wringing the air from her being. Maybe she's already too late. Too late to say her goodbyes. Too late to return the amulet to Egypt. Too late to break the curse.

She splutters through the attack, trying to remember where she left her bottle of eucalyptus. Her eye falls on it, perched on the dressing table, and she crawls. One hand in front of the other. Her back arching with every cough. Convinced that this is it, that she'll never make it. Each breath is surely her last.

But she does arrive, pulling herself up with the will of a woman not to be beaten. If not for herself, then for her sister. She pulls the cork from the bottle, spilling eucalyptus over the floor and her hands and focusing on inhaling every drop. So much has been taken from her, but she will fight for what's left.

That's what this is all about. The taking of artifacts, the taking of liberties, and the taking of her loved ones in return. Now the time has come to give.

Her breathing eases, slowly, so slowly. The fatigue crushing, leaving her leaden. A pile of stones she's swallowed, dragging her down into an abyss she hasn't even known was there.

She rests on the floor, in the stain of spilled eucalyptus, aware that she has to pick herself up, to go, to say her goodbyes. This attack lasted longer than any she's had yet. Rosetta's mania is worsening. The sisters are the only two of their family left, and they're getting weaker as the curse gets stronger.

They're running out of time and it's up to her to save them.

Threats

THE CANDLE IS BURNING LOW, and Apep still hasn't moved. Clemmie has been waiting for what feels like forever. It's possibly only been a few minutes. Horatio is probably returning to the *daha-beeyah*. He'll be ahead of her, so if she goes now, hopefully she won't cross paths with him. She'll have to move soon if she doesn't want Mariam to get help. What if she already has? It wouldn't do for Horatio to find out where she's been and what she's learned.

In the time she's been sitting here, she's tried to comprehend her discoveries. As she considers the constricting truth snaking around her, it all makes sense. The inheritance. Horatio's intimacy with Clement, like son and father, shutting her out. Cutting her off. Or that's what he thought. He got the estate, just as he wanted. But he didn't get the five human mummies, the embalmed cats, dogs, snakes, or even an ibis that she once pretended was the actual *Bennu* bird, and the numerous amulets. *The* amulet. She comprehends more clearly now that together the mummy of the twins and the amulet were her father's most valuable possessions besides the house.

You kill him for nothing.

She pictures Horatio visiting her father's sickbed. Leaning over him. Taking up the pillow in his hands. Pushing it over her father's face, then assembling the scene so that no one would suspect. Is that how it happened? They never questioned it when he came out of the room, his eyes wild, telling them to come quickly. That he feared it was all over.

And her mother? Sickened, she thinks of finding her body on the floor. A freak accident, she'd presumed. Yet she recalls that Horatio had left the sisters by the Chelmer, supposedly heading to the stables. Did he stop at the house first? Did he kill the woman whose existence kept him from inheriting Bickmore?

It was Horatio all along. How can she comprehend this, after all she has been through? Was he some kind of instrument of the curse? No, she sees now that the glyphs could indeed be harmless, as she first thought. An unusual funerary text, that's all. Was there ever reason to fear the amulet's words? Has she been haunted by nothing more than superstitions founded on gothic fictions and spurred by cruel circumstances? Clarity filters through her mind, both a release and a burden. Not a hieroglyphic malediction, then. Horatio is her family's curse.

Mariam's face appears at the opening and Clemmie stands to reveal her hiding place. Her friend beckons her over but Clemmie isn't sure if she can command her limbs to work. She casts one final glance at the body on the floor. Apep's hand has twitched a few times, so she knows he's alive. She even heard him groan once, and now she's afraid he might revive and find her.

The woman. She did this to me.

She inches her way out from behind the crates, her feet numb, one of her legs prickling its way back to life. The tent flap is restless in the gathering breeze, urging her to go, and she heads for it. Mariam's expression tells her to hurry.

Behind her, there's a gurgle, and while a part of her wants to run, she turns and looks back.

Apep lifts his head slightly. A line of blood runs down his forehead, coursing down either side of his one good eye and making him scrunch up his face. He's reaching out his hand toward her, and she's torn between revulsion and pity.

Between his bleeding gums comes a rasp of a voice. A voice that chills the way the monsters of *Tuat* do when they gather in the shadows, in the mountains and ravines, ready to attack.

"He will kill you when he finish with you." The man's breath is a rattle. The hiss of a snake ready to strike. "And if not, I kill you myself."

PART THREE

Blood

I am dying, Egypt, dying!

Ebbs the crimson life-tide fast,

And the dark Plutonian shadows

Gather on the evening blast.

— WILLIAM HAINES LYTLE, *Antony and Cleopatra*

I have come to hew in pieces. I am not hewn in pieces, nor
will I suffer thee to be hewn in pieces. I have come to do
violence, but I will not let violence be done unto thee,
for I am protecting thee.

— The Flame of Nephthys, *The Book of the Dead*

Unwrapping

1891

THE WINDOW IS DRAPED WITH lace, setting patterns on the walls as the light infiltrates the baroque swirls. The sill has been turned into a seat of sorts, and perched on that is Rosetta. Her blond hair is tangled and undressed. Gnawed, peeling fingers prize the curtain apart to look out of the window. The view beyond? Trees. The Chelmer. A child's imagined Nile.

Clemmie's heart bursts with love for her, but, as is the case when things rupture, she's also seized with pain. She clasps the locket at her throat, lifts it to kiss the engraving.

No one else hath loved thee more than I.

Rosetta turns, and in her dilated pupils and cold sneer, Clemmie fails to see the woman she once knew. The one she called her sister.

"You dare to show your face?"

Is this a reproach for preparing to go to Egypt? For leaving her? No. She knows that it isn't. For it is the scripted line from a childhood game. A game in which Clemmie would wait for a jealous sister to confront her.

Now standing, Rosetta could be seen as something immortal the way the sun glances on her. How it makes her glow. A delta of veins marbles her wide gray eyes. Her movements are slow at first, but punctuated at the end with a sudden violence. First a graceful step forward, then a hasty rubbing of the hands. Next a creeping smile, then the burst of a mirthless laugh rocking her head uncontrollably.

"You stole him from me."

"I stole no one," she argues.

"Osiris is mine!"

They're close enough now that Rosetta's spit showers on Clemmie's face. Rosetta pulls herself taller, the haughty lift of her chin shrinking Clemmie down to the size she was when they used to play the game for fun.

"You'd do well to remember who you speak to, Nephthys. Last-born. Husband stealer. I am the powerful one. I am the wife of Osiris."

Here, once, she would have responded: *We are both daughters of Seb and Nut. Both of us the sisters of Osiris and Set. And I can change my form into that of a kite, just like you.*

But she holds her tongue, because while she usually doesn't mind what people think, she very much cares now. She lets her sister continue and thinks of the ship that will soon take her away from all of this. Her heart floods with guilt. Is she running?

"It is I whom Osiris clung to in the womb. It is I whom he married. It is I you have betrayed. Do you even remember who you're speaking to?" Rosetta jabs her fingers into her breastbone, each word punctuated by the striking of her bosom. "I. Am. Isis."

"I have come to say goodbye," she says, but Rosetta begins to circle around her. Ignoring her words.

"What do you have to offer me, Nephthys? What excuse? What penance?"

How did she once answer in the game of Myths? Didn't she pass a feather over as a token of the shape-shifting magic of Nephthys, to show that she was willing to give a piece of herself to make up for what she'd done? She has no feather to make peace between them. In her pocket she has but her bottle of eucalyptus. Only able to offer her love, she opens her arms.

Rosetta assesses her, turning her head slowly, her body swaying to imagined music—the songs of Isis and Nephthys, perhaps. She takes a step closer, considering the proposed embrace.

The two sisters, in such close proximity, are so nearly a whole. Clemmie thinks of how Isis and Nephthys were restored in their story. Mightn't the same happen for them?

She's so busy in her thoughts, she never sees her sister reach out her hand to grasp the locket at her throat. Only hears the snap of the chain, sees the look of cold disdain as Rosetta tosses it to the ground.

Her heart breaks along with the metal links.

Murderer

THE DESERT'S FACE IS WRINKLED, bearing the pockmarks of strangers. A lifetime of scars that the sand tries to erase, though it never succeeds. Now two fresh trails run tear marks down this land's cheek. Clemmie staggers as Mariam pulls her along, trying to run, but making little progress. The sand is drawing her down, pulling at her feet, pawing.

At last, she can go no further. As the sky pales, she heaves up her lungs, along with all the pent sorrow within her, and howls. She is jackal-headed Anubis crying for his mother. She is lamenting Isis, weeping over a hideous murder. She is Nephthys, bruised Nephthys, aching from hurts caused by someone close.

Mariam is at her side, holding her close. The way Etta used to comfort her. Clemmie clings on, her face burrowed in the hollow beneath Mariam's clavicle. No need for words. Even if Mariam didn't hear what the men said in the tent, she seems to understand that Clemmie cannot utter the dreadful things she has learned.

Horatio is a murderer. Her father is dead because of him. No doubt her mother is too. She's starting to realize what he's capable of. Her cries are cracked with wheezes, strewn with coughs. Broken, just as she is.

"Come," Mariam says at last. "We must get you back to the *dahabeeyah*."

It is a blessing that Mariam is here, else Clemmie would be lost. Which way is the Nile?

Grit finds the wet of her cheeks, forming a second skin. How can she ever face Horatio again? She can see it all as it must have happened. Horatio discovering that she'd left the cottage, racing to her room and knowing what was missing, putting two and two together. Contacting Apep to track her down. Of course, it all makes sense now. She'd wondered how Horatio had found her in such a vast place.

In her heart, she still doesn't quite know what to think. Whether the amulet is her curse, or if Horatio is. If it wasn't bad enough discovering that her father's—no, *her* collection of antiquities—was gained by illicit means, that when her father and Horatio shut her out it was because they were dealing with a market that shouldn't even exist, then beyond that, the loss of her parents has been raked up afresh and turned all the more bitter.

It's almost light when, in her dazed wanderings, she sees the coil of the Nile and their lone *dahabeeyah* waiting for them. *Hapi* is a beacon of hope, but it also holds the man she dreads and despises. Would the others believe her if she told them that Horatio is a murderer? She has no actual proof, only an eavesdropped conversation. Would he tell her companions about Etta and make them think that she's as mad as her sister, just as he persuaded them to believe that she's his intended? He has such a way with words, his uniform inspires confidence and respect. Won't they trust him rather than the woman who was crazy enough to creep onto Philae in the middle of the night?

She wants to confront Horatio herself, to tell him that she's found him out, but if she lets on to him what she overheard, who knows what he'll do to her? Yet how can she keep it from her face? How can she spend a moment in the company of the man who murdered her parents?

When they are nearing the bank, Mariam stops Clemmie.

"What will you do now?"

"I've seen written proof that the dealer is unlicensed. He is dangerous," Clemmie says. "Horatio is too."

Mariam nods. "I could tell the soldier was a bad man from the anger in his voice. You are at risk."

"It's . . . worse than I thought."

"Do you think the soldier saw you?"

Clemmie shakes her head. Apep did, but not Horatio.

"We can report them. We can stop them, *ya aanesa* Clemmie."

Exhaustion takes over, and Clemmie stumbles.

"You need food," Mariam says. She tries to help Clemmie toward the boat, but struggles to support her reeling form. "Wait here."

Still clutching her knife, she hurries back to the *dahabeeyah*.

Murderer. That's all Clemmie can think. She's sat with her parents' murderer. She's talked with him. Been kissed by him. Once, she even liked him. Acid sears her throat.

Her arms coil around herself, despite the day already getting warm. Her clothes stick to her skin. The wind blows strands of her chopped hair into her mouth, and she gives up on swiping them away. Too dizzy to move, she digs a hole in the sand with her toes.

There's a vague movement on the deck, and as she sways, she almost doubles over in terror. Is it *him*? If Horatio sees her, he'll know she went to the village, that she heard him talking to Apep. He'll kill her too.

The figure raises a hand. It edges forward across the plank, reaching the bank. Slow and cumbersome at first. Then picking up speed.

She only allows herself to fall when he's within reach. Rowland's hands are there, keeping her from dropping to her knees as her cheek brushes his shirt. The contact makes the sand on her face cut in. Everything burns.

Priceless

S HE SEES IT IN HIS eyes, the fear of something that hasn't happened. As she looks down at herself in the gathering light, she's
aware of what an image she must present. Her blouse tucked in but
unbuttoned at the back, falling loose and revealing her shoulder.

He cups her face in his hand, and his thumb is surprisingly gentle as
he brushes away the sand. It makes her want to cry again, but she dams
her emotions for now. What if Horatio hears?

"Is he there?"

"Who?" His forehead tightens. His blue eyes are intense, pupils
large and round. Mortified at what he believes has happened.

She whispers the name she fears so much, then presses her finger to
her lips. Urgently. Eyes pleading for his silence.

"He did this?"

She shakes her head. "It's not what it looks like."

He clearly doesn't believe her, so she takes his hand, tugs on his arm.
She can't speak here, in this exposed space. They must go somewhere
else to talk. But where?

You cannot run from curses.

A low moan comes from her mouth and she bites her lip, looking
frantically around her. So much desert, so many rocks. And sand. Sand
everywhere. No place to hide.

"Come with me," he says. "I'll take you to your cabin."

Still holding hands, he guides her toward the *dahabeeyah*. She hesitates before boarding. Rowland is patient with her, allowing her to make up her mind. But she can't do it. Shaking her head, she mouths that name again. He nods that he understands, but he doesn't. How can he when even she's been duped for so long?

He waits, a gesture that moves her more than she can say. Even if she merged all the languages she knows, she couldn't articulate it. Some emotions have yet to be put into words, and are expressed only in hearts, a touch, a look.

"I'll make sure you're safe," he promises.

Safe? The French for that is *sûre*. One of the Latin words is *salvus*. Yet for some time now she hasn't been safe, or sure, or known physical salvation from her calamities.

She allows him to help her onto the deck, because she wants to believe that he's right. That she can be safe again. Even if she's not certain what that is anymore.

All the things Clemmie has ever been convinced of become ruins. They crumble around her, so that she doubts all she knows, everything around her, even herself. If she could be so wrong about Horatio, mightn't she have made other mistakes along the way?

Rowland sits her gently on the edge of her bed, shutting the door to her cabin and offering her water and the bowl of dates and almonds that Mariam provided as they boarded. She sips the water but shakes her head at the food.

He makes to sit beside her, then reconsiders, and squats stiffly in front of her, masking a grimace. Taking her hand and patting it gently. Trying to stir her focus, to bring her from the dreadful place her mind has entered.

You kill him for nothing.

Rowland implores her to tell him what's wrong, his jaw tensing as he readies himself for whatever she might reveal. His voice is kindly, and he insists that she takes her time.

"Horatio has been dealing in illegally sourced relics."

His face is blank. This isn't what he expected. He drops her hand so he's free to move and the mattress shifts as he lowers his weight next to her, making their shoulders brush. It anchors her to the present, helps her find her voice.

"Horatio met with Apep."

"Apep?"

She explains whom she means. Going right back to Rhoda and describing her first encounter with the man.

"He attacked you? Why on earth didn't you say?"

"I didn't want you prying into why a thief might target me. But you know about the amulet now, so it doesn't matter."

He almost smiles. "You nicknamed him after the serpent of darkness?"

Not for the first time, his knowledge catches her off guard, and she thinks of his suggestion of a partnership.

Then she remembers the reason she followed Apep. She was alerted to his presence because Rowland met with him. She bunches her hair behind her neck and turns on Rowland accusingly, demanding what he was doing talking to the smuggler.

Rowland doesn't look abashed. "You know I want to start up a business."

"By illegal means?"

"Yes, I'd be engaging with unscrupulous traders, but only for the greater good. It would save the antiquities. I'd be building a collection that would be looked after respectfully and I could use it to educate others, rather than those same pieces ending up owned by rich enthusiasts who don't know an Eye of Horus from an Eye of Ra. Don't you see?"

She throws her hands in the air, shorn tresses tumbling over her shoulders. "You're the one who doesn't see. Dealing with them will only encourage their trade."

When Rowland told her that he wanted to take relics away from illegal diggers and traders, she hadn't realized that he meant doing business with them in order to do so. She'd never stopped to think about any of this before. At Bickmore, so set apart from the seedy truths of sites like the one she encountered last night, she'd been so blind. Now she's seeing the world of antiquities in a whole new light, and it dazzles uncomfortably. Mariam was right. The preservation of Egypt's heritage must be advanced. It requires more people like Mariam to help conserve what's left. Conservator. The English word is the same as the Latin, meaning defender, keeper, preserver. Has the time come for Clemmie to be a *shâdûf*?

"I found something."

Clemmie tells him then, about her father's letter. How she and Mariam followed Apep in the night and discovered what he kept in his tent. Rowland tries to interrupt, to scold her for endangering herself and the captain's daughter, but she holds her hand up. She must let it all out.

She explains about Horatio and Rosetta's relationship, about the will and the inheritance, filling in the gaps to the story she relayed only recently. Only then does she allow herself to speak the words that still drive the breath from her body.

"Horatio killed my parents."

Rowland stiffens. "What proof do you have?"

"Apep said that Horatio killed my father for nothing. Horatio didn't just want Bickmore. He'd have got that eventually through marrying my sister. What he wanted was my father's collection. He wanted the twins and the amulet."

Something he thought he could get through eliminating her parents who desired the match with Rosetta, and then moving his attention on to Clemmie. The daughter who had what he wanted. She never really thought seriously about all the money that could be made until now. Anyone with an interest in Egyptology would know that such artifacts, especially if paired together, would be priceless.

But Horatio did put a price on them, and that price was blood.

Proof

ROWLAND PACES THE FLOOR OF her cabin, muttering words of revenge. He is angry, raving, as if Horatio had killed his own kin and not hers.

"Please," Clemmie says, pushing herself to stand. "You can't tell anyone. You can't let on that you know."

"And allow him to get away with this?"

"We need evidence. If he knows that we know, then he *will* get away with this. He could get away with more."

He stops pacing. Understanding her meaning. Clemmie is at risk. Horatio could try to silence her, just as he eliminated her father and mother.

"Is the amulet really that valuable?"

She was only ever concerned about the text, but now she stops to ponder its monetary worth. Impressive size, intricate hieroglyphs, and unique design: that of a Double *Tyet* instead of the commonplace single knot. She'd never seen a Double *Tyet* before that night, and hasn't since. And it's plausible that the wording of the hieroglyphs made the amulet a new discovery in the world of Egyptology.

Her father never included her in the accounts. His study was too disorganized for her to make sense of it. She was only ever interested from a scholarly perspective, not one of fame or capital. Yet, being here, she's seen evidence of greed and it's shown her what people will do when avarice sets in.

So yes, it's valuable. And perhaps she's always known it in her heart. That's why she kept it concealed when she brought it here. That's why she hid the twins back at home. Collectors could go mad for the two artifacts together.

Egyptomania.

It's that which has made Horatio's desires insatiable, his hunger for money, the collection, and Bickmore controlling him. Perhaps she can find justice through what Horatio has abused.

"He nearly killed Apep," Clemmie says. "The dealer has every right to hate him. Maybe he'd testify that Horatio told him he killed my father."

She hesitates. Apep also hates her. Why would he do what she asks of him?

"It's worth trying," Rowland says. Besides which, if they return to Apep's excavation site, maybe they can find proof of Horatio's dealings with him, just as she found evidence of Clement's involvement. What they have been doing is a crime and could perhaps get Horatio and Apep arrested. It isn't enough, but it would be a start.

He bundles the dates and almonds in a handkerchief as she slides her feet into some shoes, and they leave her cabin. Rowland presses a finger to his lips and turns the handle to Oswald's door, slipping inside. She waits fretfully, eyes on Horatio's room, afraid that he'll emerge at any moment. The *dahabeeyah* creaks softly. Somewhere, there is a gentle snore. It is a blessing that Rowland is an early riser, that he came to her when she needed him, that he believed her and is prepared to help on this, her latest mission. He is back in the corridor in moments, shutting the door quietly behind him. In his hand is Oswald's shotgun. She's glad he thought of it. They both fill their pockets with cartridges from the box of ammunition as they pass through the saloon.

Clemmie whispers their plans to Mariam on the deck, then asks her to remain behind, keep her ears open, cover for her and Rowland, and distract the others. Mariam agrees, filling a wooden canteen with water and giving it to them. It is nestled in a leather harness, and Rowland hangs it on his shoulder.

"*Yalla,*" Clemmie says to Rowland. Let's go.

Ruins

THE DESERT LETS THEM TRESPASS at a price, the sands bleeding their energy with every step. Rowland's efforts are hampered by his limp, and she fears that the trek will be too much for him. He doesn't complain, though. What made him want to work with her? When do you decide that someone can be trusted?

They keep walking.

Above them, two feathered arcs gyrate. Hard to tell if the birds are guiding or pursuing.

They come across the site more by accident than from Clemmie's skill at directing them. Sandbanks lie in shifting mounds, rocks protruding like sleeping monsters beneath a quilt of gold. Canvas lungs fill with air and deflate. The largest canopy at the end bears the appearance of a king's war tent.

Clemmie and Rowland conceal themselves together behind some rocks, and he rubs his forehead, whispering: "What is the plan?"

She points at the largest tent, but doesn't move. In the young daylight, she feels foolish for even coming here. The site is quiet, no one yet stirring. Almost ghostly. This place doesn't look right, and she isn't sure why until it suddenly comes to her. Apep's horse is gone. It isn't outside his tent. Where could the mare be?

The only evident life is a Nubian ibex as it ambles through the camp, horns curled like an ammonite. Seeing such a creature in the flesh, Clemmie understands the etymology for the fossil, how the word was derived from *cornu Ammonis,* after the ram-headed Egyptian god Amun. A name meaning hidden. It puts her in mind of secrets, of what they must uncover.

Rowland is ready to act, and he moves forward. For just a second, she falters. Apep said he wanted to kill her. What half-wit would go in search of the man who said that? Shaking herself, she hurries after Rowland, knowing that she must see her new quest through. This is no time to be timid.

She joins Rowland at the entrance, and his eyes ask: *Ready?*

Together, they throw the flaps open.

Blood. That is the first thing she sees. Apep's blood has formed a stain on the ground, already brown at the edges. Rowland enters, stooping down. Dipping his fingers into the center, he rubs the stickiness together. Slightly wet. Apep has lain there some time, then, but now he has gone.

"Here."

She leads him to the crates and shows the stacks of boxes. Page upon page naming Apep's buyers. No doubt it could be proved that they do not have the legal permissions for these sales.

"We can't just carry them back to the *dahabeeyah,*" Rowland says. "There are too many."

"One box?"

"Do any of them have Horatio's name on?"

Together they start rifling through, but it's a thankless task. None of these seem to be from Horatio. Just various customers from England, France, even America. She spies a second and third letter from her father, dates preceding the one she read earlier.

"These are old papers," Rowland says, pocketing a few as evidence against Apep. "All the dates are from the last decade. We need something recent."

What they need is the dealer. Has he picked himself up, cleaned his wounds, and carried on? That hardly seems likely. Horatio left him half dead. Maybe one of his companions found him and has carried him to their tent to nurse him. The camp could stir at any moment, although she hopes their nocturnal activity gives them more of a reason to sleep late. There isn't time to go through all the letters until they find an incriminating one from Horatio.

"This is it," Rowland says. "Look."

He passes her a brief chit.

No more artifacts required at present. You will hear from me in the future. I have eliminated the first obstacle. Will keep you informed.
H. Devereux

Rancid saliva clogs her throat as she reads *the first obstacle*. Is Horatio speaking of her father? If so, this could help prove that he killed him.

Rowland squeezes her shoulder and softly suggests that they look around the camp. Reluctantly, she agrees.

Back outside, the sun is almost blinding after the shade of the tent. It is climbing its eastward ladder, pulsating in the sky until she can feel it burning behind her eyes. She scans her surroundings. Everything is so quiet. Something doesn't feel right.

Pressing the find into her pocket, she edges toward a tent. Squaring her shoulders, both she and Rowland nod as they mutely count.

One. Two. Three.

She hopes to see Apep lying inside, but when they toss aside the flap, it is empty. Frowning, she moves on to the next, and the next. All abandoned. Apep's team have gone, cleared out, but they must intend to come back. Either that or they were in a hurry. Where would they go?

Rowland moves toward the outskirts of the camp, and she scurries after him to point out that he's going the wrong way. They need to pass back through the site to find the river.

He's scrambling over the rocks. Pausing. Inspecting them. As she gets closer, she can see that amid the larger heap of rocks, the hilly outcropping is more than just boulders. The smaller ones, and what she thought were discarded crates, have been placed carefully to cover something. So easily missed in this sea of yellow. Her heart quickens.

If this is what she thinks it is, then they're about to uncover a hidden, illegal excavation site. Within, so many possibilities. The antiquities she

260 RACHEL LOUISE DRISCOLL

imagines beneath their very feet are what her heart has learned to crave, but if life has taught her anything, then it's to fear what she also yearns for.

Rowland flashes her a boyish smile. "I think there's a whole parcel of proof right here. What do you say we find out?"

They roll away the rocks and packing cases, sweating, scraping their palms. Their efforts gradually reveal a stone frame of sorts, a jagged crack along the top evidence of either time's wear or man's destruction. She blows, brushing the dust away, and her fingers find carvings that must mean nothing to Rowland, but that speak to her. The raised arms of the *ka*, the ghostly double of the dead. The human-headed bird shape of the *ba*, another spirit-like burial symbol.

"It's a tomb."

They work quicker now, taking short intervals to breathe, assuring each other that they can see the opening, checking that the camp remains silent and still behind them. At last, the wide mouth yawns invitingly.

It's black within. She knows that most tombs would have a slope or steps leading down, but when she tests a foot inside, there is only air beneath her shoe. Squatting, she feels for some kind of way in, her skin catching against rough stone, beading with blood. This isn't the work of the careful architects who once constructed this place. The entrance has been hacked at, mutilated. But with what?

Clemmie considers the inevitable drop, how high up they probably are. What might she land on were she to lower herself in? Human remains? Sharp rocks? An old spear positioned to impale her? That's ridiculous, but she can't help wondering if she's opening herself up to more trouble by invading this sacred ground. Peering into the blackness, the sun vaguely tints what she thinks is the floor. A sizeable drop, but manageable. She casts Rowland a quick glance, and jumps before he can protest. Seeing it in his eye before she disappears: the fear for her safety.

The ground is a slap, sending a sharp jolt through her body. Just a kiss of light from above, and the sand weeps after her, making her splutter. Her arm burns where she caught it on the wrecked entrance as she fell. She runs her hands over the uneven wall, feeling the jagged edges of broken steps that no longer exist. This damage hasn't been caused by time. Man has done this. How did anyone destroy a whole stone staircase?

Rowland calls down, asking if she is all right, and his words echo eerily, giving ten, twenty versions of his voice to the darkness and whatever else is down here with her. She wants to tell him to hurry after her, but she also wants to keep this for herself. She's inside a tomb. An actual tomb. If only she had a light.

That's when she recalls her pickings from Apep's tent, and she rifles through her pocket. A snap of a lucifer, a hiss of a blackened wick, and a small tongue of flame joins her in the tomb. She isn't alone anymore.

A vague glow forms a bubble around her body, and she holds the candle out before her, lifting it up to walls that bear carvings and paintings. Figures from mythology. Glyphs she recognizes with a twist of joy.

Rowland tosses the shotgun through the entry and she catches it clumsily. The sun illuminates the uncertainty on his face, and she assures him that the drop isn't too far, remembering his bad leg too late. He falls, emitting a stifled grunt, and she doesn't know whether it's kinder to ask if he's hurt or to indulge his pride and leave him be. She returns her attention to the chamber they're in, candle in one hand, shotgun tucked under her other arm.

Someone has been here before them. They must have been. Apep and his team have surely already raided the tomb, for along with the crumbled entrance, the room is empty. The walls hint at former dead occupants, bearing scarred images of Anubis, Osiris, Maat's feather, and the sisters, Isis and Nephthys. Indicating what this room once held. All four walls contain symbols of the funerary rites, but there are no corpses or sarcophagi in sight.

Rowland releases a hiss of pain, and she whirls around in surprise. The drop was painful, but she didn't think it that bad. Perhaps it is his old injury. What was it he told her about teaching himself to walk again? What sort of person does it take to defy medical science and expectations? She almost smiles. She knows a thing or two about such things.

"Have you hurt yourself?" She nods toward the mouth, where the ever-brightening day is leaking in, dust turned liquid in the beams.

In the scant light, she sees him shake his head. "Not really. Why?"

"You made a sound. I thought you were in pain."

He shakes his head again, and she hears it once more, coming from the right. A soft noise, whispering. Rustling. Fizzing.

They're not the only ones down here.

Clemmie raises the candle, holding it out, just as Rowland turns to face whoever arrived before them. She steels herself for Apep, his single eye crazed, dried blood crusting his face. The only thing the light reveals is the painted form of Anubis mummifying a long-ago figure, rows of canopic jars beneath the funerary bed. An image of the serpent of darkness waits underneath. Painted an ugly reddish-pink color, like drying blood. Hot wax drips onto her hand, momentarily scalding, and she lowers the candle to the floor, pressing it into the sand so it doesn't topple, and steps closer. Instinctively she reaches into her pocket and withdraws a cartridge, loading the shotgun with surprising ease the way she remembers seeing her father do it before going on a shoot.

The painted serpent appears to sway in the flickering light, the way shadows play tricks on the eyes. She turns her head, deciphering.

"What have you seen?" Rowland asks, but she's too mesmerized to talk. Remembering when her father first told her about the serpent of darkness and Ra's efforts to defeat him. It was Bast who succeeded in the end, the feline goddess earning the name Lady of Slaughter. Clemmie wants to touch the image, to feel the paint once carefully mixed. Cool. Dusty. Crumbling and yet solid.

All of a sudden, the salmon-colored snake comes to life, narrow hood spreading, preparing for a battle. Darkness against light. Myth meeting reality. As the image transforms, the snake alive and not rendered in paint, realization filters through. Behind her, Rowland asks for the weapon, but the cobra will be faster. There's no time.

She's never fired a gun in her life, doesn't believe in hunting for pleasure. But there's a difference between sport and defense, and with awkward fingers she finds the balance of the gun, discovers the trigger, and aims at the snake.

It's blown back against the wall from the power of the blast, still and lifeless. A report so violent she's rendered breathless. She's killed a living thing.

Before she can turn to Rowland for approbation, expecting that glimmer in his eyes when she impresses him, the chamber begins to quake. She spins to face the entrance. In the curtain of daylight, the sand becomes a waterfall, rocks tumbling down from overhead. Clemmie screams into the dust, her throat and eyes full of sand, as the opening is eclipsed by a rockfall, forming a tidal wave of air that snuffs out the candle.

The chamber is even blacker than she imagines *Tuat* to be, and like the dead once buried here, they are trapped.

Unwrapping

1891

S HE STAGGERS FROM THE ROOM, clutching the locket. Not wanting to let go of all it represents.

No one else hath loved thee more than I.

Staring silently at it, she's bemused. Remembering when Rosetta gave it to her with a lock of her own hair nestled inside. *So you can always keep me close.*

Putting it safely in her pocket, she considers her mission. She hasn't been able to find any details in her father's records of where the twins came from. There's nothing to indicate a location for his dig. For years she would beg him to let her organize his papers, but he'd only become defensive and affronted. Thus, she's been forced to form her own educated decision. She's spent hours reading descriptions of various sites, and has settled on returning the amulet to Denderah. It sounds right, in her mind, to take the Double *Tyet* to the place where the ceiling depicts Osiris restored.

That's her plan. And she's sure of it as she says farewell to Bickmore, creeping away in the early hours to avoid the watchful eyes of a house that was once her home. She continues to believe in her plan as the carriage takes her to Chelmsford station, from there catching a train to Liverpool Street, and finally reaching the docks, where she awaits a steamer that will carry her to Egypt.

Entombed

Darkness takes on a profundity she's never known, *Tuat's* monsters devouring at last. Her lungs and the tomb are one, both caving in on her. She has no eucalyptus, and what little air they have is full of sand and barely breathable. Not now, she thinks, fighting with the advancing onslaught of her asthma. There's no time for this.

In the drowning silence that follows the rockfall, there's a muffled grunting. Rowland. Feeling for the candle where she left it on the floor, thankfully far enough from the blocked entrance not to have been buried, she calls out his name as she stumbles toward his moans. In her pocket are the matches, and she strikes one. A fizz. A spark of light. But it goes out in the excitement of her breath. She coughs, spitting grit-peppered phlegm.

He's gasping her name, begging her to help him.

Her second match snaps. The third lights the candle again, leaving her with just one match. It casts a vague glow, enough for her to see that Rowland is on his back, his legs trapped under some rocks. His face is mostly stoic, but she doesn't miss the panic in his eyes. This is a position he's been in before, on his back, unable to move.

Dropping to her knees, she plants the candle on the floor next to them, casting its drunken glow. On the wall, the hieroglyphs dance, but maybe that's just her own dizziness. She needs to work out how to escape, but first she has to free Rowland's legs. What if this worsens his old injury? Can she rid him of the debris pinning him down?

Assessing the situation, she's relieved to see that the rocks aren't so very large. From the height they fell, they've no doubt caused injury, but she thinks she can move them. Bracing herself, she pushes and rolls, steeling herself against his moans as she frees his legs.

She scrapes her hands on the rocks, but when her hands come away bloody, she realizes it's not just hers. Tearing her petticoat into strips, she presses on the places that bleed most. Afraid that she might find a bone protruding. He gasps at the pain of her touch, but there don't appear to be any exposed breaks.

"I'm sorry," she mutters, crawling up to his shoulders and putting his head in her lap. "I'm sorry I've hurt you."

A wet line carves the dust from his eye to her skirt, and he croaks out a reply. She can barely hear him. The water. She yanks at the strap on his shoulder, struggling to release it. Pulling at the cork, she lifts it to his lips.

"No . . . you'll die of thirst down here . . ."

"Nonsense." She insists that he drinks. Knowing as she lets it spill into his mouth, watching it drip down his chin to be lost in the grit, that she's using up one of their key chances of survival.

"The pain . . ." he mutters.

She shushes him. Tells him it will be all right.

"The pain is good," he insists. "I can feel them. My legs."

Choking on a sob she didn't know was loitering, she takes a moment to assess their situation. Glancing at the walls of this tomb, at Rowland's dire state, at the meager candle. They have little water left, just a small napkin of almonds and dates in his pocket, and one match.

She'll get them out of here. She has to.

Survival

THE FLAME JERKS ITS HEAD. The chamber is rendered to an ominous pit with an unearthly glow. They will die if they can't get out. She watches the movement of the minuscule tongue of fire, hating how much she relies on this tiny thing. This is their hope, and the wax is already liquid down the side, collecting on the dusty floor. The curled wick blackened and shortening. They are trapped. Soon, they'll have no light. Time is of the essence.

"Can you stand?" she asks Rowland.

He nods briskly. His face is taut as he pulls himself up, leaning on her shoulder. When he tries to put weight on his leg, he crashes to the floor again. She watches despairingly. No matter how much she wishes she could, she can't just sit here with him, hoping that they'll be discovered. Not when they have barely any sustenance and so little air. She has to make the most of the light while the candle lasts. Standing, she brushes herself down, careful not to extinguish the flame with any sudden movements.

Just one match left.

She should be used to calamities, but no matter how tough things get, it always comes as a surprise when another blow falls. Always thinking the last was the limit of what she could take. Always knowing death was chasing her. Always afraid of who might be next: her or Etta.

Will she die down here, or will her sister die on the operating table?

Standing beneath what was once the entrance, she holds the candle upward. The sand still finds small gaps, trickling down to prove the existence of a desert above their heads. An outside world they can't get to. She tries to get ahold of the remains of a step, but she loses her purchase. The stone is rough, slicing through her palm. She utters a cry.

"Are you hurt?"

"Just a graze."

"I'm no use to you at all," he says, driving a fist into the dirt floor. "No blasted use."

Using the butt end of the shotgun she hammers at the boulders above her, only succeeding in causing a fresh shower of debris to fall on her head. Her cough starts up again, unraveling at the ends with a wheeze.

The flame of her candle continues to tilt. As though it's nodding. Gesturing.

Of course.

She feels the pull of air currents luring her and follows that. Is it foolish to hope? All she knows is that she's not physically strong enough, or tall enough, to hack at the entrance.

For almost her whole life she's been obsessed with mummified remains and Egyptian funerary symbols. It's an ironic twist that she'll die this way, entombed.

Shadows

S HE LEAVES ROWLAND WITH THE shotgun because she feels guilty leaving him at all. He says that he should be the one going to scout out their prison, not her, but she shakes her head. Putting on a braver voice than she thought herself capable of.

"Do you really think I'd let you explore the tomb instead of me?"

"Of course not," he says, fashioning what should be a smile but results in a grimace. "You're the Egyptologist."

"Precisely. I'm going to get us out of here."

Promising that she'll be back, she follows the bend of her flame and enters a world of shadows.

How did Nephthys feel the first time she entered the darkness, knowing that monsters hid behind each rock, every turn? Did she fear them more than Set, or had she grown so used to living with a monster that taking on some more made little difference? Clemmie squares her shoulders.

A memory itches her mind. A threat made by a man who had already tried to attack her, who bears the wound she inflicted. A man who wants revenge.

I kill you myself.

Was the rockfall caused by her gunshot? Or was it the land itself? Egypt and Nubia wanting to cover up their hidden treasures, to exact retribution on them for trespassing. Or was Apep lying in wait for them all along? Could he have summoned the strength to trap them down here?

Once, as a child, she was handling one of her father's artifacts. Made of faience, it was a broken shard of pottery, part of a vase in a former life. It had a sharp edge. Her father had warned her about it, but she hadn't realized how sharp until she cut herself. The wound was relatively small, but quite deep. It left a little white scar, one that she still bears.

You see, her mother said when Clemmie ran to show her the bleeding wound, not crying but still wanting a fuss. *That's what comes from handling all those nasty old things.*

Her mother expected her to lose interest at once.

The next day, Clemmie returned to her father's study. She picked up the blue fragment first, holding it differently this time, more carefully. Flora found her later and tutted loudly.

I thought you'd learned your lesson.

The truth was, she had. The lesson was to take care, but not to concede defeat.

Clemmie has pride in her scars, both physical and unseen. They tell a history, and she's become a stronger person because of them. She's scarred in ways no one will ever see, but each time she's been cut, pierced, or broken, a new layer of skin has grown back.

You cannot run from curses.

That's what the fortune teller told her, and she was right. You cannot run. But you can face your opposition, chin lifted, eyes blazing.

Clemmie is swallowed by the darkness as she passes through the tomb. She is Ra, ready to battle Apep. She is Isis, willing to overcome death. She is Nephthys, eager to harness the darkness. She is also more than that, greater than a story to be retold and reshaped by others.

She is Clementine Attridge, a woman who will not be defeated that easily. She has fought a hundred battles already, and she will fight again.

Crates

As is common, the walls depict the funeral of Osiris, his sisters working to piece his body back together. Passing through the empty tunnels, Clemmie runs her hand over depictions of the myth that she treasured as a child. Here, the sisters arrange the dismembered body parts. There, Anubis mummifies his uncle. In this section, Isis and Nephthys sing their songs of lamentation and healing. In that portion, Osiris is revived.

The myth of these Egyptian siblings is one of murder, of brokenness, betrayal, loss, and pain. The ending is one of healing, of togetherness, and it lends her a hope that burns brighter than her weakening flame. She treads dust that once caressed the painters of these images, binding her to bygone times in ways that she can't even comprehend.

Not sure how far she's come, she can hear only the deadening silence of entering the core of history. She steps into another room, stopping in the entryway, breath stolen.

Monstrous shapes loom around her, shifting in the feeble candlelight. She approaches one outline cautiously, and as she gets closer, she sees the grain of wood, the dull shine of a hastily hammered nail at a crude angle. With one hand, she prizes the top of the box open, a splinter stabbing her, and it comes loose easily, falling to the ground with a clatter that reverberates around the chamber, stirring dust-ghosts. Will the echoes reach Rowland where he waits? Will he wonder what's happened, if she's in danger?

Straw sits inside, and she delves her hand in, ignoring the biting stalks. A warning to stay away. Her candle gutters violently. She digs the way people before her have dug. Her hand closes around something cylindrical. She pulls it out.

What she holds is a stick of sorts. It resembles a candle, with a string standing erect from the center. It isn't made of wax, though. She turns it over, sniffs it. A powdery smell that's vaguely putrid and metallic. She almost drops it when it occurs to her what it is. Dynamite.

Of course. The ruined entrance, the wrecked stone that should have been a staircase or slope. That's how the disrespect of the dealer is made complete. Blasting tombs that have been hidden by time, not caring about the damage, only needing to find a way in. She looks around her, almost expecting to see an exit made by blasting powder—but like the other chambers in this tomb, the walls are intact. These sticks of destruction must have been used to uncover boulders off the entrance that has since closed in on them. No doubt causing the massive crack in the stone lintel. Just the right amount of dynamite, so that the tomb didn't cave in completely and twice bury what lay inside.

Moving on to another crate, she uncovers this one too. Expecting more explosives. How much would Apep and his men need to run their murky business? Her fingers pass from straw to something cold, hard, and familiar. She sweeps the last of the chaff aside, and she's met with an eyeless stare.

She doesn't scream. The mummified body appears to be sleeping. It's almost peaceful, lying here in its wooden bed. The bandages that once wrapped it have come loose, slipping away from the head, leaving the face shamefully naked and exposed. Maybe she should shrink from the body, but instead she studies it curiously.

She wants to whisper: *Who were you? What was your name?* Yet it seems disrespectful to speak. For years she's stared at embalmed bodies in her father's study, watched them being bared and displayed. This is the first time she's seen one in its natural place.

Only, it's not entirely natural. Scanning the room with candle and eyes, she can see the many crates stacked along the walls. These mummies are boxed up, ready to go to homes they don't belong in. This is

Apep's latest hoard. The kind of proof she came in search of. Her heart leaps with excitement, stifled only when she remembers she has no way of getting out and revealing her finds.

Why put the mummies here? Surely it would make more sense to store them in the chamber closest to the entrance? Perhaps the dealers feared that the tomb would be discovered, hoping that the initial empty chambers would put any explorers off searching further. The flame shivers more, her hands shaking. She's come to the end of the tomb, only to learn that there's no second entrance. They really are trapped.

There's a coldness to this reality, a chill that the darkness wears, and it wraps itself around her ankles, her bare throat, her hands. Sucking her deeper into this place. Spend too long in a tomb, and you become a part of it. The spilled straw scratches her bare legs beneath her skirt, rustling as she circles her confinement. But what if it isn't straw? She remembers the red cobra and jumps away from the shifting floor, knocking into a wall and dropping her candle.

The straw-covered floor catches fire at once. Spreading like spilled water. She watches in horror as it advances, parched ground a feast for this ravenous blaze. The chamber is drowning in amber, its course like a river at flood. Heading for the dry wood of the crates and the dynamite within.

Fire

THE ROOM IS BRIGHT NOW, as if Ra really has descended into the darkness to fight Apep. Light battling dark. Sun against shadows. There's enough dynamite down here to rend the tomb in two, bringing the desert down upon them.

They're going to die.

Despite this certain fact, Clemmie's survival instincts charge through her.

The dust she stands on can be used to her advantage. Kicking, she wields her fear to feed her energy. Her rage to fight the flames. Her fortitude to find strength she didn't know she had, shoving the crates out of the way, buying her more time.

Only when a savage pain pierces her leg does she look down and realize her skirt is on fire, and she crashes to the floor, rolling in the sand. Slapping the fabric with her hands. Putting it out. The fetid stench of scorched flesh chokes her.

Fighting the fire is a losing battle, but she's used to such things, and she pours her determination into seeing each flame extinguished. Grit wins out, both hers and the land's. When the chamber is reduced to darkness again, when the last spark of light has been snuffed by dust and her own feet stamping on them, she drops onto the scorched floor with smoke in her nostrils and blooming in her lungs.

She only perceives that she's crying when the liquid salt navigates burns she didn't know she had. Her leg is a furnace. The palms of her hands pulsate. She has one match left, and she must not light it to find her way back to Rowland. She needs it to help them escape.

The fire has given her an idea, and it solidifies the more she plays it out in her mind, wrapping her hopes around the security of it.

Using the backs of her tender hands she feels for the crates. Everything she touches has the prick of fangs, the venom of a snake. Many times she releases a sharp cry, hot tears providing more pain than relief. Straw stabs her seared flesh. Often, the pain is so severe she feels her mind sway from her body, and she clutches the wall, the boxes, the sturdiness of her own limbs, to keep herself from losing consciousness. The air has thickened from the smoke. She imagines one of Nephthys's canopic jars, ready to be filled.

Clemmie brushes against the rough grain of wood. Painfully, she discovers the dynamite, her fingers wrapping around a narrow tube, tail of string brushing her cheek. She puts one in her pocket. Then a second. Not sure how many they'll need. She doesn't want to make two trips. She's running out of energy. Her chest is heavier than she's ever known it.

Standing is an accomplishment that requires every ounce of resolve she's ever possessed. Walking is even harder. She drags her injured leg behind her, her melted shoes catching on the ground. With her gait so hampered, she's fleetingly reminded of Rowland. Will he be able to help? To move fast enough? Won't he think she's lost her mind?

The walls are her guide, branding themselves on her broken skin. She imagines the paintings that she touches but can no longer see, commingling, her blood meeting Egypt's substance. Never has each second felt so long, pain so cruel. Her body is assailed with every movement, making her want to cry out, to break down with sobs that will fracture her body into irreparable pieces.

I won't break, she thinks, knowing that she must get back to Rowland. Praying for God to give her strength.

She might have been staggering for hours or only a few minutes, but she knows when she's back in the first chamber. His voice is a cool breeze to her aching frame.

"Clementine?" he calls to her. "Is that you?"

When she's next to him again, she wants to touch him—his hands, his face—to remind herself of what it is to be with another living human being. Never has she felt such a need not to be alone.

"You smell of smoke," he says.

"Never mind that now. I've found some dynamite. I was thinking we could blast ourselves out."

The plan is so fragile that, spoken aloud, it already seems to shatter around her. So much that could go wrong. Blowing themselves apart. Causing the roof of the tomb to fall in on them entirely. Burying themselves indefinitely.

Yet a small spark of hope exists, and, used correctly, sparks can do immense things. Apep must have used the dynamite to open the entrance of the tomb, after all, and the tomb is still standing. Just the right amount, and they could be free.

"You were in the army, weren't you? You understand how to use powder."

"The cavalry," he corrects.

"But you know something of artillery?"

"I picked up a thing or two."

A spark. So little. That's all they need.

"You'll have to lift me."

He snorts. "I can barely stand."

"Well, neither can I. There was an accident with the candle—a fire—I'm hurt too. Do you want to live?"

"You're hurt? How badly?" His voice lowers with concern, but she barely knows the extent of her injuries herself. Trembles shake her body, building in intensity. Is it her body registering distress? Shock? There's no time to relent.

She finds his hands and pulls. He grunts, his breath quick and labored, but he is up. She can feel his body sway, and then the stiffening of his resolve. United in their tenacity. They will do this. They have to.

The trickle of sand is so silent, it could easily be missed, but she can't strike her match to find the old opening. She has to save it for lighting the fuse. She stands quietly, bearing some of Rowland's weight as he balances on his injured legs. They help each other move, and she listens. Holds her breath. Picturing the chamber as if it were lit and she could see it perfectly. Remembering the layout of it when she'd seen it earlier. She uses the backs of her hands to brush the walls, to feel for the staircase that was blasted to oblivion. At last, she touches something solid. Rough.

A small tickle runs down her face, so faint it could be a spider. She cups her hand, feels the sand slowly building in her palm. Something so gentle, yet it might just as well be rocks on her raw flesh. This is it.

She tells him to pick her up.

"I'm not steady," he says, each word hewn with pain. "I'll drop you."

"Pick me up," she says again.

A moment's pause, then his arms are around her waist, then her legs, and she rises. Slowly. Her body rocking as he tries to anchor himself. The press of his face is against the softness of her belly, his hot breath dampening the fabric of her blouse. She ignores his closeness, the way their bodies fit so strangely and yet so perfectly, his nose finding the indentation of her navel. Reaching above her, she pats the wall, feeling for where the roughness of demolished stone gives way to looser rocks and dirt. The landslide. A door waiting to be opened.

Digging with her fingers, she widens one of the crevices. If only she could see what she's doing, but it's as dark as *Tuat* down here. Several times she cuts her already ruined hands on a sharp piece of rock, gasping at the pain. Rowland asks if she is all right, but she hardly registers his question.

Her mouth is dry, but she works up a moisture. Spitting, she pushes her saliva into the gap that's now as wide as two of her fingers, forming a paste of sorts with the grit. Then she reaches into her pocket. Rowland loses his grip slightly, oscillating like a date palm in the sandstorms, but she waits for him to regain his hold. Willing him to be steady. Amazed at how much she trusts him. His grip bruises, but it also heartens. She returns her focus to the job at hand. If she doesn't hurry, they'll have no air left.

Withdrawing her hand, she follows Rowland's instructions as she fixes the stick of dynamite in place. One is enough to blast a tree stump from the ground, so one is enough to blast the entrance.

"Pack it tight. Make sure it can't fall." He pauses before adding, "This could kill us."

It could save us, she thinks.

Once more her hand finds her pocket, closes around the little box that sits there. It sticks to her palm. Pain makes her back arch and Rowland clutches her tighter, conveying through touch that he's with her. That she can do this.

They don't speak at this point, aware of how crucial this small stick of imprisoned fire is. Shaking now, she picks up the last match with the tips of her fingers where her skin is less damaged, determined not to drop it. If it snaps, they'll have no way to light the fuse. If she puts it out with her breath, with a sudden wheezing cough, if the trickle of sand extinguishes it, there will be no way to get them out of here. No one knows they're here—not even Mariam would guess. No one will rescue them. It's this, or nothing. There's no other way.

With a silent prayer, she strikes the end of the match against the wall, and the trembling flame brings the chamber to life once more. By her head, the stick of dynamite waits to be lit, to do its damage. She hesitates, feeling the increasing heat as the flame travels down toward her fingers. If she does this, they might be dead in a few seconds. If she doesn't, they will die slowly, suffocating like Osiris in his chest.

The flame is beautiful, and she's never wanted to live as much as she does in that moment. Clemmie holds the match to the fuse, hears the kiss as fire meets string, and then Rowland releases her and she's falling, sliding down alongside his body, feeling the brush of him against her. They've become accustomed to the shape of each other, learned how to see by touch, and his hands appear in time, stopping her from crashing to her knees. Guiding each other, they hobble into the deeper shadows. Feeling for the tunnel, for the chambers beyond.

The fizz of a spark devours the darkness behind them.

Y

Air

*B*REATHE.

The canopic jar is opened. Releasing her lungs. A butterfly freed from a net.

Breathe.

She is transforming from woman to kite. Unfurling wings. Feathers fluttering. A breeze fans her.

Breathe.

The Nile is flowing through her body. Through her windpipe. A delta of water that cleanses. Her chest inflates, liquid and airy.

Breathe.

Rosetta is smiling at her, nodding. Encouraging.

"Breathe. That's right. Breathe."

Clemmie opens her eyes, and it isn't Etta leaning over her. Instead, she looks into the bloodshot eyes of Rowland. His hands are *tap, tap, tapping* her face. Sand coats his skin, his hair, his clothes, the way it did in the storms. Crow's feet carve branches to the tips of his ears, hinting at the peach of his skin beneath. She brushes her hand along the ground, wincing at the pain of this small movement. The sun brands. Wind licks hair across her face.

"How . . . ?"

"It worked." Rowland's face is eggshell, dust falling. For a moment she thinks he might cry, but then he smiles, and it's a wonderful sight. "It actually worked."

He tells her how the explosion caused so much dust that she had an asthma attack, and she has a vague memory of her lungs giving up on her at last. Of thinking: *So this is how it ends.*

"You collapsed," he says. "I managed to scramble over the rockfall and drag you out into the air."

And they are in it. The sun that smiled on pharaohs is a furnace on her skin, its warmth reviving. With sentience comes pain. Everything hurts. Her chest, her eyes, her flesh. She's not sure how they'll get back to the *dahabeeyah,* uncertain how they'll walk. But they're safe.

Then she remembers Horatio and Apep. Maybe they are alive and have escaped the tomb, but she still doesn't know how they got trapped down there. A landslide, the gunshot, the dealer. It could be any of those things.

The truth is, they're not safe. Not really. And it's safer to accept that so that they can be on their guard. They need to get back to *Hapi,* and they must get away from those who want her dead.

Wounds

"**W**HAT ON EARTH HAPPENED?"
Oswald's face is a picture when finally, clinging to each other, Rowland and Clemmie stumble onto *Hapi*'s deck. His eyes travel from their dusty, torn exteriors, to their wounds bound in her shredded petticoat, to the fowling piece Rowland has used as a walking stick.

"Is that my gun?"

Celia emerges from the saloon, her brow unusually troubled. She stops when she sees them, her hand flying to her mouth. The deck is remarkably unstable, so that Oswald and Celia move like pendulums. Clemmie thinks she might be sick and swallows, the dust of a desert sitting heavily in her stomach.

"Major Devereux," Celia calls. "They're back!"

"Rowland . . . Rowland needs a doctor . . ."

Clemmie hears her voice parting from her body like a spirit from a corpse. As she fights the exhaustion, the press of agony, she hears a heavy step on the deck. A face swims into her vision as everything dances in and out of focus.

Familiar hands separate her from Rowland and she cries out in pain. In the fug of her brain, she knows who's touching her.

"Rowland . . . a doctor . . ."

Strong arms pick her up, and there's a haze of red fabric like seeping blood, the cold burn of a button against her cheek. Sometimes, the only way to fight is to pretend that you're weak, the way an animal plays dead. She goes limp in his arms as Horatio carries her to her cabin.

Mariam brings water, and while Horatio tries to get answers from Clemmie—*Where were you? What were you doing with him, and dressed like that? What happened?*—Mariam shoos him away. Clemmie manages to muster a weak smile of thanks.

Finally alone with Sphinx, Clemmie angles the dressing table mirror to look at her body. Slowly, agonizingly, she peels the fabric from her wounded frame. Her skirt has stuck to her burnt leg, and she has to soak it off slowly. Twice, she nearly loses consciousness. Acid burns her mouth, her roasted flesh pulsing. She can still smell smoke.

Her cat rubs against her, and even that gentle motion sets her body throbbing. Tears escape her eyes. She blames them on the pain, knowing they're rooted more deeply. Celia and Mariam offered to help her, but she needs this time to be alone. To sort the jumble of her thoughts. To see the damage done without the shock showing on her friends' faces.

Once she's unclothed, Clemmie stands as straight as she can muster. In this manner she assesses her reflection. The parts not caught in the glass she looks down to see. Livid flesh curls at the corners where she caught fire. She touches the stickiness apprehensively, winded by the pain and withdrawing her finger shakily.

Distracting herself, she inspects her abdomen. She's somewhat bereft that there's no mark on her midriff where Rowland held her tight. Only the memory of his proximity. She sweeps her hand over the space, closing her eyes, re-creating the moment. His breath, the point of his nose in the nook of her belly, the intimacy of their shared need to survive.

When she opens them again, she's standing taller.

The handle of her cabin door turns. She bolted it for privacy, but she still jumps, looking for something to cover her modesty. The handle begins to shake violently. Sphinx darts under the bed and Clemmie stills her breath, waiting for the rattling to stop. It does, finally, followed by a hush so dreadful her knees almost buckle.

His voice is like smoke, curling into the room, choking her.

"You can't hide in there forever."

Horatio's departing footsteps are the sound of a hammer beating nails into her coffin.

She thinks of Rowland's courage, blazing along with hers. His gentleness, binding her raw limbs. His nearness. His passion to see her avenged. She is dazed, lost in these excruciating pangs, in her utter exhaustion from wandering the sands of both desert and time. She is driven by a need to sleep and forget everything. Despite this, she lies there and thinks of him.

What does it feel like to love? She knows the love she has for her sister, that tie that has always been so strong. The unity of their minds that has often made people marvel, presuming them to be twins. Clemmie understands that kind of love.

There's also the love for her family, a loyal love. The love that made her hunger for a partnership with her father. That made her ache for her mother to accept and understand her. A love that's grounded in blood.

She's recently discovered an amicable love. That unique love reserved for kindred spirits. People who aren't relatives but have earned the right to be close.

But a romantic love? What does such a love feel like? She isn't certain if she deserves to know. Once, she might have felt an attraction for Horatio—she admits that now, folding into herself in horror and shame. It was a fondness for him that betrayed Rosetta, but also failed herself.

Love is too broad a term for something so complex. Her life has been dedicated to Egyptology and family, yet in her almost four-and-twenty years, she's never truly understood what love—that specific, intimate, passionate love—is. There's just one thing she's certain of. The English language tries to sum these emotions into one appellation, but the Greeks knew better, reserving different words for different kinds of love.

Philia. Agape. Storge. Eros. Even *mania.*

Unwrapping

1891

IT IS THAT STRANGE TIME between Christmas and the coming year when the days dress in the clothes of their neighbors; when a Tuesday could very well be a Thursday and people debate on which it actually is. In a matter of a few months, eager spectators in New York will gather for the opening of Tennyson's play *The Foresters,* hearing those words of promise: *Hope smiles from the threshold of the year to come whispering "It will be happier."*

On the cusp of 1892, very much hoping that it will be a happier year than the last five, which have haunted her, Clemmie boards a ship bound for Egypt. The ship, the year, the far-off country, each hold new possibilities. A season of hope; of leaving former mistakes in an obsolete annum and reaching out to a virginal one.

She wasn't meant to travel to Egypt alone. How can she forget the promises made when she was twelve? The day she became a woman.

Clemmie had tiptoed into the room that Rosetta now had as her own, too old for the nursery. It didn't stop them from sharing a bed when Nurse Pugh wasn't looking. A new game for Clemmie to sneak down and find the warmth of a bed already filled with another body, the openness of two arms ready to hold her, the softness of feet that would tickle her own.

Rosetta was seated on the edge of her bed, her face buried in her palms. Touching her older sister's trembling shoulders, she'd asked what was wrong. Rosetta had looked up, her face blotched, saying that she knew, that Nurse Pugh had told her. And she couldn't bear for her little sister to change.

We're growing up, Rosetta had said, and Clemmie had replied: *You've already grown up, but we're still sisters.*

Sitting there on the bed, they held each other for a while. Lulled by the rhythm that their breathing made. By the sameness of its music.

Then Clemmie spoke. She said that there was one good thing about growing up. It meant that they could go to Egypt together. One day, when they were both a little older, they would go.

So they promised each other.

I promise, Rosetta said.

I promise, Clemmie replied.

They'd see the Nile. The ruins. Those depictions of mythical sisters in preserved artwork. They'd see them all. Together.

I promise. I promise. I promise.

Now she's here on the ship without her sister by her side. Trying to break a curse, but breaking a promise instead. The curse is quicksand. Each move she makes to free them only sinks her in deeper, swallowing her up. Soon it will cover her, so that not even her fingers are visible, reaching for the one person she has left.

She makes a new promise. She will restore things so that her sister can join her in Egypt one day, so that they can see the Nile, and the carved and painted artwork. So that they can be together.

I promise. I promise. I promise.

Downriver

THE *DAHABEEYAH* CHANGES COURSE with a groan that echoes deep inside Clemmie. Sleep will fortify her, time will heal her body, but how will her heart mend? Staying away from Horatio will be easy. No one questions her need to rest. But she already misses Rowland, who also keeps to his cabin.

She hears Celia come and go, hears herself whispering through a voice that's thick with dust and smoke a version of what happened. Her wounds are washed, the bowl of water bloody and full of sand. Every part of her aches for the Nile, to lower her molten body into the balm of those waters.

Celia fusses constantly, and only leaves when Clemmie urges her to share the carefully scripted version of events with the others.

Clemmie wanted to explore. Rowland was awake early and said he'd come along to offer her protection, helping himself to Oswald's fowling piece. They came across a tomb that caved in on them. There was a fire when Clemmie dropped her candle. They were both hurt.

She doesn't mention how she discovered crates of mummified remains, or the dynamite. Better that they presume a second exit was found, like an air shaft in a mine. Better that Horatio doesn't suspect that she's uncovered Apep's unlawful excavations. She can only hope that Apep stays away from Horatio and doesn't reveal that she was hiding in the tent when the two men met.

Giving her no time to sleep, Celia and Mariam return with a bottle and rolls of what looks like cerement. Celia goes to stand by Clemmie and strokes her brow. Mariam sits on the end of the bed, and Sphinx comes to investigate. Pawing the strips of cloth.

It's one of Celia's petticoats, ripped into bandages. Mariam lifts Clemmie's nightgown enough to reveal the injured leg, and Celia pales. The afflicted area is plummy, scorched skin crimped like withered flowers. Mariam's and Celia's eyes meet momentarily, Celia swallows, and Mariam gestures with her head.

Reaching into her pocket, Celia withdraws a flask. "Ossie says it might help."

Her hands are too raw to turn the cap, so Celia does it for her, holding the vessel to her lips and encouraging her to drink. Liquid dynamite courses down Clemmie's throat and through her veins. She's ready.

With just a brief hesitation, Mariam pours oil onto the wound. Clemmie bucks against the mattress, tears leaking onto the pillow, the bedsheets soaking at her back. Celia guides the flask back to her mouth and she chokes down a second helping.

"Talk to me," Clemmie murmurs to Celia as Mariam begins binding. She wants to squeeze her friend's hand but her own are too blistered.

"About what?"

Clemmie crushes her eyes shut, but it doesn't smother the pain. "Anything."

Happy to oblige, Celia babbles about her Michael back at home. The man she's been sent here to avoid. The scandalous affair. She strokes Clemmie's shoulder as she talks, periodically encouraging her to imbibe more brandy. Mariam finishes with Clemmie's leg and moves on to her hands, wrapping them until they're bulbous and just her fingers are visible.

Clemmie's thoughts drift away. Maybe it's the pain, or the brandy. Perhaps a cocktail of the two. Who knows? When she closes her eyes, she allows herself to remember an affair of her own.

She and Rowland, alone in a tomb. Not exactly the sort of romantic setting Celia might design for her tête-à-têtes with Michael. More of a gothic romance. She can't help but smile, and that's how she falls asleep. Smiling, with her hand draped across her middle. Allowing her mind to slip to the moment when Rowland swayed as he held her, and he clasped tighter. How, along with his grip, something shifted.

When she awakes, Mariam is still with her. Seated at the bottom of the bed, the captain's daughter watches her closely. The light in the room is different. Brighter, somehow, which is odd, because shouldn't it be darker by now? She can't feel the boat moving, and there is a surprising number of voices outside. Hard to tell if they come from the *daha-beeyah* or the shore.

"You have slept a long time, *ya aanesa* Clemmie. It is morning," Mariam says. Her voice lowers confidentially. "There's something you should know."

The noises outside are crushing. Clemmie palms her head to push them out, the bandaged mitts encumbering her movements. The scorch of a thousand deserts is in her throat, and a relentless sun behind her eyes. Mariam helps her sit up and passes her a glass of water. Beautiful, sweet water. She's never tasted anything more delicious.

When she's drunk the whole glass, her voice is back and she asks Mariam where they are. The external voices are interspersed with a clanging sound. A *chip, chip, chipping*.

"We've moored," Mariam says at last. "*Hapi* has another small leak— the last repair didn't hold up. My *baba* says it's nothing to cause alarm, but we have to wait here whilst his crew see to it. We know you need to get to the hospital at Cairo, but the major is more interested in the excavation onshore."

Excavation? In Mariam's eyes, Clemmie sees the reflection of that night they shared together. The memory played out in the glimmer of her friend's dark eyes. The starlight. The shadows. The hole she dug. A necessary wound made on an island to return a precious amulet.

"We're at Philae."

Secrets

F UNNY THAT BEFORE, ALL SHE could think about was getting to
Philae, but now the name of that place fills her with dread.

Dig up the whole damned island for all I care.

Now the empty camp makes sense. After Apep's beating, the diggers
left to get to Philae. Because, like her, they were afraid of Horatio. Her
body pulses with the venom she feels for him, and she wishes that she
were a snake so she could spit in his eyes and blind him. Poison him.
Destroy him. Maybe there is a way to do that, but until she can think of
one, he's a threat to her, to the amulet, to the twins, and to Etta.

If he uncovers the amulet, what will happen to her sister? No, she's
reverting to thoughts of a curse again, and Rowland was right. Curses
don't exist, at least not the kind that she once believed in.

She needs to get a telegram sent home, to ask Nurse Pugh what's
been happening. Has the operation gone ahead? How is Etta? What
will Horatio do once he's found the amulet? For he will find it, she
knows he will. Never did she think someone might disturb the ground
of Philae. Why would they? When she and Mariam considered the
meaning behind the hieroglyphs, discussing the perfect resting place
for the Double *Tyet*, she presumed that no one would think of digging
around the Temple of Isis.

But then, she hadn't reckoned on Horatio turning up.

Won't someone notice the excavation and demand to see a permit? Will no one stop them? Or will Apep's team get away with this, just as they have got away with blasting the site near Korosko? Are tourists likely to interrupt a team of diggers and suspect them of illegal digging? It's more probable that they'd start asking what's for sale.

The amulet still belongs to her by her father's will, and she'll use that reasoning to fight Horatio. Of course, she doesn't really believe the amulet belongs to her.

How can she own something twice stolen?

When she finally feels able to leave her cabin, she does not go to Horatio to beg him to stop the digging, or to Youssef, to ask him to work faster on the repair, to hurry *Hapi* downriver to Cairo, or at least to Assûan so she can send a telegram. Her breath is excavated from her lungs as she makes herself stand. Teaching herself to walk with her injured leg. Mastering a shuffle that makes the sound of Rowland's walk.

That's who she goes to. Heading to Rowland's cabin, she doesn't even knock, doesn't consider the impropriety of being in a man's room. After all they've been through together, it hardly seems to matter.

"Horatio's digging on the island."

"I know."

There's a silence that's thicker than the dust they waded through the day before. She meets his eye, and he holds it as securely as he clutched her waist in the tomb.

"How are you?" he asks.

It seems one of those strange, typically English questions, where, whatever the truth, the norm would be to respond: *I'm very well and how are you today,* when in fact, she's in agony. Not just from her burns.

"What about your leg?"

"Youssef has cut me a walking stick from one of his *dahabeeyah* poles. Wasn't that kind of him?" He reaches for it and manages to stand, using it as a crutch. Hopping over to her with one leg bent. She sees that it is tied with splints and he follows her gaze. "Not too much damage done. A small break, I think. Could have been worse."

"I'm so sorry." Again, someone has been hurt because of her.

"Don't be."

"I'm worried," she admits. "About the amulet."

"Clementine, I . . ."

Rowland gathers her wrists. The skin on his hands is chapped and scratching. Her body burns in a new way, and she can't comprehend this feeling, but she accepts it. Slowly, he lifts her bandaged palms to his mouth and kisses them with the softness of clouds, a gentleness that unwraps the bindings on her heart. His mouth hovers before hers, and every part of her strains to feel his lips, to kiss him, to know the press of his body, his touch, and caress him in return. Her fingers tingle with a need to trace the contours of his muscles, to study him the way she would a hieroglyph. The intensity of her desire is shocking and delicious. She's unsure. She is certain.

A man in a uniform. You don't love him. But you will.

Clemmie remembers the fervent grind of the old woman's hand on her wrist. All this time she thought the words implied Horatio. Did the fortune teller see Rowland when she spoke?

He pulls away. Her naked heart shudders at its own vulnerability. Has she been reading him wrong? His eyes have always been a riddle, it's hard to tell what he's thinking. She is shaking.

"You don't have to worry," he says. A tremor of uncertainty enters his voice.

Her heart is still throbbing.

"What do you mean?" she asks, already forgetting why she first came here.

"Clementine."

His voice is edged with apprehension. What might he have to say? Her heart wants to hear only one thing.

On the bank of the Nile, he offered her a partnership. She hasn't forgotten that. Now she beholds the man before her, and she aches to be with him. Interpreting her own feelings is shocking but freeing. Breathlessly, she waits for him to speak. To reveal the secrets buried deep within his heart, so that she might do the same, and share with him how she feels.

"I never talk about this to anyone."

That's when she realizes that he isn't going to present her with his heart. Rowland has a history of his own, and he's finally going to reveal it.

Skeletons

H E TELLS HER THAT THEY'RE alike, the two of them. However, he doesn't speak with fondness. He says it coldly. Distantly. Bitterly. When she waits for him to go on, his body rocks with the weight of what he's about to share.

His story begins with childhood, and comprehension pulses through her veins as Rowland's words paint an image of two boys—brothers— playing a game of soldiers. A picture of siblings, something she resonates with. Perhaps if so-called innocent games influence life so much, parents should be more careful with what amusements they permit their offspring to partake in.

They encourage it, he says. All the fighting as children. The adults seeing the boys grabbing sticks, pretending they're swords. Applauding the show of make-believe. He helps her imagine the attraction they felt for the uniforms gleaming, to understand the drive as boy sprouts to man, thinking: *That'll be me. I'll be a soldier.* Never pausing to consider the blood and the killing and the rats feeding on cadavers.

Archie. That was his name. Archibald Luscombe. Rowland's younger brother. They both went to war. Soldiers in their game, and soldiers as men. Thinking they could continue their antics, that they could preserve their childhood. That it was merely sport.

It wasn't like that, though. He describes how Archie became ill, developing asthma, but how he didn't want to be discharged. Desiring always to remain with Rowland. Brothers together, through everything. That's how Rowland learned how to tend to someone when their lungs gave up on them. Lifting the arms above the head. Using eucalyptus. Steam.

The war, it was awful. They'd drink to forget, because why not? Why not have a drink or two and get a bit jolly and somehow find a way to laugh it all off? Rowland and Archie did their duty in Egypt. They did what they were supposed to do. No one could call Rowland a coward, but he hated every second of it.

They survived the Moonlight Charge together, side by side. Always looking out for each other. Brothers in arms and brothers by blood. Archie could have got away from the regiment with his lungs, but he stuck by Rowland's side, hiding his asthma from his seniors. Unwilling to leave Rowland to face the fighting and his nightmares alone.

A few years passed. They were home on leave, getting ready for a dinner party. They always had plenty of invitations, eligible daughters of their hosts pressing fan handles coquettishly to their lips. Both the brothers had been drinking at home before leaving. It was the only way Rowland knew how to bolster his act. Without liquor, he couldn't bear to be merry in front of a gathering, how fake it all was, after what they'd seen.

Kassassin. How to sum up Kassassin? The hell of it. The fear. The taste of blood splattered on eyes and lips, the screams of dying men, the smell of spilled guts. The dinner they were going to was around five years after the Moonlight Charge, but the ghosts of that battle lingered. Kassassin stayed with Rowland. It had changed him. Charging like that, wanting to kill to save himself, his brother, and the rest of his unit, but knowing that the opposing side was thinking just the same. That they had brothers and comrades of their own whom they were trying to save. It was harrowing.

Rowland was drunk when they got into the carriage. He'd had much more than Archie. His younger brother didn't hate the fighting quite to the extent that Rowland did, and didn't drink half as much. But Rowland was the elder. He had to look out for Archie *and* himself. The responsibility made his fear of what could happen greater. He'd drink anything he could get his hands on—brandy, port, gin. Even ale was better than nothing.

He started singing some stupid song, and Archie laughed but told him to get some air and sober up before the ladies saw them. Rowland hooted and climbed out of the carriage before it got moving, the night air hitting him but not managing to get through his skull. He called to Archie to follow, took the reins, and dismissed the driver. With a crack of the whip, they were off.

Archie climbed out, telling him to stop as they tore along. They went faster and faster, so fast Rowland knew they could crash but he only relished the danger. The thrill of it, with the liquor in his veins, pushed Kassassin—all of it—from his mind.

Hurry up and get into the seat, he called. *It's marvelous up here.*

But Archie was still clambering up the side of the carriage, clinging on as they raced along.

They reached a hill, Devonshire being riddled with them. They were going so fast down it that their stomachs were in their throats. Archie, now begging him to slow down, was still hanging on to the side. Was Rowland going to listen? Did Archie get through to him? It was too late to find out. The momentum had a mind of its own and the carriage toppled. It rolled over and over, them with it.

He doesn't remember much. They had to shoot the horses. Their legs were broken, and they did it to be kind. It wasn't that simple for Rowland. For weeks he wanted them to shoot him too. He'd have done it himself.

I suppose we all have skeletons in our closets.

That's what Rowland said back in Cairo, as they shared Lumps of Delight while perusing the bazaars. And now his closet is open before her, Archie's remains laid bare.

Rowland wasn't injured at Kassassin. He was injured the same day he killed his brother.

Only now does Rowland's voice break.

"Well, aren't you horrified?"

"It was an accident," she says. "And you must have realized that, because you said you wanted to learn to walk again."

"I learned to walk for Archie's sake. To live his dream."

"What dream?"

Rowland swallows. "When we were serving in Egypt," he says, "all Archie could talk about was the history of this place. He'd caught the mania sweeping the world."

He goes on to explain that after his brother's death, he adopted that dream. Egyptology became his interest. Archie's plan to build a collection to display became Rowland's plan.

Egyptomania. The partnership offer makes sense now. She'd wondered why Rowland, of all people, would want to start such an enterprise. To honor a brother's memory. *Isis and Nephthys. Osiris and Set.* The bond of siblinghood. Who can comprehend it except those who have known it for themselves?

"When you first told me about the mummy," he says, "the one with two heads, I didn't tell you that I already knew about it."

She falters. The first time they met, at Shepheard's, he'd felt vaguely familiar. He can't have been at one of Bickmore's events, though. She knows he wasn't. She'd have remembered.

"Archie was there that night."

Her muscles jar. She remembers the hesitation she'd felt in the Cairo hotel, questioning whether she'd seen Rowland before, wondering how he knew her and her father's history so well. She'd considered countless times whether he'd ever been to one of their unwrappings. But it hadn't been him. It had been Archie Luscombe.

"The redcoat," she gasps. "He was your brother."

It's incredible. What I would do to own a specimen like this.

Rowland is saying something about Archie wanting the Double *Tyet* and the mummified twins. How he'd offered a price but her father had refused it. Torn between keeping the artifacts, or relinquishing them for a much vaster sum.

This is the moment when he picks up his jacket, slung across his bed. His crutch slows each of his movements, so that everything happens slowly. He pulls something from the pocket. Hidden there. Holding it out toward her like a gift. The room is liquid. Her ears pump with molten blood, her heart a fuse ready to detonate. She is in the tomb again, waiting for the moment when the explosion comes. When the roof caves in on top of them.

Light fingers its way through the window, onto the object in Rowland's hand. In his palm is a locket. A silver locket engraved with words

296 RACHEL LOUISE DRISCOLL

that she's read countless times, words credited to Isis in an old text. The broken chain is around a mane of long hair, threads of copper and even a single line of blond cutting through brown. Binding them all together.

It's her hair. Her locket. But how can that be when she buried them? There is no denying that they are here before her in broad daylight, so where is the amulet?

Maat

ONE OF HER FAVORITE REMEMBRANCES *of her father begins like this:*

In his study, with Clement's hands clasped around Clemmie's middle, a pose usually reserved for the telling of myths. The smell of book dust, of antiquities, of the things that bound them.

"Once," he said, "when the dead in Egypt were ready to go to the underworld, Anubis would take the heart of the person who had died, and place it on a set of weighing scales. When you use scales, you have to use a counterbalance. Do you know what he'd use?"

She shook her head.

"A feather."

This answer was surprising. Surely everyone knew that you couldn't use a feather as a balance.

He went on to tell her that this wasn't just any feather. It was the feather of Maat, the goddess of truth. When a wicked heart was weighed against the feather of Maat, it was heavy with its sin, and the scales toppled from the weight.

Here, he dropped his knee and pretended to let her fall, although he still had his arms wrapped around her. She squealed.

"When a good heart was weighed," he continued, "it proved to be as light as a feather. And the scales would stay balanced."

She asked him what happened to the heavy hearts, and he told her that crocodile-headed Ammit, the eater of the dead, would devour them. At this point, he buried his face into her chest. Making gobbling noises.

"One more thing," he said. "Who was the Egyptian god of wisdom?"

"Thoth." She scowled at the easiness of the question.

"Well, Thoth was married to Maat. So, you see, Wisdom and Truth, they really go together. You can't have one without the other."

She can hardly believe her eyes. Her hair and locket are before her, here, in Rowland's cabin. Does that mean that the amulet is no longer safe in the ground? She thinks of Etta's apparent recovery and then her relapse. Horatio is the instigator of her family's misfortunes, she knows that now, but the old superstition niggles.

Despite the bandages, Clemmie forms fists. Paltry fists that don't seem enough to beat down this man who's ruined everything, but she tries just the same. She beats his chest over and over, wanting to hurt him, even though each slap is a knife through her palms. She wants to break him, and he doesn't stop her. He stands there and takes it silently.

"How could you?"

"I did it for Archie. He'd told me about the amulet, and when our paths crossed in Cairo, when it occurred to me that you were hiding something and what you had with you, I couldn't believe my luck."

"You're a thief. I never should have trusted you."

Now he grabs her wrists, holding them tightly. Not to bruise, but she knows it might if she tries to pull free.

"The amulet is safe. I've shipped it back to England—I was afraid you'd find it and be angry, and perhaps a part of me feared that I'd change my mind the more time I spent with you—but I kept your hair and locket, waiting for the right moment to tell you. It was always my intention to pay you for the amulet, I just needed more time to get you on my side. Maybe even see if you'd reconsider the business proposition. Can't you see what I'm trying to tell you? Horatio can't get the amulet."

She doesn't listen, thinking of the hieroglyphic text on the Double *Tyet.* Kites. Storms. The myth everywhere.

Isis. Nephthys. Osiris. Set.

"What if the curse is still on us because of you?"

He releases a sound of exasperation.

"Listen to yourself," he says. "Even if you were right and you had to return the amulet, how could my taking it prolong your afflictions? You weren't part of my removing it from Philae, and if I hadn't, another person would have done, be it Horatio, or someone else entirely. All of Egypt is being excavated."

"I can't ignore that we're still suffering. Yes, Horatio is to blame for so much, but . . . oh, I hardly know what to think anymore."

He steeples his fingers together, holding them to his mouth.

"People always look for explanations for things that happen when it's just life."

She shakes her head. Even if she accepts that, she can't ignore that Rowland betrayed her.

"I know you've come to be ashamed of your father's work. Aren't you just trying to come to terms with your own guilt? Don't succumb to that. Superstition is a bindweed, and it will choke the life from you."

His words convict her. If she hadn't been disrespectful, would her father have acted so recklessly by cutting the twins apart? Has she permitted the idea of a curse as a way of dealing with her own remorse, caught up in her sister's mania? How can she separate what is real from what is imagined?

"I want to believe you. I do believe you. But I've been wrestling with this for so long. I wanted the amulet to remain buried. You had no right to go against my wishes."

"It's an antique with old icons inscribed on it. It's beautiful and magnificent, but it doesn't have power, Clementine. Trust me."

Trust him? How can she do that when he has betrayed her? Their misfortunes have been the product of circumstance and Horatio's greed, not something caused by texts naming mythical figures. Yet that doesn't absolve him from meddling with her efforts to remedy her family's wrongs.

She thought he was different, but he's just like other collectors, selfishly procuring precious things with no thought of the consequences. A thief, twice over. First, he stole the amulet, keeping the truth of his actions concealed from her.

And then he stole her heart.

Hunger

T RUST IS A VIRGIN GIVEN into someone's care, to be respected, honored, protected. Clemmie had every confidence in Rowland, but he has defiled her trust.

Her mind travels over the carefully planned steps of her old mission as she totters from Rowland's cabin with the locket restored to her pocket, her hacked mane of hair scattered at his feet. They're well rehearsed, imprinted in her inner being. Keep the twins safe, return the amulet, bury it by the images of mythical siblings, bring healing.

She'd never accounted for Rowland.

In her cabin, she barely notices that Sphinx doesn't come running to greet her, the way she usually does. Should she stop the operation on her sister's tumor or is it already too late? Distracted by this new burden she misses the movement in the mirror. Only when her cabin door snaps shut behind her does she spin around, her own speed nearly crippling her with pain.

Horatio sneers at her, a cocksure swagger to his walk.

"You took your time."

She eyes him the way a rabbit might a predator, and she hates that he makes her feel this way. How he preys upon her, drawing her sweat to the surface, making her flayed skin burn all the more. Oxygen and pulse fight for room in her throat.

He nods toward her cabin window and the island beyond, but she doesn't move, doesn't take her eyes off him. He's parading in front of her, bragging about his minions and their excavation, waiting for her to bite.

"Of course," he says, "you could just tell me where it is. Save us all this fuss."

"You'll never get it."

His grin is condescending, shaking his head at her naïvety. It's that which makes her incensed enough to turn her back on him. Through the window she can see the diggers, their tools, earth flying. They'll destroy the island, and she shudders at the blight of greed. Will Horatio never give up? If he's prepared to kill for her home, wouldn't he do the same for her father's collection?

"Even if you found it," she says, "it's not yours."

"But we're going to get married." His voice is suddenly right behind her. His breath scorching her ear. "And then it will be mine. We can work together, just as we used to."

Another partnership offer. This one makes her skin shrink. She's afraid that he's going to touch her. Those hands, did they pin her father down, choking the breath from him? Did they shove her mother down the stairs?

"You don't want to work with me," she says. "You pushed me away, came between my father and me."

In both life and death.

"Your knowledge could prove useful now."

So that's it. He thinks she'll increase his chances of making a fortune. Using her skill to date specimens, to value them, so he can get the right price. All those years ago, did she misinterpret his interest in Egyptology to be akin to hers when it was merely financial?

"Is that why you haven't killed me?"

She can almost hear him stiffen. A click as he straightens. His breathing a little faster, falling hot on the back of her neck. There's a pause as he measures his answer.

"I don't know what you think you know, but if I wanted to kill you, I'd have done it a long time ago."

He's so close now that she daren't turn around, else she'll be pressed close to him, her lips near his. Her blood churns the way the Nile did in the storms.

"I won't marry you, Horatio. You'll never get the amulet or the mummy."

He grabs her waist, twists her around, crushing her back against the wall. She bites down a cry. Pinning her wrists on either side he leans into her, eyes ablaze.

"I always get what I want."

In this position, he reveals what he's capable of.

"I could have you admitted to an asylum faster than you can blink. If you fight me, if you pretend to know anything about me that might drag my name in the dirt, then I swear that I'll draw everyone's attention to your sister's mania as proof of your own, and they won't even question me."

Her eyes widen at his threat. He's right, of course. Everyone would believe him, a man. Who would listen to her? Invisible.

She doesn't understand. If he hates her so much, why would he want to marry her? Maybe he sees the question on her face, for in that moment he comes closer, if possible, an appetite naked on his face that frightens her. It stirs memories from years ago when he would kiss her cheek—like a brother, she'd think—and his jaw would tense in a way that confused her. When she sometimes saw him watching her instead of Rosetta, his fiancée. When they'd discuss a recent arrival—a mummified dog, perhaps—and they'd reach out to touch it at the same time, fingers brushing. And she knows in a flash of clarity that while he was engaged to Rosetta as her father wished, in his warped heart he lusted for her.

"I know what you are," she spits before he can make another move. "Murderer! Take your hands off me."

She draws her knee up, connecting below his stomach and winding him. As his head flies upward, her wrapped hand connects with his face. Once for her father. A second time for her mother.

"I know about your arrangement with that dealer, that you had him follow me. I saw you beat him senseless after he mocked you for killing my father, and I won't rest until the authorities know what you've done."

The blows send him back a few steps, and he holds his jaw, panting. She wants to keep hitting him, but she stays where she is, watching him consider what she's just done and said. Finally, he draws his sticky fingers away, a line of blood cutting the corner of his mouth. A storm brews in his eyes, flashes foretelling a coming strike.

"You're going to be sorry you did that."

He's there in one stride, and she flinches, bracing herself for the slap. It doesn't come. Instead, he's laughing. In his face, she can see why he won't kill her. Because he enjoys the fight. Because he wants to break her spirit, to dominate her. She's just a thing for him to master.

"Don't you touch me," she snaps. "I'll scream."

"You think your cripple will rescue you?"

She grinds her teeth. Rowland isn't hers—he's betrayed her—but she still hates to hear Horatio speak of him.

"Oswald will come," she says. "And Oswald has a gun. I will tell them all what you've been doing. I've seen evidence that the authorities will be only too glad to hear about."

Time is an accordion, stretched and compressed. The fabric of her blouse pulses above her chest. Horatio doesn't move, pondering her threat.

Eventually, he steps back. Nursing where the blood is already starting to crust. Licking it.

"All right," he says. "All right. But don't get any foolish ideas. I will own you, just as I'll own that amulet."

She picks up her jewelry box, finds the ring, and throws it at him. Let that be her answer.

It rolls in a circle, stopping inches from his feet. A dot of blood winking. Horatio picks it up in a sweep and pockets it with a lingering look. As if it makes little difference.

Own her.

For years she has yearned to belong. Until his confession, she dared to hope she might find her place at Rowland's side, to be his, and for him to be hers. But to be owned? Is Clemmie a piece of Bickmore that Horatio hopes to acquire as part of his property? No different from the drive that leads to the house, or the portion of the Chelmer River on their estate? If she's any of those, then let her be the river, flowing free.

Not all rivers lead to freedom. That afternoon, Mariam brings news from her father. *Hapi*'s leak is still causing problems that require more time to repair before they tackle the cataract. They can't leave Philae, can't even get to Assûan to send a telegram home. They're trapped, and

Clemmie can't help but wonder whether to blame Horatio. Did he tamper with the *dahabeeyah*? Is this all part of his plan to gain control, to give the dealers a chance to find the amulet?

Only they won't find it. Even though she hates Rowland for betraying her, for interfering and stealing the Double *Tyet*, she's glad that Horatio won't find what he seeks. One good thing among so many calamities. She holds on to that.

A little while later, Sphinx creeps out from under the bed, and Clemmie is impressed that the cat knew to keep out of Horatio's way. She does the same. Mariam kindly brings her meal to her cabin and checks how she is, sitting with her a short while to keep her company.

Observing Philae, Clemmie sees no sign of Apep. Perhaps the dealer has learned to stay away from the man who almost killed him. Horatio seemed surprised when she said that she'd overheard the conversation in the tent, so Apep can't have told him that she was there. From her window, she witnesses Horatio keeping to the island, shouting and prodding his workers, pacing up and down. He grabs one man roughly and asks him something, the Egyptian shaking his head in reply, and she wonders if he's looking for Apep, to tell him that Clemmie's on to them. Perhaps she's alarmed him after all.

When she's certain that the others are in the saloon, eating the turkey and rice Mariam's prepared, Clemmie slips out of her cabin to visit Oswald's room.

It smells of cigar smoke, linseed oil, and desert dust. At the base of his bed is a chest. If she were Oswald, that's exactly where she'd keep it. She lifts the lid.

Lying inside is his shotgun. Clemmie picks it up, cold metal a chilling kiss. There are cartridges left in her other skirt pocket back in her cabin, and that thought steadies her. She killed a snake when she had to—couldn't she do the same again? She denies any knowledge of the weapon when Oswald later knocks on her door, apologizing for disturbing her but wondering if she might possibly know what has happened to his beloved firearm.

She takes the shotgun to bed with her that night. Entwined with it, like lovers.

Osiris

THE NILE IS A BEAUTIFUL, writhing water serpent teeming with fauna in its belly. Harmless. Deadly. All kinds of creatures. There are crocodiles and fish and hippopotami. There are things that allude to life, and those that can bring about death. The Nile is stunning, and it is hostile.

After first searching for their brother's body parts as kites, Isis and Nephthys return to their human forms. Nephthys suggests a boat—a papyrus boat, for crocodiles are said to be repelled by them—and they procure one with haste. Sometimes they call Osiris's name while they float along, but then they stop and remember: He is gone, he cannot hear us, he is in pieces.

They look everywhere. In the plants at the water's edge, even plunging into the river to see if any parts have fallen and sunk to the bottom. They take turns, one of them looking for the telltale ripples, the horny disturbance of the filmy water, the unblinking eyes of a predator.

What might they find? Will it be a foot on its own, or will that foot be attached to the lower limb? To the whole leg? Will his head be complete or the ears severed off? The nose missing?

Isis goes ashore to search, and Nephthys continues alone in the boat made of papyrus. Singing a song that could be for the *Bennu* bird wading near the bank, could be for her lost brother, or could be for herself. At last, she sees a wink of green that isn't the Nile and isn't sedge. It beckons, almost like a curled finger . . . it *is* a curled finger. She's found the first piece.

Nephthys wades along the river's edge in her eagerness, wet *kalasiris* tying her legs together. Slowing her movements. Arriving at the finger, picking it up, she kisses it. Weeping. Cradling the severed hand it's attached to like when she first held Anubis.

She climbs back into the boat. The Nile is as still as a corpse. Decay isn't far away.

As she sails along the river, she can see shapes coming toward her, flowing downstream. They must be crocodiles, and immediately she's glad of the papyrus boat, that it should ward off the beasts. As they get closer, she sees that the objects are smaller than reptilian monsters, that they are smooth. Approaching, the shapes become distinct, a parade of body parts. An arm here. A foot there.

Her heart chants the words: How many?

How many are here? How many more to find? How many more days until her mission is complete? How many?

Set cut the body of Osiris into fourteen pieces. Seven scattered to Upper Egypt, and seven to Lower Egypt. Fourteen of them—she has found one, and the remaining float around her, encircling her boat.

She leans over, gathering them up. A harvest of body parts. The skin not green as she'd first thought. More pinkish white. When she gets to the head, only the back is visible. She has to turn it over. It sloshes in the river as she rights it, revealing the drowned features.

The eyes that stare back at her are a poisonous red. The mouth an ossified scream. This isn't the head of Osiris, and she isn't Nephthys. The face she holds is Rowland's.

The scene dismembers into as many pieces as Osiris's broken body and Clemmie jolts upright, her bedsheets awry. The room rings with the quickening of her heart, but otherwise all is silent.

Somehow, it feels as though she's heard a noise, the way the night bears the scar of a sound that's come just before. A sound made while she was dreaming. The echo of something bloodcurdling and shrill perforates the air. In her heart she knows something is wrong, just as she's always known when her blight has spread a little further.

The dream was trying to tell her something. Rowland is in danger. Of course, it makes sense, for he stole the amulet. The dream was a foreshadowing of what's coming for him.

The curse of Osiris.

Prey

THE EARLY MORNING IS A wispy garland around her neck. As she steps onto the deck, Oswald's shotgun now loaded and in her arms, the air caresses her open throat with unseen claws. It isn't warm. It isn't cold. Just in between, like the hour. Walking in a realm that is neither night nor day.

Death is here. So close she can almost touch it. A familiar figure in her life, so much so, she thinks she could pick it out from a crowd, describing the features easily. Inky arms. Breath that blows a furnace one minute, ice the next. A leering look that says: *I'm coming for you*.

As she slides one foot across the deck, there's a creak behind her. She turns, but there's nothing there. Nothing to see, that is. It could be her fears, messing with her mind. It could be death, come at last.

Her movements are slowed the way they are in dreams, but she knows she isn't dreaming. She isn't Nephthys, she is Clemmie. And she's being hunted.

The bruised shore beckons to her, and she shouldn't listen, of course she shouldn't. It must be Death's whisper in her ear. Acting the part of mermaids, reeling her in only to drown her.

Here she is, at Philae. As the air knifes her lungs, she thinks it a fitting place to die. The island where she tried to make things right. The island where she fell short and failed so pitifully.

For it is her fault, even if she blames Rowland too. She failed to make sure the amulet, once buried, wasn't disturbed. She failed to keep Rowland off her scent. She failed from the moment she agreed to travel with companions, once more being selfish and putting her needs, her wants, first.

This land has been reduced to what it is because of selfish gain. After all she's been through, she should have known that Rowland was a temptation that she should have said no to. A test that she failed.

Cursing in whispers only ghosts are capable of hearing, she struggles to maneuver the plank with her injured hands and, giving up, lowers herself over the side of the *dahabeeyah*. She has to wade for a few steps through water, holding the shotgun above her head. The Nile is metal. Clamping on her. She absorbs it, the river flowing in her, chilling with every change of course; through her limbs, her belly, her heart. Here it meets that blood-pumping organ with the charge of a cataract. Egypt has got under her skin, and she'll face it with her plea. Has she not sacrificed so much already?

But maybe it isn't her for whom death has come. She thinks of her dream, of Rowland's part in all of this, and while she fiercely resents him, she also can't quite forget the way she's come to see him. The connection that has formed between them. A bridge letting two banks meet.

She walks the shore of a gouged island in nothing but a white cotton nightdress. The bindings on her leg are lost in the river, her heart a rabid animal that makes itself seen in the exposed notch between her clavicles.

Each step on the island is the sound of bones breaking. *Crunch.* She pauses. Tries to breathe. *Scrunch.* It's all around her. They are. Whatever it is, she's being surrounded. *Crunch.* Is Apep out there? Is he waiting to fulfill his threat?

I kill you myself.

The men completing Horatio's dirty work sleep around the temple complex. She glances up that way now, but sees no movement.

Who is the greater threat? Is it Apep, the man who bears the scars she inflicted, with his need for retribution?

The woman. She did this to me.

Is it Horatio, with his belief that he can coerce her into a brutal marriage or have her locked up in an asylum? Either way, he'll get his hands on her father's collection. He's a man with a lawyer for a father. He'll find a way.

I will own you.

Or is it that old hieroglyphic text? The one that Rowland doesn't believe in, but she was once so sure of.

Isis and Nephthys.

Is she really able to stand up to all these things?

The glow from the sky is a sun that wants to rise, but is too heavy to bear the burden of another day. It's a weight Clemmie understands, but rise it will, and so must she. Her feet continue on the path that calls to her. Instinct tells her to look up.

There they are. The kites. She hasn't seen them while hiding in her cabin, and now they're back above her head. Circling, like the sisters when they first searched for their brother's body parts.

They fly on and she follows, keeping in step with them. Remaining under the canopy of their outstretched wings. Her eyes train on them, not watching where she's going or what she's stepping on. It's the sole of her bare foot that tells her that she's trodden on something plump.

She retracts her toes, crouching, sinking slowly. The air adopts the texture of sand. Dropping the gun, she picks up that *thing*. The something that gave way when she stood on it. In her hands, it's unpleasantly soft. Her bandages catch on something vaguely sharp. She looks closer. Sees the faint white crescent of a fingernail.

A surge of comprehension rushes through her and she drops it. Too late, the finger leaves its trail, a red stain on her wrapped hands. She runs to the water. Scrubs and scrubs, but the residue clings in pink streaks and won't come clean. Sand in her eyes, salt on her cheeks. She unwinds her palms, doesn't care that they're raw underneath, doesn't cry out as she tears her flesh where the cloth has stuck. The bandages drop into the water, curling on the surface. Bloody cerement snakes that gradually grow heavier and sink.

A whimper rises from deep within, something that begins tremulously and builds to a crescendo, gasping and panicky. The dream has come true. It was telling her what had already happened. Rowland is dead.

She doubles over, heaving up everything her body has consumed lately. Her dinner. Her fears. Her poisoned hopes.

A scream interrupts her vomiting. She swipes the back of her hand across her acrid mouth. Her peeling lips sting, but she barely notices. Everything hurts.

Above her, the raptors release their haunting cries. Arresting her attention, they press on. She doesn't know how she moves, her sodden nightdress hampering every step, but she follows after them. Pitching and rolling like *Hapi* in a storm, her eyes on the birds.

She falls to her knees, sand finding the tenderness on her hands and clinging there. But the sand isn't the brown and golds of this place. It's red. Her nightdress, limpid to the knees where the Nile has painted it, takes on a new hue. Red seeps through, coating everything she touches, till she's bathing in Rowland's blood.

Shuddering with her tears, she looks around her and sees the marks of dragging. A scuffle.

The river makes the tinkling sound of opening its door, of letting something in, and she stares ahead of her. Squints. Her eyes following the dip of the shore up ahead where the Nile meets it. Only just seeing the horny tail disappear beneath the river's folds.

A crocodile. *The* crocodile. It could be any reptile, but she believes with a certainty that it's the same one they saw that night, the one that came for her, Mariam, and Celia. Rowland is really gone.

Her legs have no strength left and her hands are destroyed. She crawls forward, sobbing with every move. Wading through the gore-smeared sand, to the point where the kites are waiting. They've landed now, picking at something that sparkles.

When she's barely three feet from them, she's surprised that her moves don't startle them away, that they look at her with their bright, scathing eyes and cock their heads to sum her up. Is she found wanting?

One kite, the slightly smaller one, drops what it holds in its beak, and the two birds unfold their wings and fly away. Clemmie watches them go, becoming mere specks, then disappearing completely in the brightening mass above her.

When she looks down, she considers what the kite tossed toward her and reaches her hands out. It takes several attempts to make her fingers work. To pick it up. The metal sticks to blood.

She sits up. Inspects it closer. Can't quite believe what she's holding, what it means.

In her fingers is a gold ring, gore-smeared diamonds grinning at her. In the center is a large faceted ruby, bleeding the identity of the man who fell prey to the land.

Siblings

THE STORY OF OSIRIS GOES something like this. Once, an Egyptian god was murdered by someone he thought he knew because of something he did, and after the life was stolen from his lungs, his body was cut into fourteen pieces. Thirteen of those were discovered by his faithful sisters, but the fourteenth was swallowed by a fish. Isis was resourceful and not easily prevented, and she molded that fourteenth piece out of clay in order to make Osiris complete. The two sisters sewed their brother back together so that Anubis could embalm his body, preserving him. Healing something that seemed beyond repair. Mending a broken thing.

Clemmie has been cut into pieces. She's been hurt by the people she thought she could trust. She's even been hurt by the very thing she's dedicated her life to: Egyptology. While she's been the Osiris of her story, she has also been the Set—partaking in a destruction that she regrets—the Isis—resourceful—and the Nephthys—helper and healer. The past is oozing with wounds, but now they must be bound back up. There comes a time to be dead to the past, and alive for the future.

In her blood-sodden nightdress, with the shotgun back in her arms, Clemmie does not go after the creature that has played the role of Ammit, devourer of the impure. She doesn't shoot at the place where she saw it slide into the river. The last time she saw Horatio, he put the ring she threw at him into his pocket before striding onto the island, angered by her threats. Now he is gone.

The sun lifts its head on the bloody shoreline of Philae as Clemmie climbs onto the deck. She's met by a frazzled Oswald who's been looking everywhere for his missing shotgun. When he sees the spectacle of her—a bloodied, ghostly figure with sand-knotted hair and his weapon balanced on her elbows, hands issuing more blood—his face blanches.

She cries then, but this time they're the tears of release. Horatio is dead. That means that her parents are avenged, and the twins are safe.

With *Hapi* patched up and sailable once more, they return to Assûan and moor there. They still need to get to Cairo to seek medical attention at the hospital, but the pause is necessary. Horatio's death must be reported.

Oswald, Youssef, and Khalil go ashore to do this, leaving Clemmie and Celia on the deck, and Rowland resting his leg in his cabin. Clemmie wonders if he's also too ashamed to emerge, afraid of facing her after his confession. She hasn't seen him once since she informed their group of Horatio's fate.

Celia cried when she heard what had happened, commiserating with Clemmie before musing that Horatio's handsome face quite reminded her of her Michael back at home.

Clemmie is stunned by it all. She sits in a silence that clearly makes Celia flustered. Bringing Sphinx to cheer her, Celia tries to encourage her to talk, to tell her what's been going on. Suggesting that sharing can be a comfort and that, after what they've been through together, they are sisters of a kind.

Mariam emerges from her kitchen, bringing lemonade and dates, and Clemmie asks her to join them. The captain's daughter sits on her right, and, with a friend on either side, Clemmie prepares for one final unwrapping.

It's fitting, really, that the women who helped her bury the amulet are the ones to hear her now. She considers what Celia said, about being sisters, and realizes that there is a form of sisterhood that goes beyond blood. Celia and Mariam listen patiently as they all sit on *Hapi*'s deck, Sphinx purring on Clemmie's lap. From the night the twins were unrolled to the present, she leaves nothing out. The shadow the hiero-glyphs left on her life, her secret sister, Horatio's wicked deeds, even all of Rowland's revelations. She utters her history one section at a time, in English and halting Arabic, so that both her friends can hear her.

"What will you do with the unburied twins, *ya aanesa* Clemmie?"

Mariam's voice is sorrowful, and it's no wonder. They are her ances-tors, people who lived and belonged here, their corpses stolen and taken to foreign places. Clemmie wouldn't want someone to dig up her parents' bodies and ship them across the world.

"I've often wondered whether to bury them at home."

Even as she says it out loud, she knows it isn't the answer. A part of her considered bringing the twins with her on this trip. She went over it in her head so many times, yet it never felt right. There was respect and disrespect in every option.

Mariam touches Clemmie's hand.

"In the Bible, Joseph, son of Jacob, died in Egypt. He made his kin take an oath that they'd carry his bones, his embalmed body, out of that foreign place to be buried with his people. Moses did so in the great Exodus, just as they had sworn. Our bones don't belong in a foreign place, *ya aanesa* Clemmie. They should be buried in their home coun-try."

Repatriate. That's what Mariam means, what she longs for. Clemmie doesn't know the Arabic for that word, but Mariam is right. Just as she's been right about the need to irrigate a land being ransacked.

"So your sister was better whilst the amulet was here in Egypt?" Celia asks.

Clemmie nods as she scoops Sphinx close to her chest. Nuzzling her head.

"And then as soon as the amulet left Egypt's shores, she relapsed?"

There's something in Celia's words. Clemmie's spine straightens, and Sphinx wriggles from her arms. She looks at her friend's gleaming eyes. The kind of look she imagines Sherlock Holmes would wear in an il-lustration in *The Strand Magazine* when he's solved one of his mysteries.

Is it really as simple as that? Is it the stealing that's the curse? Treat-ing these ancient bodies the way a pickpocket would a silver vesta case? The way Horatio and her father treated the smuggled antiquities?

"What do you think, Mariam?" she asks. After all, it was Mariam who suggested Philae instead of Denderah, a proposal that made so much sense.

The two Egyptologists share a look, both understanding. Osiris, the river. Isis, the land. Not an island, then, but the whole country. Egypt. Home.

Rising gently from her rattan chair, she hobbles toward the saloon and the cabins beyond.

"Clemmie, wait a moment," Celia calls. She waits for Clemmie to return before continuing. "I do believe Rowland did what he did because he loved his brother. Even if Ossie is a terrible bore at times and treats me like a child, well, I am very fond of him. I think we both know what it is to love a sibling."

Clemmie nods. The sun is in her eyes, making them water.

"I know that, but even if I understand a sibling's bond, it doesn't change the fact that Rowland betrayed me. He should have respected my wishes for the amulet to remain at Philae, just as we should respect the wishes of the people who once died here, never expecting to be borne from their tombs and displayed far from home."

"Rowland admitted what he'd done," Celia says. "I think that shows that he didn't want to keep any more secrets. Perhaps he regrets his actions."

Can she forgive Rowland in light of his motivations? How must he have felt in the wake of Archie's death? Two brothers who fought side by side. Death would have been ever present, to the point where he might have anticipated losing his brother, but not by a freak accident. Celia's right. As Clemmie pictures the Luscombe brothers, she grasps a faint understanding of why Rowland did what he did. It was for his brother. Still, her resentment niggles.

She knows what she has to do.

Home

ROWLAND'S BODY MAKES THE SHAPE of Isis's hieroglyph. Using the edge of his bed as a perch, he plays fitfully with his fingers. His shirt is stained with sweat, the smell of it thick and sickly in his cabin. He hasn't heard her approach, and when she touches his arm, his head jerks upright. Eyes meeting hers with a transparency that terrifies her.

She hardens herself, turns her heart into a dead thing. Devoid of feeling. Even as she does so, remembering that dead things still need protecting.

He hurt her—unwittingly, that's true. Still, his actions have caused pain. For her. Possibly for her sister. She summons these reminders to combat the emotions building inside her. She detests this man. She does.

"You have to return the amulet," she says.

She stands before him. The bridge that had stood between them has been wrecked. She once believed that something broken could be mended. Now she isn't so sure.

"It wasn't yours to take, and it needs to come back to its homeland."

His voice has been sanded by Egypt's storms and his own inner tempests. "I know."

She has to test her hypothesis, to have the amulet back here. What if burying the amulet wasn't what was required? What if all she had to do was return it to Egypt, to the country of Osiris and Isis, of river and land? To have it back where it belonged. She could give it to the Egyptian authorities. Khalil mentioned the Khedive's palace museum. Maybe that would be the perfect place for it.

What about the kites? The asthma attacks and the dust storm? These things happened when the amulet was here. Clemmie doesn't have answers to everything, but when Nurse Pugh sent the telegram about Rosetta's recovery, she said *E has been better.* Not E *is* better, but *has been.* Something she'd missed at first, but now she wonders if that means Rosetta started to improve as soon as the amulet was home. Home in Egypt. Coincidence or not, she feels the pull—stronger than ever—to bring the amulet, her father's whole collection, back here. Would it be enough for the Double *Tyet* simply to be back where it had come from?

Home. It's a word that isn't quite Bickmore anymore. What makes a home a home? If Etta dies under the trephine, Clemmie will never want to see Chelmsford again. If Etta lives, then they made each other a promise long ago that they'd come here together. They could still fulfill that vow. Perhaps it's the Egyptian sand that's got beneath her skin, finding an entry through her pores and wounded flesh, through her dust-filled lungs, encouraged by Mariam's offer to join the work of restoration. Could this be her home now?

"I've asked Oswald to send a telegram for me," Rowland is saying, cutting through her thoughts. "That night at Philae, my dead brother's dream was my priority. After your father's event, he had so wanted the amulet. I couldn't afford for you to stop me from honoring one of his last wishes. I needed to ensure it was with the rest of my collection of antiquities, in the care of my man, Stone, out of your reach. But I see I was wrong now, I really do, and I'm arranging to have the amulet returned."

He's acted already, then. She's inclined to thank him, but it's his duty. His responsibility. A part of her is relieved, but there's also a cavern inside her. The day Rowland revealed his betrayal, he blasted a hole in her heart so wide that it aches.

She will pack it with sand. With the desert and the sun. With the Nile that Nephthys would bathe in to soothe her Set-inflicted bruises. She will heal it by working with Mariam, each of them a *shâdûf*. They can be vessels of irrigation with a mission to protect antiquities and see illegal dealers brought to justice. She will fill this hole with everything except the shape of the man who caused it.

When she's at the door, his voice grates through the silence, and she's glad to be leaving because it's almost more than she can bear.

"I hope it makes things right between us."

Sphinx comes to her in her cabin, and Clemmie holds the cat in her arms. Burying her face in the solace of fur. Isis forgave Nephthys for her betrayal. Like the sisters in the myth, Clemmie has overcome so many obstacles along the way.

Why does it feel as though forgiving Rowland is one too many?

Letters

THE STEPS AT THE FRONT of Shepheard's are carpeted through the middle, the Turkish design faded with dust. Clemmie passes through the foyer that she once entered as a new arrival, when she had a definite mission before her. And she still has, although her plans are a little hazier than before. Her wounds have been seen to and dressed, and now she can only hope and pray that they don't become gangrenous.

She's barely seen her companions since they arrived back in Cairo. Youssef and Mariam have already been hired by some tourists who want to visit Luxor, the old city of Thebes. Rowland keeps to himself, aided by a new pair of crutches while his fractured tibia heals, and she avoids dining at the popular hours when she might see him. Celia and Oswald speak of returning to England imminently. The Egypt that Clemmie has known over the last few weeks is shifting around her, the way the desert appears altered after a storm.

Letters, so many letters. She has sent one to the consul general describing the camp and the man she marked with the shard of glass, and containing one of the stolen papers from Apep's tent. She has also written to the director of the Department of Antiquities, sending him another filched paper, and explaining her discoveries of the dealers and of her own father's involvement, how she wants his help to arrange for the return of her father's collection of antiquities in a respectful manner, how she wants to give the relics back to Egypt, and, if permitted, find a way to work with the museum. In this letter, she made clear her desire to help protect Egypt's heritage. Finally, she wrote home to Horatio's father to tell him about Horatio's death, and to a lawyer of a rival firm asking him to take her case with details of Horatio's crimes and the letter implicating his involvement with Apep. If the dealer testifies that Horatio killed her parents, then that will help prove her case. They can fight for Bickmore, her and Etta's rightful inheritance. She doesn't want to go back to that house and its ghosts, but selling it will fund a future here.

"Miss Attridge."

The clerk is beckoning to her from behind his counter, and just as she did on her first day in Cairo, she marvels at his skill for remembering the names of each guest. She approaches him eagerly, hoping for a message from home. There are three communications awaiting her perusal, but not one is a telegram.

The first two look official, and she puts these in her pocket. The third is written in a hand she doesn't know, but she senses what could be inside. She doesn't open any of them until she's in her room, standing by the window with Sphinx tying herself in knots around her ankles.

Already she aches for the river. She finds herself waiting for the smell of Mariam's cooking, listening for Youssef's booming laugh. The ground shifts in a way the *dahabeeyah* didn't, and her limbs miss the rhythm they'd adjusted to. It helps when she assesses Cairo from up here, when she can see the city in all its glory.

The music of the country calls to her as vendors shout their wares, flea-ridden dogs whine for food, and two cats yowl at each other over their domain. From here, she can almost smell the bitter notes of coffee on the breeze. Looking over the city, she's furnished with a view she will never tire of. Verdant palm trees wave their majestic fingers as people pass by on foot, in a brougham pulled by a sweating pair of horses, or on donkeys with fringed bridles. The sun reflects off a minaret in a blinding white spot that stains her eyes and everything else she looks at.

Tearing the note open, she reads the following:

Dear Clementine,

I write to you sending my warmest regards. In truth, I wish to offer you more than just my regard.

It is too late for that, you will tell me, and so I write not to win your heart but at least to restore your favor. Firstly, I desire for you to know that I have come to agree with you that dealing with illegal traders will only encourage their unethical business. Should I build a collection, know that it will only be done with the permission of Egypt's government, to further knowledge, and in memory of a brother whom I miss dearly.

The main reason I'm writing, however, is one which I hope will bring you much relief. The amulet, that object which has become such a thing of contention between us, is once more in the country of its origin. I shall arrange delivery to you at your convenience. Is there any chance that you would permit me to return it in person?

I remain at Shepheard's, should you find it possible to relent enough to see me. I pray that you will forgive my persistence. However, I wish to outline one final time why I made the decisions I did. I have suffered, the pains of which no person can imagine unless they, too, have caused the death of one they loved more than themselves. If ever I came close to believing in curses, then the blight of war cursed me, and I consequently cursed my brother. You have known the pain of loss, the weight of suffering. You have a sister, and I ask that you consider what you might do were you to bring about her death. Would you not do everything in your power to honor her memory and her wishes? Just so, I have acted out of the bond of brotherhood. May you forgive me for my unintentional sin.

I am your humble servant,
Rowland

A strong breeze is blowing, the kind that would be perfect for starting up the Nile. In the *dahabeeyah*-studded port of Boulak, a fresh vessel sets out with its passengers. It's a game, albeit one fed by jealousy, to guess how far these tourists will be going. Will they make it to Philae? Beyond that? Will the travelers ride the donkeys and camels that Clem-

mie and her companions rode? Will they look at the ruins with ignorance, pleasure, or shame, regretting what their fellow man has done to
mutilate them? Will the feet of these strangers pass over the place
where Horatio was devoured?

A *dragoman* barters with a *Reïs* on behalf of a European traveler. A
waiting crew begin a lively beat on their drums, singing their local
songs. It's a sound that was unfamiliar at first, but after spending so long
on the Nile, she's grown accustomed to this music. Perhaps even fond
of it.

The paper in Clemmie's tender but healing hands flaps in the river's
breeze. It is Nurse Pugh's latest telegram. The one that arrived mere
hours after she'd finished considering Rowland's letter, knowing that
the amulet is back in Egypt. That the knots of Isis and Nephthys are
home.

Now she reads the words sent from Nurse Pugh. She'd already heard
that the tumor had been removed, but since arriving in Cairo, she has
awaited news that Etta is awake and strong enough to talk. Because
Clemmie has lived with fear for so long, her hope deferred time and
again, it's hard to accept that the danger is really gone.

Hope deferred maketh the heart sick.

Yet in the brief message she's received, she can almost hear that lilt-
ing voice of her childhood guardian trying to soothe her:

E woke up—Isis no more

She almost forgets about the other two letters in her excitement. The
amulet is back, and just hours later, her sister is reported well again.
Can that be a coincidence? She doesn't know if myths are curses, or
curses are myths, but whichever is true, this blight has seemingly
passed. Just as the storm swept over them in *Hapi* and was gone. They'll
bear the scars of it in the loss of their parents, in the time it takes for
Etta to heal and join her here, in the ache of memories, and in the pain
of explaining Horatio's betrayal and death to her sister, but scars are
evidence of healing.

Already it feels easier to breathe, the peace inside her stretching her
lungs to their full capacity. Have her fears made everything worse,
sparked by superstitions and fantasies? Easy to blame the mysterious,

the amulet with its arcane hieroglyphs, but much harder to see that the source of suffering was someone she thought she knew. She was blind to the truth, just as she has been blind to the fate of artifacts.

Back in her hotel room, she focuses on the responses from the director of the Department of Antiquities and the consul general, the latter assuring her that the dealers to whom she's drawn his attention will be brought to justice, and the former making an interesting proposition. The director's last paragraph is the one that she keeps reading, playing over the possibilities in her mind:

> *Regarding your interests in the field of Egyptian antiquities, I would have it known that it is most unusual for me to consider the services of a woman in these respects, and yet, here we are. You find yourself wanting to help, and I find myself in a position where I am unable to refuse. Egypt is being thieved daily, behind our backs, when we close our eyes to sleep at night, when the eager tourist uses word of mouth to find the dealers who will supply them with illicitly gained antiquities. We must flush them out. The work of excavation is necessary to further grasp Egypt's history, but the preservation of artifacts in the land of their origin is equally vital. You mention knowing Youssef and his daughter, so it may come as no surprise to you that they already work for me in an essential capacity. As they take tourists up and down the Nile, they keep me informed on sightings of illegal digs and dealers. Their work is invaluable. They are part of a team I've been building, an operation supported and guided by our local historians. Some of my volunteers discover unethical practices, and send their observations my way. Others take the role of the tourist, the collector, the museum custodian, and their job is to befriend the dealer, and then report him to me. It has the potential to be dangerous, and I would understand if I ask too much of you. The character whom you and Mariam lately uncovered is a man we have been trying to find for some time—now we have another who we believe operates near Denderah, but that is all we know. Your mission would be to release the news that you are seeking artifacts and let the dealers come to you. Your guise could be the English tourist, or, indeed, a curator of antiquities—you may use your imagination for the part you choose to play. You already have*

a willing captain and his daughter to direct you with their local knowledge and expertise, which gives me the faith that this partnership could work. Take the time you need to consider my offer.

Her father didn't protect his family. He didn't protect the mummies he acquired illegally. Ever since the evening of the unwrapping, Clemmie has been burdened with the need to right his wrongs. The time has come to respect the past if there is to be any hope of a future.

The amulet was made to protect the twins. She set out to protect her sister. And now she has a chance to help protect what remains.

That's what Clemmie thinks when she sits down to form her responses, and while the future seems a little uncertain, there are two things that are vaguely within her control.

A man in a uniform. You don't love him. But you will.

It isn't easy holding the pen, so she writes the same short but clear message to both Rowland and the director:

I accept.

EPILOGUE

That man of all the men I ever knew

Most touched my fancy.

O! what days and nights

We had in Egypt, ever reaping new

Harvest of ripe delights.

—ALFRED, LORD TENNYSON, excised stanza from
"A Dream of Fair Women"

I am Nephthys, thy sister who loveth thee. Thine enemy is

    vanquished,

he no longer existeth!

I am with thee,

protecting thy members for ever and eternally.

—*The Lamentations of Isis and Nephthys*

Nephthys, to whom they give the name of Finality and the

    name of Aphroditê,

and some also the name of Victory.

—PLUTARCH, *Moralia*

Protection

Several months later

THERE IS A *DAHABEEYAH* MOORED up by an island near the first cataract. It has seen many sandstorms, this boat, many adventures on the Nile. The wood has been polished to a smooth patina over time, and the name painted on its prow is barely visible. Just a faint *H*.

On the lower deck, a *Reïs* smokes a *chibouk* so long he could trip over it were he not an expert. He stands near a little hut from which come smells of onion, rice, spices, and lamb, all worthy of the term *lazeeza*. Within the hut, a kitchen of sorts, a woman with a blue tattoo on her wrist stirs a pot with one hand, while she peruses a map and makes notes.

A movement on the deck, and an Englishwoman steps across a plank from the boat, her eau de Nil skirt blowing, revealing petticoats and, beneath, a large pink scar on one leg. Her brown hair is unpinned, tumbling past her shoulder blades and flapping about in the breeze. From a distance, those feathery locks could be mistaken for a pair of wings. She calls behind her, and a man appears from the saloon. He joins her, and they walk beside each other onto the shore of the island, him limping, her purposely slowing her steps for him to keep up. Here, in the shadow of a vast sanctum, they seem to be talking. The wind doesn't steal their words, so their conversation is lost on the observer. There's been enough stealing, after all.

330 RACHEL LOUISE DRISCOLL

The smell of paint is on the air, and, coming closer, there's evidence on the upper deck of a sign being painted. The border is made of Gothic swirls and the corners bear hieroglyphs.

A throne. A house with a basket.

Isis and Nephthys.

The central words still require a second coat to make them stand out, but they're clear enough to read, headed by an emblem in the shape of a *shâdûf*.

The Floating Museum:
An exhibition of the Gîzeh Museum

Rumor has it that there's a collector of antiquities who sails on a *dahabeeyah,* curating pieces for the museum in the Gîzeh palace. Wherever the *dahabeeyah* passes, they meet with excavators who work legally—and some who do not. Over time, the questionable dealers have been disappearing. No one knows where. Many have their suspicions.

It's even alleged that the collector can read the mysterious hieroglyphs of that long-ago age and charges a fee for artifacts to be translated, but very few understand those early shapes, so this is highly doubted. In some regions along the river, it's whispered that the hieroglyphist is a woman, although people shake their heads and say it cannot be.

On the deck of the *dahabeeyah* is sprawled a desert-colored cat. Beside it, a gray one. Next to that, one peppered in spots. Perhaps the owner of this *dahabeeyah* isn't just a curator of antiquities. The living need protecting, as well as the dead.

The woman and man have stopped talking, and the wind whips up the sand around them. The Nile releases a jubilant roar at its cataract as their two shapes become one. The Egyptian sun drips from the sky. A glimmer that's reflected in the Nile, in the sand, in a band on the woman's finger.

There are many forms of being conjoined. Some are born that way. Others feel it by blood, by something invisible. Others, by the rebuilding of a broken bridge.

The *dahabeeyah* seems to rock, and from the living quarters emerges another figure. Her movements are rather slow and she's wrapped a little too warmly for the climate. Pale skin inclines the viewer to believe she's an invalid, perhaps come to Egypt to recover from an illness or period of confinement. On her head she wears a scarf, but it has slipped, revealing a surprisingly short crop of golden hair beneath. She disembarks, joining the man and woman who seem to be waiting for her, and the man remains behind as the women press on, hand in hand, toward the temple.

There is a myth of two sisters who worked to piece the broken body of their brother back together. They brought healing. They were victorious.

There is a story of two women who are sisters who worked to piece together the brokenness of their lives. Some say they are still healing. They are also victorious.

There is hearsay of two sisters who were stolen from their homeland, broken apart, and then finally bound back together and brought home to be buried with their Double *Tyet* amulet. There's victory in that.

Where do you draw the line between myths and reality? Between mania and an obsession? Between curses and misfortune?

On the island, the two women have reached the center of the temple complex. They don't look alike, but there's something in their movements that seems to connect them. Sisters.

All around them: orange stone, carvings of mythical figures, and hieroglyphs—like people—waiting to be translated.

Above them, a beautiful blue sky. The Egyptian sun keeping darkness at bay. And two kites soaring overhead, wingtips touching.

Author's Note

My love for Egyptology began the same way as Clemmie's: holding a mummified cat. I was seven years old. My incredible mum had arranged a private artifact-handling session for my sister and me at our local museum, and the thrill of the moment has never left me. As I held a cat that had been alive in another age, some seeds were sown inside me that people might call Egyptomania. Now, many years later, I've finally written a book that's been sprouting in me since that day.

I set out to create a novel that married two eras I was fascinated by. I'm a Victorian at heart—my mum read my first Dickens to me at the age of three, and I've been hooked on the period ever since—so I definitely wanted the book to be set in the nineteenth century. It was my intention for this novel to be a celebration of history, siblings, antiquities (and cats!), and I hope I've achieved that.

At the time the story is set, the Egyptian god Geb was more commonly known as Seb, which I decided to remain true to in this book. Likewise, some of the other gods, goddesses, and ancient Egyptian words have variations, and I chose the ones appropriate to translations of the period; Bast is another example, perhaps better known as Bastet, Set is also called Seth, and *Tuat* is often referred to as *Duat*.

Clemmie might have believed that it was unlikely for the Temple of

Isis to be tampered with, but this has, in fact, happened. In the twenti-
eth century, due to flooding, it was relocated to Agilkia Island.

I have Amelia B. Edwards to thank for her magnificent memoir *A
Thousand Miles up the Nile.* She was once called "the most learned
woman in the world," and her book gave me a fantastic view of Egypt
in the nineteenth century, and of the work of destruction that she tried
to thwart by co-founding the Egypt Exploration Fund in 1882. She
learned to read hieroglyphs and even translated Gaston Maspero's
Manual of Egyptian Archeology. Amelia B. Edwards passed away in
April 1892, the year in which this story is set, after catching the influenza that was ravaging Europe. The spellings of the place names in
Egypt and certain terminology throughout the story (such as Gîzeh and
dahabeeyah) are unusual to our current spellings, but are in fact true to
those stated in various sources of the time period, including by Amelia B. Edwards—and who am I to argue with the Queen of Egyptology?

Alongside Amelia Edwards, I found the stories of Kate Bradbury
Griffith and Margaret Benson inspiring. Kate was a friend of Amelia
Edwards, executor of her will, and supporter of the Egypt Exploration
Fund, and Margaret was an Egyptologist and the first woman to be
granted a permit by the Egyptian Department of Antiquities to operate
an excavation site. I think these three women would all have been role
models for Clemmie, and perhaps, as Margaret first visited Egypt in
1894 (accompanied by her brother), the two might have become firm
friends.

Other resources that helped me with my research and that you may
find interesting are Plutarch's *Moralia; Egypt's Place in Universal History, Vol. V* by C. C. J. Baron Bunsen with additions by Samuel Birch;
and the Egyptian texts *The Songs of Isis and Nephthys* from the Bremner-
Rhind Papyrus, *The Lamentations of Isis and Nephthys,* and *The Book of
the Dead.* I also valued the use of *Ancient Egypt in Poetry: An Anthology
of Nineteenth-Century Verse* edited by Donald P. Ryan, and the poem
"At Kassassin" by Arthur Clark Kennedy. Louisa May Alcott's *Lost in a
Pyramid, or The Mummy's Curse* and Edgar Allan Poe's "Some Words
with a Mummy" were reads that I found interesting in the initial stages
of plotting. JSTOR remains a brilliant digital library that I am so grateful for.

In my early days of research, *Gods and Myths of Ancient Egypt* by

Robert A. Armour, and *The Complete Gods and Goddesses of Ancient Egypt* by Richard H. Wilkinson were really useful. I also referred to *Egyptian Myth: A Very Short Introduction* by Geraldine Pinch. Perusing *The Rape of the Nile* by Brian Fagan helped me consider the vast issue of illegal antiquity dealing. The World History Encyclopedia is always a great resource. Chapter XVIII of *Modern History of the Arab Countries* by Vladimir Borisovich Lutsky aided my understanding of the British occupation of Egypt. National Museums Scotland have many interesting articles on the subject of antiquities, and the Smithsonian website was also of interest. Throughout my research I've flicked through many resources, and if I've not mentioned them here, then it is only because, in my enthusiasm for the actual writing of the novel, I've lost track of every article, website, and book I've dipped into.

I found www.bibalex.org extremely useful for understanding hieroglyphs and the development of the ancient Egyptian language. Etymonline was a tab open constantly on my laptop to double- and sometimes triple-check many words in the book, and I hope that I've avoided using any that had not yet entered the English language at the period of this novel. I must thank Mark Hurn, the departmental librarian at the Institute of Astronomy at Cambridge who, many years ago when I was exploring a different writing project, advised I use Stellarium to see the night sky of any date and location I required. Stellarium has been invaluable for not just this book but also others already written and, no doubt, more to come.

The subject of historical fashion is one that I am slightly obsessed with, and, as such, throughout each draft of this novel I was wedded to my treasured copy of *Handbook of English Costume in the 19th Century* by C. Willett Cunnington and Phillis Cunnington. My nineteenth-century reproduction corset from the historical costume shop Prior Attire really got me into character when I sat down to write. (Although it was hard to wear during the summer heat wave, and I felt for Clemmie and Celia in Egypt!) I also found the fashion plates of the era to be great pictorial aids, and if you are interested in the same subject, I tweet and post on my author social media accounts under the hashtag #FashionPlateFriday.

My own asthma, once quite bad but now so much better, was used as a reference for Clemmie's health. The artists from ancient Egypt who crafted beautiful carvings, structures, and paintings provided me with stunning visual resources that have guided many of my descriptions. Bertha Müller's *Portrait of a Coptic Woman* helped inspire Mariam. I enjoy immersing myself as much as possible when writing, so I can assure you that copious amounts of Hotel Chocolat's Turkish delight (or "Lumps of Delight") were consumed during the course of writing this book.

Unlike Clemmie, I am no linguist, so I hope that I have not misrepresented any languages or cultures in my efforts to celebrate them. Historical accuracy is really important to me, but I am a writer of fiction, so I can only apologize if I have unintentionally misused any facts or details.

Sensationalism and conspiracy theories have long gripped people with tales and hypotheses of cursed tombs and mummies. *The House of Two Sisters* touches on the gothic tropes of such thoughts, but also reinvents them to focus on a greater curse: that of mistreating antiquities. The legal work of uncovering, preserving, and protecting history is a wonderful feat, but the troubling illegal practices happening in Clemmie's era still go on today. Some vague warnings have been found on tombs, but whether they were intended as curses is debatable. The Victorians were often superstitious, and a series of unhappy events could easily be misconstrued as something supernatural.

Acknowledgments

GETTING A BOOK READY FOR publication requires the support, expertise, and talent of many individuals whom I would like to thank.

First, I want to thank God, the Author of my life, for opening these doors for me.

I can go no further without thanking my amazing agent, Sarah Hornsley, for believing in me and this book. Thank you for being the best agent I could ask for. Also, thank you to Lisette Verhagen, who stood in as my temporary agent whilst Sarah was away.

I really want to thank Wendy Wong, my U.S. editor, and the whole team at Ballantine Books, PRH, for all you've done to bring *The House of Two Sisters* to the USA. I've loved working with you on this exciting journey. Also, many thanks to my UK editor, Liz Foley, and the team at Harvill Secker and Vintage for everything you've done to publish my debut (under the title of *Nephthys* in the UK). And huge thanks to everyone else involved in my novel; I realize it takes a lot of people to release a book, and I don't take any of you for granted.

In 2020 I won the CBC Write from Home three-month scholarship. HW Fisher sponsored my place on that course, for which I shall be forever grateful. I wish to extend my thanks to the whole CBC team (especially Jennifer Kerslake and Abby Parsons), who have cheered me on all the way through my journey. Thank you to my tutor, Andrew Michael Hurley, and my CBC course mates from both the three-month online course and the six-week Edit & Pitch Your Novel course. Particularly, a big thank-you to the talented and lovely Write-Inners for being the best writing group ever. And many thanks to Naomi Rebis.

I was longlisted for the Bath Novel Award 2022 with a different novel—but BNA have been so supportive of all my writing. Thank you!

I want to thank the book bloggers, the booksellers, and you, the reader, for choosing my novel.

My grandads would have loved to have seen my book published, but both have passed away now. Grandad Gregory supported me so much, helping fund my laptop, buying a printer, and paying for the report on my six-week CBC course. He never doubted that I'd get published. Thank you, Grandad. Having got married prepublication, Driscoll is now my nom de plume as I had the honor of taking my husband's surname. Whilst I would have liked to publish under my new name, the last time I saw Grandad Driscoll before he died, I told him that I would keep the family name going in print. So, whilst I am now proudly a McPherson, Driscoll will be in print, just as I promised my grandad.

Thank you to Mummy and Daddy for being the best parents in the world, for all the sacrifices you've made for me, and for always believing in me and never stamping out my dreams. Daddy, thank you for all the lifts; they cut down my commuting time and enabled me to spend more hours at my writing desk. Thank you for your hard work so that Mummy could be a full-time mum as I grew up. Mummy, thank you for being my teacher and raising me on the finest literature, for always being ready to hear me talk a plot point out loud, for beta reading for me, and for getting just as excited as me (to the point that you were the one who actually screamed!) when I had the call about my offer from Harvill Secker.

Etta and Clemmie are not copies of my sister and myself—far from it—but there are little nods to Rebekah and myself in this novel. Our sister relationship was a huge influence in the writing of this book, and I want to thank Rebekah for all the memories. Also, thank you to her lovely husband, Tom, for being the brother I always wanted.

Thanks to all my family and friends for the support shown for this novel.

Thank you to Tabitha, my feline companion whilst I lived with my parents before I got married, for being my writing buddy.

I've saved someone very special to last. When I wrote the first draft of this novel, I was single, but between getting my book deal and publication, I met the love of my life. My beloved husband, David, thank you for showing your interest in my writing from day one. Thank you for your love, your encouragement, your support, thank you for believing in me, for always being there, and for making it possible for me to give up work so I can be a housewife and author. I couldn't write a hero that would come close to you, even if I tried. I love you.

ABOUT THE AUTHOR

RACHEL LOUISE DRISCOLL is a former librarian and winner of the Curtis Brown Creative scholarship. She lives in the northeast of England with her husband and her cat, Cleopatra. *The House of Two Sisters* is her debut novel.

X: @RachLouDriscoll
Instagram: rachel.louise.driscoll

ABOUT THE TYPE

This book was set in Caledonia, a typeface designed in
1939 by W. A. Dwiggins (1880–1956) for the Mergan-
thaler Linotype Company. Its name is the ancient
Roman term for Scotland, because the face was intended to have a Scottish-Roman flavor. Caledonia is
considered to be a well-proportioned, businesslike face
with little contrast between its thick and thin lines.